Pokémon™ Adventures
HeartGold & SoulSilver

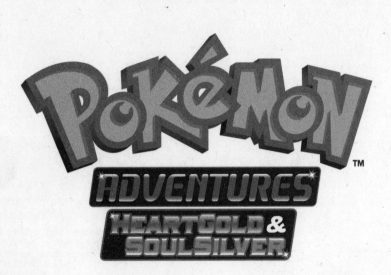

Pokémon ADVENTURES
HeartGold & SoulSilver
Volume 1
Perfect Square Edition

Story by **HIDENORI KUSAKA**
Art by **SATOSHI YAMAMOTO**

© 2013 The Pokémon Company International.
© 1995–2013 Nintendo / Creatures Inc. / GAME FREAK inc.
TM, ®, and character names are trademarks of Nintendo.
POCKET MONSTERS, SPECIAL Vol. 41
by Hidenori KUSAKA, Satoshi YAMAMOTO
© 1997 Hidenori KUSAKA, Satoshi YAMAMOTO
All rights reserved.
Original Japanese edition published by SHOGAKUKAN.
English translation rights in the United States of America, Canada, the United Kingdom,
Ireland, Australia, New Zealand and India arranged with SHOGAKUKAN.

English Adaptation/Bryant Turnage
Translation/Tetsuichiro Miyaki
Touch-up & Lettering/Annaliese Christman
Design/Shawn Carrico
Editor/Annette Roman

Printed in the U.S.A.

Published by VIZ Media, LLC
P.O. Box 77010
San Francisco, CA 94107

10 9 8 7 6 5
First printing, August 2013
Fifth printing, October 2017

PARENTAL ADVISORY
POKÉMON ADVENTURES
is rated A and is suitable
for readers of all ages.
ratings.viz.com

www.viz.com

INTRODUCTION

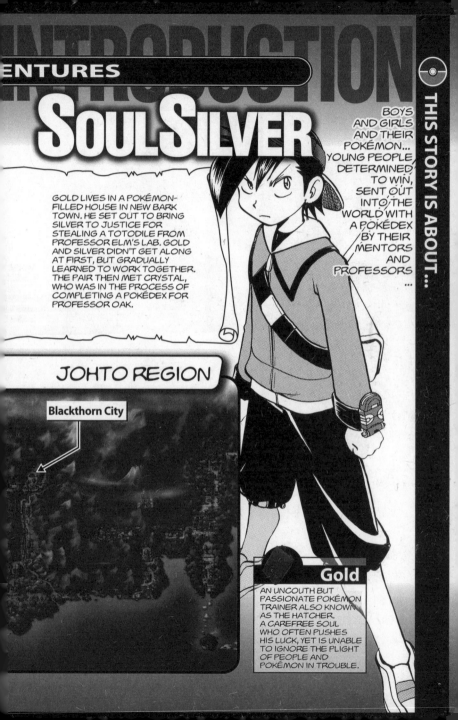

ENTURES

SOULSILVER

THIS STORY IS ABOUT...

BOYS AND GIRLS AND THEIR POKÉMON... YOUNG PEOPLE DETERMINED TO WIN, SENT OUT INTO THE WORLD WITH A POKÉDEX BY THEIR MENTORS AND PROFESSORS...

GOLD LIVES IN A POKÉMON-FILLED HOUSE IN NEW BARK TOWN. HE SET OUT TO BRING SILVER TO JUSTICE FOR STEALING A TOTODILE FROM PROFESSOR ELM'S LAB. GOLD AND SILVER DIDN'T GET ALONG AT FIRST, BUT GRADUALLY LEARNED TO WORK TOGETHER. THE PAIR THEN MET CRYSTAL, WHO WAS IN THE PROCESS OF COMPLETING A POKÉDEX FOR PROFESSOR OAK.

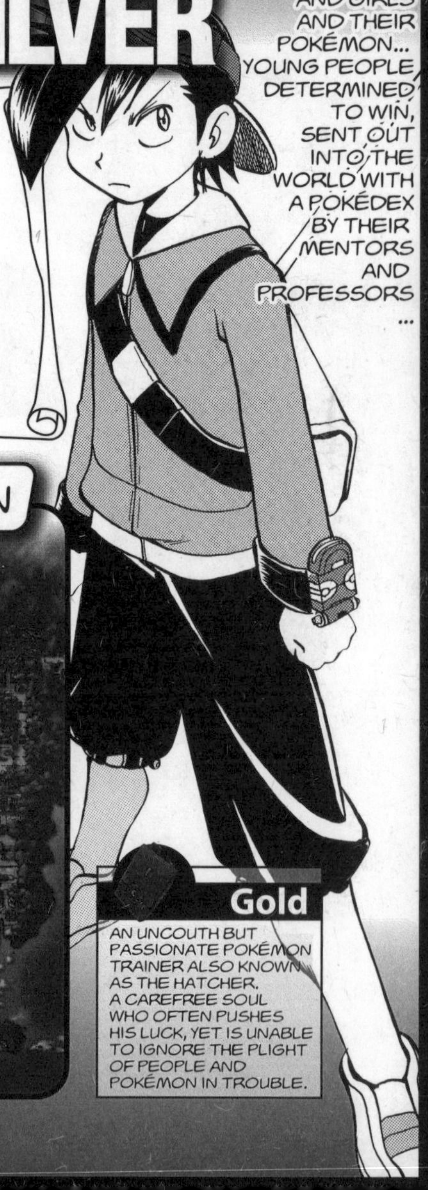

JOHTO REGION

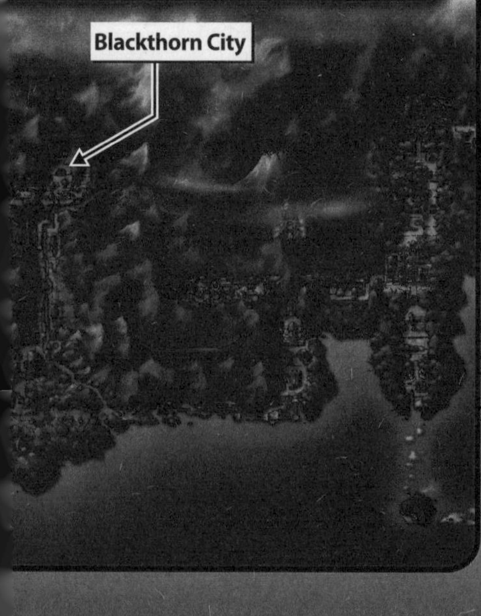
Blackthorn City

Gold

AN UNCOUTH BUT PASSIONATE POKÉMON TRAINER ALSO KNOWN AS THE HATCHER. A CAREFREE SOUL WHO OFTEN PUSHES HIS LUCK, YET IS UNABLE TO IGNORE THE PLIGHT OF PEOPLE AND POKÉMON IN TROUBLE.

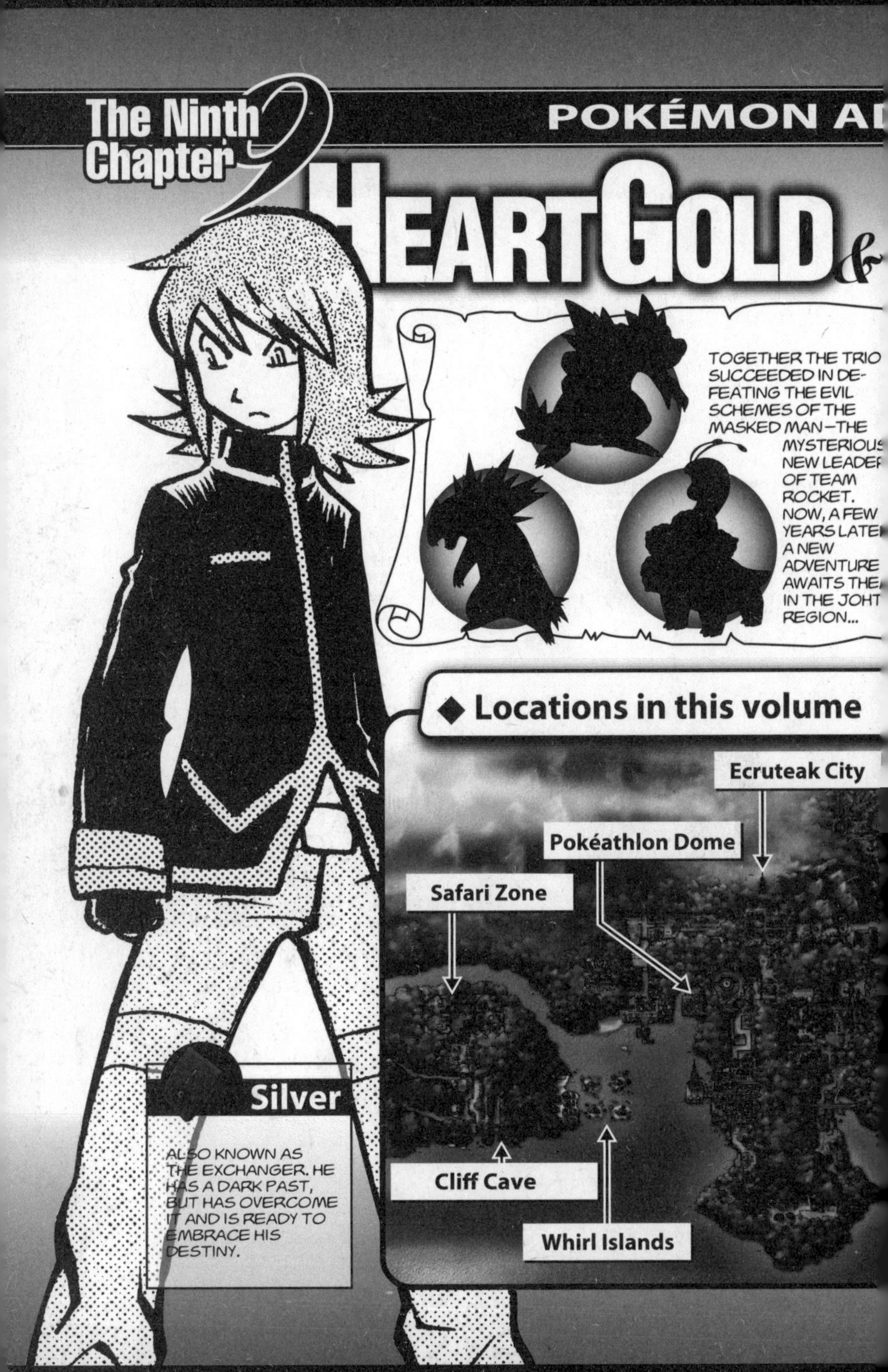
The Ninth Chapter 9
POKÉMON AD
HEARTGOLD &
TOGETHER THE TRIO SUCCEEDED IN DE-FEATING THE EVIL SCHEMES OF THE MASKED MAN—THE MYSTERIOUS NEW LEADER OF TEAM ROCKET. NOW, A FEW YEARS LATER A NEW ADVENTURE AWAITS THEM IN THE JOHT REGION...
◆ Locations in this volume
Ecruteak City
Pokéathlon Dome
Safari Zone
Cliff Cave
Whirl Islands
Silver
ALSO KNOWN AS THE EXCHANGER. HE HAS A DARK PAST, BUT HAS OVERCOME IT AND IS READY TO EMBRACE HIS DESTINY.

POKÉMON ADVENTURES
HEARTGOLD & SOULSILVER

1 VOLUME ONE

CONTENTS

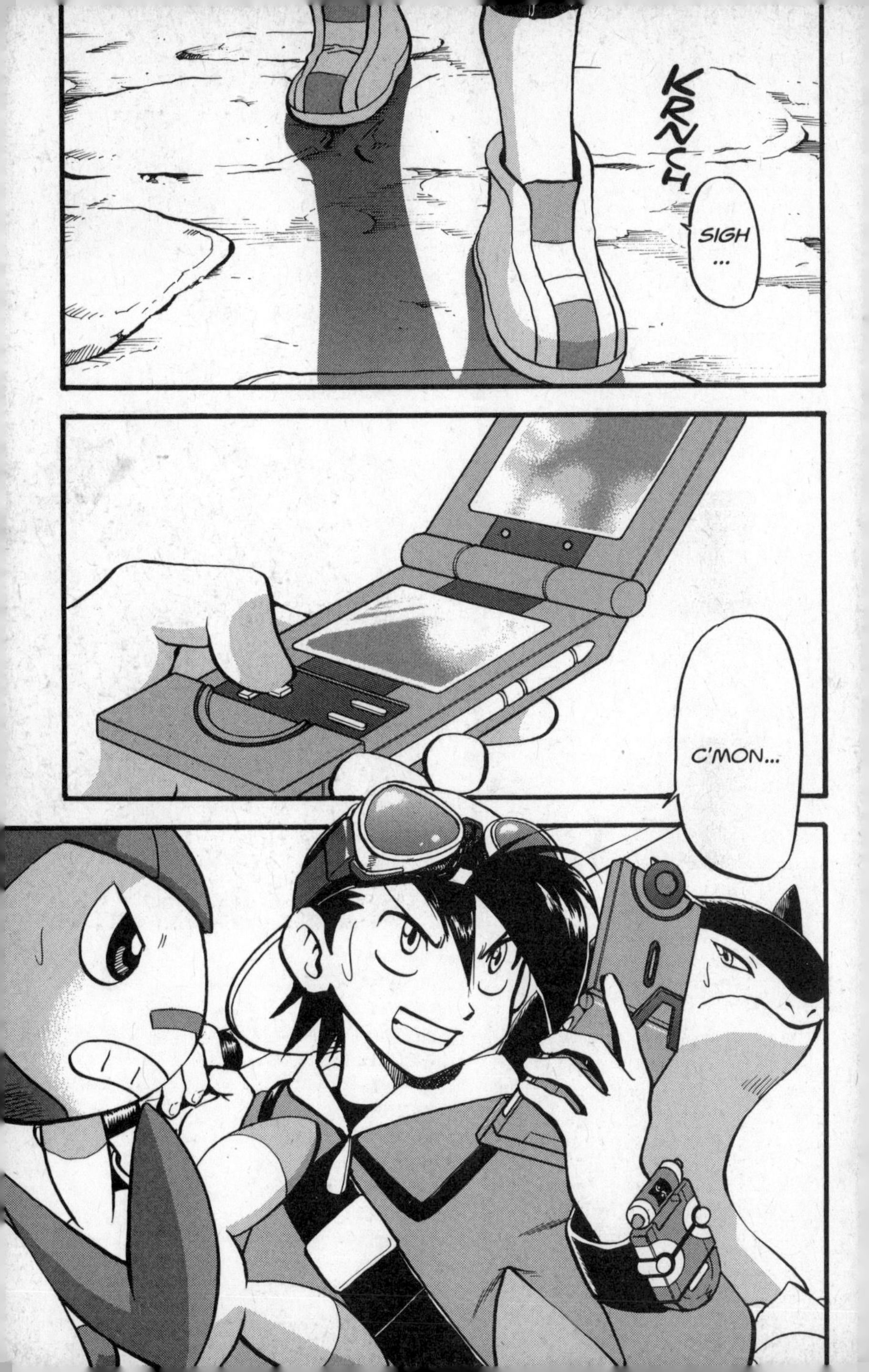
KRNCH
SIGH...
C'MON...

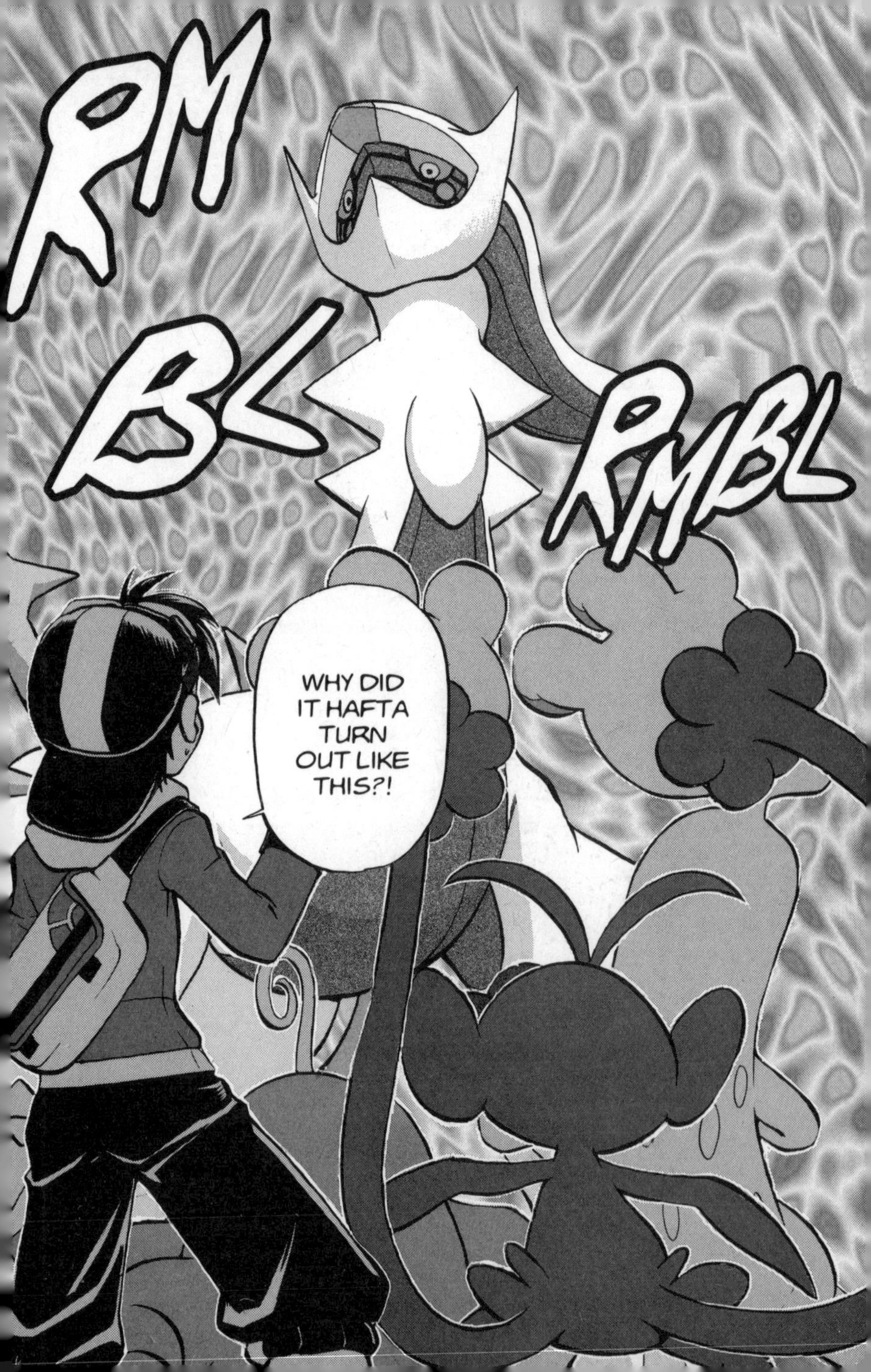
RMBL
RMBL
WHY DID IT HAFTA TURN OUT LIKE THIS?!

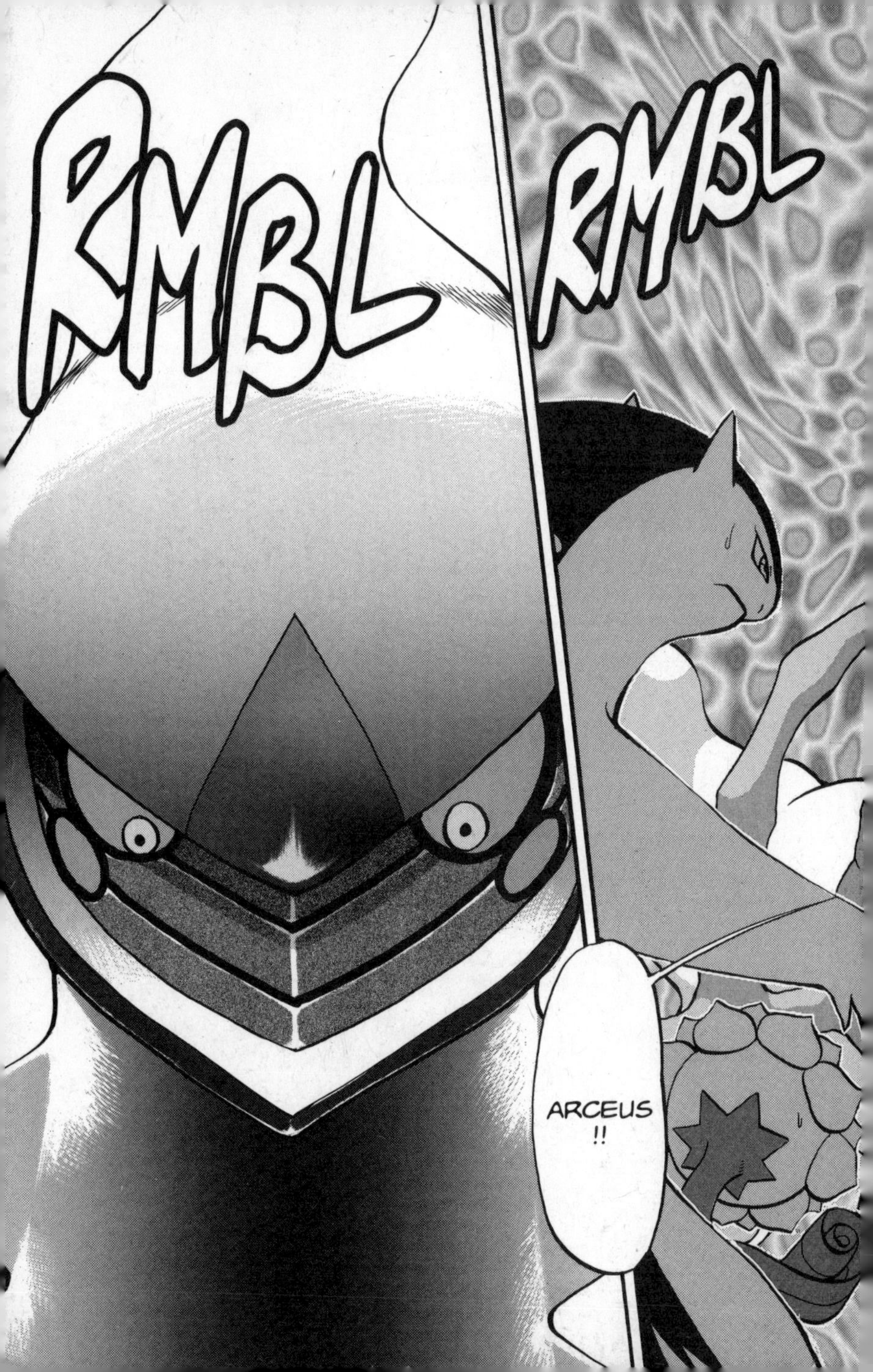
RMBL
ARCEUS !!
RMBL

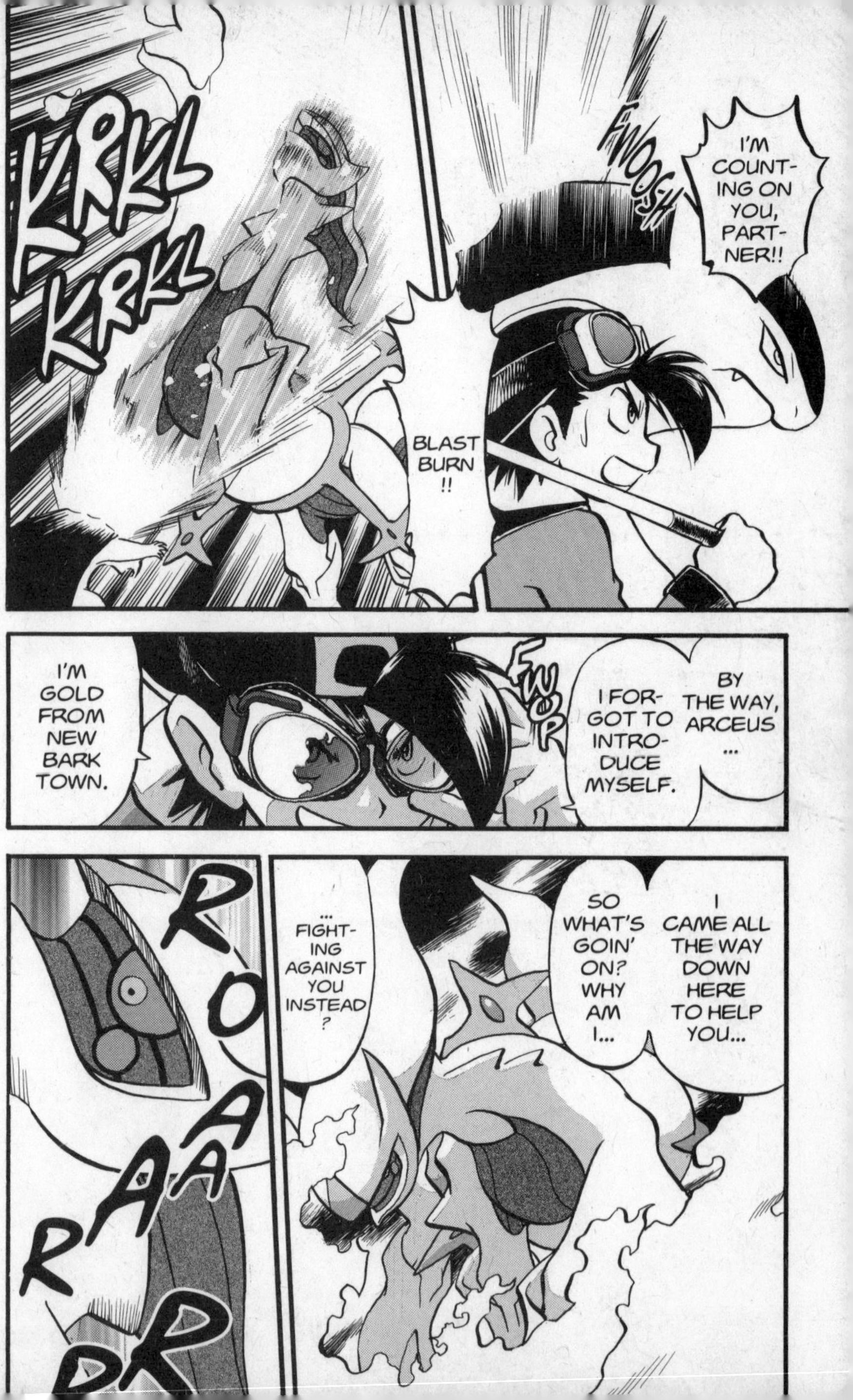

FWOOSH
I'M COUNTING ON YOU, PARTNER!!
KRKL KRKL
BLAST BURN!!
BY THE WAY, ARCEUS...
I FORGOT TO INTRODUCE MYSELF.
FWOP
I'M GOLD FROM NEW BARK TOWN.
I CAME ALL THE WAY DOWN HERE TO HELP YOU...
SO WHAT'S GOIN' ON? WHY AM I...
...FIGHTING AGAINST YOU INSTEAD?
ROAAARRR

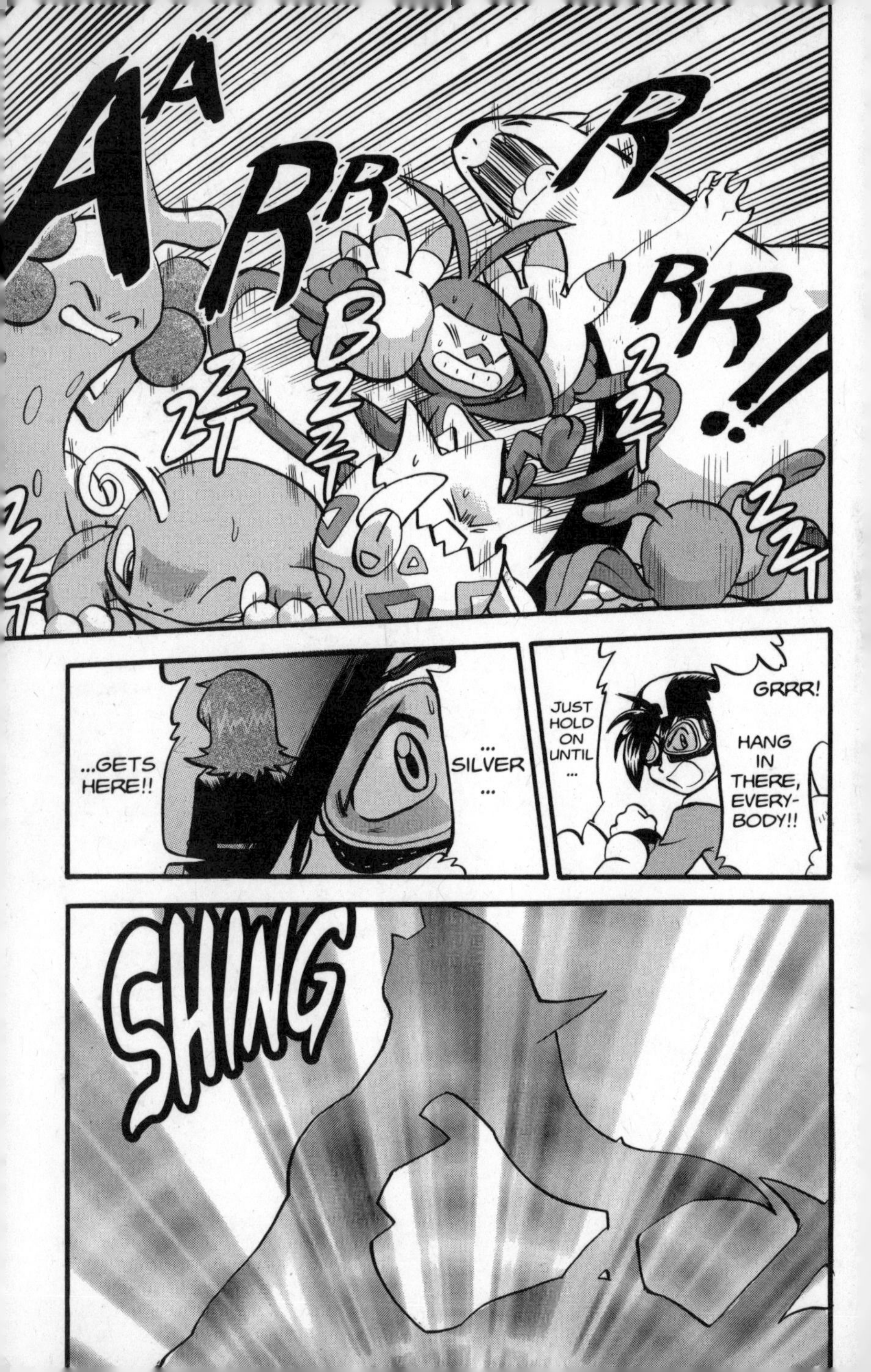
AAARRRRRR!!
ZZZT
BZZZZT
ZZZT
ZZZT
ZZZT
GRRR!
HANG IN THERE, EVERYBODY!!
JUST HOLD ON UNTIL ...
... SILVER ...
...GETS HERE!!
SHING

Pokémon™ Adventures

The Ninth Chapter 9

HeartGold & SoulSilver

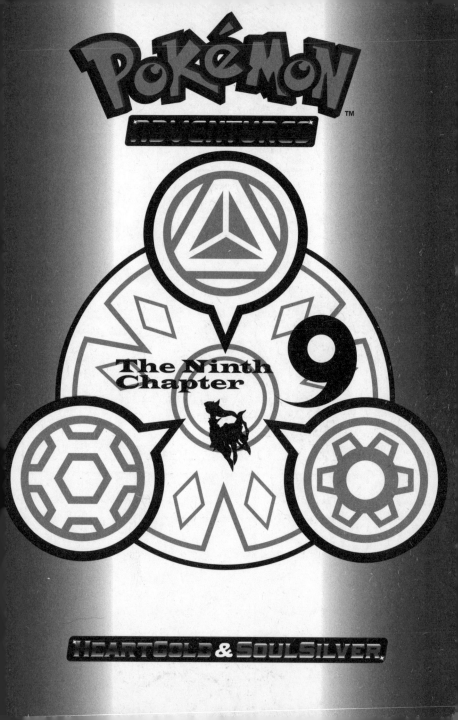

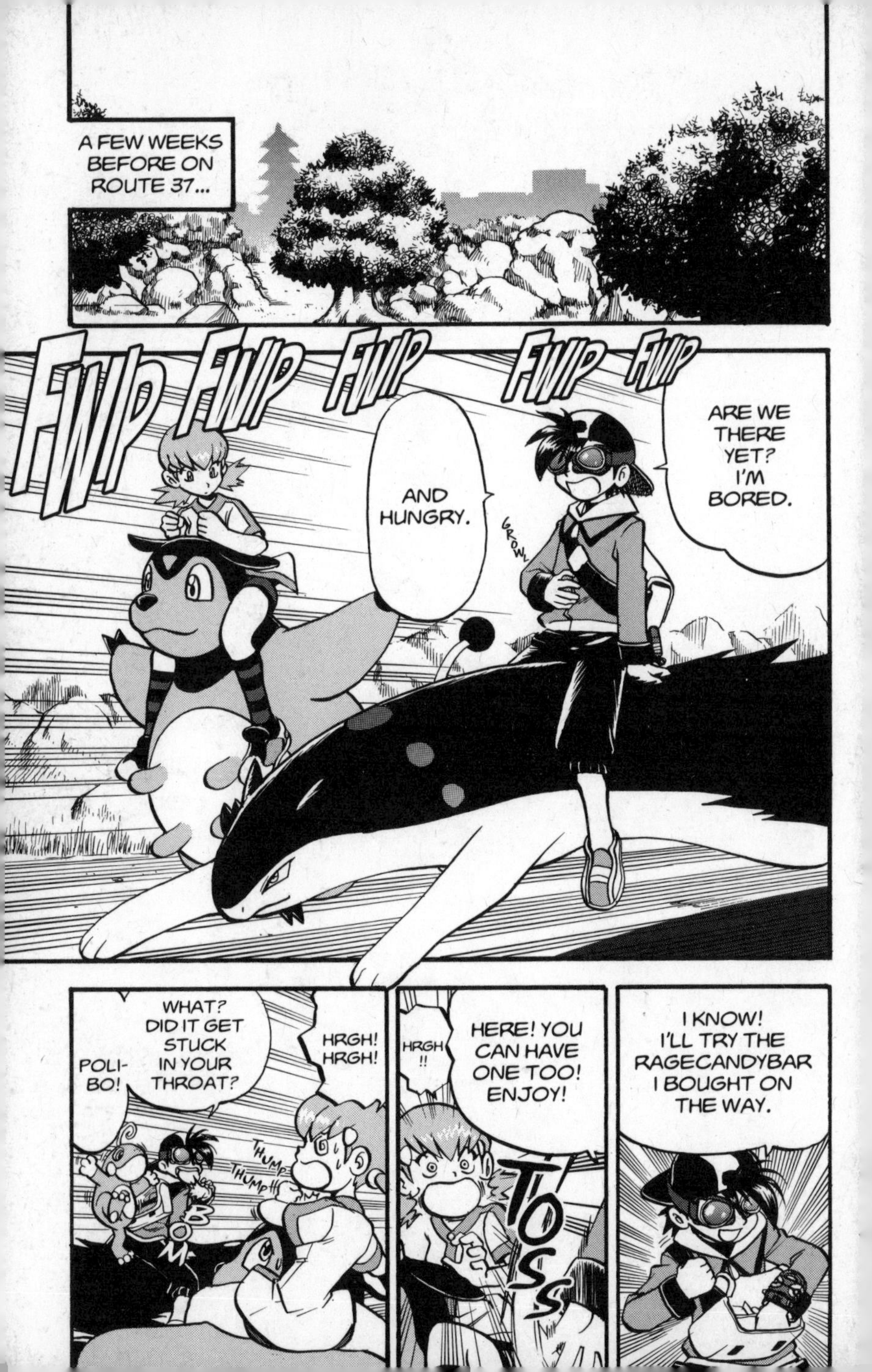
A FEW WEEKS BEFORE ON ROUTE 37...
FWIP FWIP FWIP FWIP FWIP
ARE WE THERE YET? I'M BORED.
GROWL
AND HUNGRY.
I KNOW! I'LL TRY THE RAGECANDYBAR I BOUGHT ON THE WAY.
HERE! YOU CAN HAVE ONE TOO! ENJOY!
HRGH !!
TOSS
WHAT? DID IT GET STUCK IN YOUR THROAT?
HRGH! HRGH!
POLI-BO!
THUMP THUMP
BOM

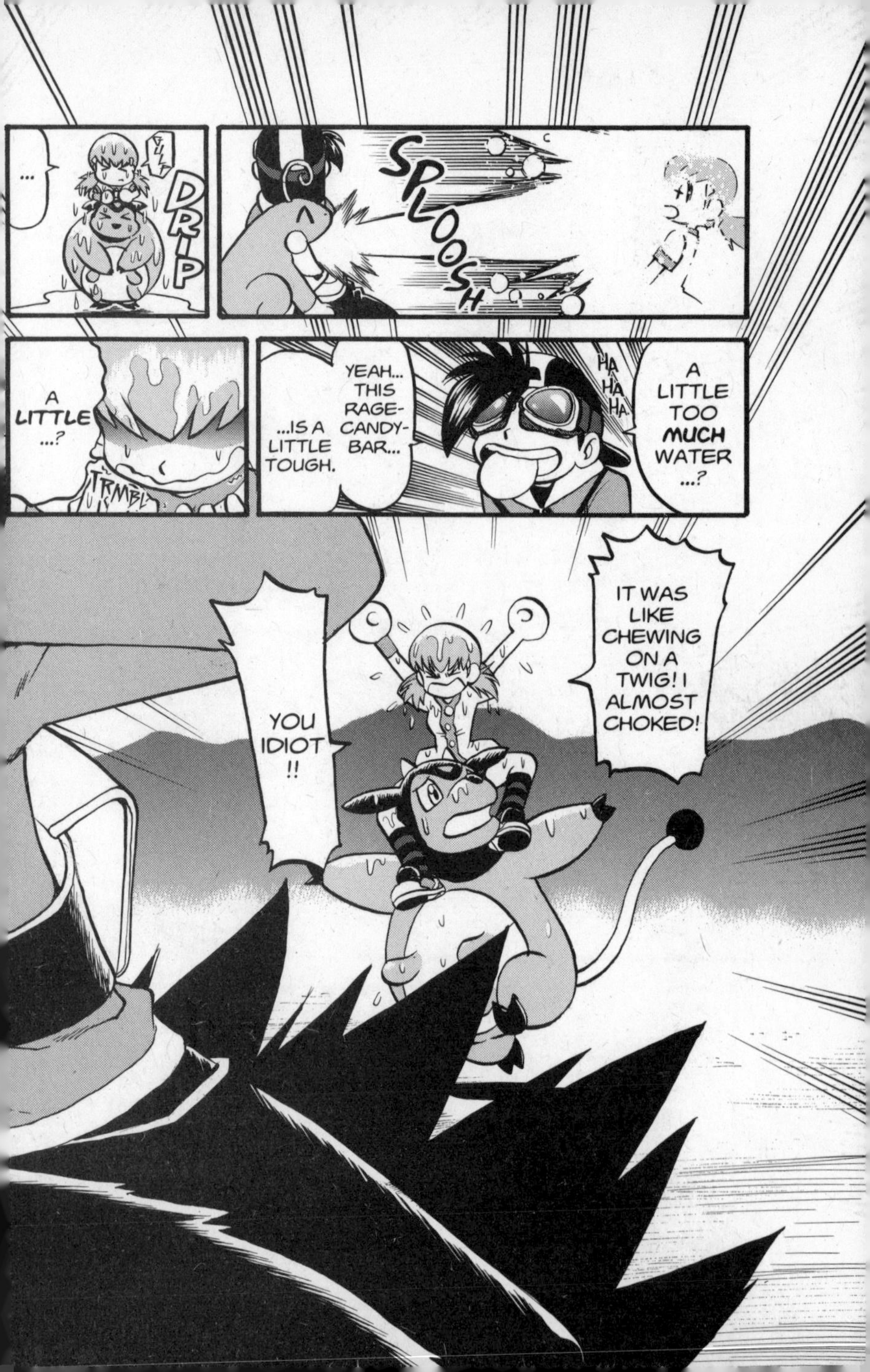
SPLOOSH
...
DRIP
HA HA HA
A LITTLE TOO MUCH WATER ...?
YEAH... THIS RAGE-CANDY-BAR...
...IS A LITTLE TOUGH.
A LITTLE ...?
TRMBL
IT WAS LIKE CHEWING ON A TWIG! I ALMOST CHOKED!
YOU IDIOT !!

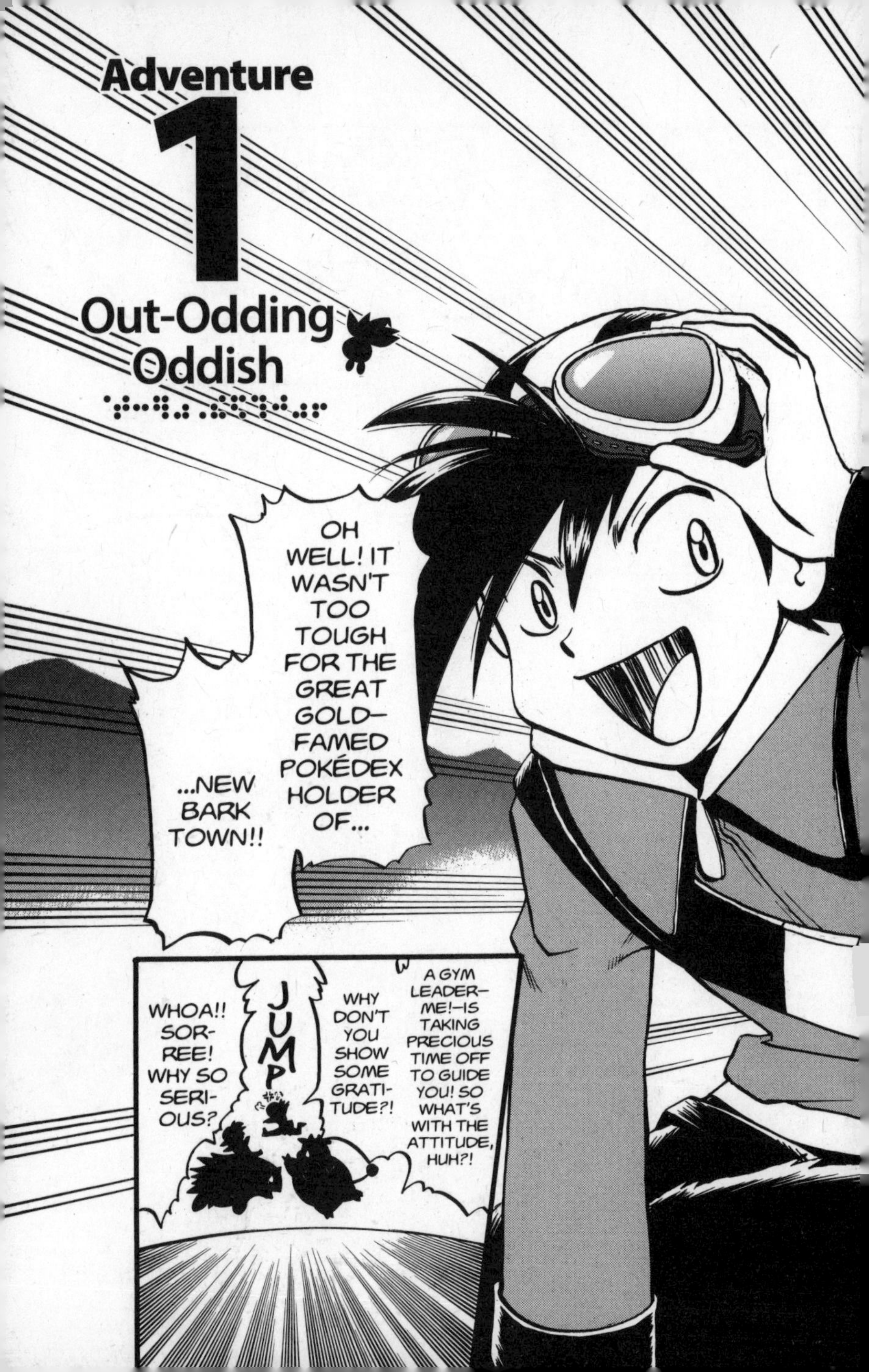
Adventure 1
Out-Odding Oddish
OH WELL! IT WASN'T TOO TOUGH FOR THE GREAT GOLD-FAMED POKÉDEX HOLDER OF...
...NEW BARK TOWN!!
A GYM LEADER—ME!—IS TAKING PRECIOUS TIME OFF TO GUIDE YOU! SO WHAT'S WITH THE ATTITUDE, HUH?!
WHY DON'T YOU SHOW SOME GRATITUDE?!
JUMP
WHOA!! SOR-REE! WHY SO SERI-OUS?

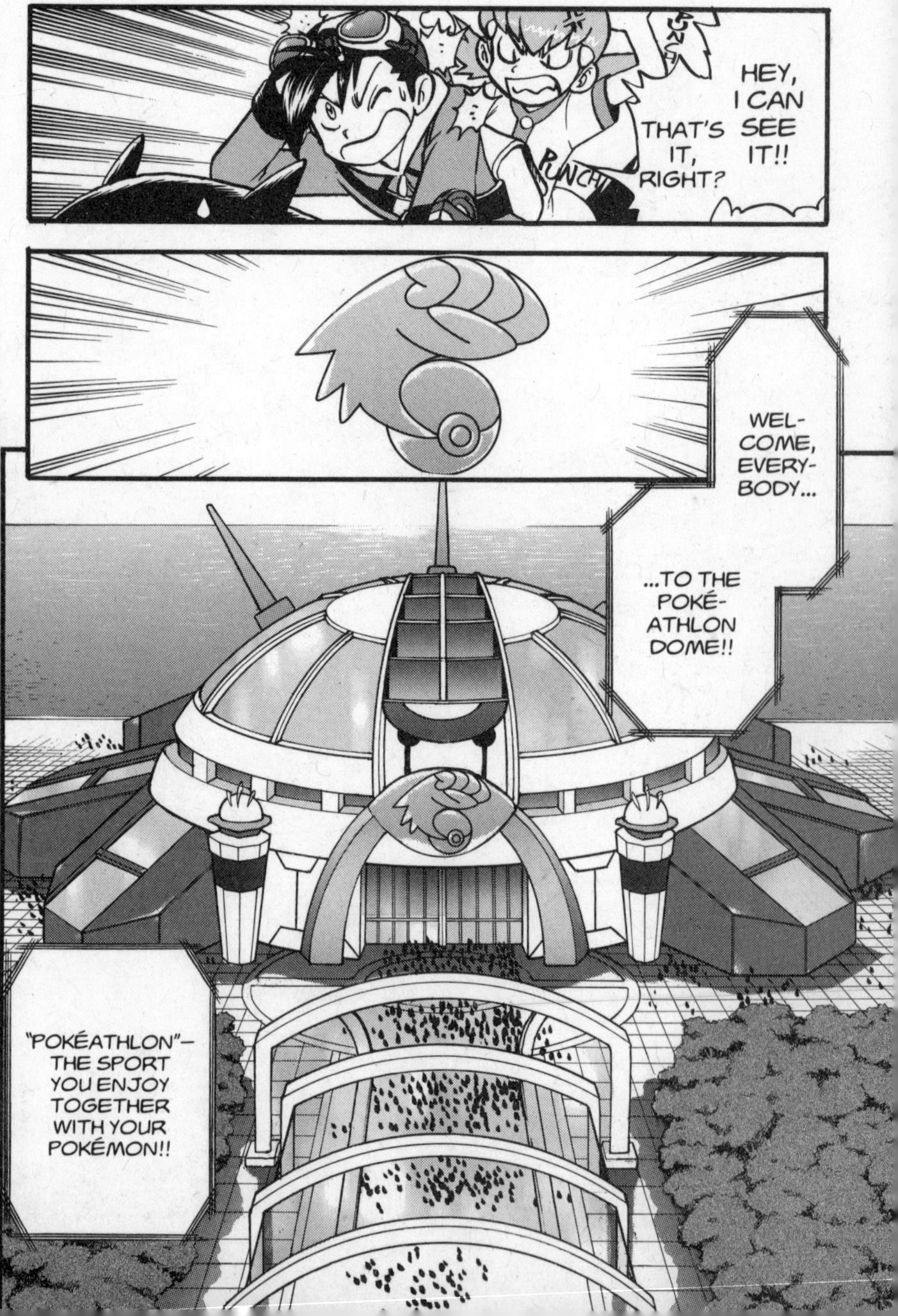
PUNCH
HEY, I CAN SEE IT!!
THAT'S IT, RIGHT?
PUNCH
WEL-COME, EVERY-BODY...
...TO THE POKÉ-ATHLON DOME!!
"POKÉATHLON"— THE SPORT YOU ENJOY TOGETHER WITH YOUR POKÉMON!!

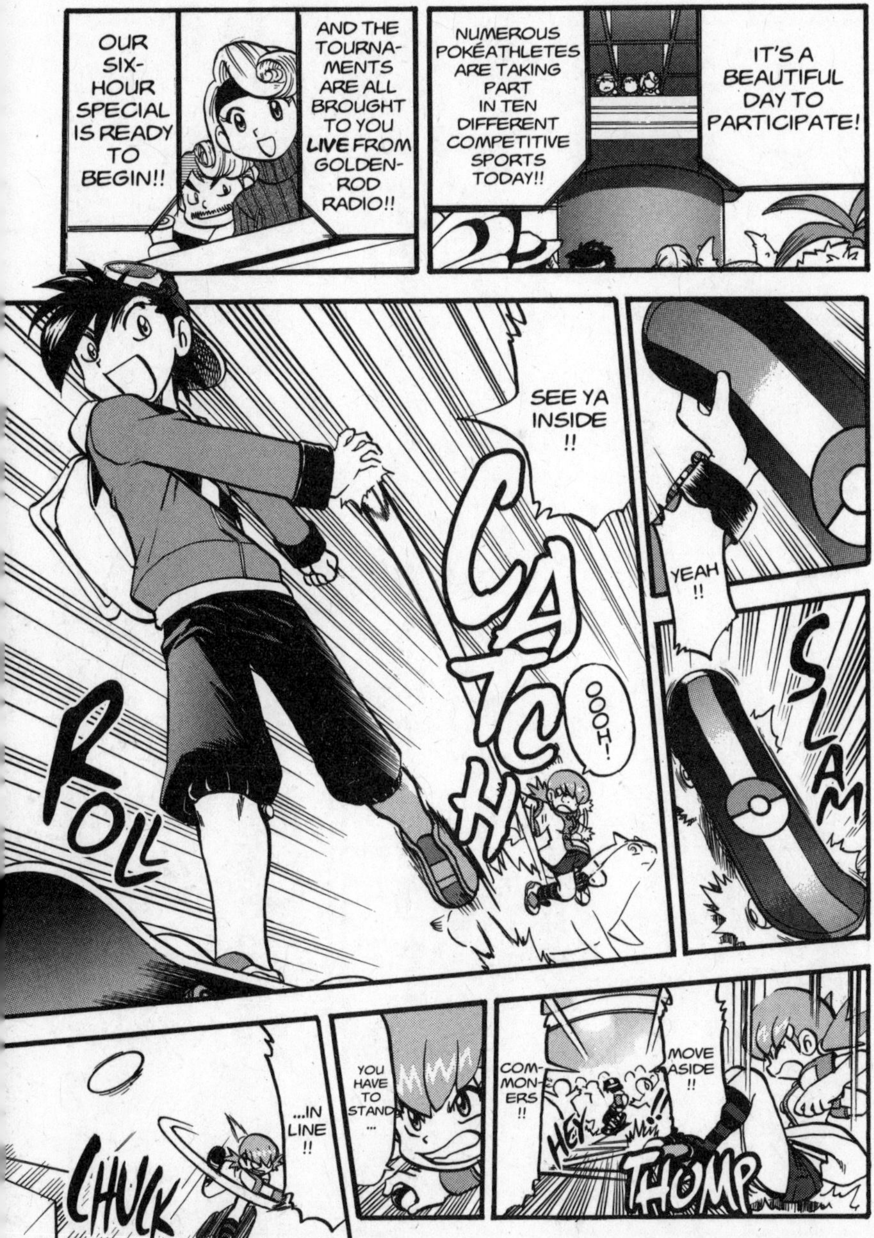
IT'S A BEAUTIFUL DAY TO PARTICIPATE!
NUMEROUS POKÉATHLETES ARE TAKING PART IN TEN DIFFERENT COMPETITIVE SPORTS TODAY!!
AND THE TOURNAMENTS ARE ALL BROUGHT TO YOU LIVE FROM GOLDENROD RADIO!!
OUR SIX-HOUR SPECIAL IS READY TO BEGIN!!
YEAH!!
SLAM!
SEE YA INSIDE!!
CATCH
OOOH!
ROLL!!
MOVE ASIDE!!
COMMONERS!!
HEY
THOMP
YOU HAVE TO STAND...
...IN LINE!!
CHUCK

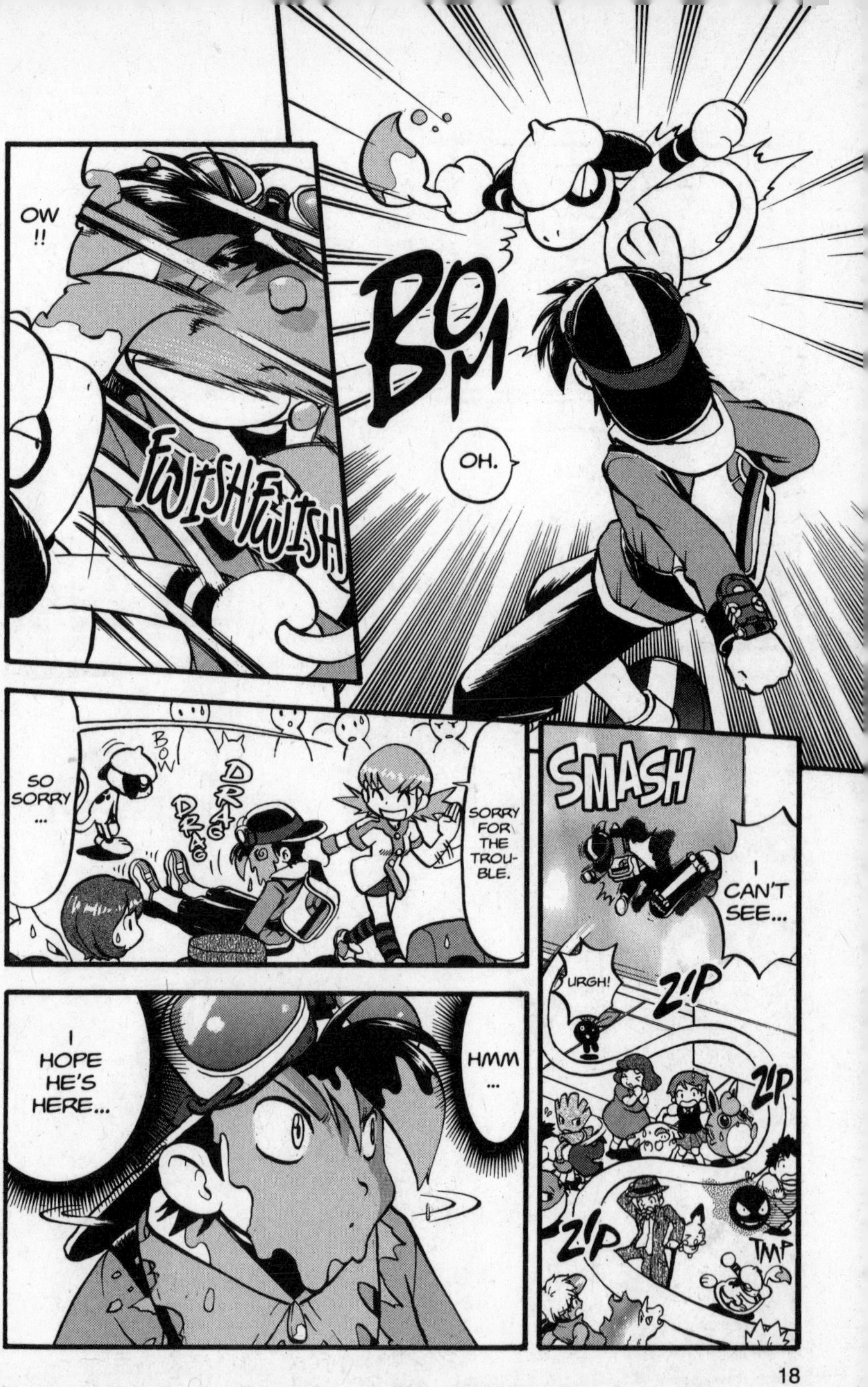
BOM
OH.
OW !!
FWISHFWISH
SMASH
I CAN'T SEE...
URGH!
ZIP
ZIP
ZIP
TMP
SORRY FOR THE TROUBLE.
DRAG DRAG
BOW
SO SORRY ...
HMM ...
I HOPE HE'S HERE...

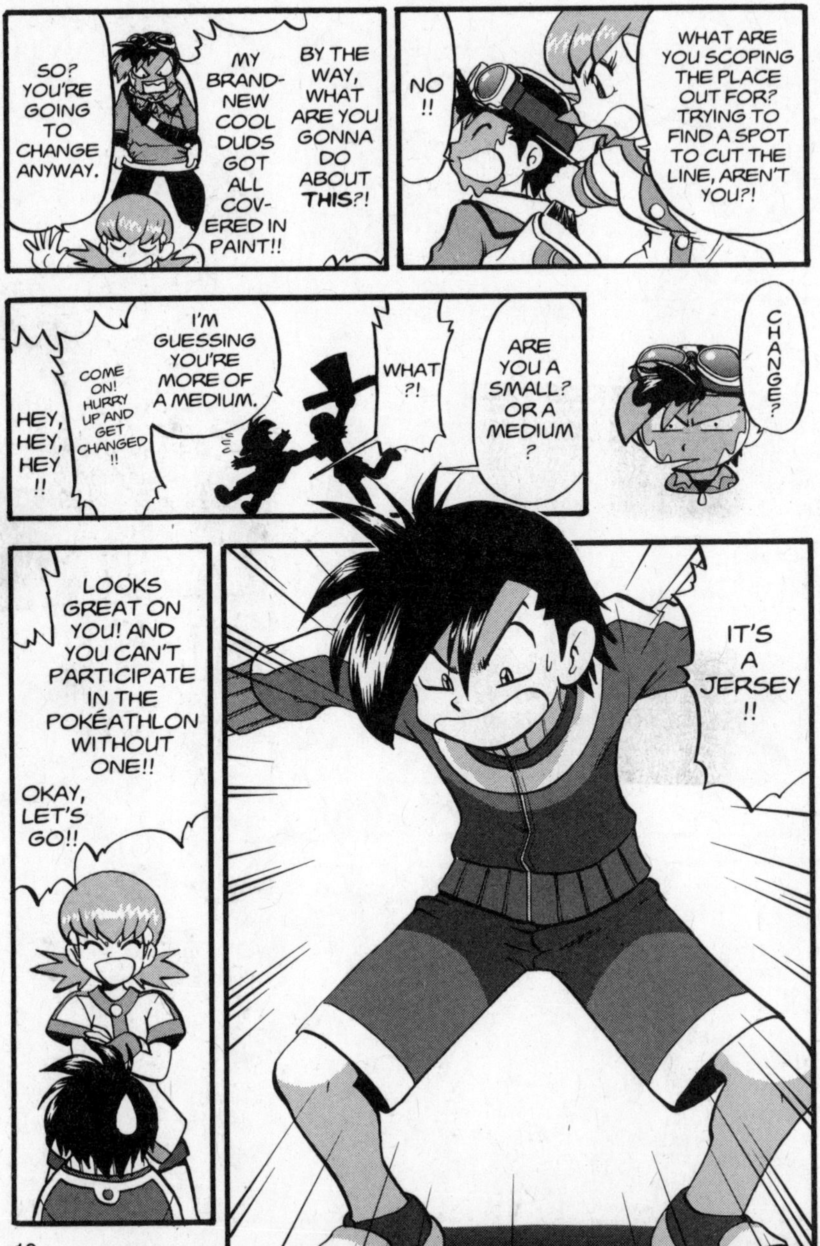
WHAT ARE YOU SCOPING THE PLACE OUT FOR? TRYING TO FIND A SPOT TO CUT THE LINE, AREN'T YOU?!
NO !!
BY THE WAY, WHAT ARE YOU GONNA DO ABOUT **THIS**?!
MY BRAND-NEW COOL DUDS GOT ALL COVERED IN PAINT!!
SO? YOU'RE GOING TO CHANGE ANYWAY.
CHANGE?
ARE YOU A SMALL? OR A MEDIUM?
WHAT?!
I'M GUESSING YOU'RE MORE OF A MEDIUM.
COME ON! HURRY UP AND GET CHANGED!!
HEY, HEY, HEY!!
IT'S A JERSEY!!
LOOKS GREAT ON YOU! AND YOU CAN'T PARTICIPATE IN THE POKÉATHLON WITHOUT ONE!!
OKAY, LET'S GO!!

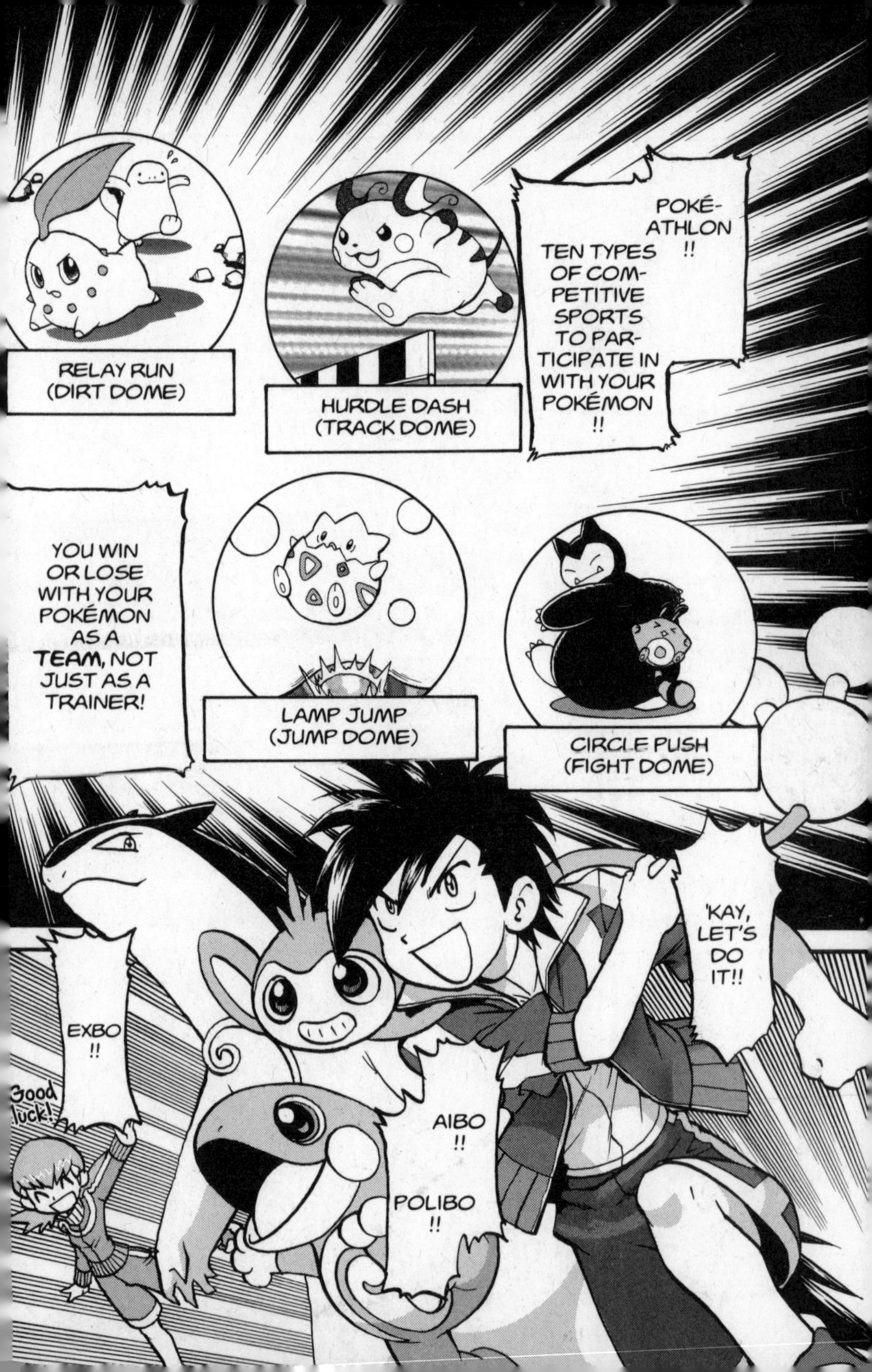
POKÉ-ATHLON !!
TEN TYPES OF COM-PETITIVE SPORTS TO PAR-TICIPATE IN WITH YOUR POKÉMON !!
HURDLE DASH (TRACK DOME)
RELAY RUN (DIRT DOME)
CIRCLE PUSH (FIGHT DOME)
LAMP JUMP (JUMP DOME)
YOU WIN OR LOSE WITH YOUR POKÉMON AS A **TEAM**, NOT JUST AS A TRAINER!
'KAY, LET'S DO IT!!
EXBO !!
AIBO !!
POLIBO !!
Good luck!

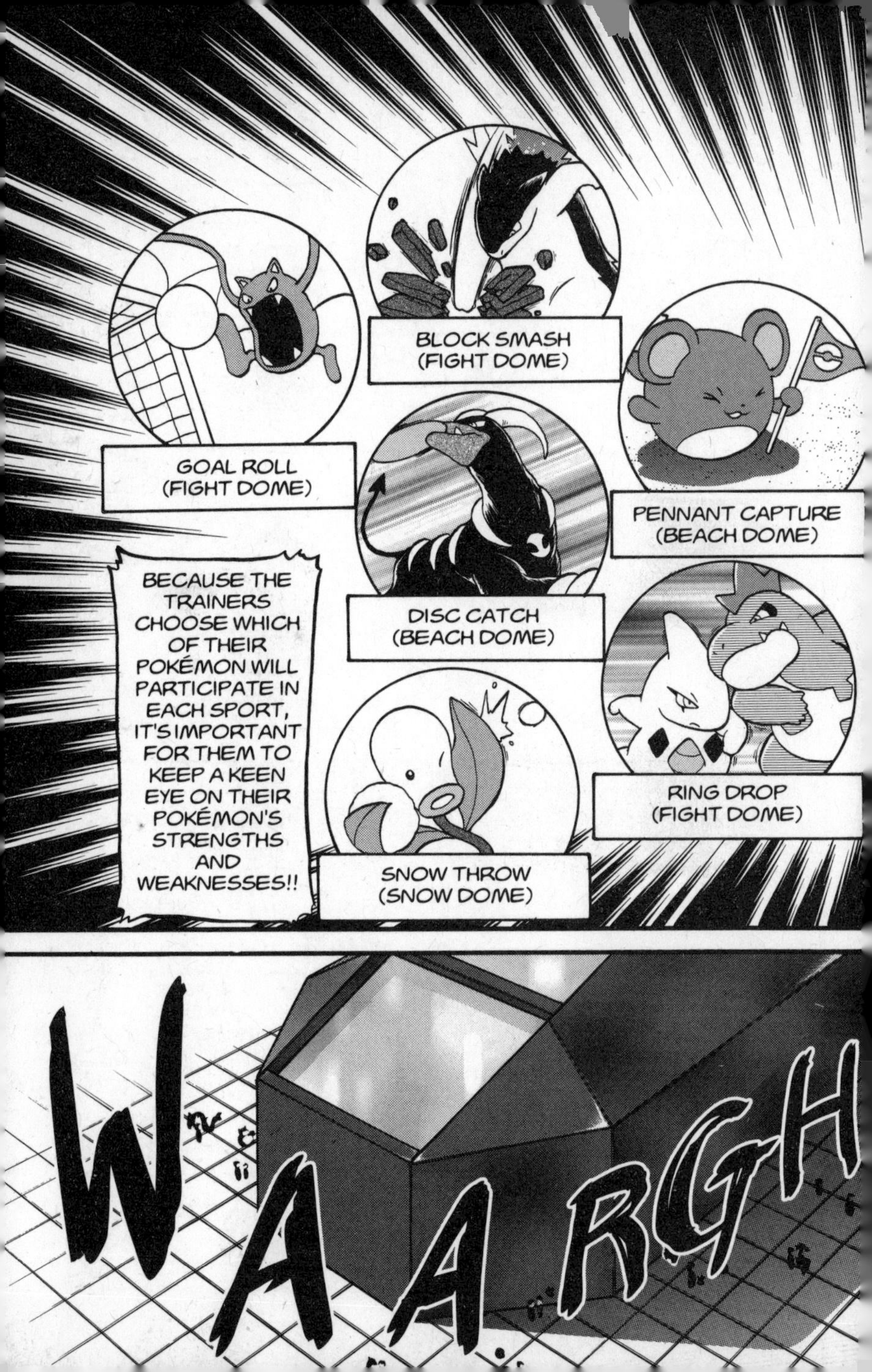
BLOCK SMASH (FIGHT DOME)
PENNANT CAPTURE (BEACH DOME)
GOAL ROLL (FIGHT DOME)
DISC CATCH (BEACH DOME)
RING DROP (FIGHT DOME)
SNOW THROW (SNOW DOME)
BECAUSE THE TRAINERS CHOOSE WHICH OF THEIR POKÉMON WILL PARTICIPATE IN EACH SPORT, IT'S IMPORTANT FOR THEM TO KEEP A KEEN EYE ON THEIR POKÉMON'S STRENGTHS AND WEAKNESSES!!
WAARGH

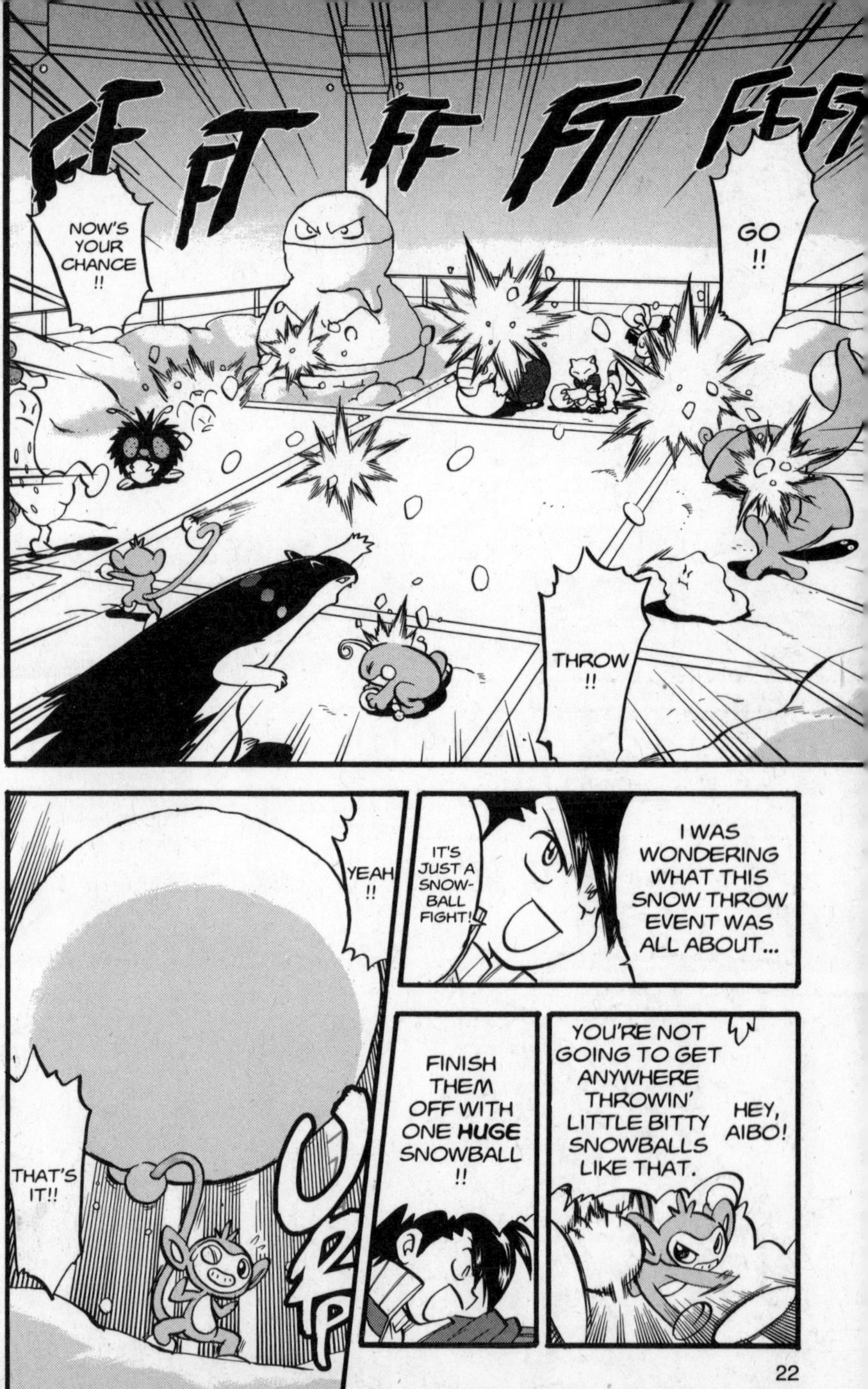
GO !!
NOW'S YOUR CHANCE !!
THROW !!
I WAS WONDERING WHAT THIS SNOW THROW EVENT WAS ALL ABOUT...
IT'S JUST A SNOW-BALL FIGHT!
HEY, AIBO!
YOU'RE NOT GOING TO GET ANYWHERE THROWIN' LITTLE BITTY SNOWBALLS LIKE THAT.
FINISH THEM OFF WITH ONE **HUGE** SNOWBALL !!
YEAH !!
THAT'S IT!!

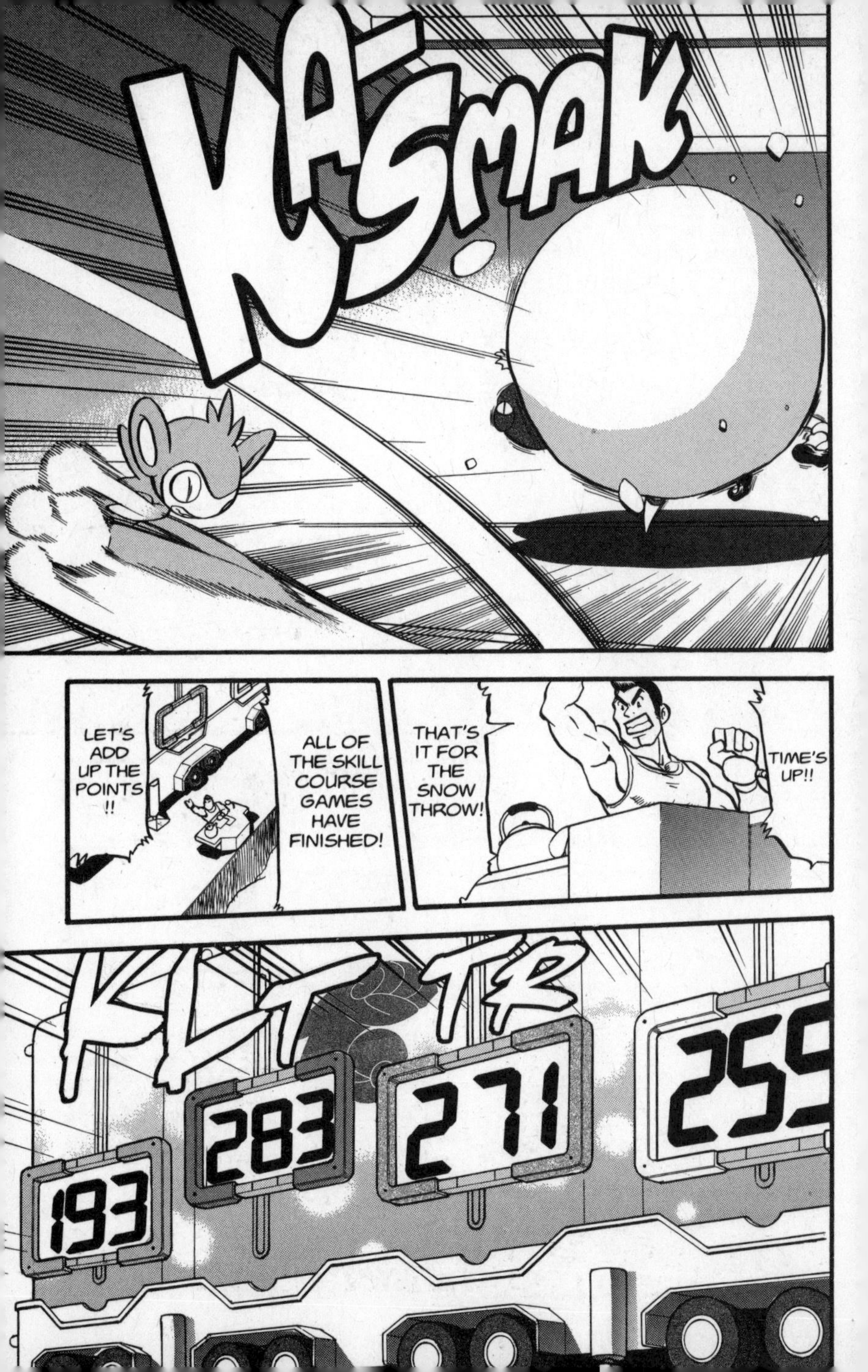
KA-SMAK
TIME'S UP!!
THAT'S IT FOR THE SNOW THROW!
ALL OF THE SKILL COURSE GAMES HAVE FINISHED!
LET'S ADD UP THE POINTS!!
KLT TR
259
271
283
193

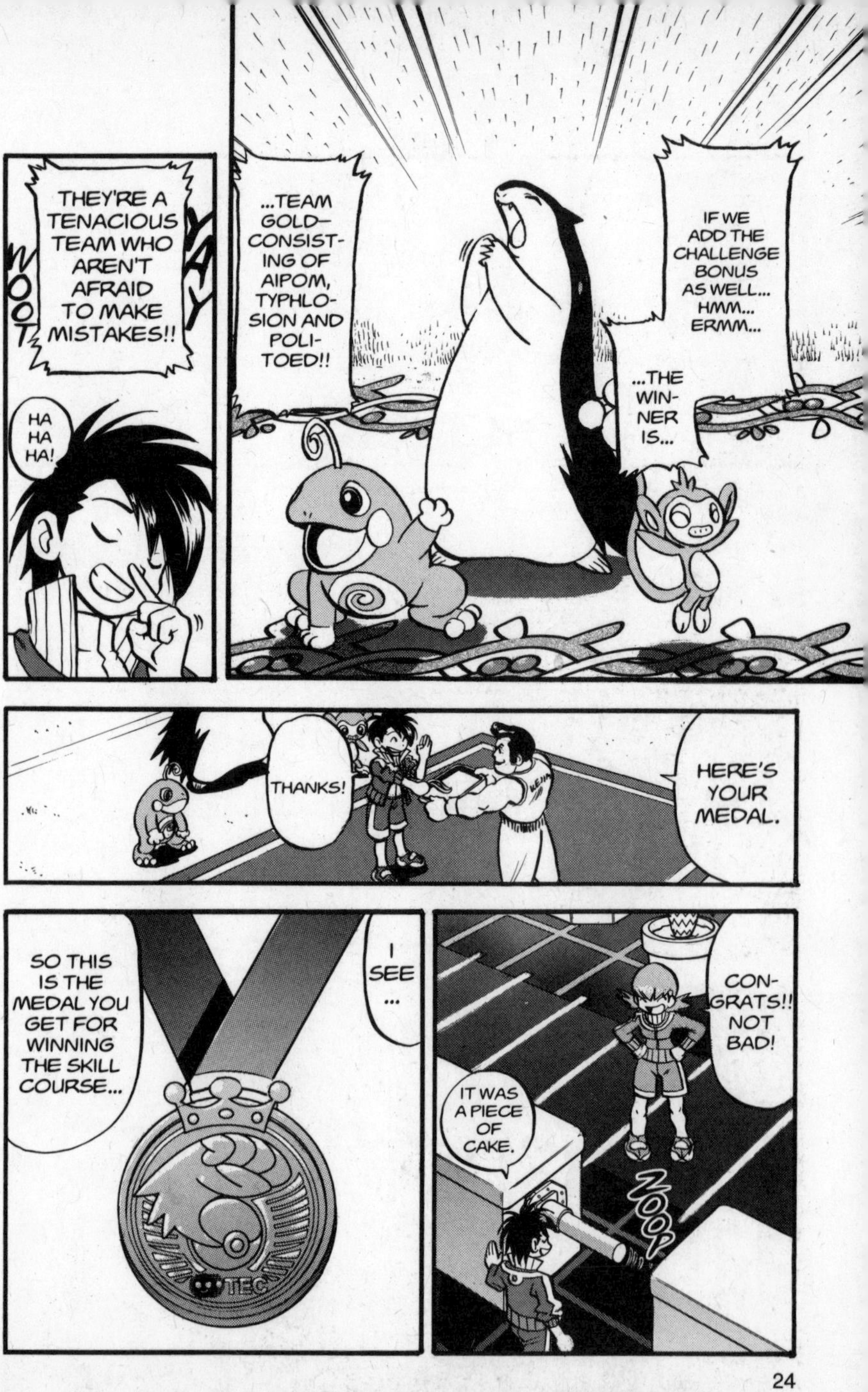
IF WE ADD THE CHALLENGE BONUS AS WELL... HMM... ERMM...
...THE WINNER IS...
...TEAM GOLD—CONSISTING OF AIPOM, TYPHLOSION AND POLITOED!!
THEY'RE A TENACIOUS TEAM WHO AREN'T AFRAID TO MAKE MISTAKES!!
YAY
WOOT
HA HA HA!
HERE'S YOUR MEDAL.
THANKS!
CON-GRATS!! NOT BAD!
IT WAS A PIECE OF CAKE.
ZOOP
I SEE...
SO THIS IS THE MEDAL YOU GET FOR WINNING THE SKILL COURSE...
TEC

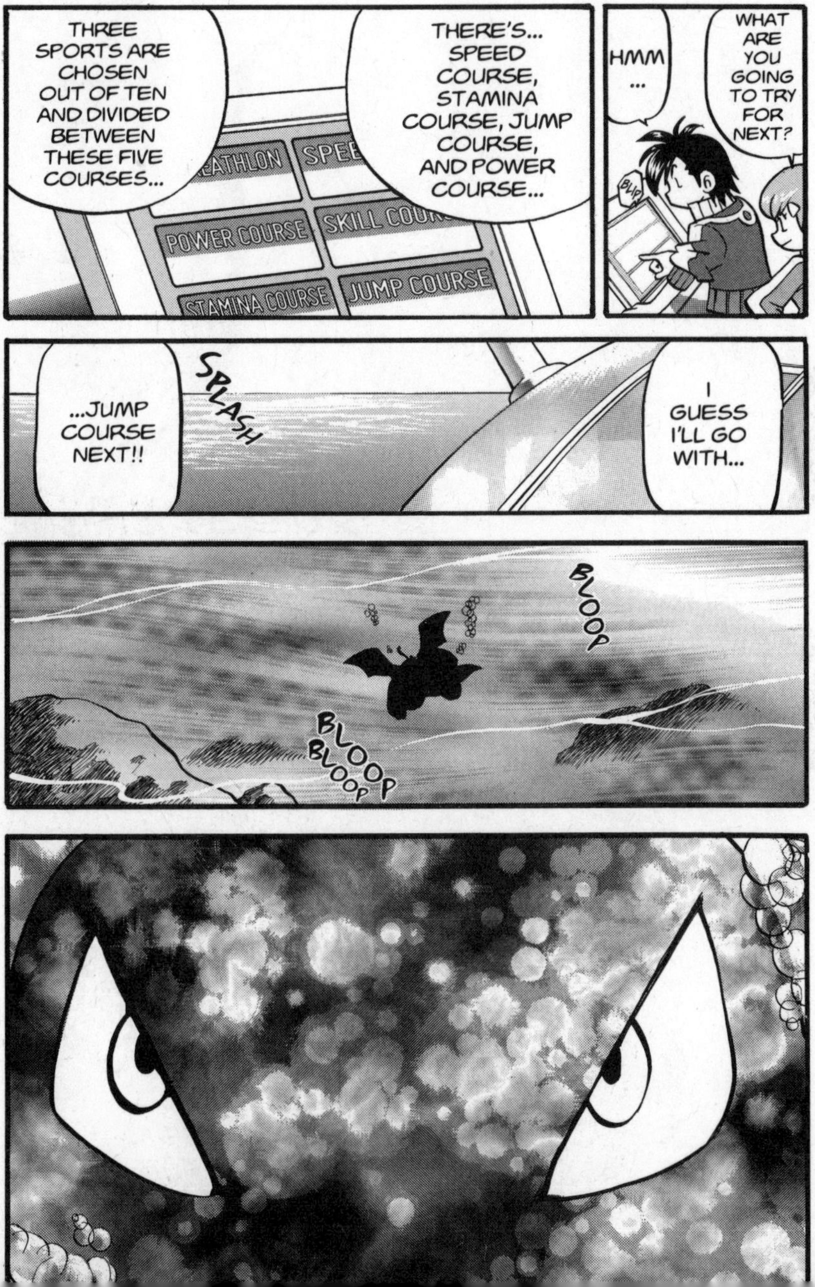
WHAT ARE YOU GOING TO TRY FOR NEXT?
HMM ...
BLIP
THERE'S... SPEED COURSE, STAMINA COURSE, JUMP COURSE, AND POWER COURSE...
THREE SPORTS ARE CHOSEN OUT OF TEN AND DIVIDED BETWEEN THESE FIVE COURSES...
POWER COURSE
JUMP COURSE
STAMINA COURSE
I GUESS I'LL GO WITH...
SPLASH
...JUMP COURSE NEXT!!
BLOOP
BLOOP
BLOOP

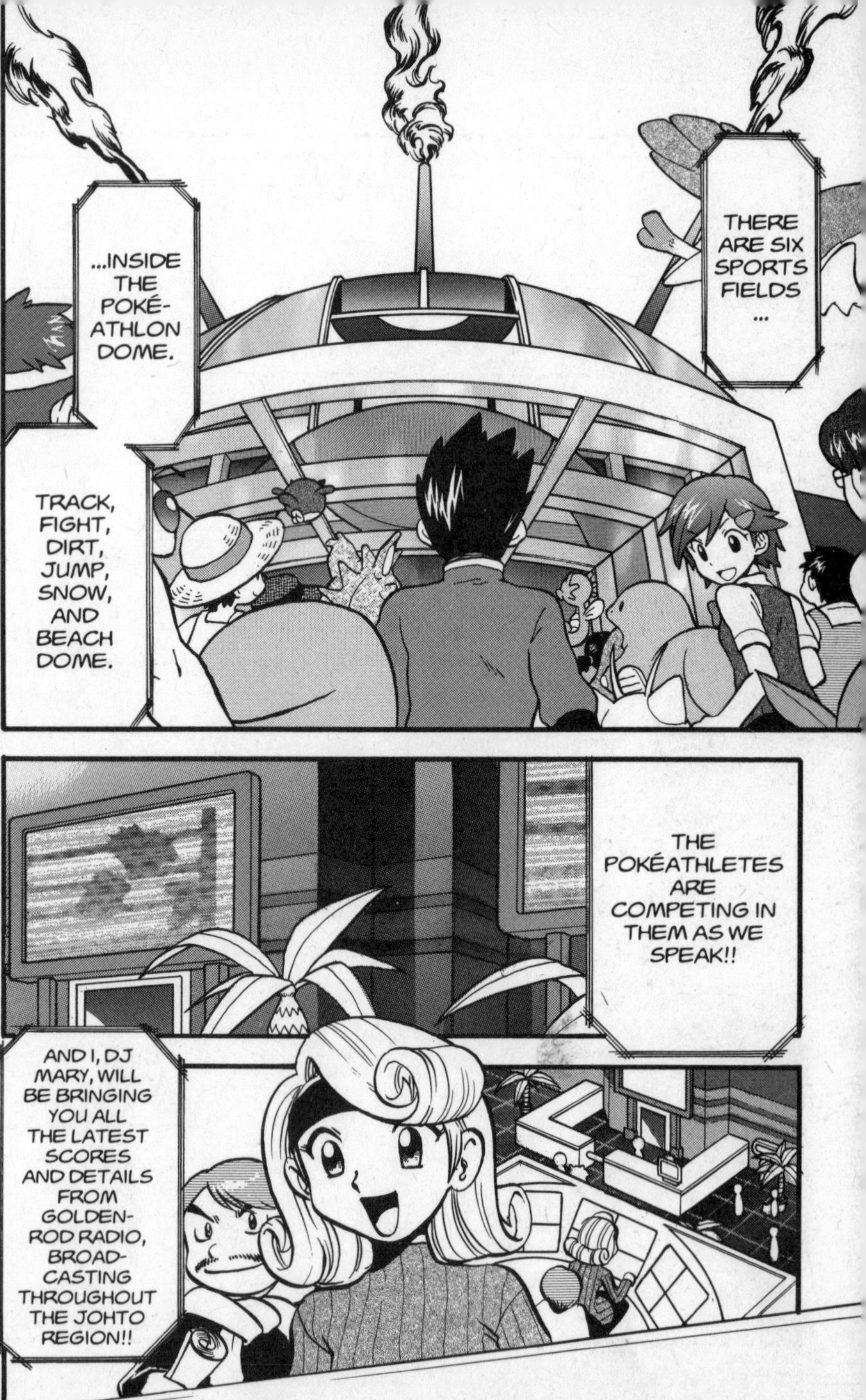
THERE ARE SIX SPORTS FIELDS ...
...INSIDE THE POKÉ-ATHLON DOME.
TRACK, FIGHT, DIRT, JUMP, SNOW, AND BEACH DOME.
THE POKÉATHLETES ARE COMPETING IN THEM AS WE SPEAK!!
AND I, DJ MARY, WILL BE BRINGING YOU ALL THE LATEST SCORES AND DETAILS FROM GOLDEN-ROD RADIO, BROAD-CASTING THROUGHOUT THE JOHTO REGION!!

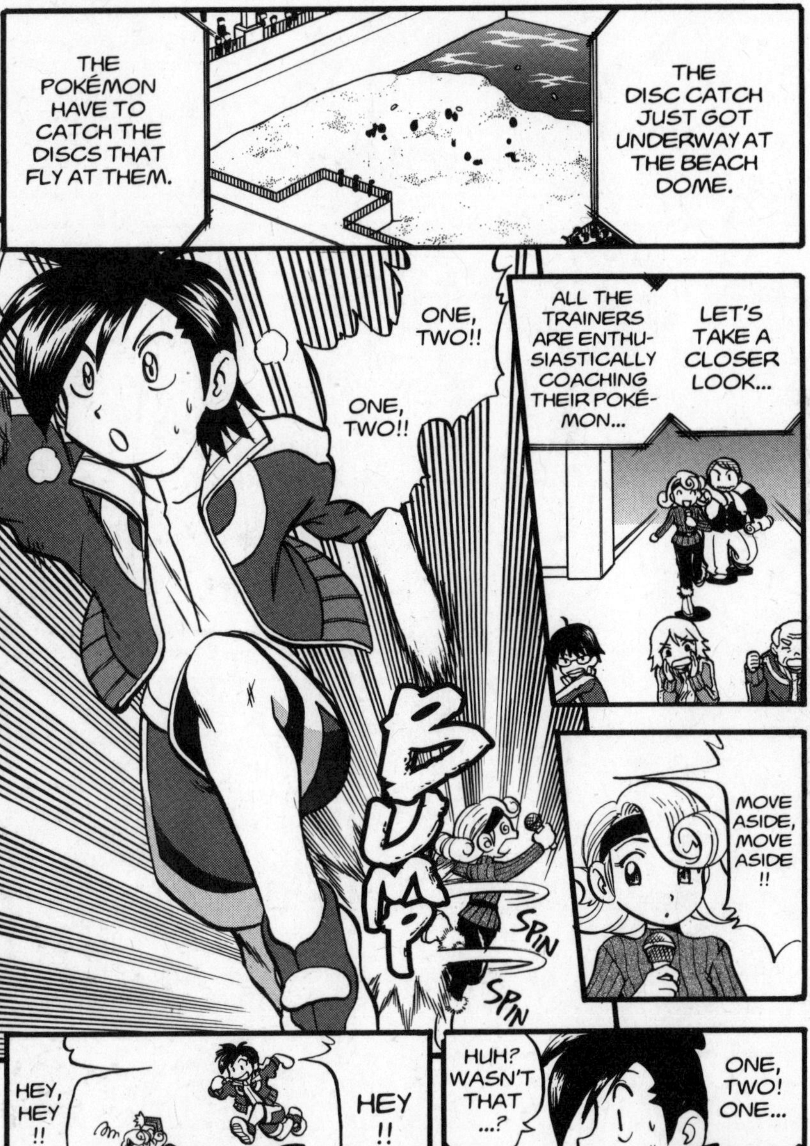
THE DISC CATCH JUST GOT UNDERWAY AT THE BEACH DOME.
THE POKÉMON HAVE TO CATCH THE DISCS THAT FLY AT THEM.
LET'S TAKE A CLOSER LOOK...
ALL THE TRAINERS ARE ENTHUSIASTICALLY COACHING THEIR POKÉMON...
MOVE ASIDE, MOVE ASIDE !!
ONE, TWO!!
ONE, TWO!!
BUMP
SPIN
SPIN
ONE, TWO! ONE...
HUH? WASN'T THAT ...?
HEY !!
HEY, HEY !!

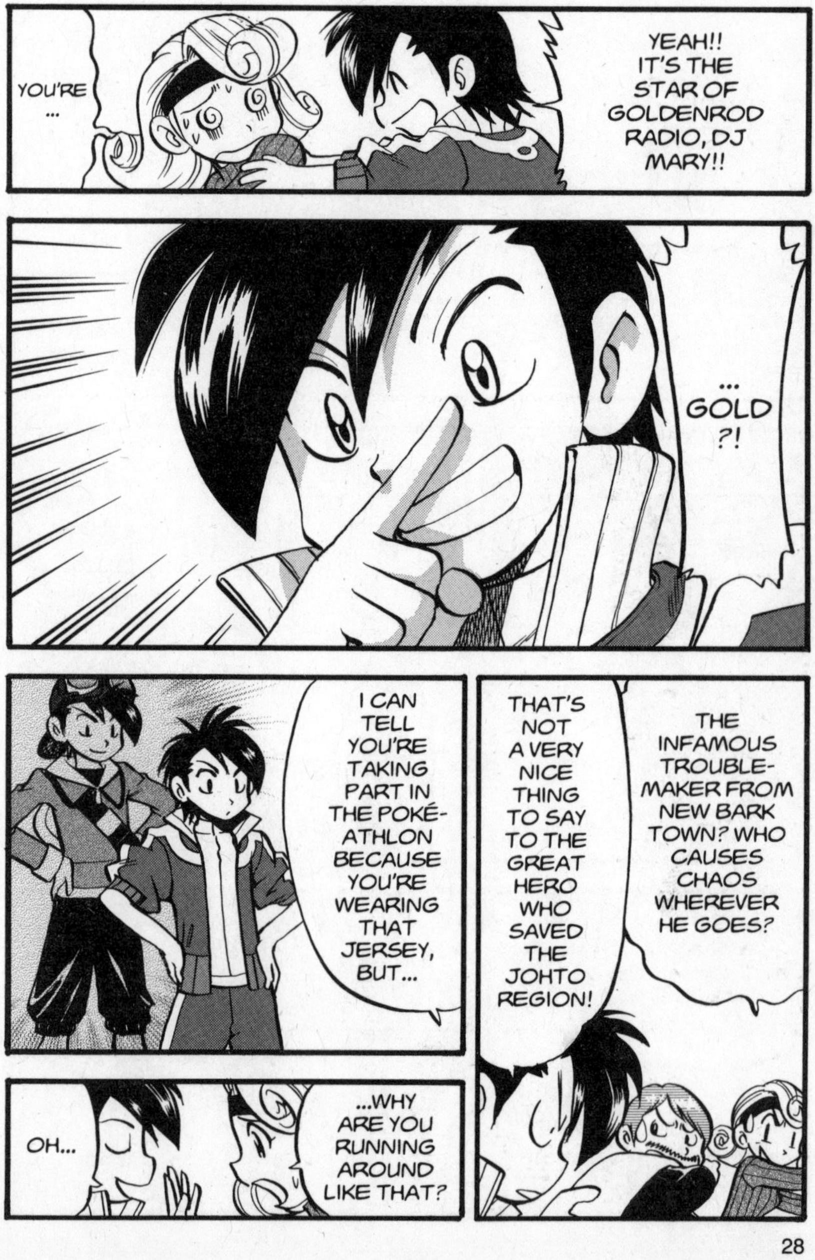
YEAH!! IT'S THE STAR OF GOLDENROD RADIO, DJ MARY!!
YOU'RE ...
... GOLD ?!
THE INFAMOUS TROUBLE-MAKER FROM NEW BARK TOWN? WHO CAUSES CHAOS WHEREVER HE GOES?
THAT'S NOT A VERY NICE THING TO SAY TO THE GREAT HERO WHO SAVED THE JOHTO REGION!
I CAN TELL YOU'RE TAKING PART IN THE POKÉ-ATHLON BECAUSE YOU'RE WEARING THAT JERSEY, BUT...
...WHY ARE YOU RUNNING AROUND LIKE THAT?
OH...

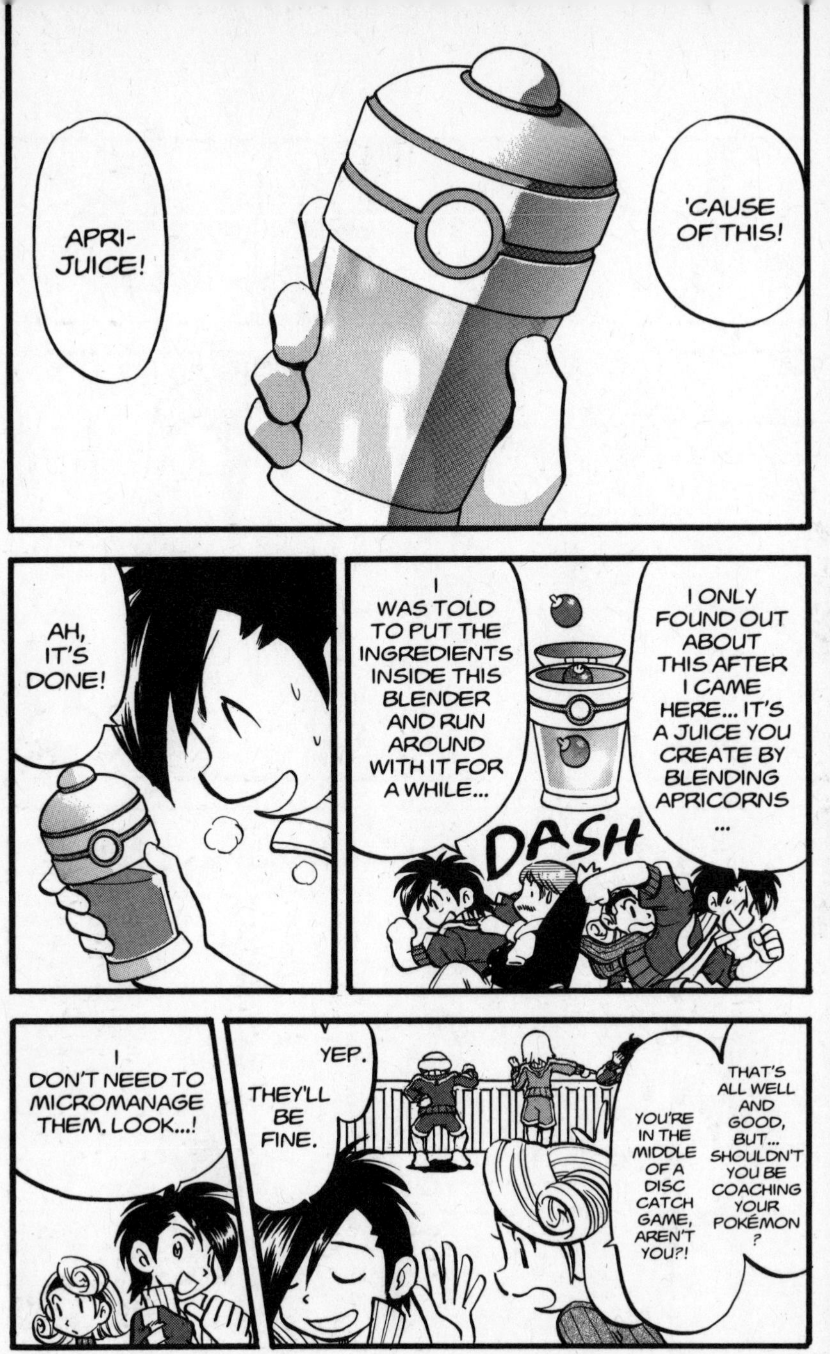
'CAUSE OF THIS!
APRI-JUICE!
I ONLY FOUND OUT ABOUT THIS AFTER I CAME HERE... IT'S A JUICE YOU CREATE BY BLENDING APRICORNS ...
I WAS TOLD TO PUT THE INGREDIENTS INSIDE THIS BLENDER AND RUN AROUND WITH IT FOR A WHILE...
DASH
AH, IT'S DONE!
THAT'S ALL WELL AND GOOD, BUT... SHOULDN'T YOU BE COACHING YOUR POKéMON ?
YOU'RE IN THE MIDDLE OF A DISC CATCH GAME, AREN'T YOU?!
YEP.
THEY'LL BE FINE.
I DON'T NEED TO MICROMANAGE THEM. LOOK...!

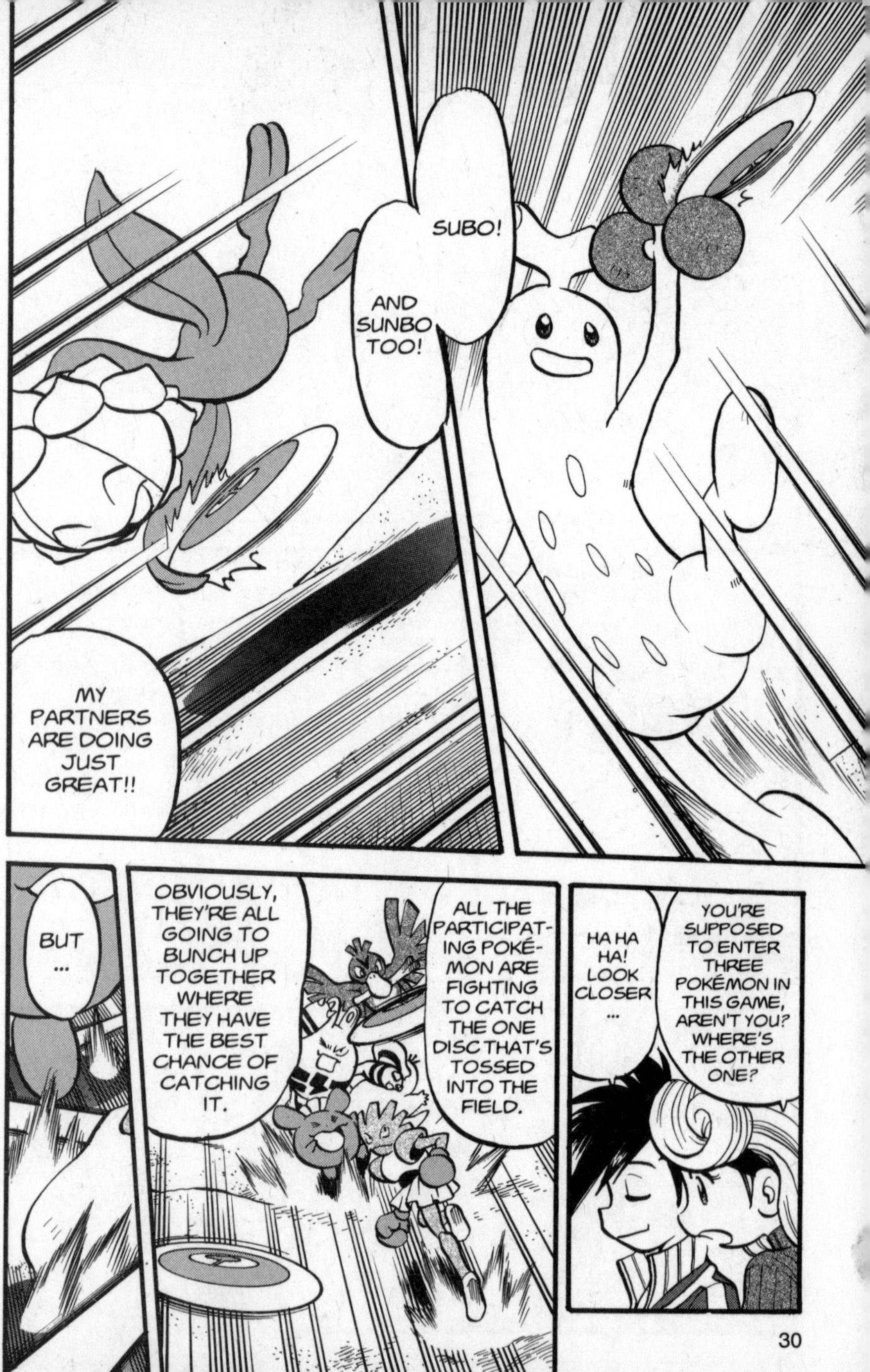
SUBO!
AND SUNBO TOO!
MY PARTNERS ARE DOING JUST GREAT!!
YOU'RE SUPPOSED TO ENTER THREE POKÉMON IN THIS GAME, AREN'T YOU? WHERE'S THE OTHER ONE?
HA HA HA! LOOK CLOSER ...
ALL THE PARTICIPATING POKÉMON ARE FIGHTING TO CATCH THE ONE DISC THAT'S TOSSED INTO THE FIELD.
OBVIOUSLY, THEY'RE ALL GOING TO BUNCH UP TOGETHER WHERE THEY HAVE THE BEST CHANCE OF CATCHING IT.
BUT ...

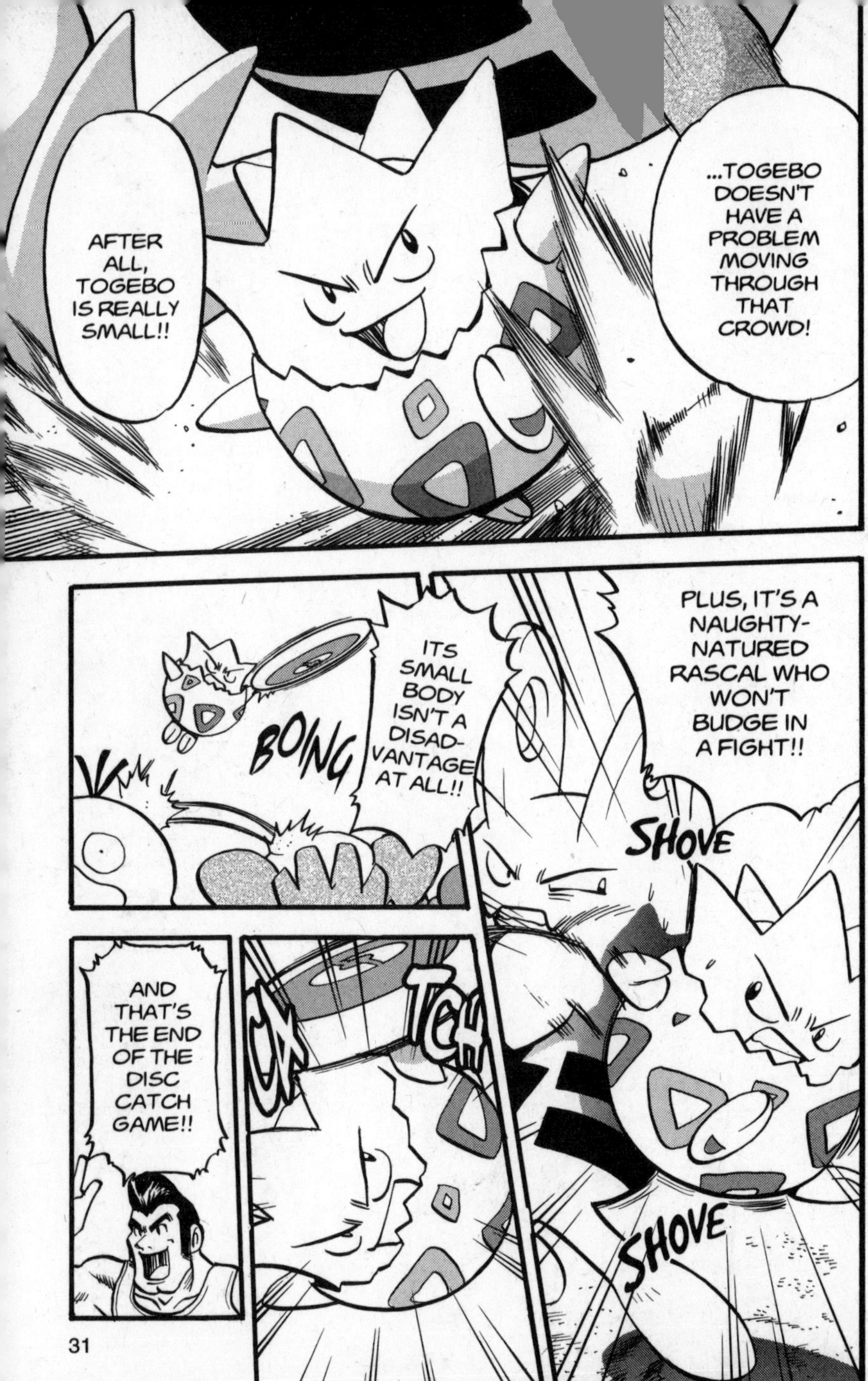
...TOGEBO DOESN'T HAVE A PROBLEM MOVING THROUGH THAT CROWD!
AFTER ALL, TOGEBO IS REALLY SMALL!!
PLUS, IT'S A NAUGHTY-NATURED RASCAL WHO WON'T BUDGE IN A FIGHT!!
SHOVE
SHOVE
ITS SMALL BODY ISN'T A DISAD-VANTAGE AT ALL!!
BOING
CATCH
AND THAT'S THE END OF THE DISC CATCH GAME!!

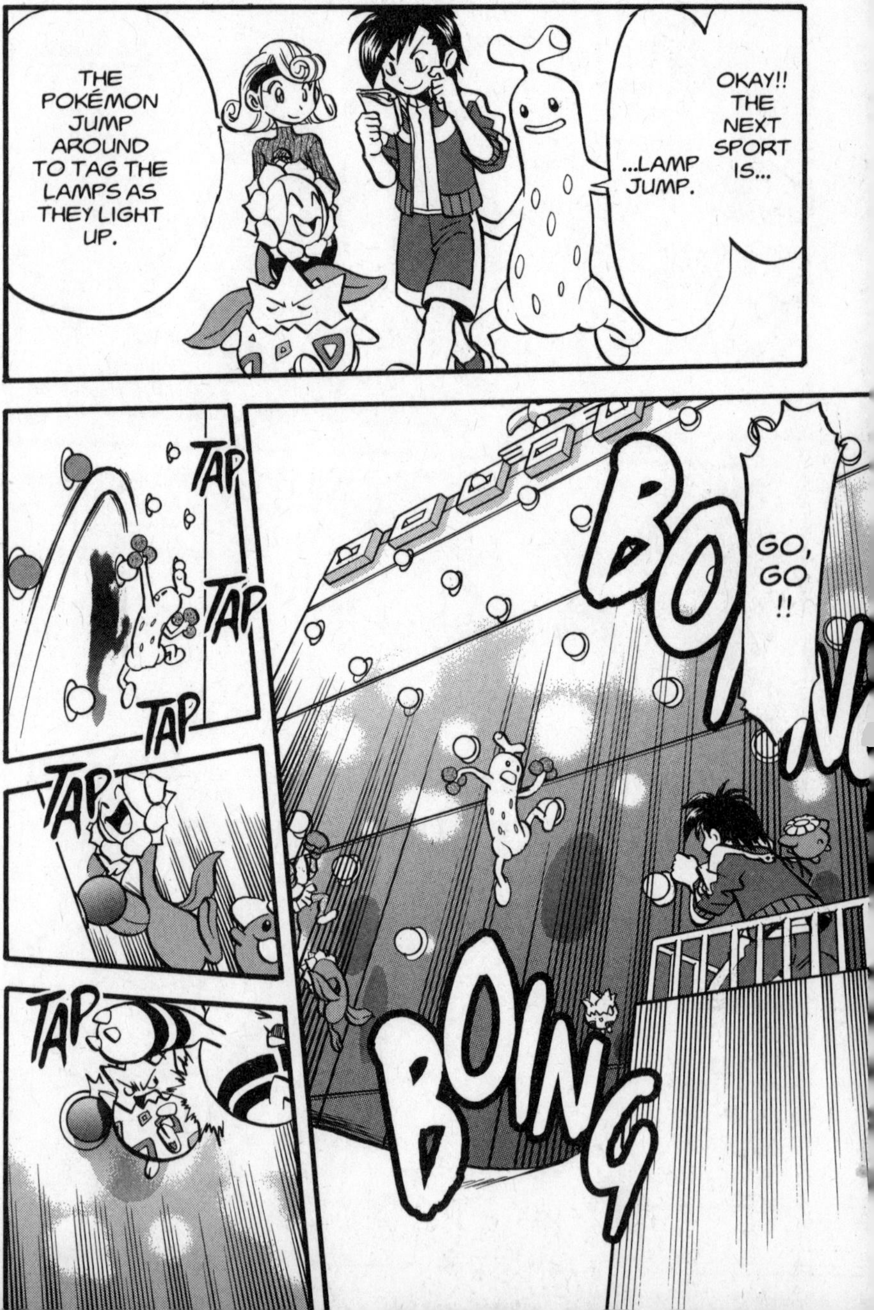
OKAY!! THE NEXT SPORT IS...
...LAMP JUMP.
THE POKÉMON JUMP AROUND TO TAG THE LAMPS AS THEY LIGHT UP.
BO
GO, GO !!
BOING
TAP
TAP
TAP
TAP
TAP

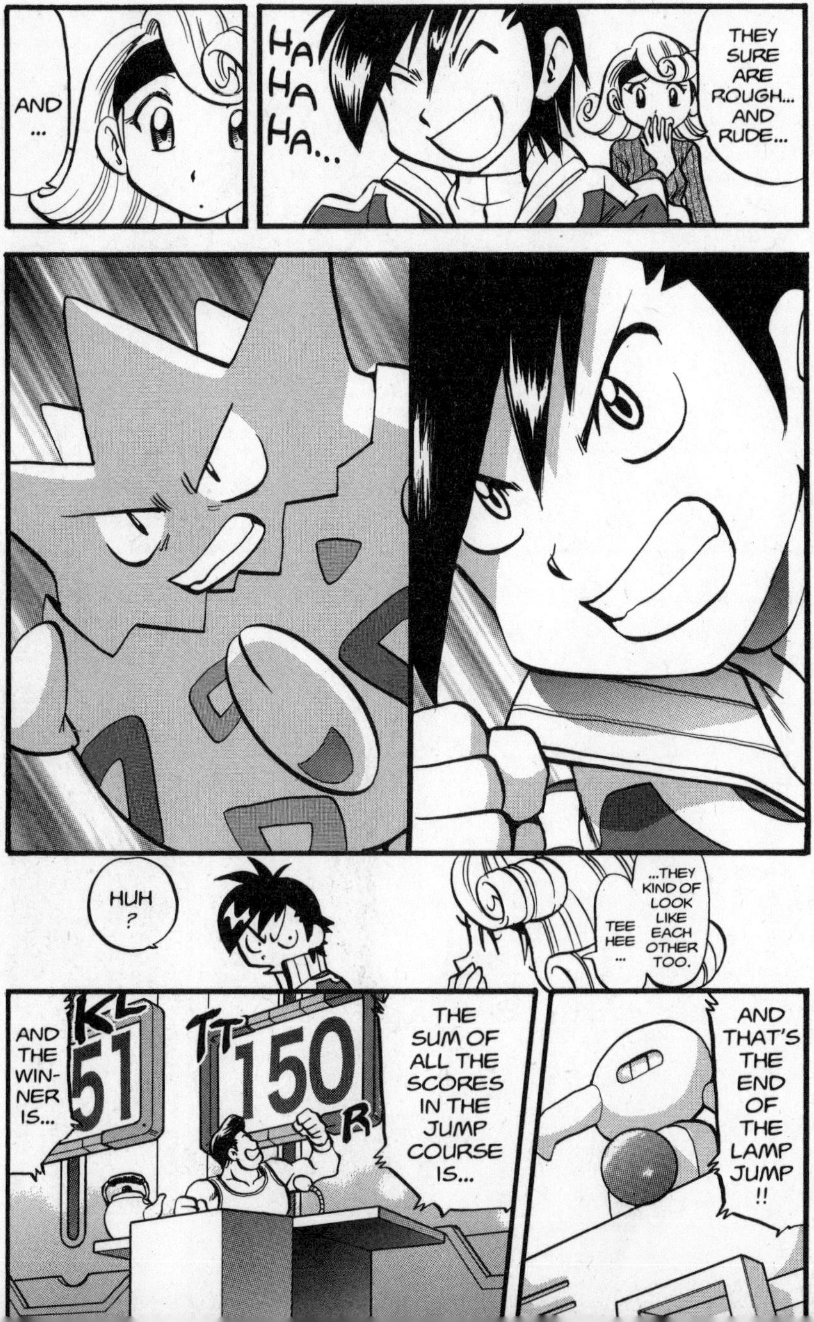
THEY SURE ARE ROUGH... AND RUDE...
HA HA HA...
AND ...
...THEY KIND OF LOOK LIKE EACH OTHER TOO.
TEE HEE ...
HUH ?
AND THAT'S THE END OF THE LAMP JUMP !!
THE SUM OF ALL THE SCORES IN THE JUMP COURSE IS...
TT
150
R
KL
51
AND THE WIN-NER IS...

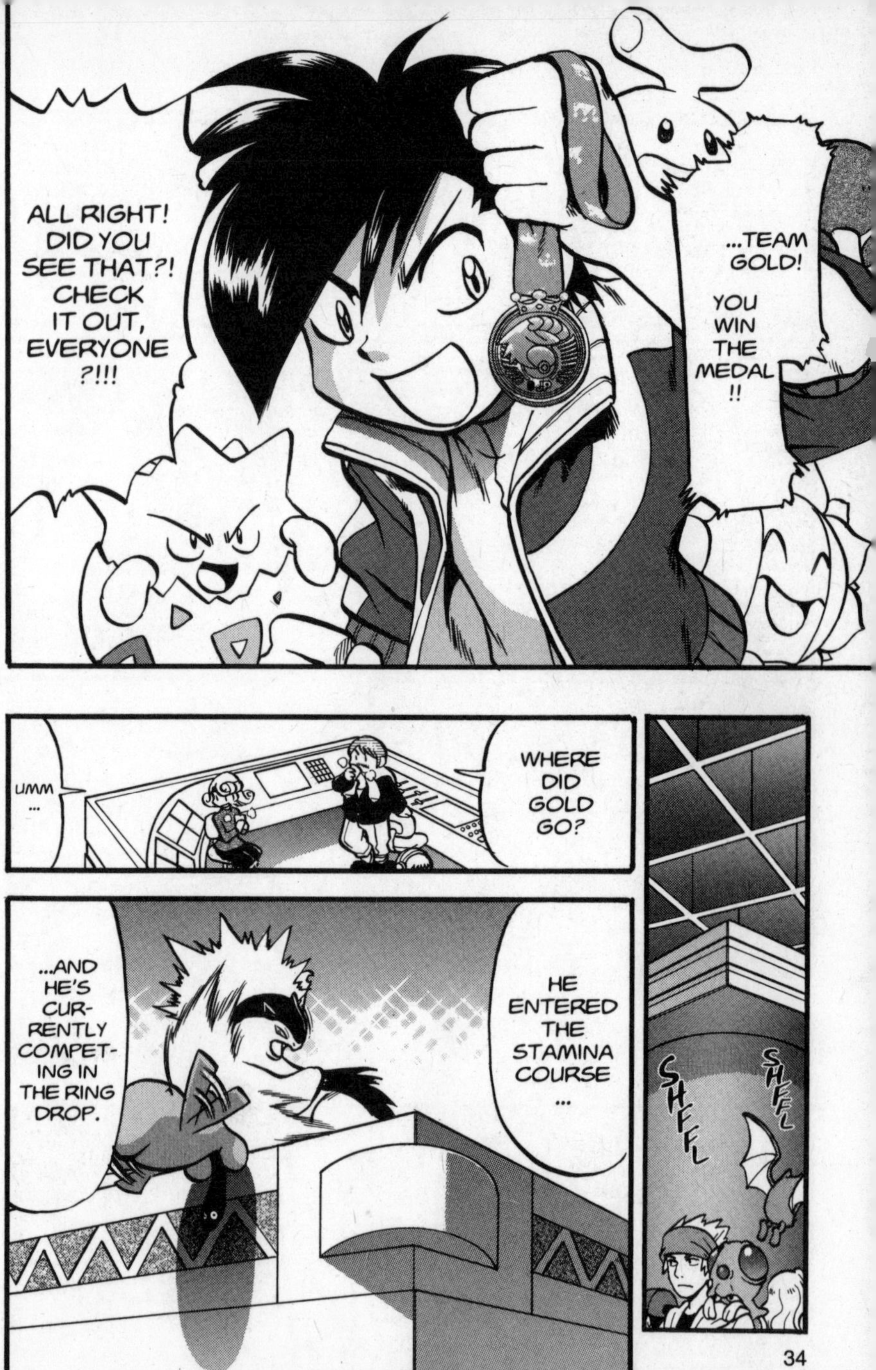
...TEAM GOLD!
YOU WIN THE MEDAL!!
ALL RIGHT! DID YOU SEE THAT?! CHECK IT OUT, EVERYONE?!!!
SHFFL
SHFFL
WHERE DID GOLD GO?
UMM...
HE ENTERED THE STAMINA COURSE...
...AND HE'S CUR-RENTLY COMPET-ING IN THE RING DROP.

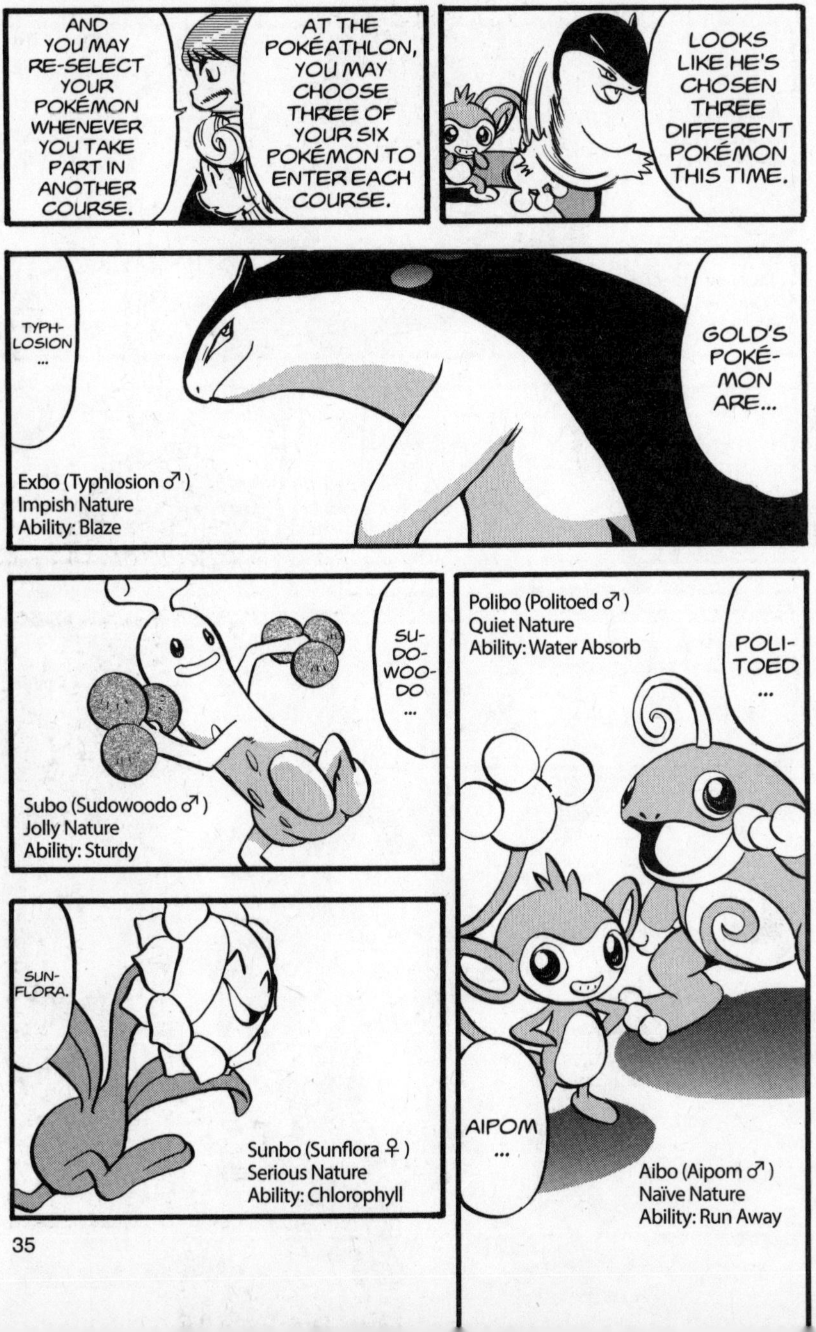
LOOKS LIKE HE'S CHOSEN THREE DIFFERENT POKÉMON THIS TIME.
AT THE POKÉATHLON, YOU MAY CHOOSE THREE OF YOUR SIX POKÉMON TO ENTER EACH COURSE.
AND YOU MAY RE-SELECT YOUR POKÉMON WHENEVER YOU TAKE PART IN ANOTHER COURSE.
GOLD'S POKÉMON ARE...
TYPHLOSION...
Exbo (Typhlosion ♂)
Impish Nature
Ability: Blaze
POLITOED...
Polibo (Politoed ♂)
Quiet Nature
Ability: Water Absorb
AIPOM...
Aibo (Aipom ♂)
Naïve Nature
Ability: Run Away
SUDOWOODO...
Subo (Sudowoodo ♂)
Jolly Nature
Ability: Sturdy
SUNFLORA.
Sunbo (Sunflora ♀)
Serious Nature
Ability: Chlorophyll

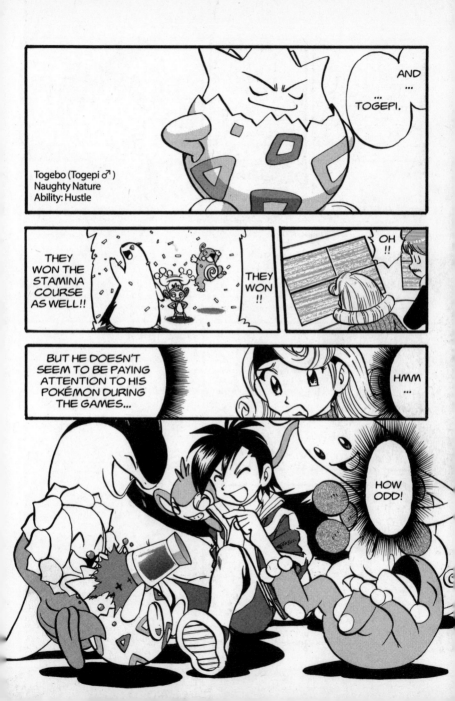

AND
...

... TOGEPI.

Togebo (Togepi ♂)
Naughty Nature
Ability: Hustle

THEY WON THE STAMINA COURSE AS WELL!!

THEY WON!!

OH !!

BUT HE DOESN'T SEEM TO BE PAYING ATTENTION TO HIS POKÉMON DURING THE GAMES...

HMM ...

HOW ODD!

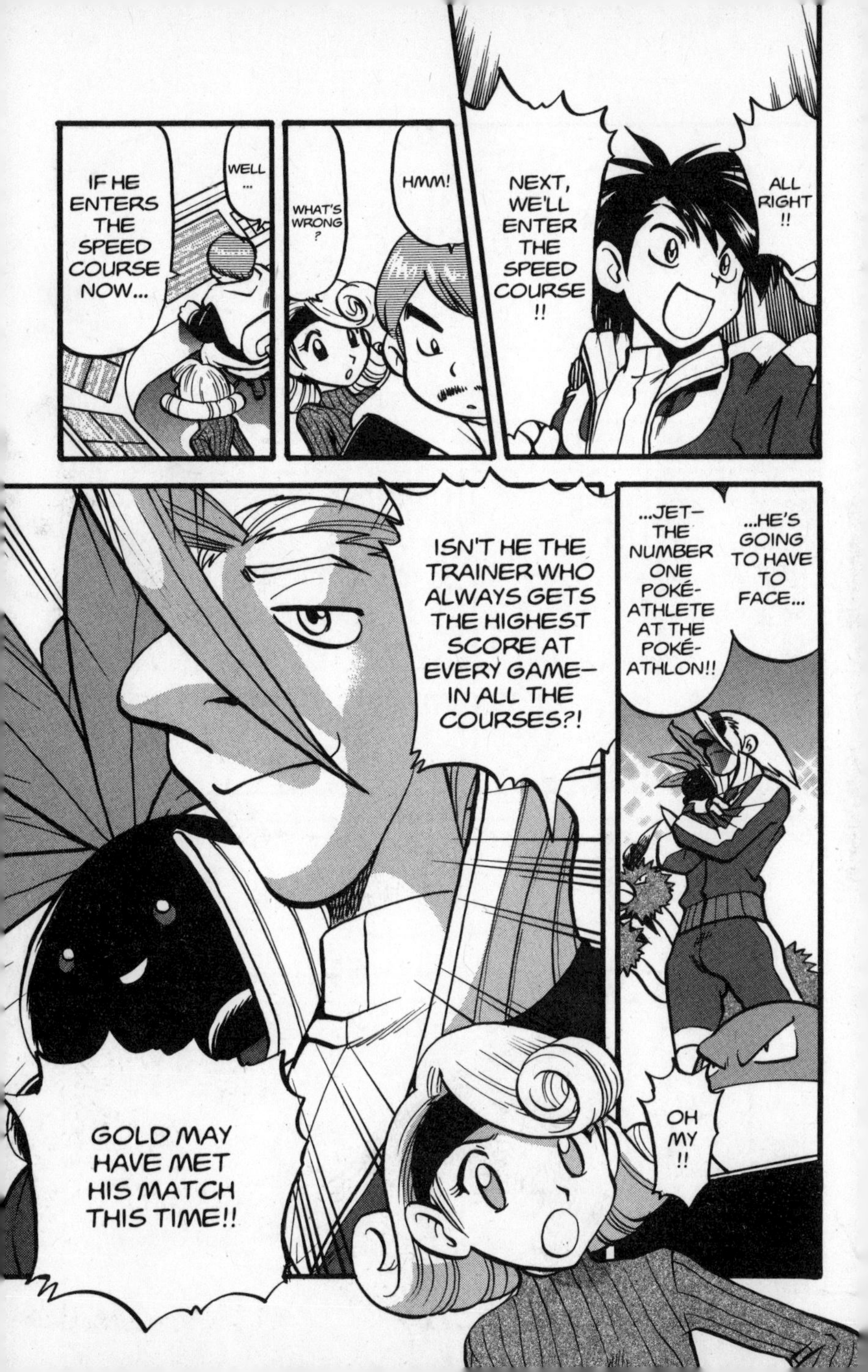
ALL RIGHT !!
NEXT, WE'LL ENTER THE SPEED COURSE !!
HMM!
WHAT'S WRONG ?
WELL ...
IF HE ENTERS THE SPEED COURSE NOW...
...HE'S GOING TO HAVE TO FACE...
...JET—THE NUMBER ONE POKÉ-ATHLETE AT THE POKÉ-ATHLON!!
OH MY !!
ISN'T HE THE TRAINER WHO ALWAYS GETS THE HIGHEST SCORE AT EVERY GAME—IN ALL THE COURSES?!
GOLD MAY HAVE MET HIS MATCH THIS TIME!!

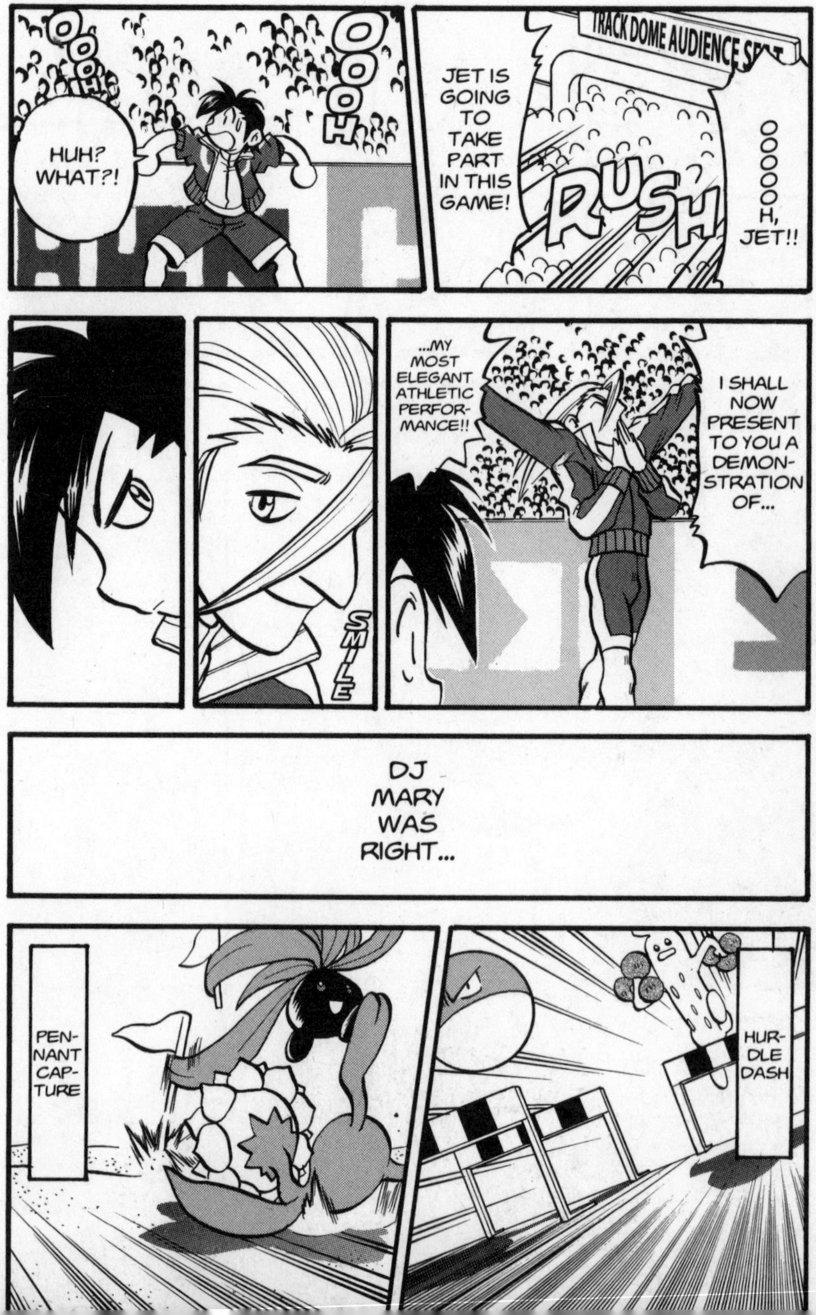
TRACK DOME AUDIENCE
OOOOOH, JET!!
JET IS GOING TO TAKE PART IN THIS GAME!
RUSH
OOOOH
OOOOH
HUH? WHAT?!
I SHALL NOW PRESENT TO YOU A DEMON-STRATION OF...
...MY MOST ELEGANT ATHLETIC PERFOR-MANCE!!
SMILE
DJ MARY WAS RIGHT...
HUR-DLE DASH
PEN-NANT CAP-TURE

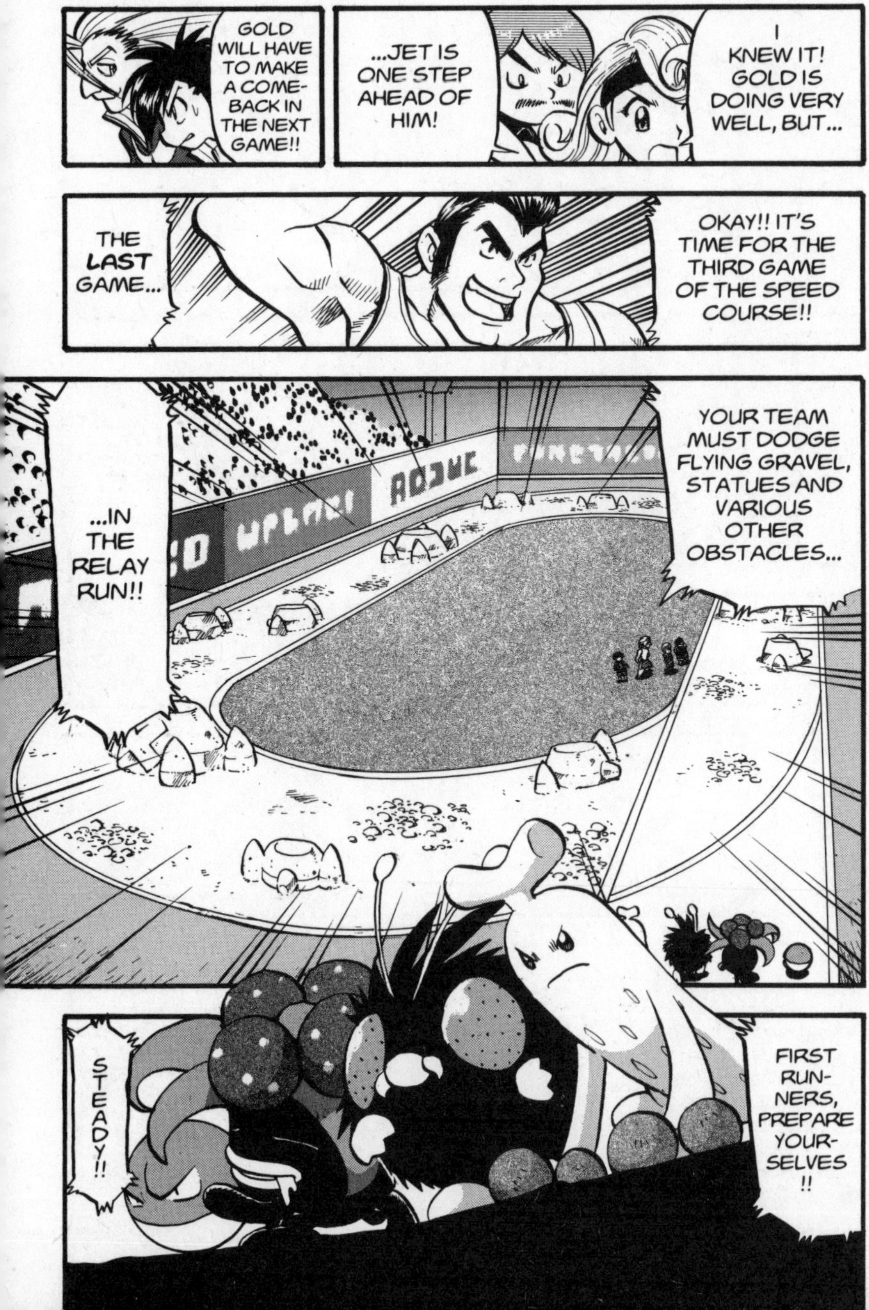
I KNEW IT! GOLD IS DOING VERY WELL, BUT...
...JET IS ONE STEP AHEAD OF HIM!
GOLD WILL HAVE TO MAKE A COME-BACK IN THE NEXT GAME!!
OKAY!! IT'S TIME FOR THE THIRD GAME OF THE SPEED COURSE!!
THE **LAST** GAME...
YOUR TEAM MUST DODGE FLYING GRAVEL, STATUES AND VARIOUS OTHER OBSTACLES...
...IN THE RELAY RUN!!
FIRST RUN-NERS, PREPARE YOUR-SELVES !!
STEADY!!

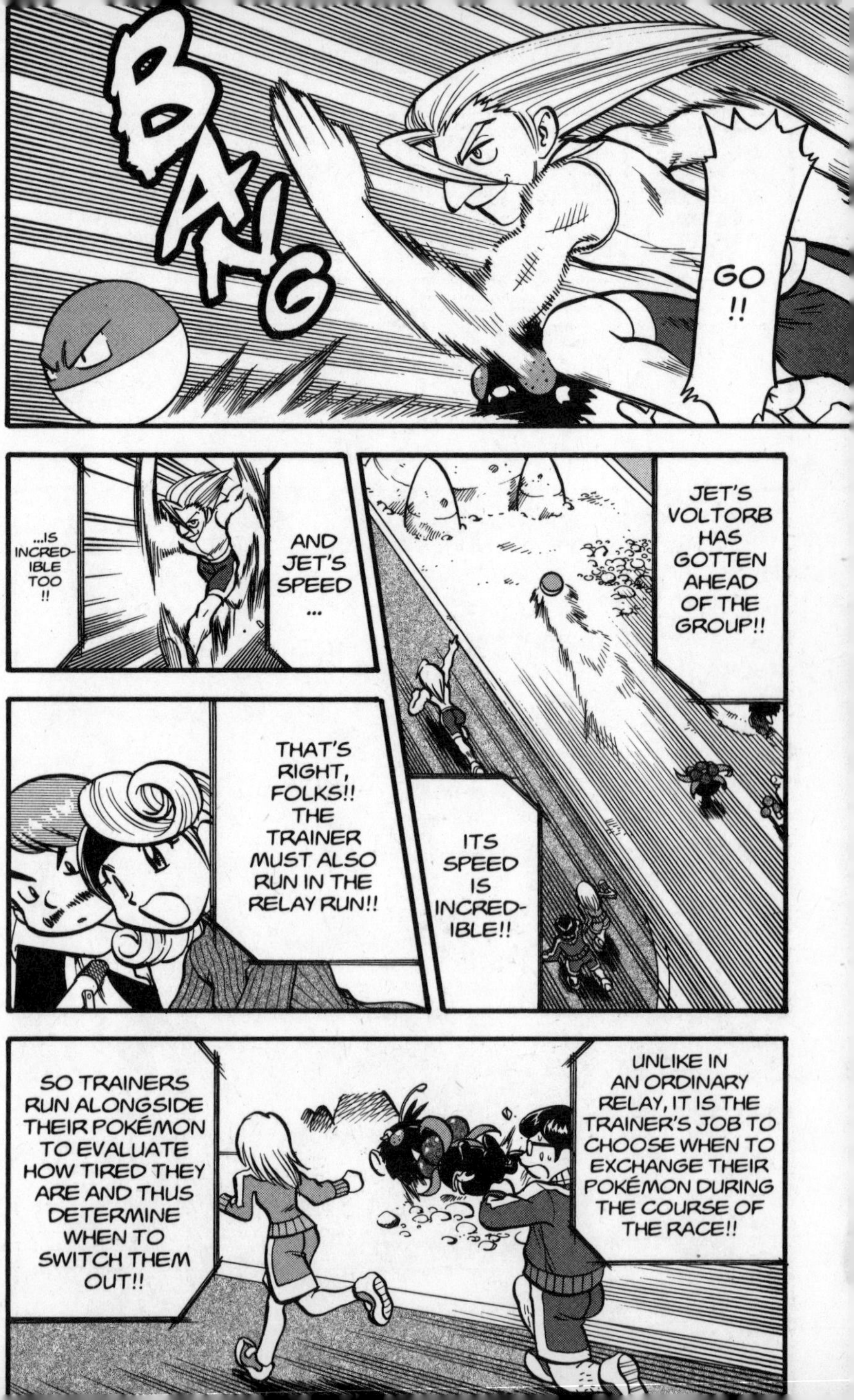
GO!!
BANG
JET'S VOLTORB HAS GOTTEN AHEAD OF THE GROUP!!
ITS SPEED IS INCREDIBLE!!
AND JET'S SPEED...
...IS INCREDIBLE TOO!!
THAT'S RIGHT, FOLKS!! THE TRAINER MUST ALSO RUN IN THE RELAY RUN!!
UNLIKE IN AN ORDINARY RELAY, IT IS THE TRAINER'S JOB TO CHOOSE WHEN TO EXCHANGE THEIR POKÉMON DURING THE COURSE OF THE RACE!!
SO TRAINERS RUN ALONGSIDE THEIR POKÉMON TO EVALUATE HOW TIRED THEY ARE AND THUS DETERMINE WHEN TO SWITCH THEM OUT!!

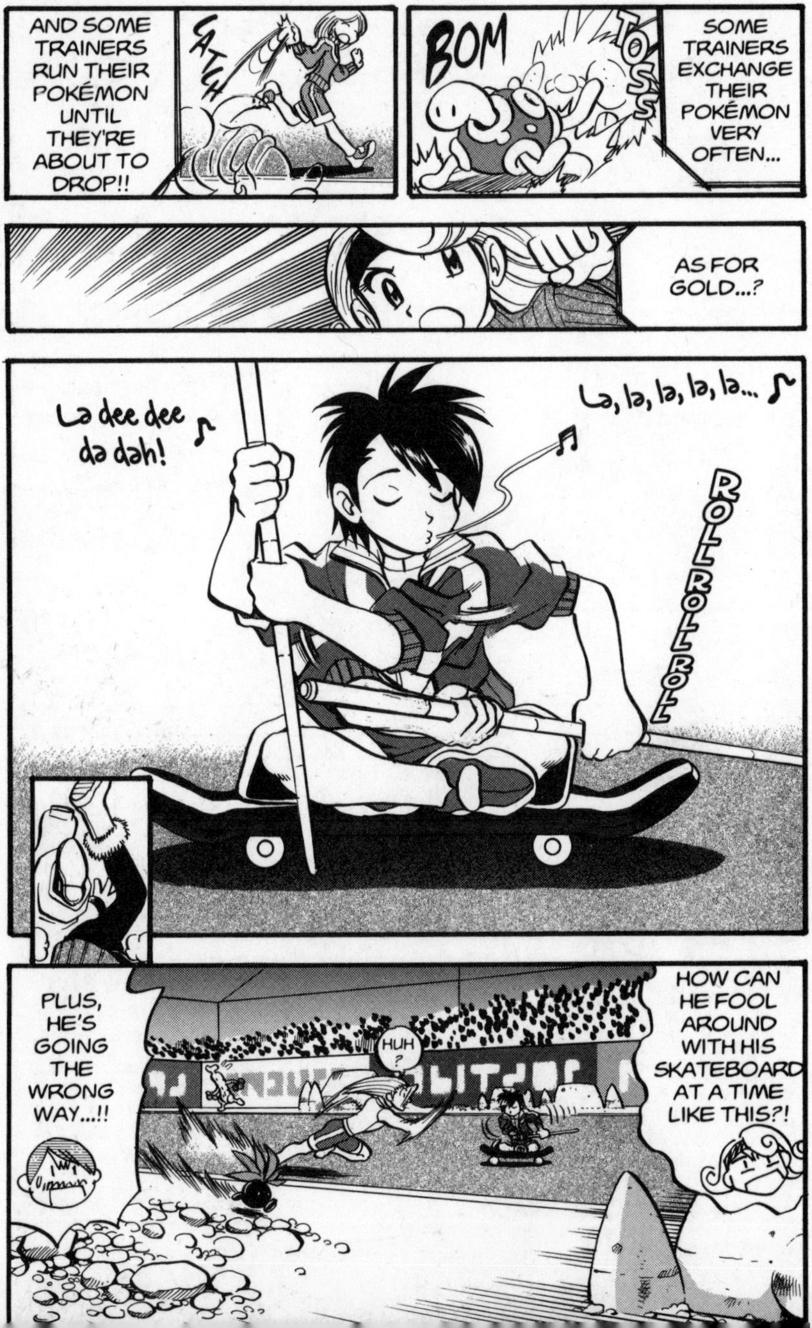
SOME TRAINERS EXCHANGE THEIR POKÉMON VERY OFTEN...
TOSS
BOM
AND SOME TRAINERS RUN THEIR POKÉMON UNTIL THEY'RE ABOUT TO DROP!!
CATCH
AS FOR GOLD...?
La, la, la, la, la...
La dee dee da dah!
ROLLROLLROLL
HOW CAN HE FOOL AROUND WITH HIS SKATEBOARD AT A TIME LIKE THIS?!
HUH?
PLUS, HE'S GOING THE WRONG WAY...!!

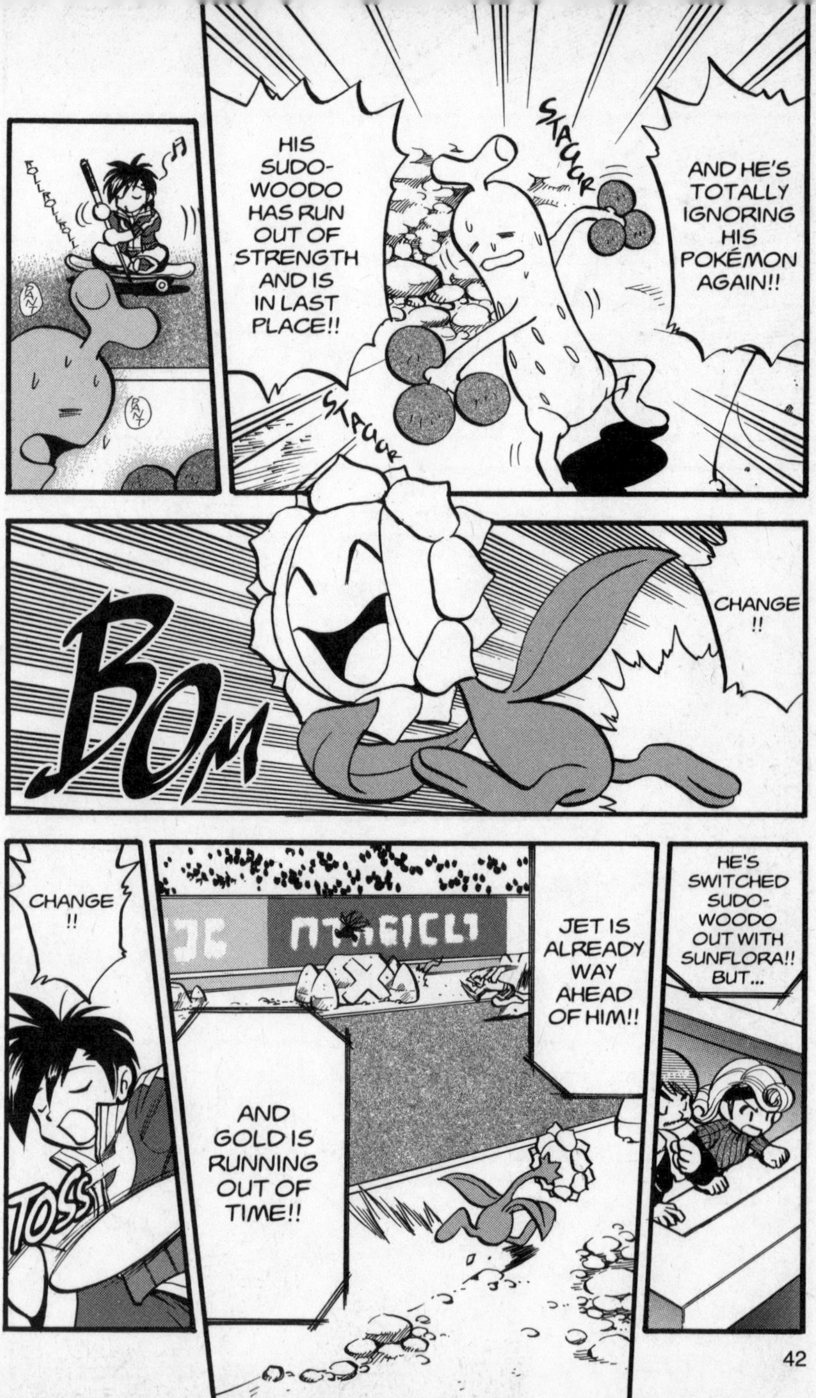
SKAGGR
AND HE'S TOTALLY IGNORING HIS POKÉMON AGAIN!!
HIS SUDO-WOODO HAS RUN OUT OF STRENGTH AND IS IN LAST PLACE!!
SKAGGR
ROLLROLLROLL
PANT
PANT
CHANGE!!
BOM
HE'S SWITCHED SUDO-WOODO OUT WITH SUNFLORA!! BUT...
JET IS ALREADY WAY AHEAD OF HIM!!
AND GOLD IS RUNNING OUT OF TIME!!
CHANGE!!
TOSS

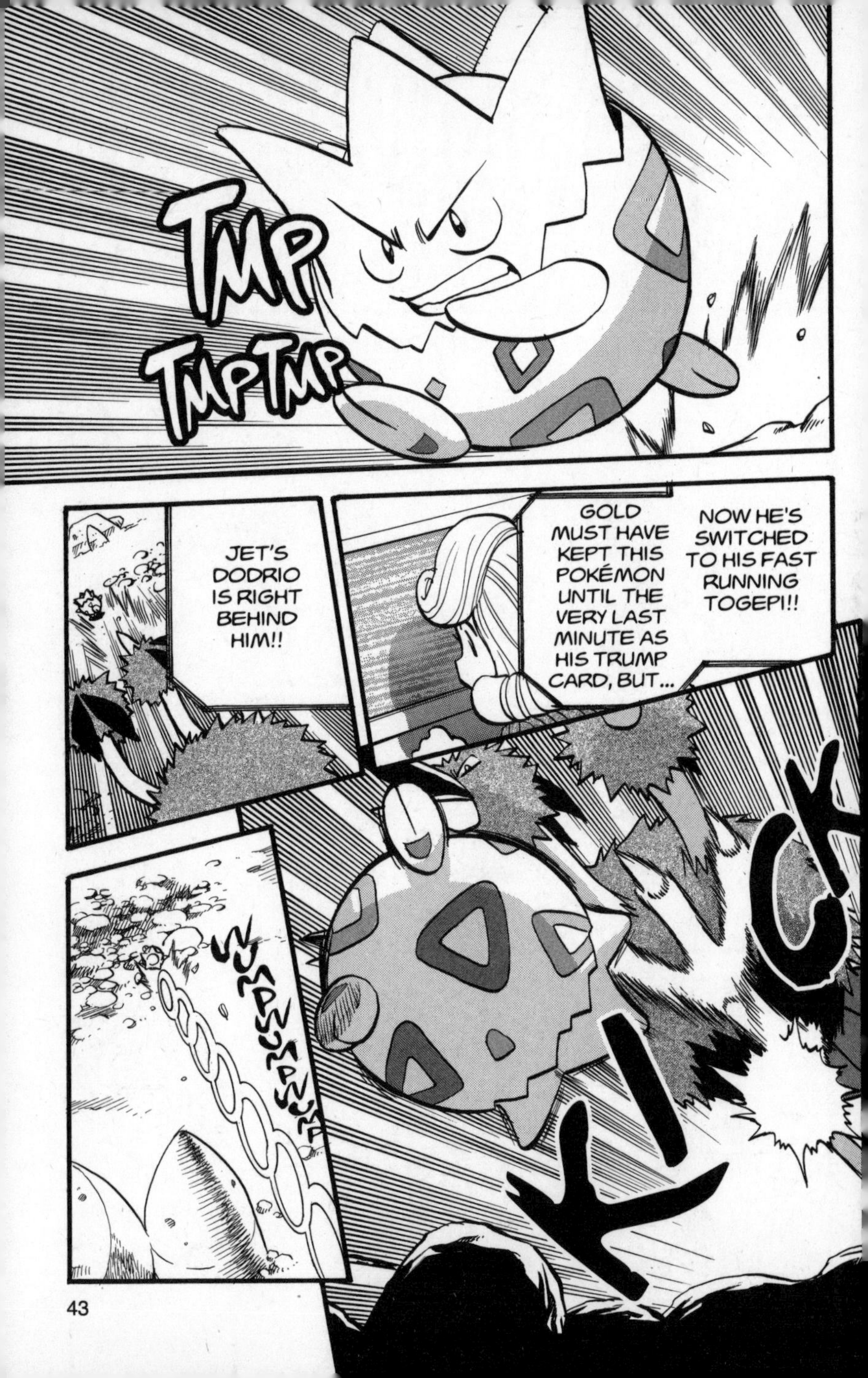
TMP
TMPTMP
GOLD MUST HAVE KEPT THIS POKÉMON UNTIL THE VERY LAST MINUTE AS HIS TRUMP CARD, BUT...
NOW HE'S SWITCHED TO HIS FAST RUNNING TOGEPI!!
JET'S DODRIO IS RIGHT BEHIND HIM!!
KINCK
WUMPWUMPWUMP

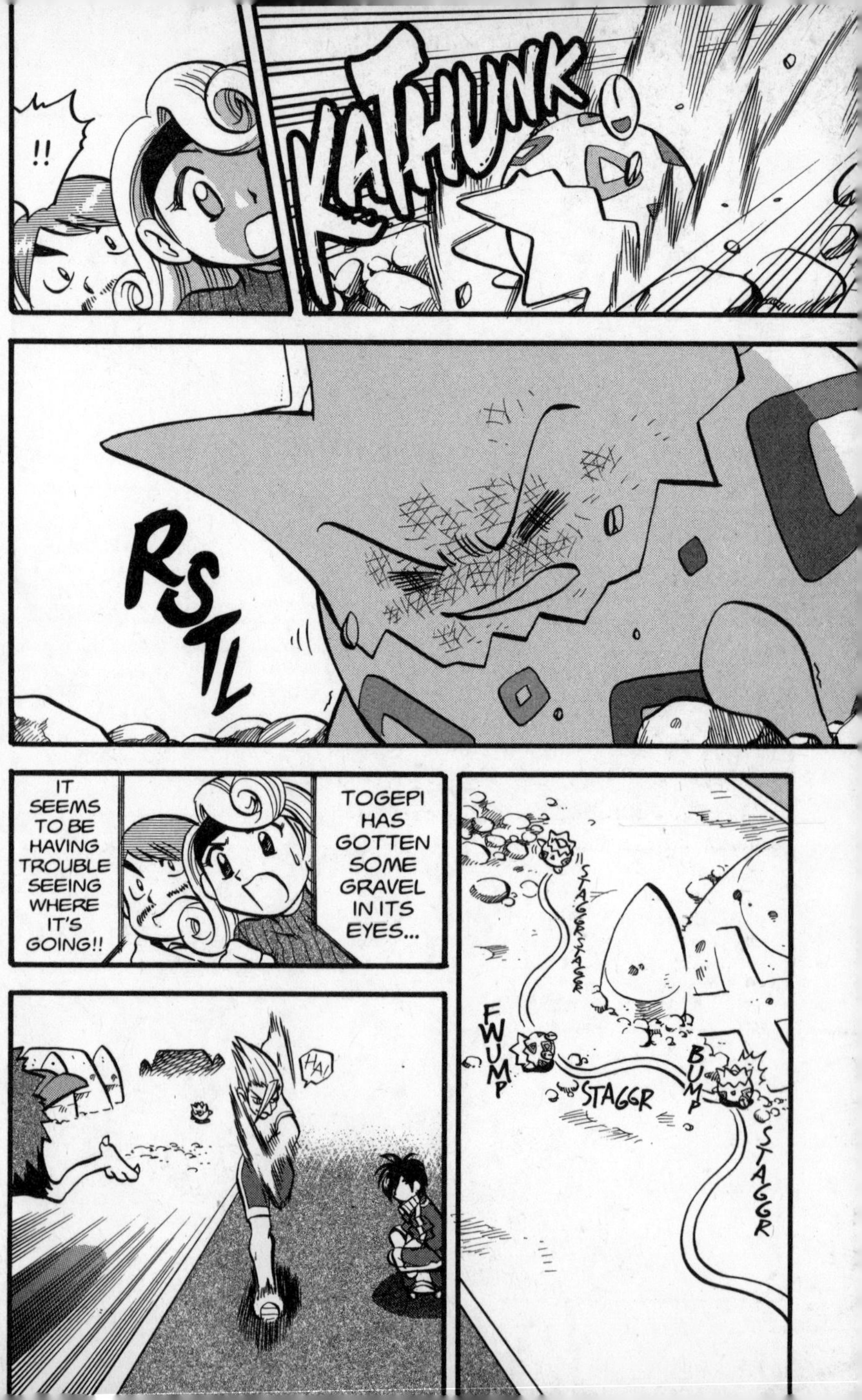
KATHUNK
!!
RSTL
STAGGRSTAGGR
BUMP
FWUMP
STAGGR
STAGGR
TOGEPI HAS GOTTEN SOME GRAVEL IN ITS EYES...
IT SEEMS TO BE HAVING TROUBLE SEEING WHERE IT'S GOING!!
HA!

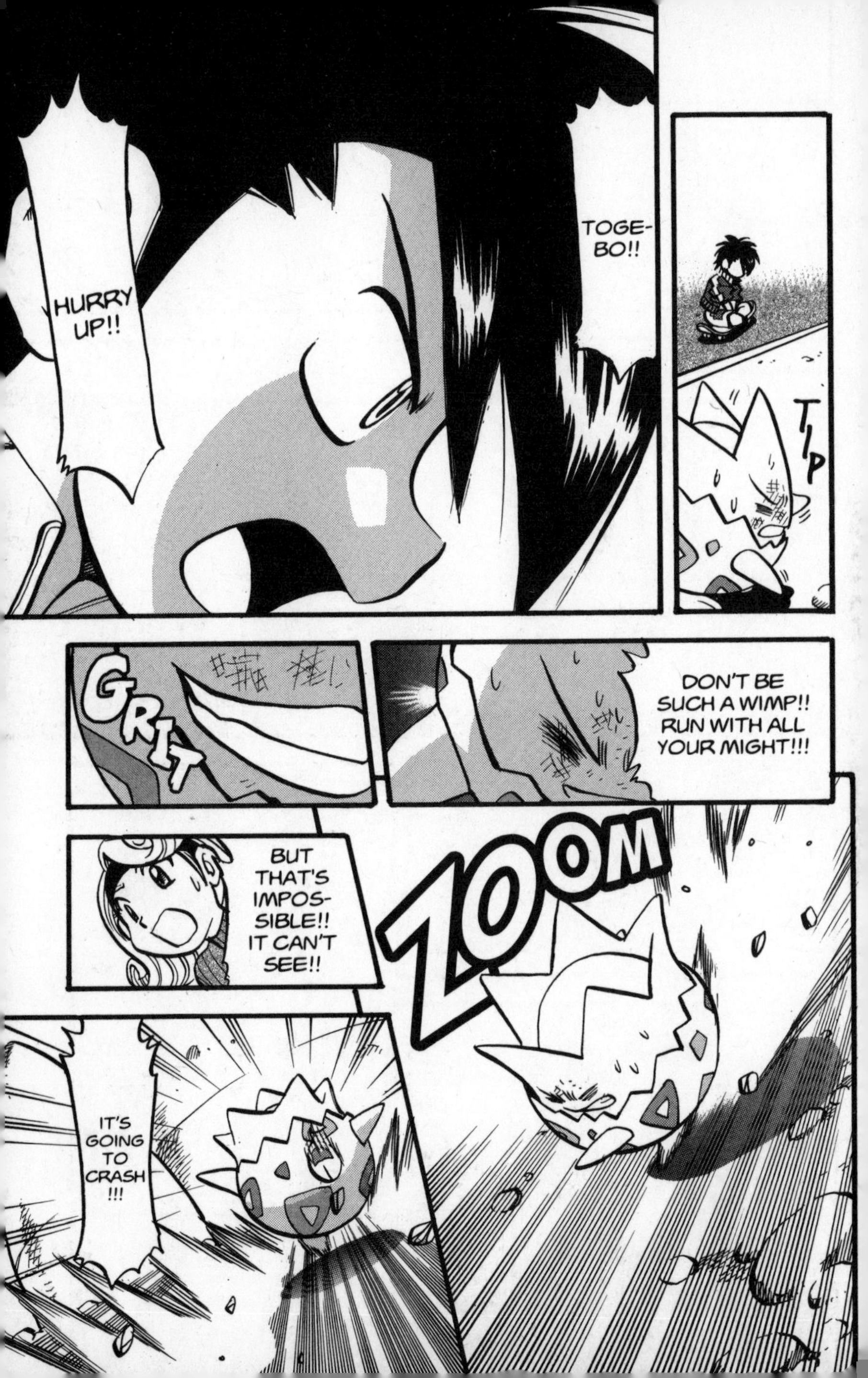
TIP
TOGE-BO!!
HURRY UP!!
DON'T BE SUCH A WIMP!! RUN WITH ALL YOUR MIGHT!!!
GRIT
ZOOM
BUT THAT'S IMPOSSIBLE!! IT CAN'T SEE!!
IT'S GOING TO CRASH!!!

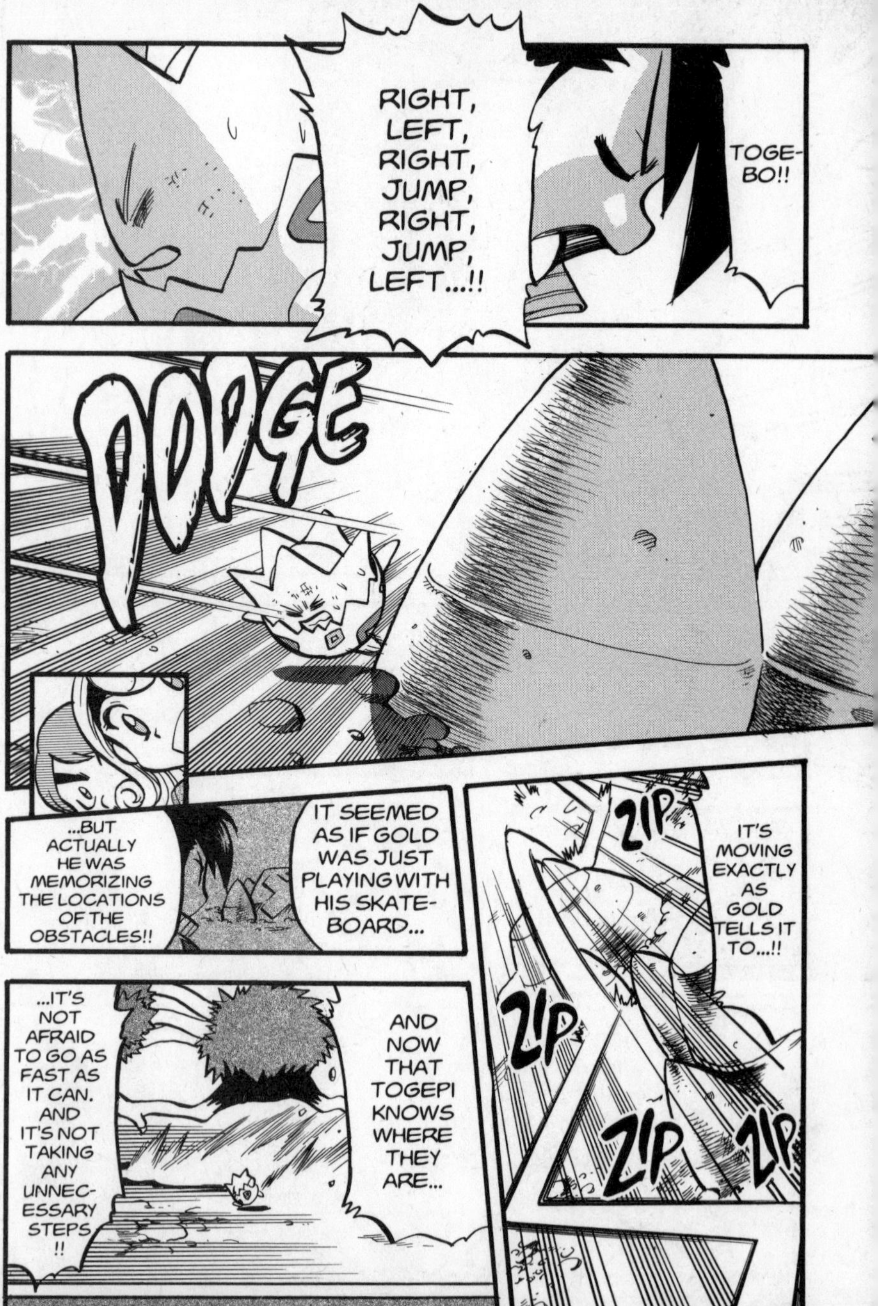
TOGE-BO!!
RIGHT, LEFT, RIGHT, JUMP, RIGHT, JUMP, LEFT...!!
DODGE
ZIP
IT'S MOVING EXACTLY AS GOLD TELLS IT TO...!!
ZIP
ZIP
ZIP
IT SEEMED AS IF GOLD WAS JUST PLAYING WITH HIS SKATE-BOARD...
...BUT ACTUALLY HE WAS MEMORIZING THE LOCATIONS OF THE OBSTACLES!!
AND NOW THAT TOGEPI KNOWS WHERE THEY ARE...
...IT'S NOT AFRAID TO GO AS FAST AS IT CAN. AND IT'S NOT TAKING ANY UNNEC-ESSARY STEPS!!

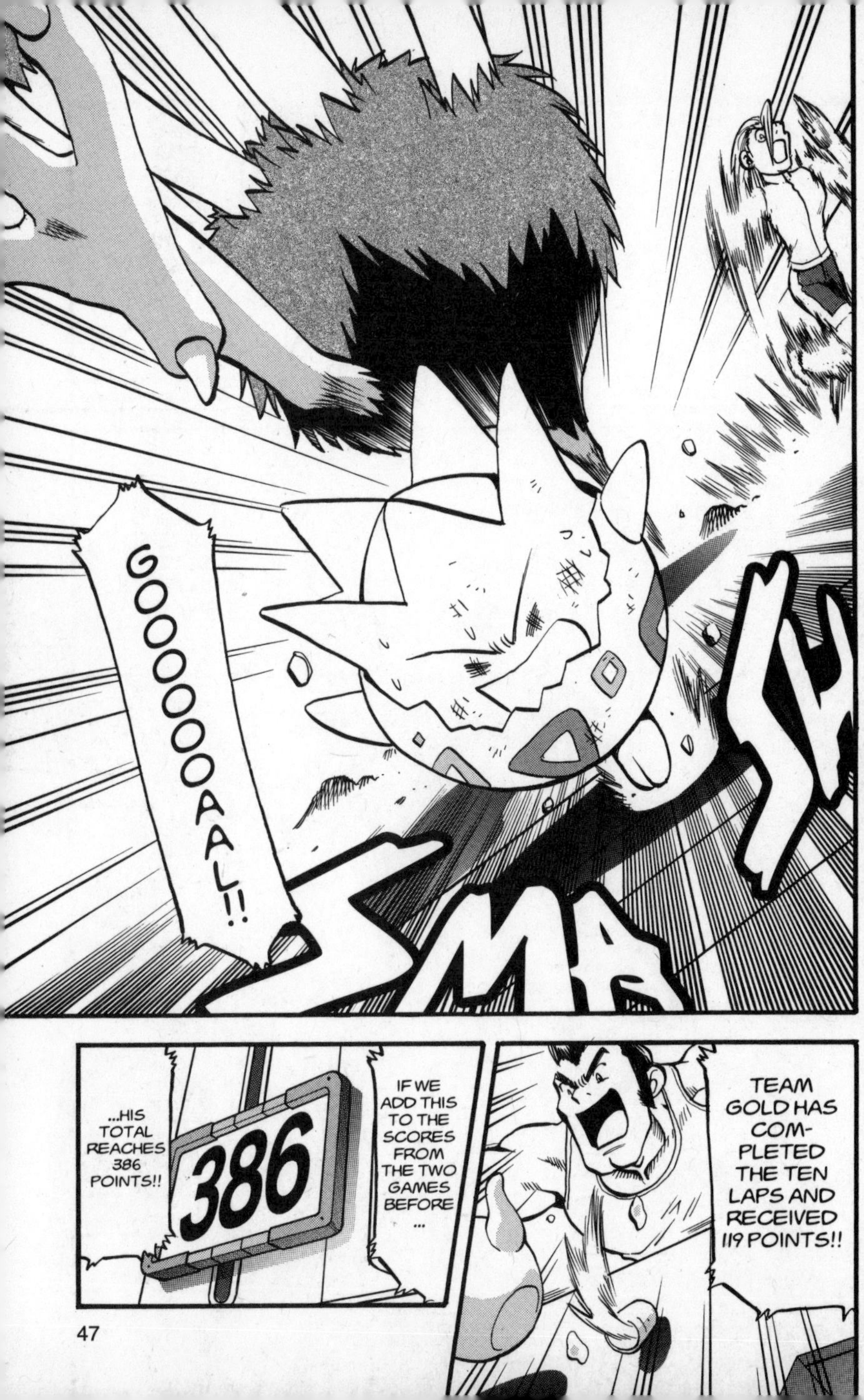
GOOOOOOAAL!!
TEAM GOLD HAS COM- PLETED THE TEN LAPS AND RECEIVED 119 POINTS!!
IF WE ADD THIS TO THE SCORES FROM THE TWO GAMES BEFORE ...
...HIS TOTAL REACHES 386 POINTS!!
386

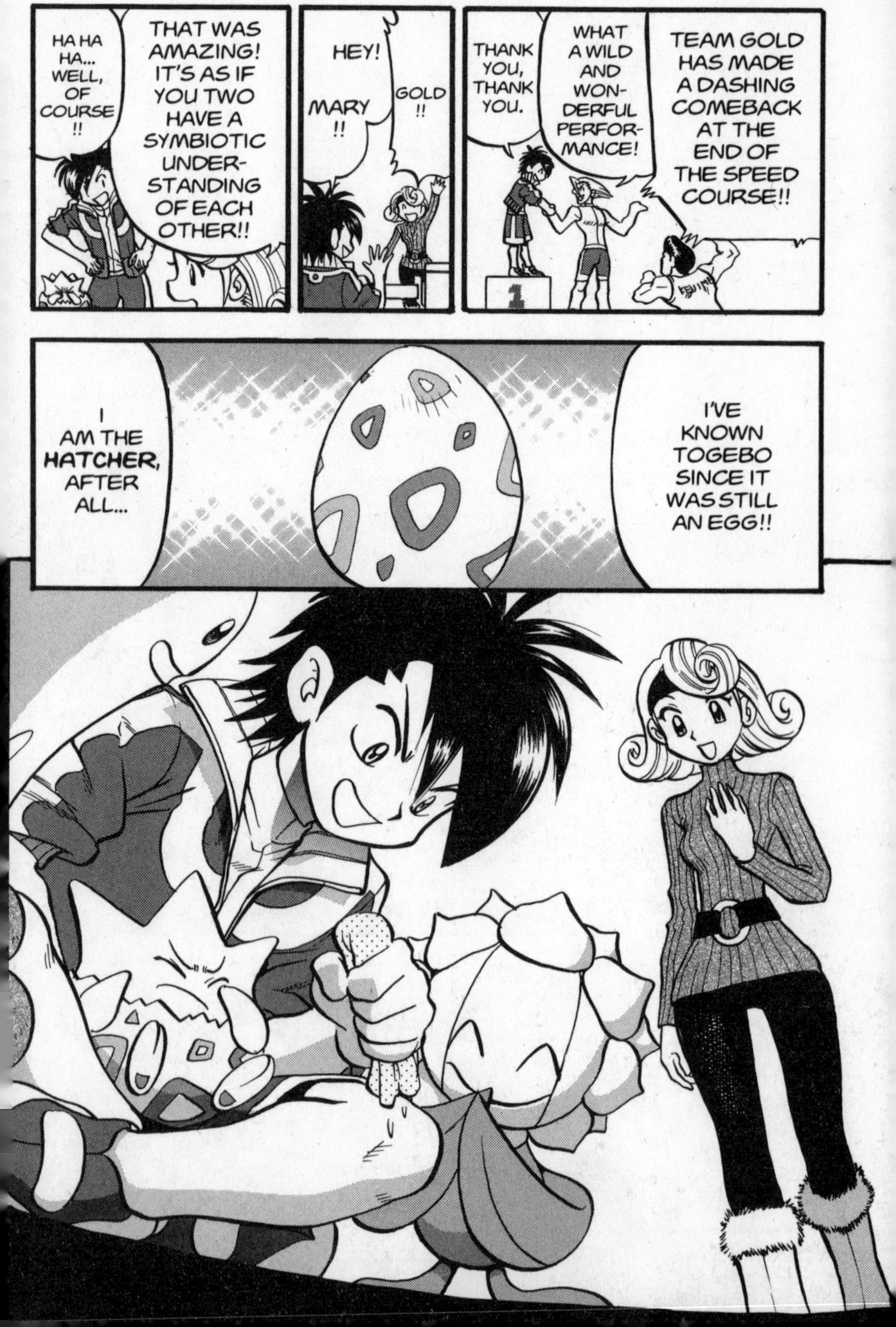

TEAM GOLD HAS MADE A DASHING COMEBACK AT THE END OF THE SPEED COURSE!!
WHAT A WILD AND WONDERFUL PERFORMANCE!
THANK YOU, THANK YOU.
HEY!
GOLD!!
MARY!!
THAT WAS AMAZING! IT'S AS IF YOU TWO HAVE A SYMBIOTIC UNDERSTANDING OF EACH OTHER!!
HA HA HA... WELL, OF COURSE!!
I'VE KNOWN TOGEBO SINCE IT WAS STILL AN EGG!!
I AM THE **HATCHER**, AFTER ALL...

Adventure 2

ATTAWAY, AIPOM!

9

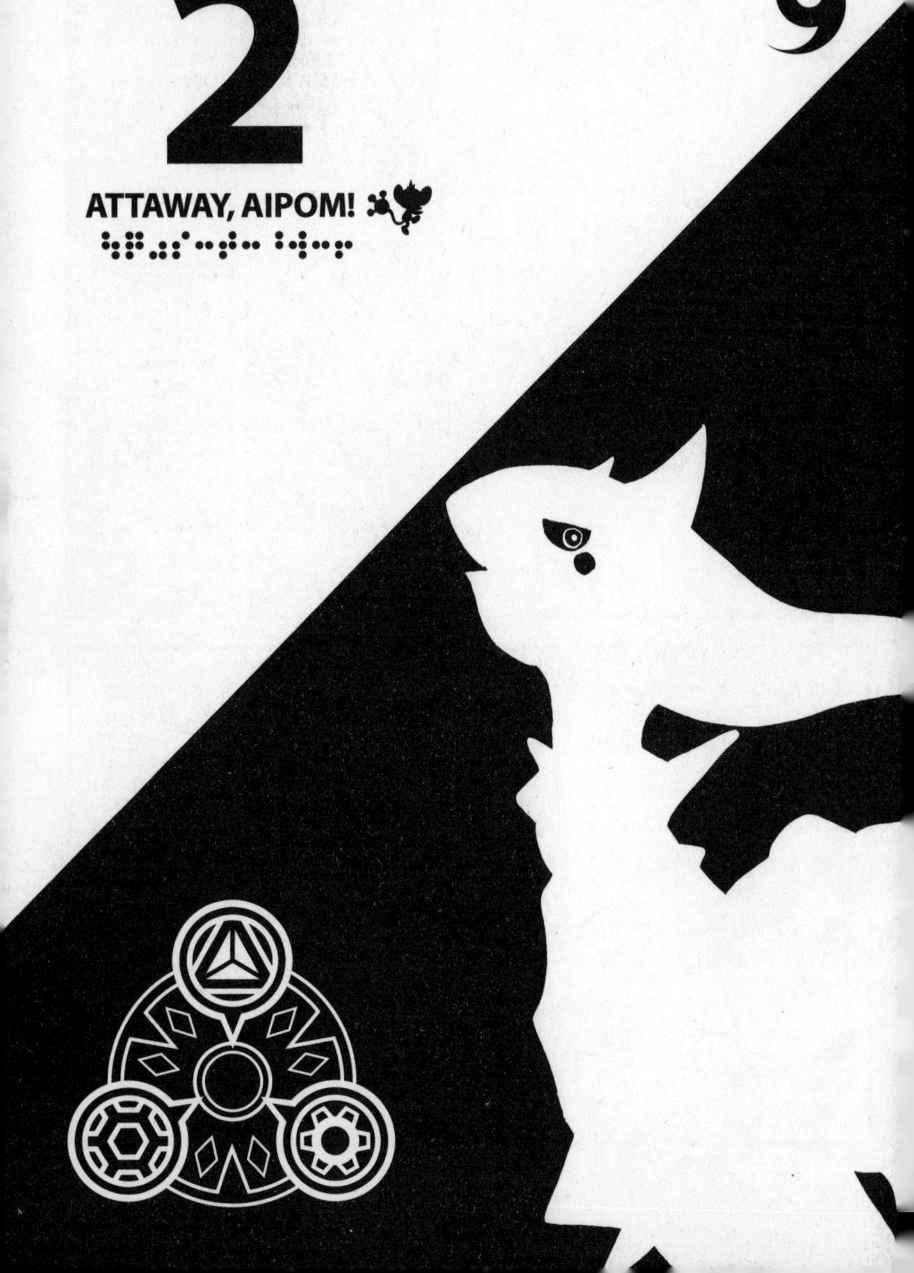

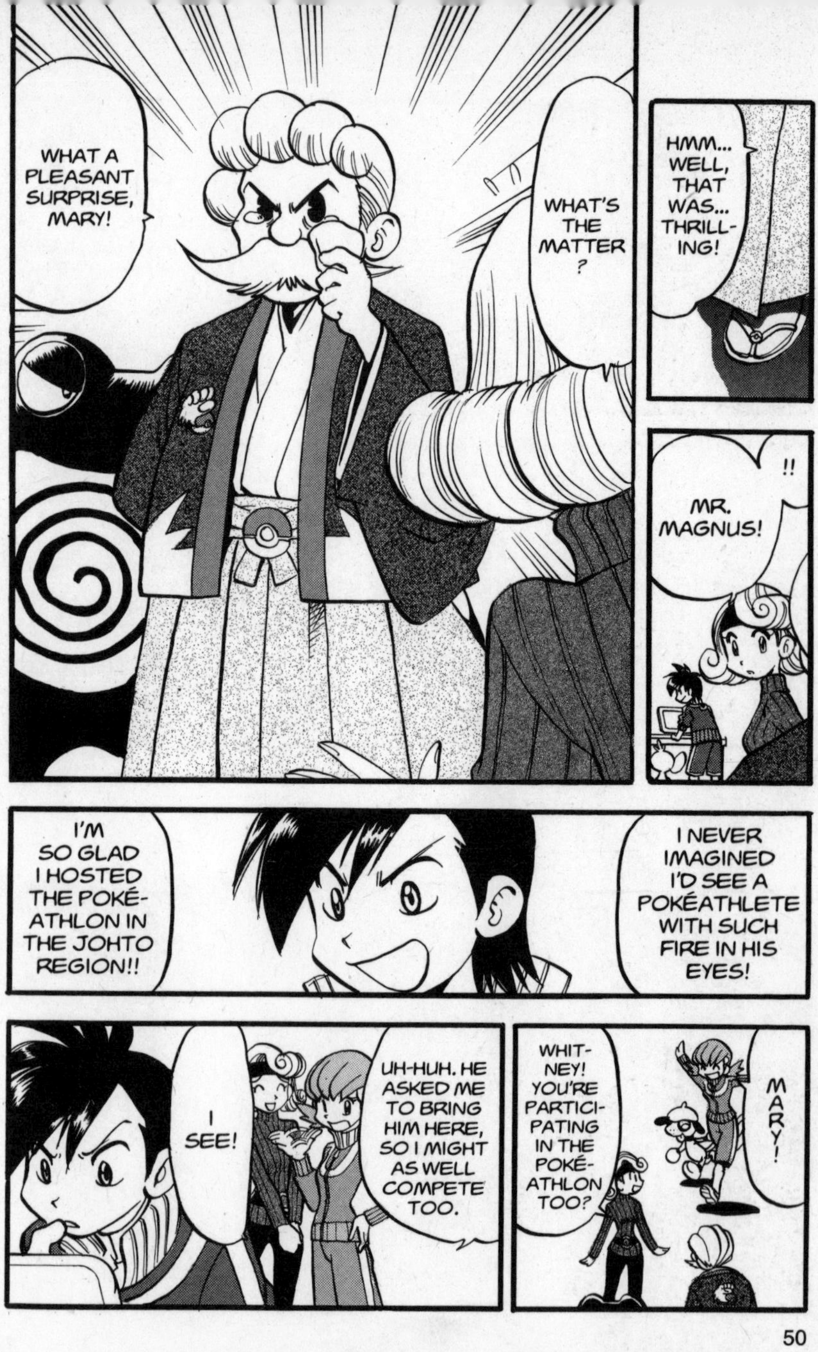
HMM... WELL, THAT WAS... THRILLING!
!!
MR. MAGNUS!
WHAT'S THE MATTER?
WHAT A PLEASANT SURPRISE, MARY!
I NEVER IMAGINED I'D SEE A POKÉATHLETE WITH SUCH FIRE IN HIS EYES!
I'M SO GLAD I HOSTED THE POKÉATHLON IN THE JOHTO REGION!!
MARY!
WHITNEY! YOU'RE PARTICIPATING IN THE POKÉATHLON TOO?
UH-HUH. HE ASKED ME TO BRING HIM HERE, SO I MIGHT AS WELL COMPETE TOO.
I SEE!

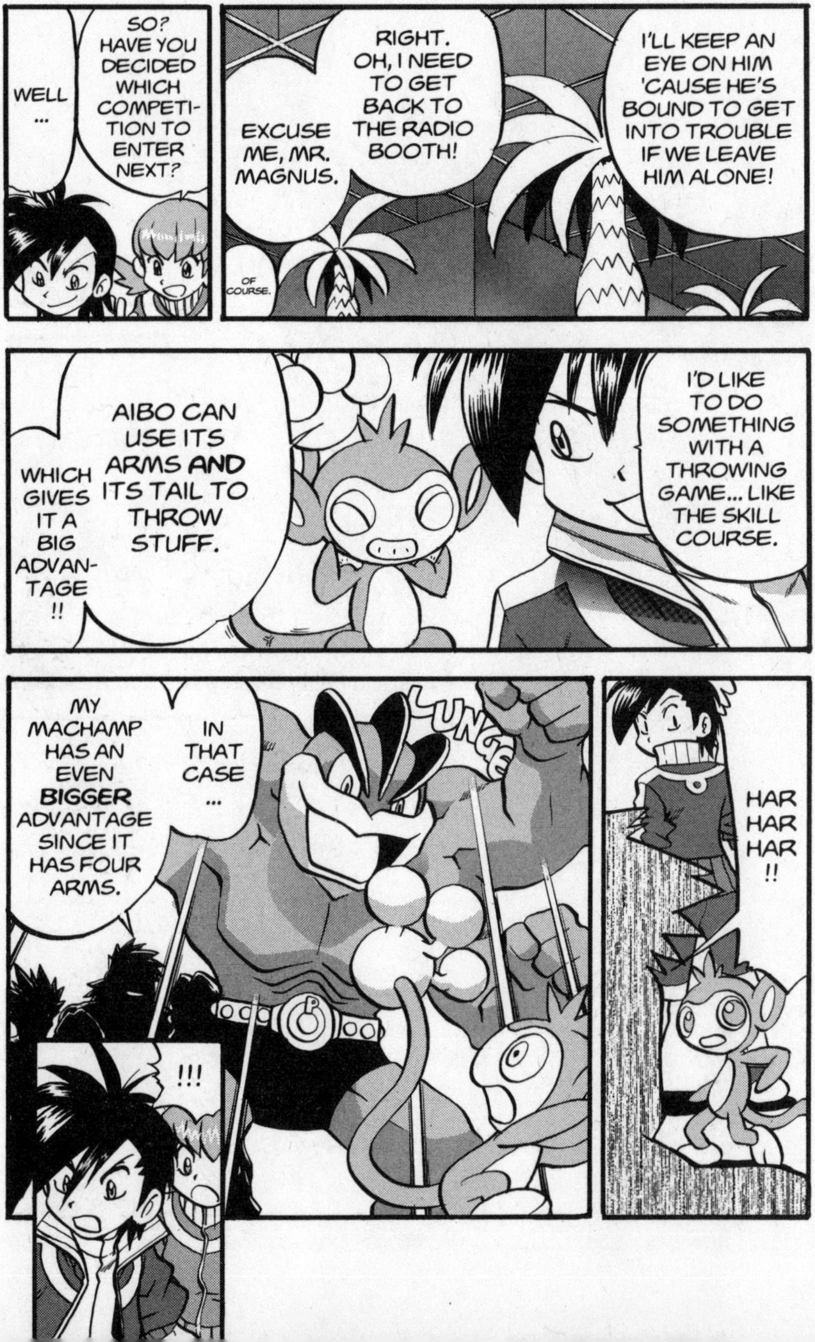
I'LL KEEP AN EYE ON HIM 'CAUSE HE'S BOUND TO GET INTO TROUBLE IF WE LEAVE HIM ALONE!
RIGHT. OH, I NEED TO GET BACK TO THE RADIO BOOTH!
EXCUSE ME, MR. MAGNUS.
OF COURSE.
SO? HAVE YOU DECIDED WHICH COMPETITION TO ENTER NEXT?
WELL ...
I'D LIKE TO DO SOMETHING WITH A THROWING GAME... LIKE THE SKILL COURSE.
AIBO CAN USE ITS ARMS AND ITS TAIL TO THROW STUFF.
WHICH GIVES IT A BIG ADVANTAGE!!
HAR HAR HAR!!
LUNGE
IN THAT CASE ...
MY MACHAMP HAS AN EVEN BIGGER ADVANTAGE SINCE IT HAS FOUR ARMS.
!!!

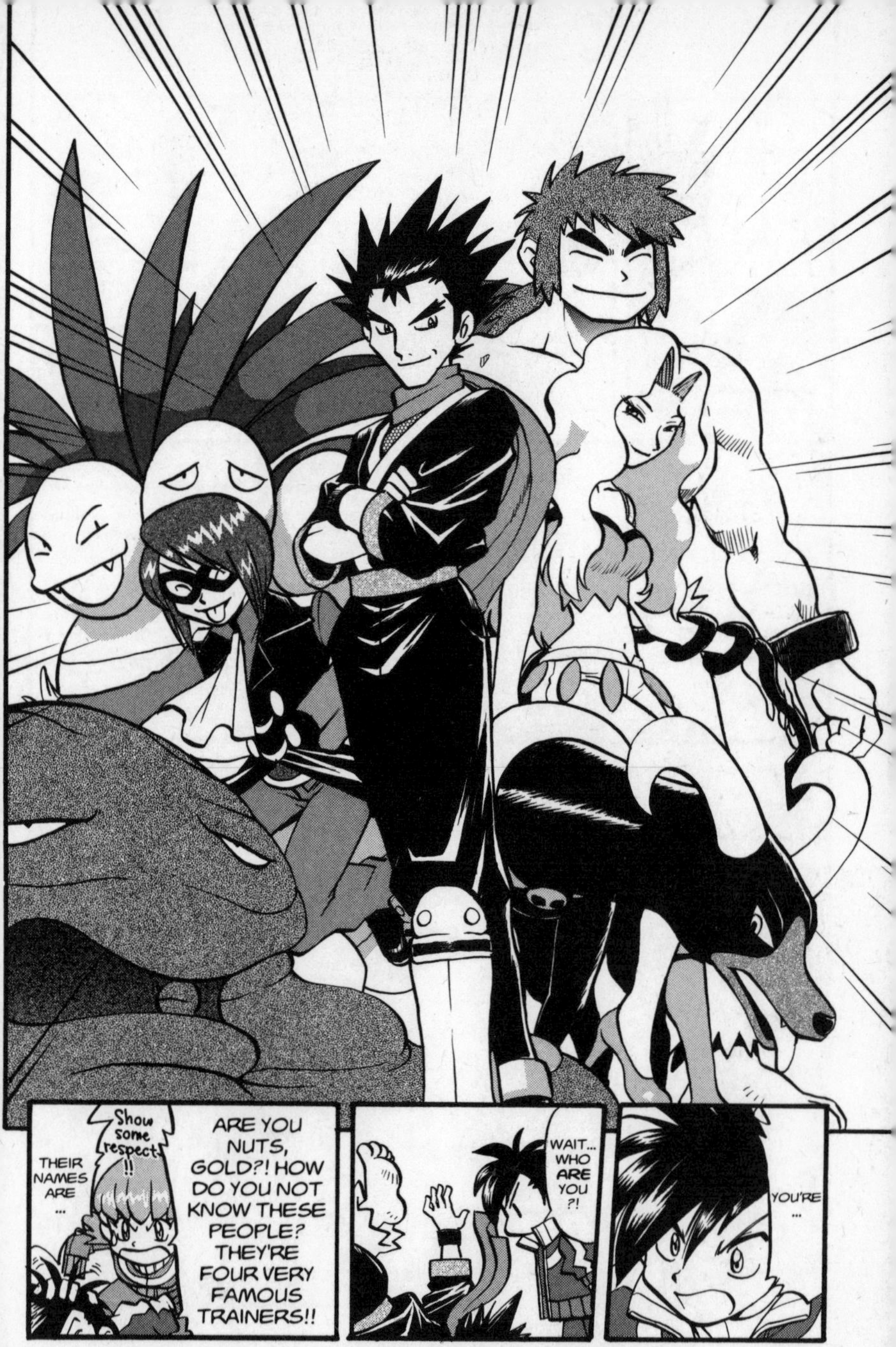
YOU'RE ...
WAIT... WHO ARE YOU ?!
ARE YOU NUTS, GOLD?! HOW DO YOU NOT KNOW THESE PEOPLE? THEY'RE FOUR VERY FAMOUS TRAINERS!!
Show some respect!!
THEIR NAMES ARE ...

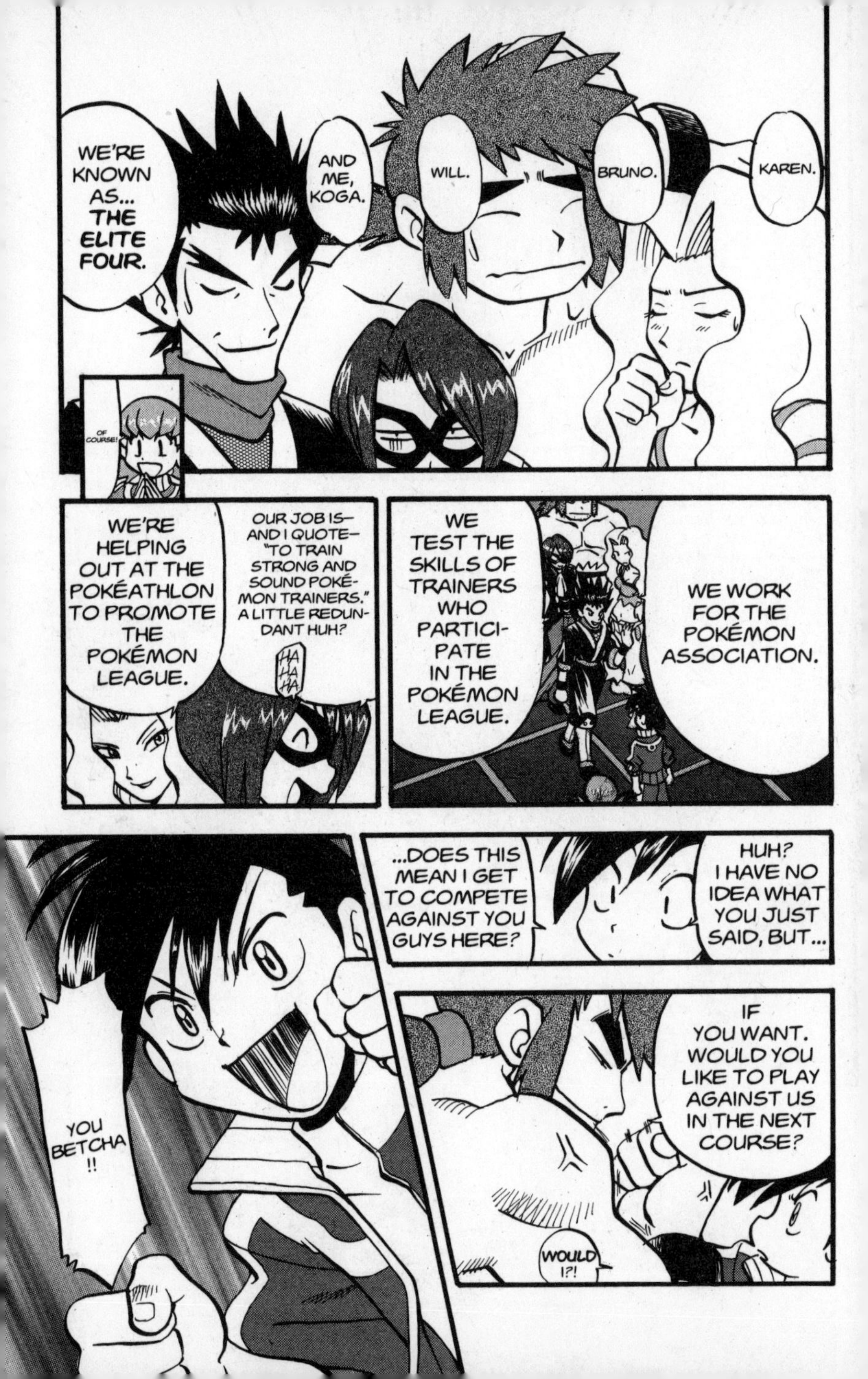
KAREN.
BRUNO.
WILL.
AND ME, KOGA.
WE'RE KNOWN AS... **THE ELITE FOUR.**
OF COURSE!
WE WORK FOR THE POKÉMON ASSOCIATION.
WE TEST THE SKILLS OF TRAINERS WHO PARTICIPATE IN THE POKÉMON LEAGUE.
OUR JOB IS—AND I QUOTE—"TO TRAIN STRONG AND SOUND POKÉMON TRAINERS." A LITTLE REDUNDANT HUH?
HA HA HA.
WE'RE HELPING OUT AT THE POKÉATHLON TO PROMOTE THE POKÉMON LEAGUE.
HUH? I HAVE NO IDEA WHAT YOU JUST SAID, BUT...
...DOES THIS MEAN I GET TO COMPETE AGAINST YOU GUYS HERE?
IF YOU WANT. WOULD YOU LIKE TO PLAY AGAINST US IN THE NEXT COURSE?
WOULD I?!
YOU BETCHA!!

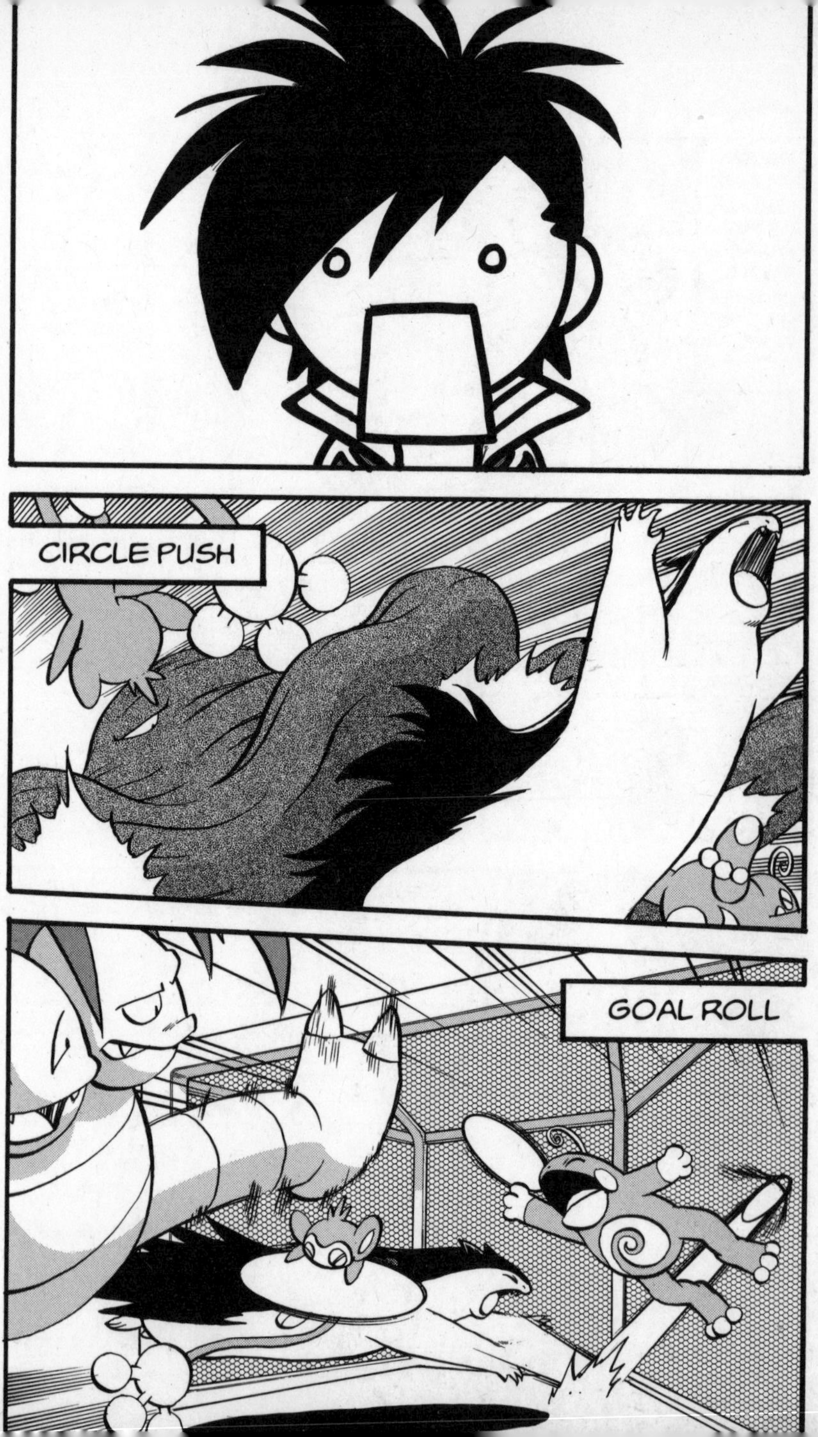
CIRCLE PUSH
GOAL ROLL

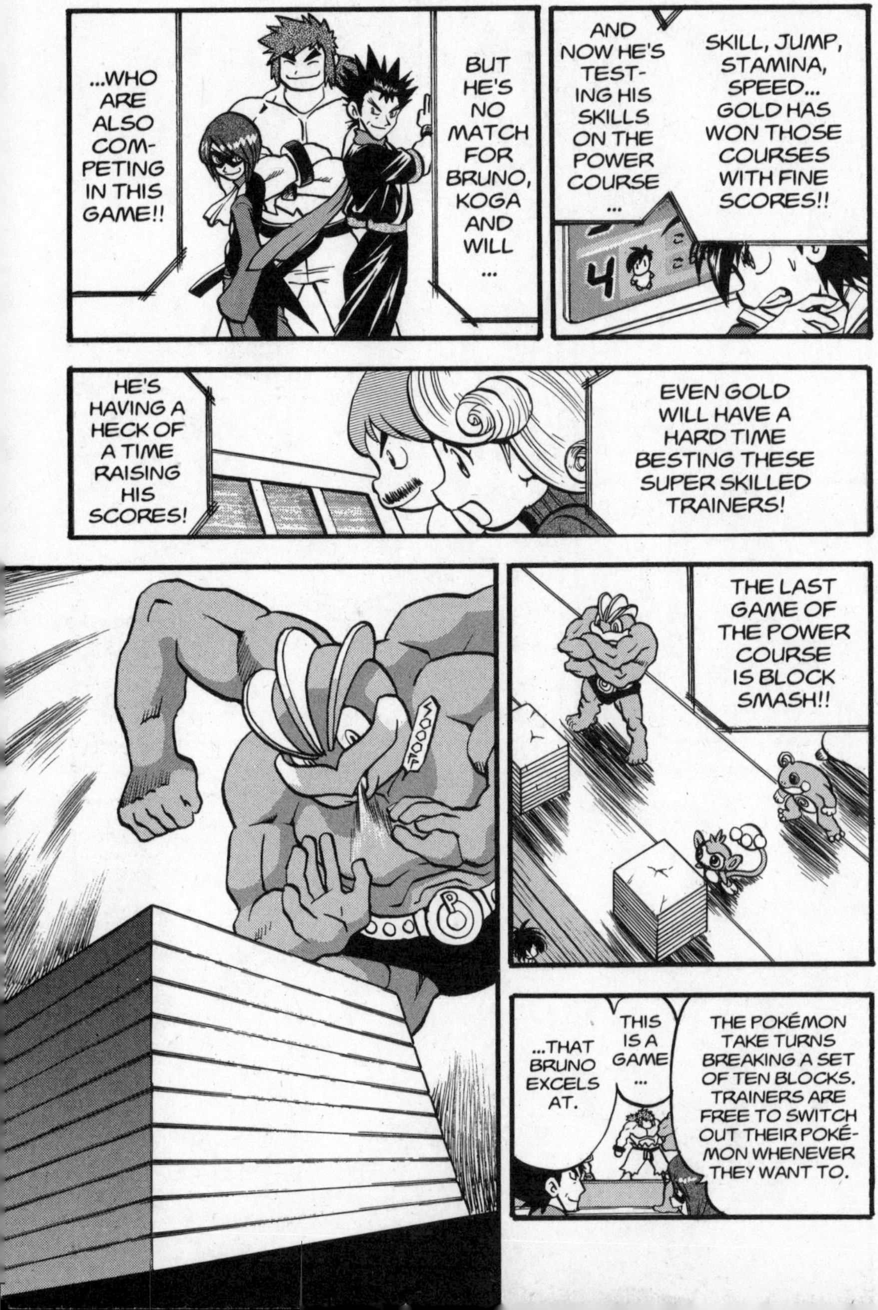
SKILL, JUMP, STAMINA, SPEED... GOLD HAS WON THOSE COURSES WITH FINE SCORES!!
AND NOW HE'S TEST-ING HIS SKILLS ON THE POWER COURSE...
BUT HE'S NO MATCH FOR BRUNO, KOGA AND WILL...
...WHO ARE ALSO COM-PETING IN THIS GAME!!
EVEN GOLD WILL HAVE A HARD TIME BESTING THESE SUPER SKILLED TRAINERS!
HE'S HAVING A HECK OF A TIME RAISING HIS SCORES!
THE LAST GAME OF THE POWER COURSE IS BLOCK SMASH!!
THE POKÉMON TAKE TURNS BREAKING A SET OF TEN BLOCKS. TRAINERS ARE FREE TO SWITCH OUT THEIR POKÉ-MON WHENEVER THEY WANT TO.
THIS IS A GAME...
...THAT BRUNO EXCELS AT.

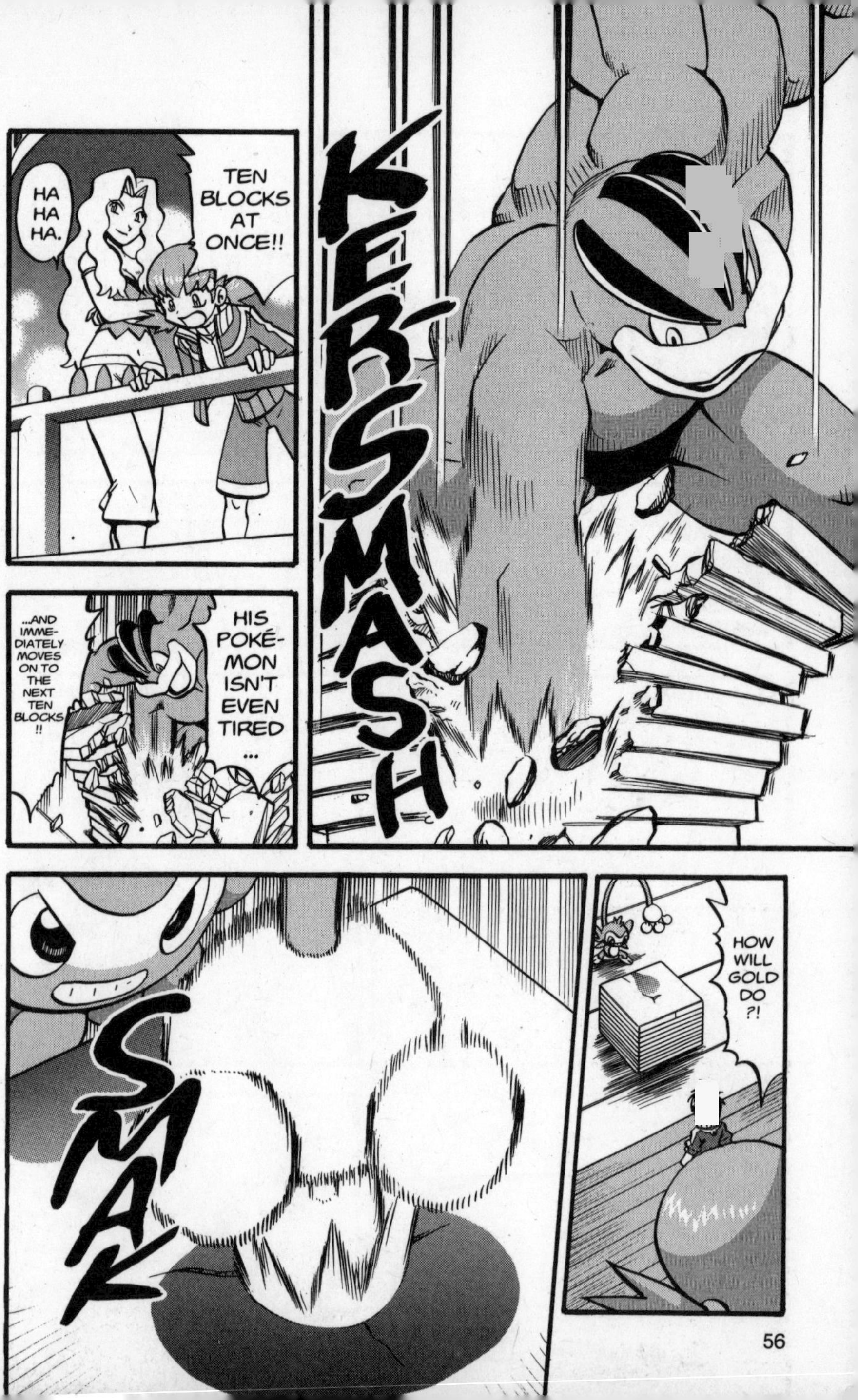
KERSMASH
TEN BLOCKS AT ONCE!!
HA HA HA.
HIS POKÉMON ISN'T EVEN TIRED...
...AND IMMEDIATELY MOVES ON TO THE NEXT TEN BLOCKS!!
HOW WILL GOLD DO?!
SMAK

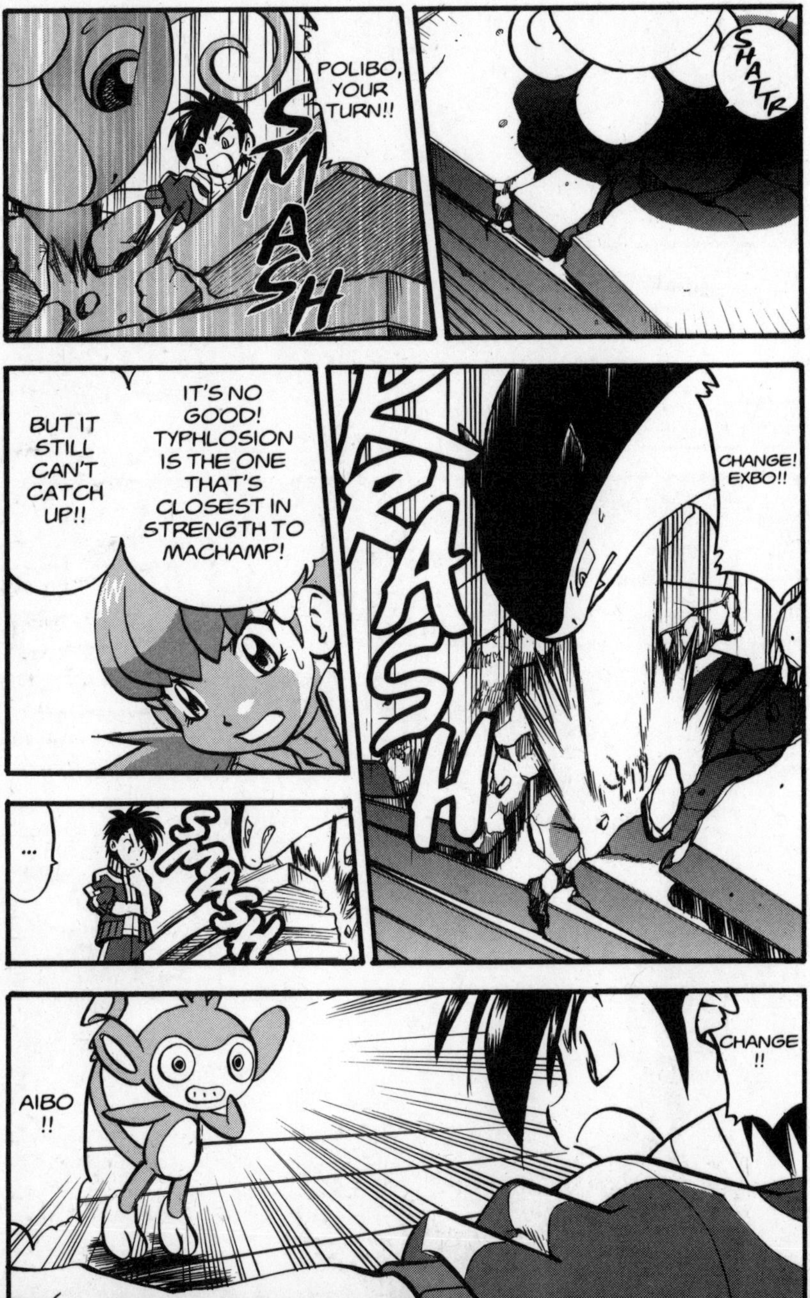
SHATTR
POLIBO, YOUR TURN!!
SMASH
CHANGE! EXBO!!
KRASH
IT'S NO GOOD! TYPHLOSION IS THE ONE THAT'S CLOSEST IN STRENGTH TO MACHAMP!
BUT IT STILL CAN'T CATCH UP!!
SMASH
...
CHANGE !!
AIBO !!

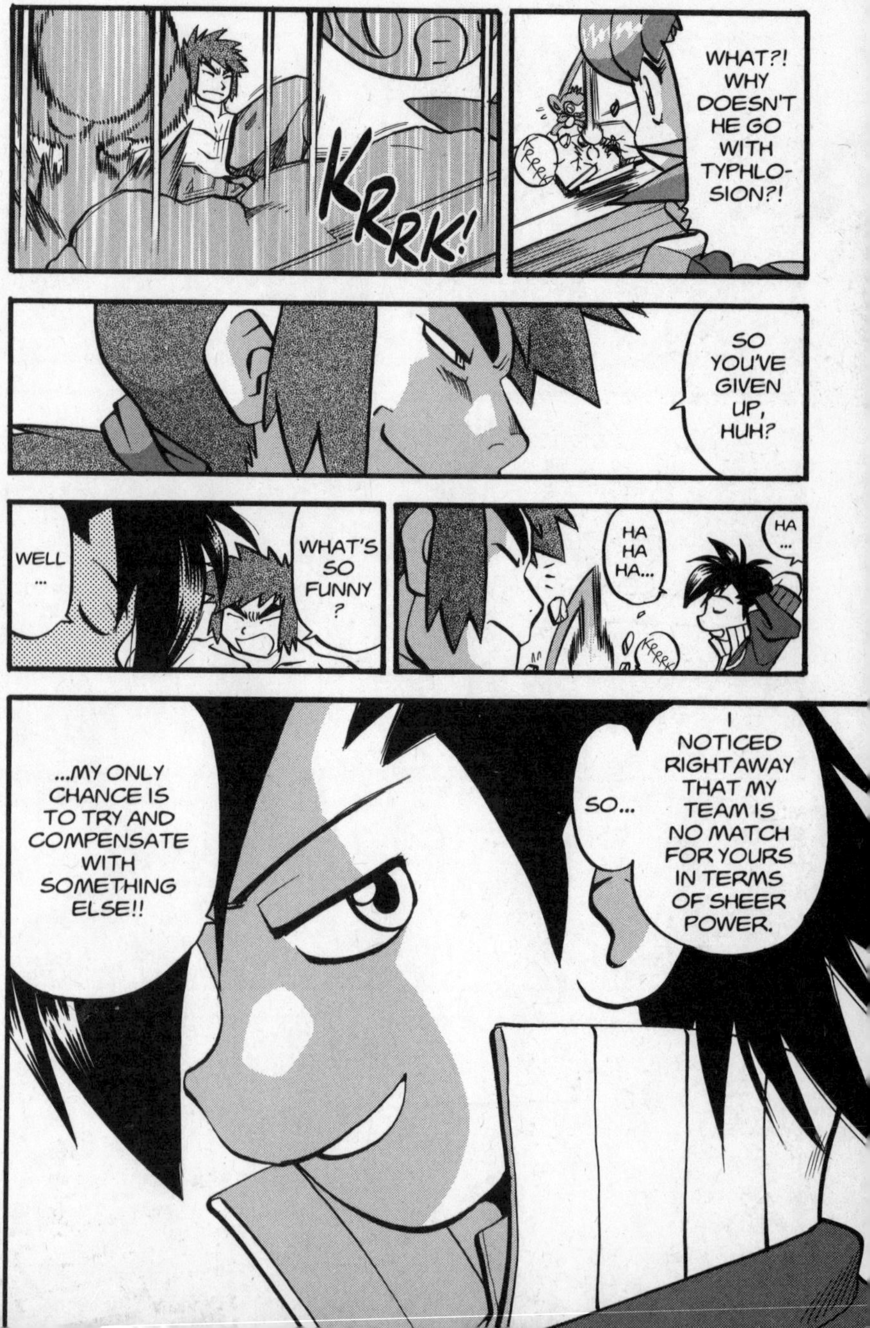
WHAT?! WHY DOESN'T HE GO WITH TYPHLOSION?!
KRRRK
KRRK!
SO YOU'VE GIVEN UP, HUH?
HA ...
HA HA HA...
KRRRK
WHAT'S SO FUNNY ?
WELL ...
I NOTICED RIGHTAWAY THAT MY TEAM IS NO MATCH FOR YOURS IN TERMS OF SHEER POWER.
SO...
...MY ONLY CHANCE IS TO TRY AND COMPENSATE WITH SOMETHING ELSE!!

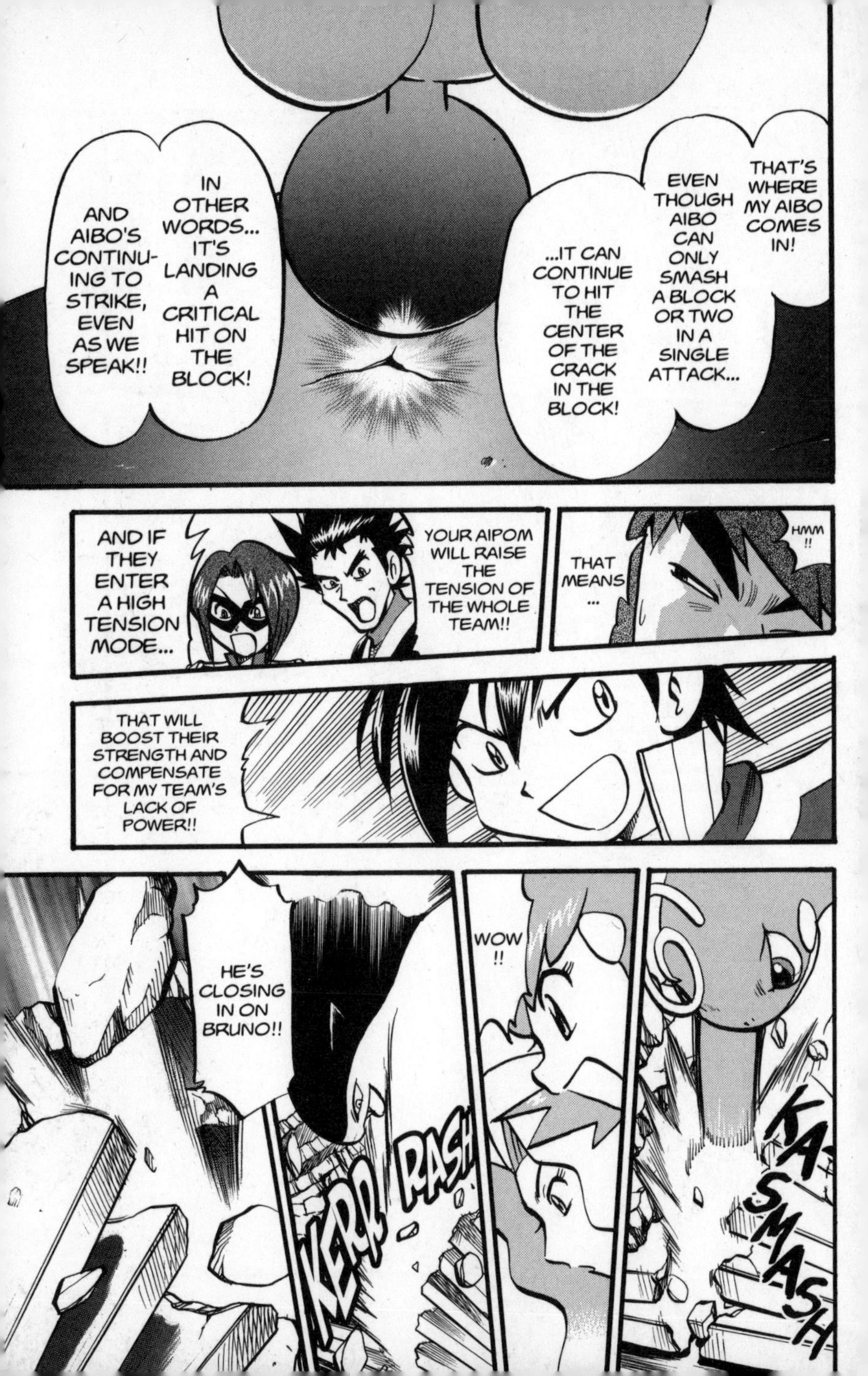
THAT'S WHERE MY AIBO COMES IN!
EVEN THOUGH AIBO CAN ONLY SMASH A BLOCK OR TWO IN A SINGLE ATTACK...
...IT CAN CONTINUE TO HIT THE CENTER OF THE CRACK IN THE BLOCK!
IN OTHER WORDS... IT'S LANDING A CRITICAL HIT ON THE BLOCK!
AND AIBO'S CONTINU-ING TO STRIKE, EVEN AS WE SPEAK!!
HMM !!
THAT MEANS ...
YOUR AIPOM WILL RAISE THE TENSION OF THE WHOLE TEAM!!
AND IF THEY ENTER A HIGH TENSION MODE...
THAT WILL BOOST THEIR STRENGTH AND COMPENSATE FOR MY TEAM'S LACK OF POWER!!
KA-SMASH
WOW !!
KERR RASH
HE'S CLOSING IN ON BRUNO!!

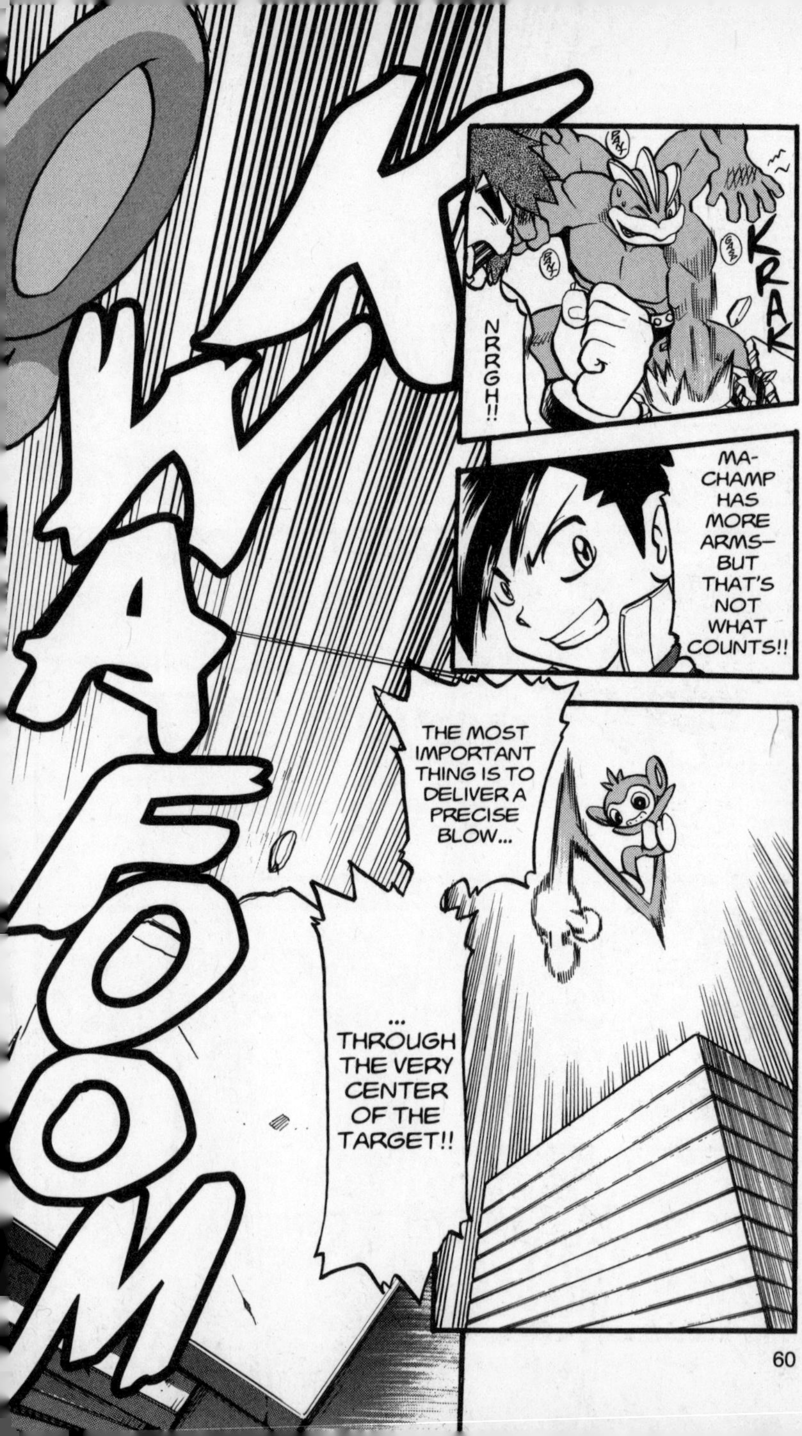
KRAK
NRRGH!!
MA-CHAMP HAS MORE ARMS—BUT THAT'S NOT WHAT COUNTS!!
THE MOST IMPORTANT THING IS TO DELIVER A PRECISE BLOW...
...THROUGH THE VERY CENTER OF THE TARGET!!
KABOOM

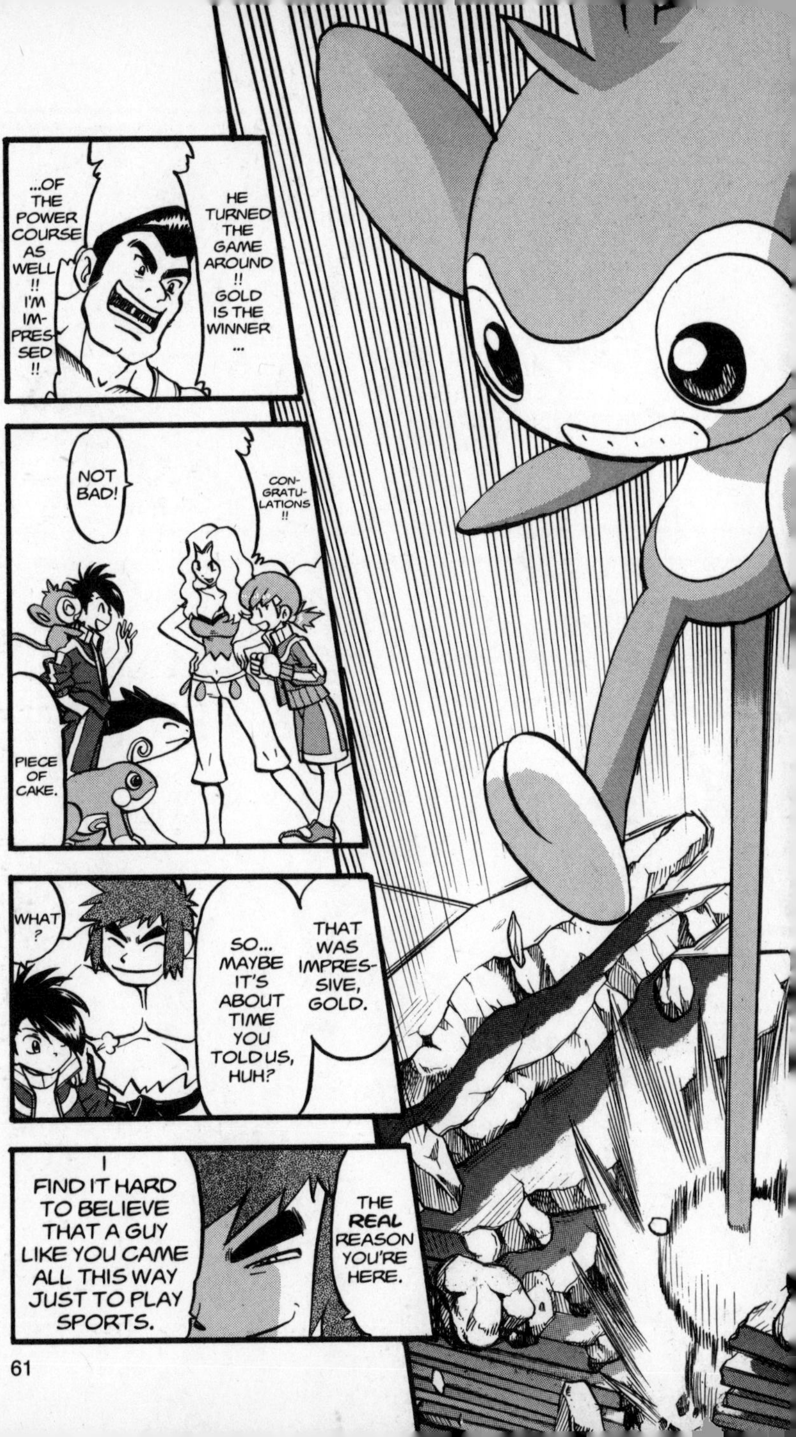
HE TURNED THE GAME AROUND!! GOLD IS THE WINNER...
...OF THE POWER COURSE AS WELL!! I'M IMPRESSED!!
CONGRATULATIONS!!
NOT BAD!
PIECE OF CAKE.
THAT WAS IMPRESSIVE, GOLD.
SO... MAYBE IT'S ABOUT TIME YOU TOLD US, HUH?
WHAT?
THE **REAL** REASON YOU'RE HERE.
I FIND IT HARD TO BELIEVE THAT A GUY LIKE YOU CAME ALL THIS WAY JUST TO PLAY SPORTS.

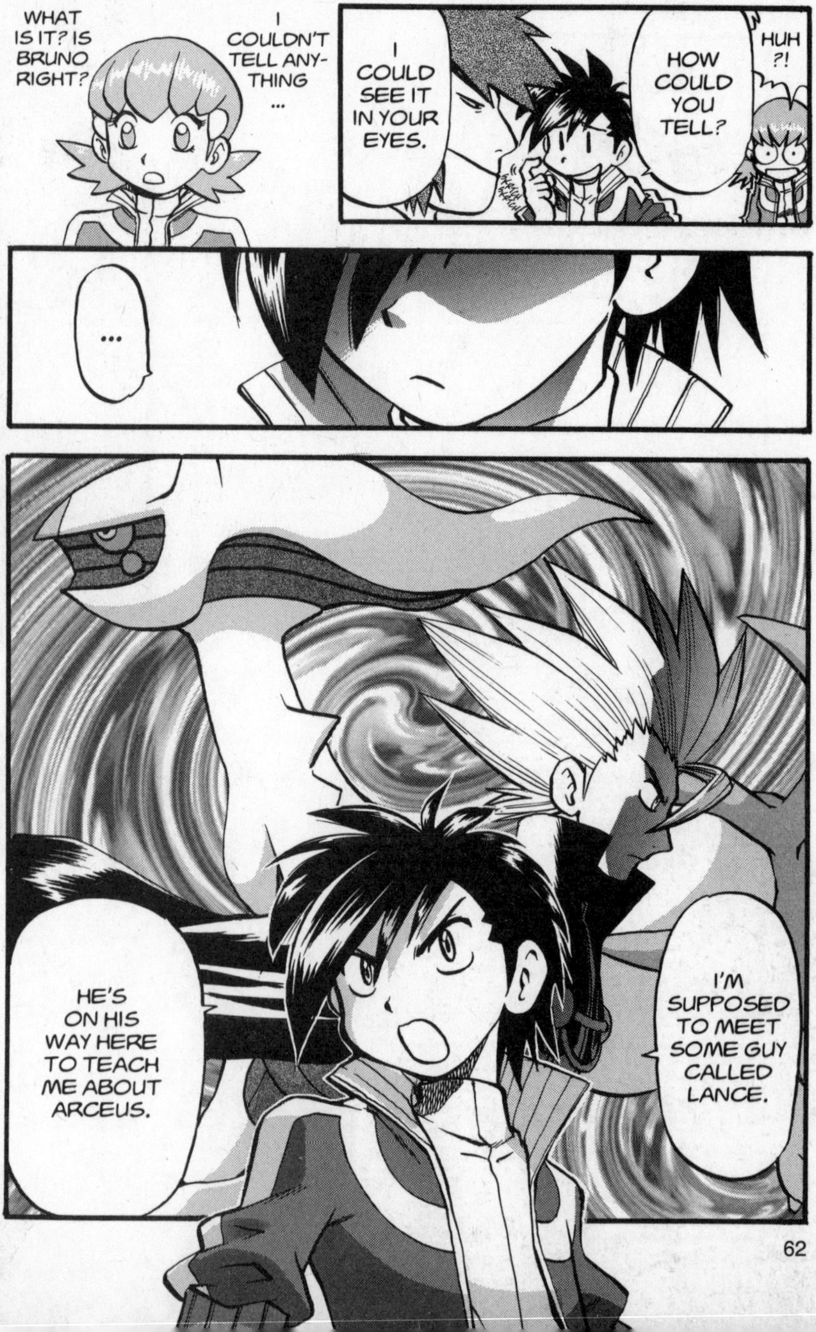
HUH ?!
HOW COULD YOU TELL?
I COULD SEE IT IN YOUR EYES.
I COULDN'T TELL ANYTHING ...
WHAT IS IT? IS BRUNO RIGHT?
...
I'M SUPPOSED TO MEET SOME GUY CALLED LANCE.
HE'S ON HIS WAY HERE TO TEACH ME ABOUT ARCEUS.

Adventure 3

9

ONE TOUGH TOGEPI

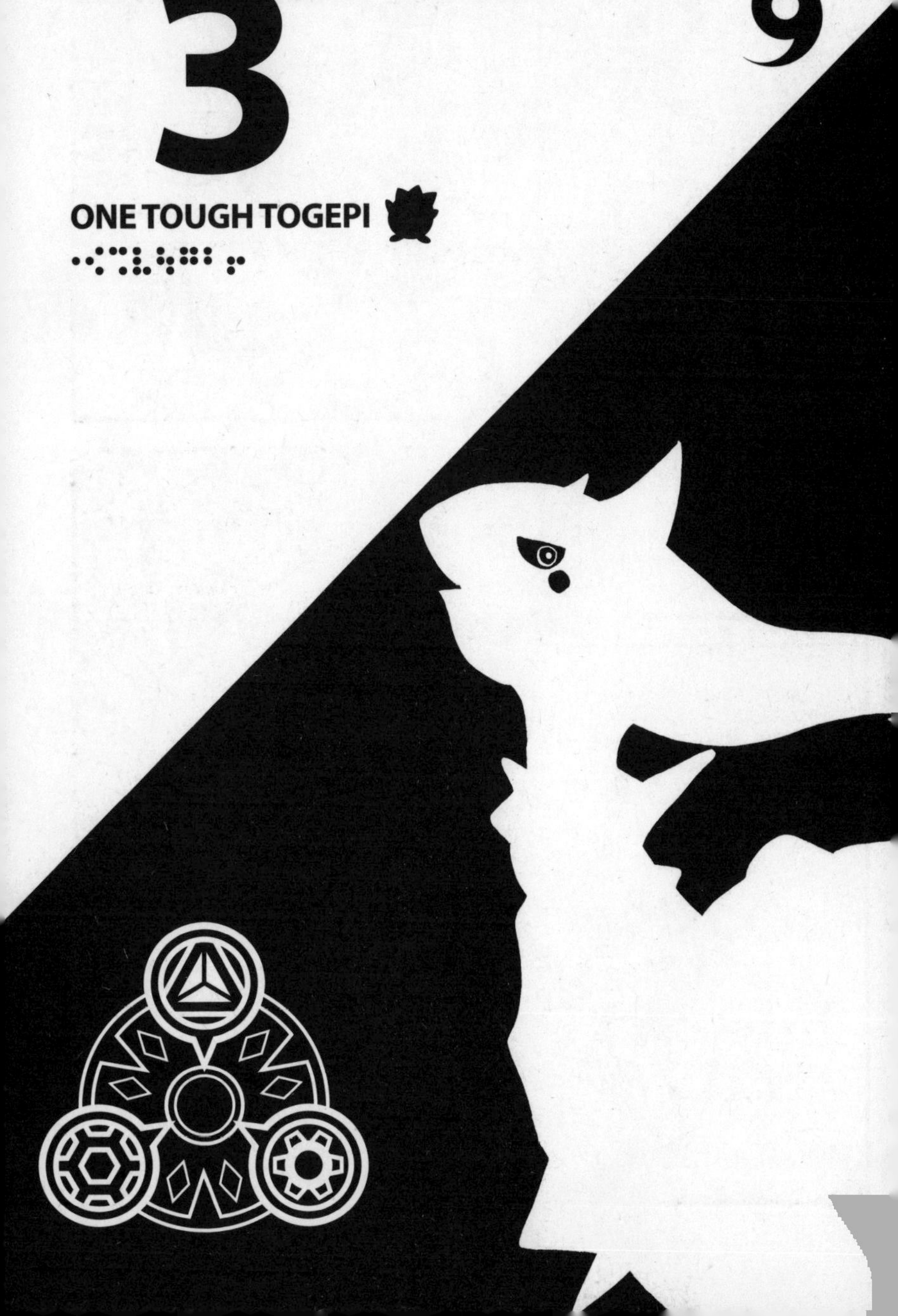

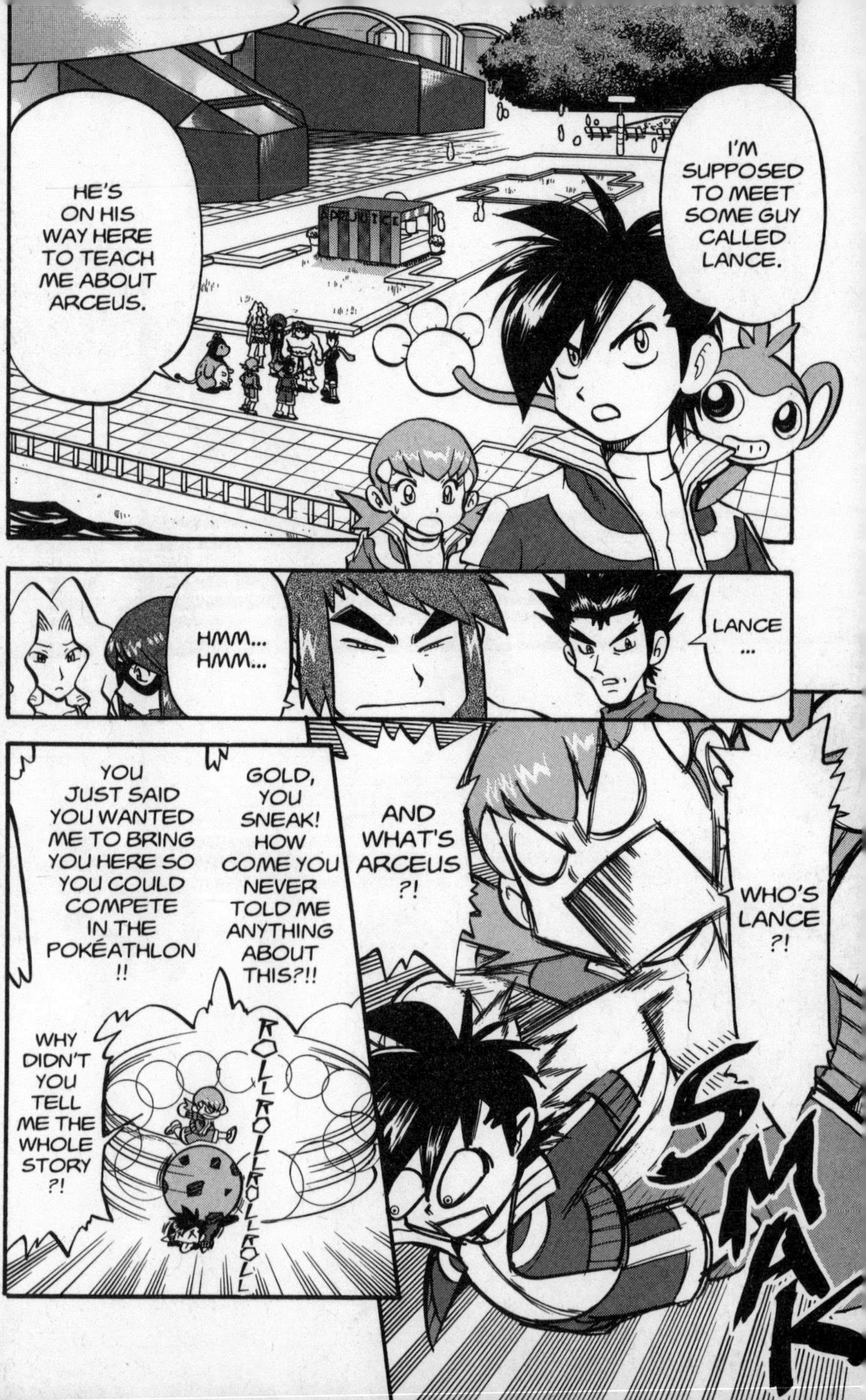

I'M SUPPOSED TO MEET SOME GUY CALLED LANCE.
HE'S ON HIS WAY HERE TO TEACH ME ABOUT ARCEUS.
LANCE ...
HMM... HMM...
WHO'S LANCE ?!
AND WHAT'S ARCEUS ?!
GOLD, YOU SNEAK! HOW COME YOU NEVER TOLD ME ANYTHING ABOUT THIS?!!
YOU JUST SAID YOU WANTED ME TO BRING YOU HERE SO YOU COULD COMPETE IN THE POKÉATHLON !!
SMAK
ROLL ROLL ROLL ROLL
WHY DIDN'T YOU TELL ME THE WHOLE STORY ?!

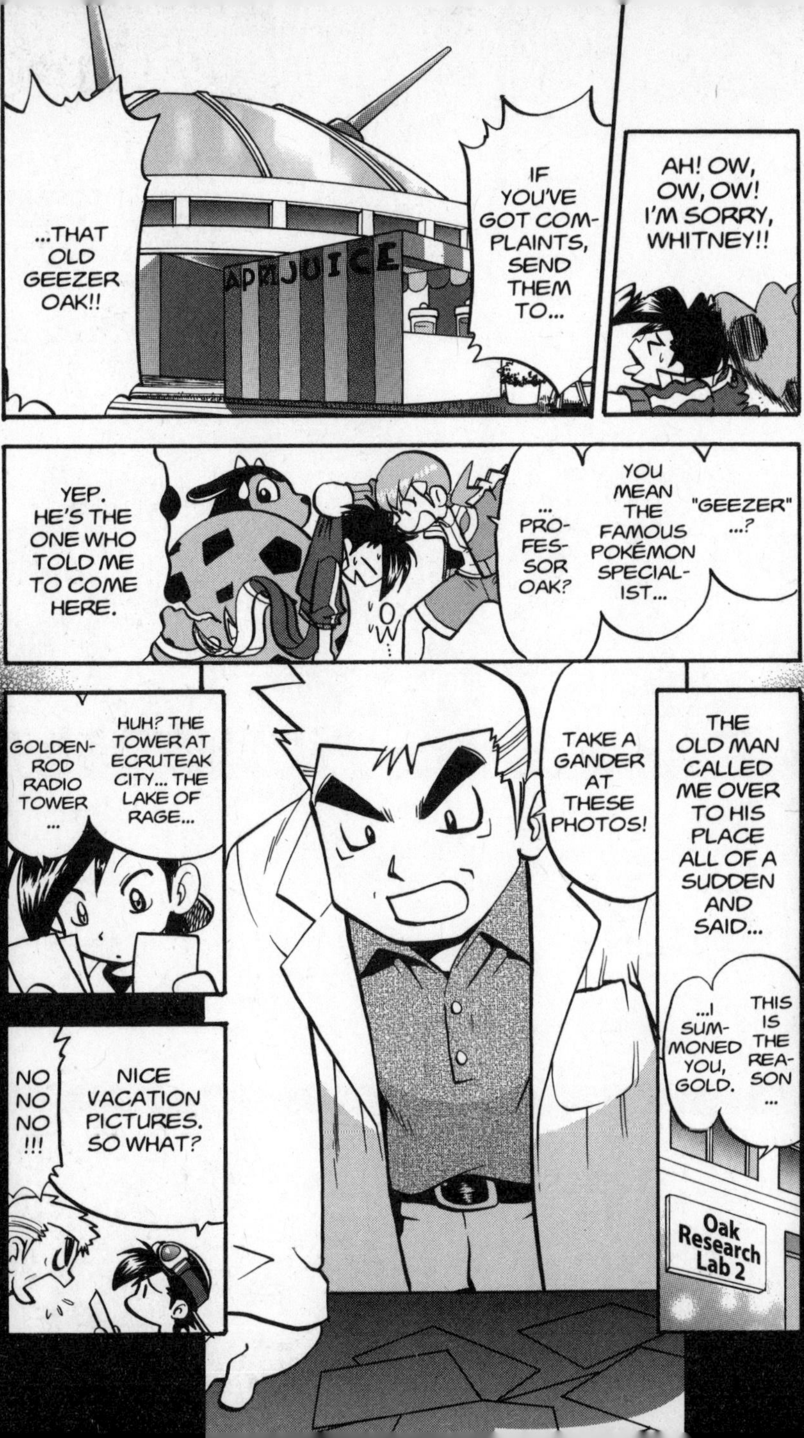

AH! OW, OW, OW! I'M SORRY, WHITNEY!!
IF YOU'VE GOT COM-PLAINTS, SEND THEM TO...
APRIJUICE
...THAT OLD GEEZER OAK!!
"GEEZER" ...?
YOU MEAN THE FAMOUS POKÉMON SPECIAL-IST...
... PRO-FES-SOR OAK?
OW
YEP. HE'S THE ONE WHO TOLD ME TO COME HERE.
THE OLD MAN CALLED ME OVER TO HIS PLACE ALL OF A SUDDEN AND SAID...
THIS IS THE REA-SON ...
...I SUM-MONED YOU, GOLD.
Oak Research Lab 2
TAKE A GANDER AT THESE PHOTOS!
HUH? THE TOWER AT ECRUTEAK CITY... THE LAKE OF RAGE...
GOLDEN-ROD RADIO TOWER ...
NICE VACATION PICTURES. SO WHAT?
NO NO NO !!!

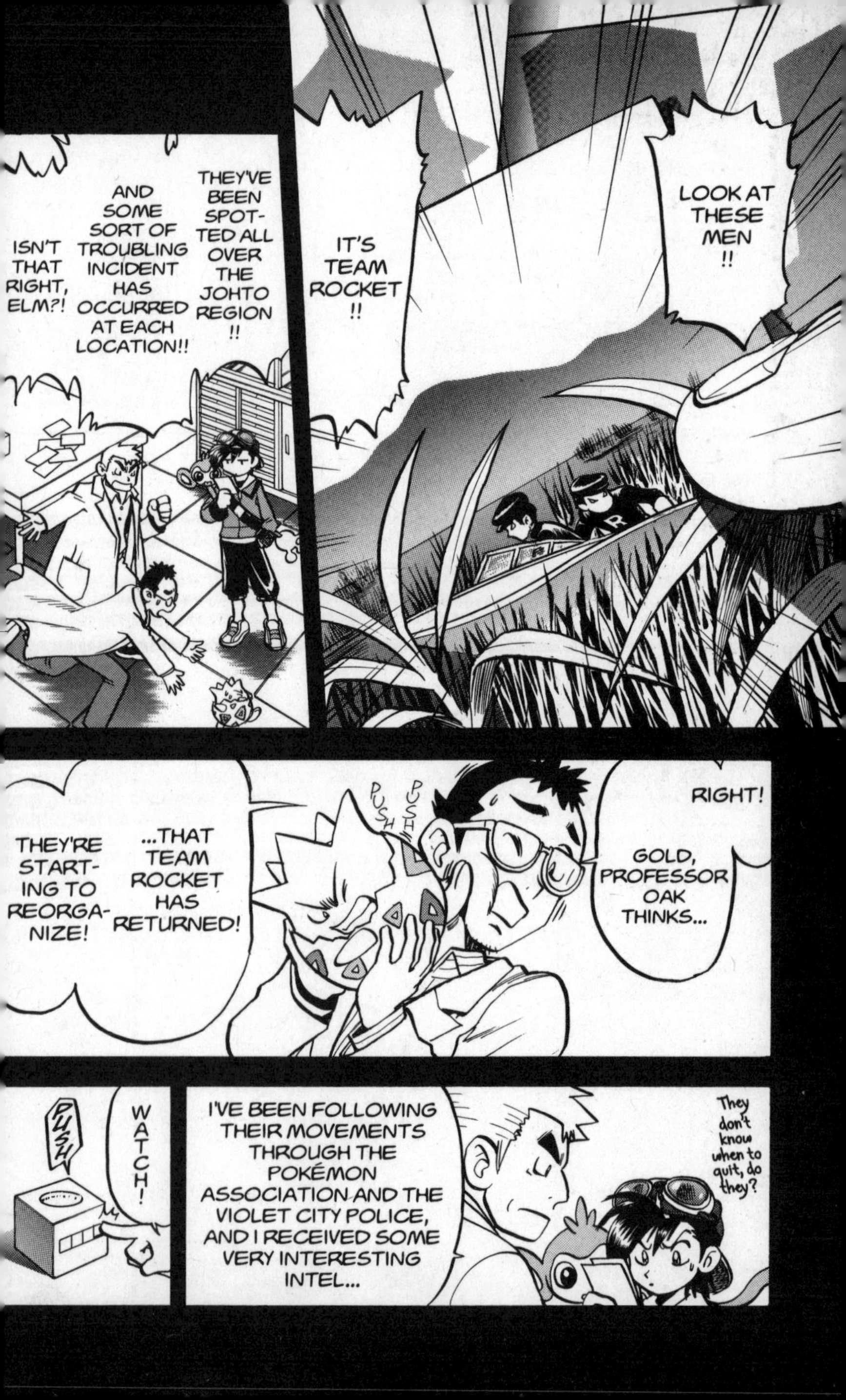
LOOK AT THESE MEN!!
IT'S TEAM ROCKET!!
THEY'VE BEEN SPOTTED ALL OVER THE JOHTO REGION!!
AND SOME SORT OF TROUBLING INCIDENT HAS OCCURRED AT EACH LOCATION!!
ISN'T THAT RIGHT, ELM?!
RIGHT!
GOLD, PROFESSOR OAK THINKS...
PUSH PUSH
...THAT TEAM ROCKET HAS RETURNED!
THEY'RE STARTING TO REORGANIZE!
They don't know when to quit, do they?
I'VE BEEN FOLLOWING THEIR MOVEMENTS THROUGH THE POKÉMON ASSOCIATION AND THE VIOLET CITY POLICE, AND I RECEIVED SOME VERY INTERESTING INTEL...
WATCH!
PUSH

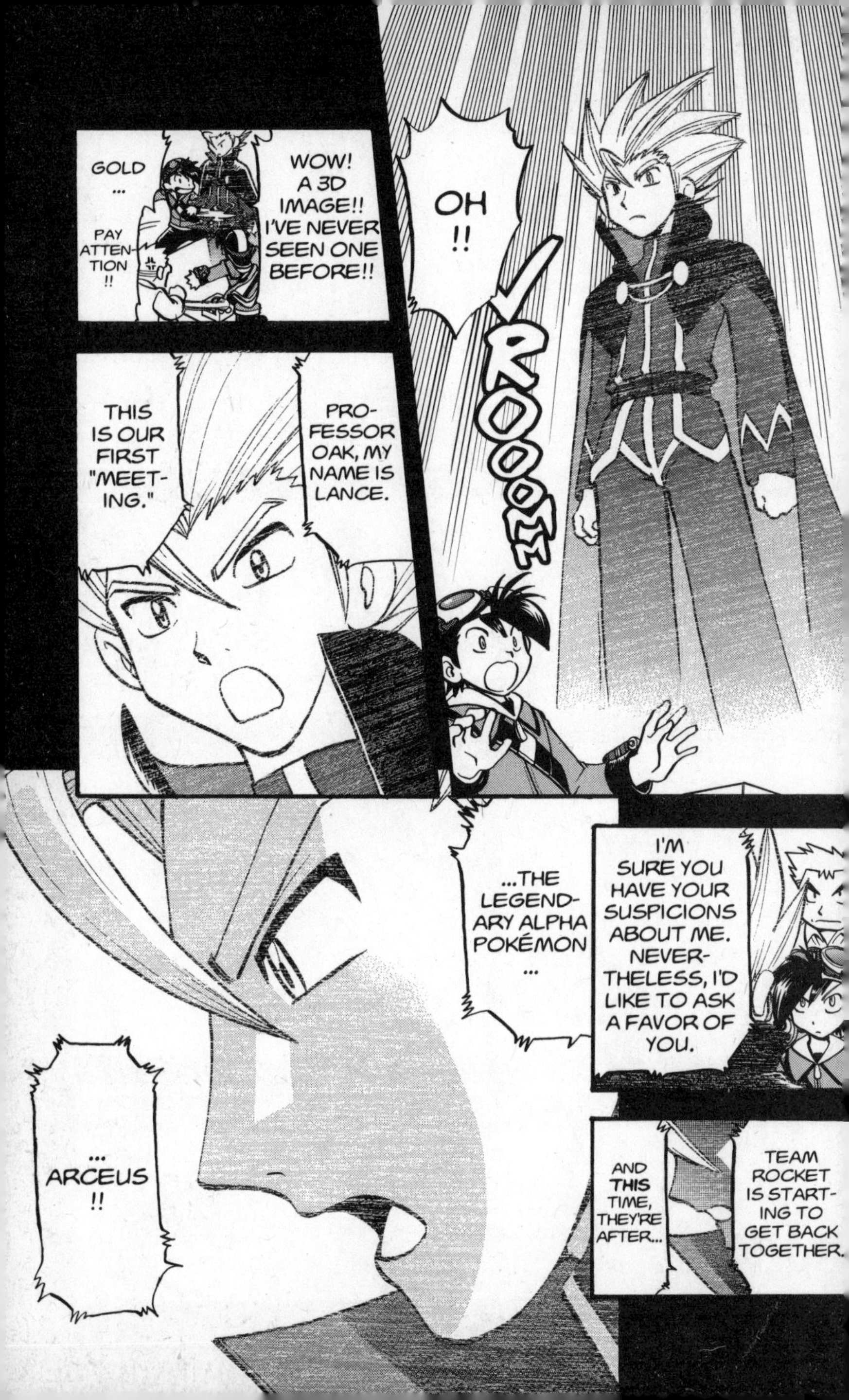
OH !!
VROOOOM
WOW! A 3D IMAGE!! I'VE NEVER SEEN ONE BEFORE!!
GOLD ... PAY ATTENTION !!
PRO-FESSOR OAK, MY NAME IS LANCE.
THIS IS OUR FIRST "MEET-ING."
I'M SURE YOU HAVE YOUR SUSPICIONS ABOUT ME. NEVER-THELESS, I'D LIKE TO ASK A FAVOR OF YOU.
TEAM ROCKET IS START-ING TO GET BACK TOGETHER.
AND THIS TIME, THEY'RE AFTER...
...THE LEGEND-ARY ALPHA POKÉMON ...
... ARCEUS !!

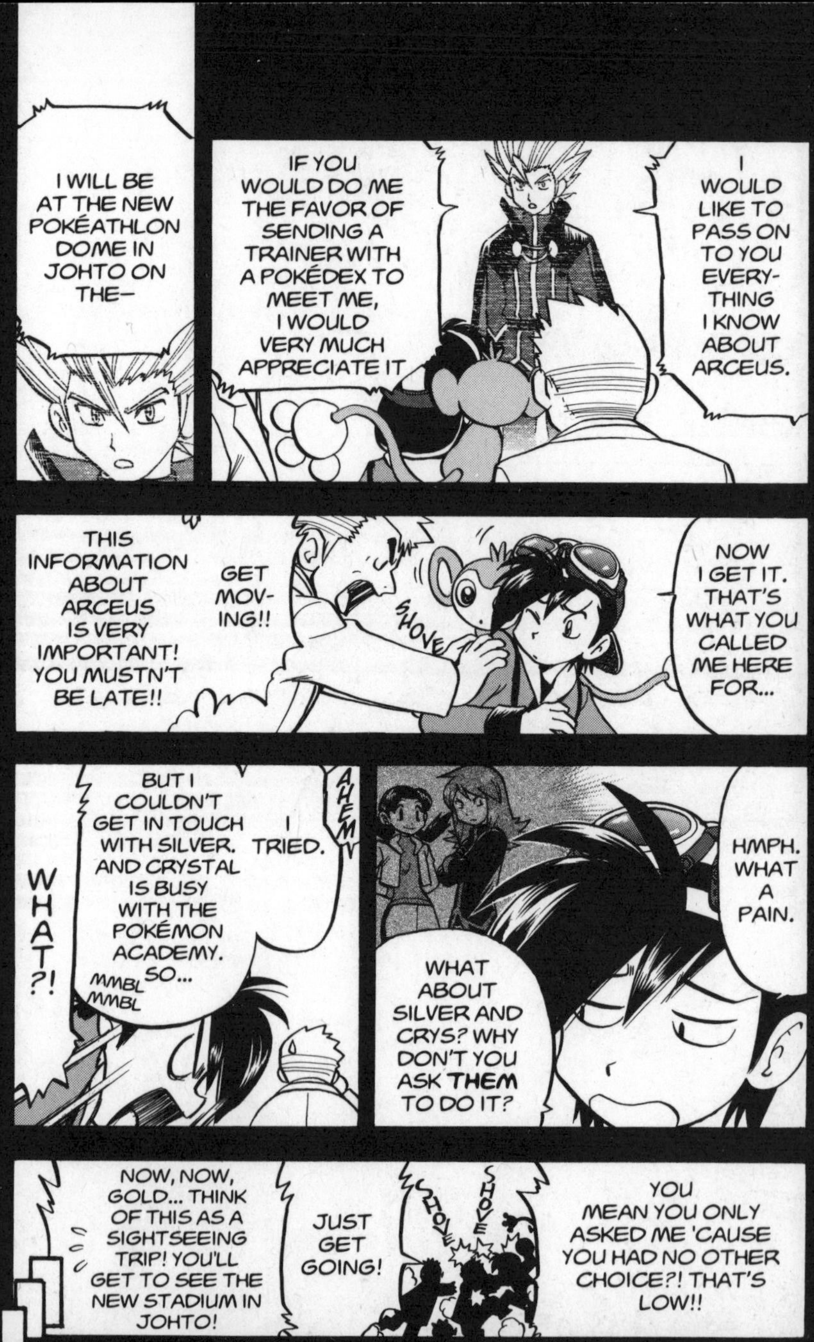
I WOULD LIKE TO PASS ON TO YOU EVERY-THING I KNOW ABOUT ARCEUS.
IF YOU WOULD DO ME THE FAVOR OF SENDING A TRAINER WITH A POKÉDEX TO MEET ME, I WOULD VERY MUCH APPRECIATE IT
I WILL BE AT THE NEW POKÉATHLON DOME IN JOHTO ON THE—
NOW I GET IT. THAT'S WHAT YOU CALLED ME HERE FOR...
SHOVE
GET MOV-ING!!
THIS INFORMATION ABOUT ARCEUS IS VERY IMPORTANT! YOU MUSTN'T BE LATE!!
HMPH. WHAT A PAIN.
WHAT ABOUT SILVER AND CRYS? WHY DON'T YOU ASK **THEM** TO DO IT?
AHEM
I TRIED.
BUT I COULDN'T GET IN TOUCH WITH SILVER. AND CRYSTAL IS BUSY WITH THE POKÉMON ACADEMY. SO...
MMBL MMBL
WHAT?!
YOU MEAN YOU ONLY ASKED ME 'CAUSE YOU HAD NO OTHER CHOICE?! THAT'S LOW!!
SHOVE
SHOVE
JUST GET GOING!
NOW, NOW, GOLD... THINK OF THIS AS A SIGHTSEEING TRIP! YOU'LL GET TO SEE THE NEW STADIUM IN JOHTO!

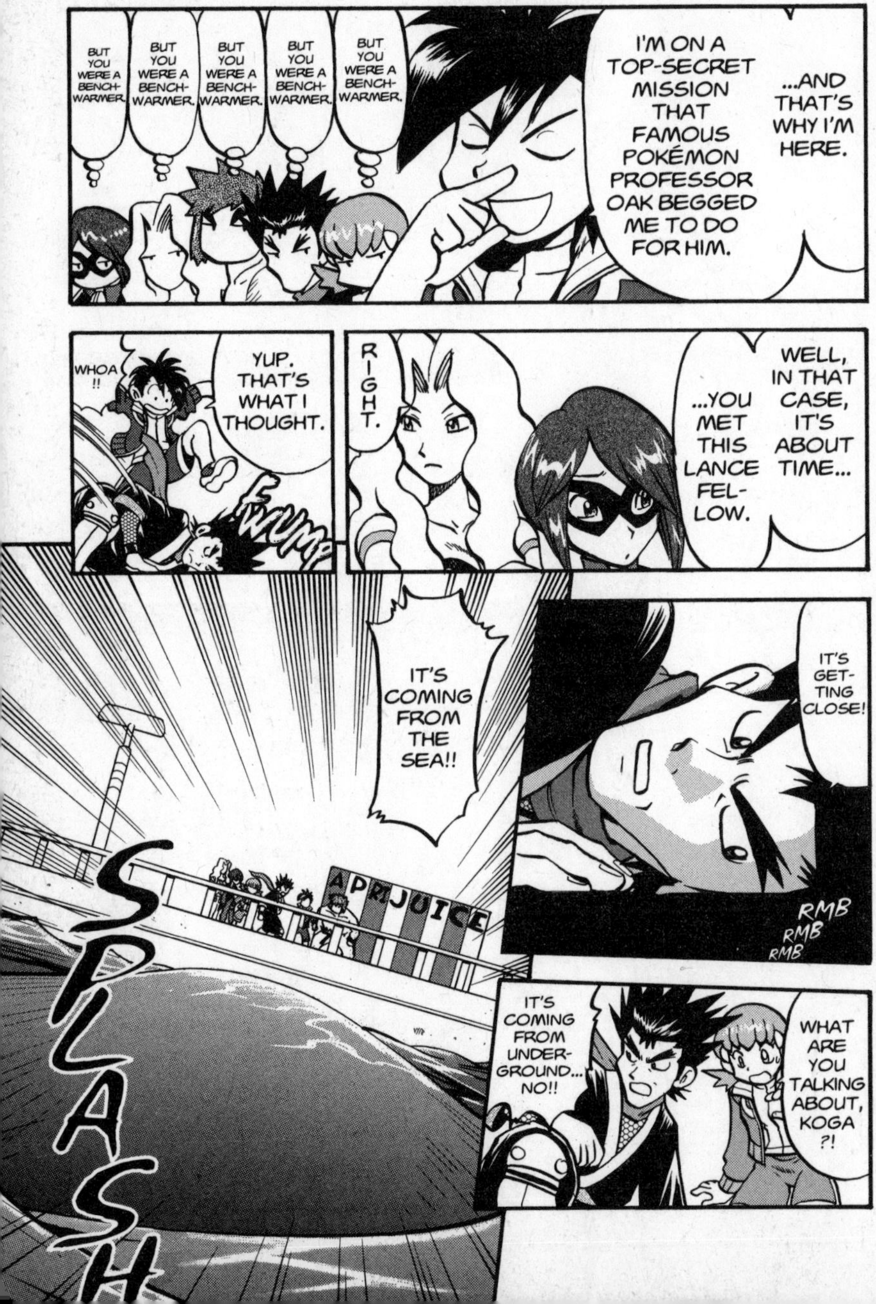
I'M ON A TOP-SECRET MISSION THAT FAMOUS POKÉMON PROFESSOR OAK BEGGED ME TO DO FOR HIM.
...AND THAT'S WHY I'M HERE.
BUT YOU WERE A BENCH-WARMER.
BUT YOU WERE A BENCH-WARMER.
BUT YOU WERE A BENCH-WARMER.
BUT YOU WERE A BENCH-WARMER.
BUT YOU WERE A BENCH-WARMER.
WELL, IN THAT CASE, IT'S ABOUT TIME...
...YOU MET THIS LANCE FELLOW.
RIGHT.
YUP. THAT'S WHAT I THOUGHT.
WHOA!!
FWUMP
IT'S GETTING CLOSE!
RMB
RMB
RMB
WHAT ARE YOU TALKING ABOUT, KOGA?!
IT'S COMING FROM UNDERGROUND... NO!!
IT'S COMING FROM THE SEA!!
APRIJUICE
SPLASH

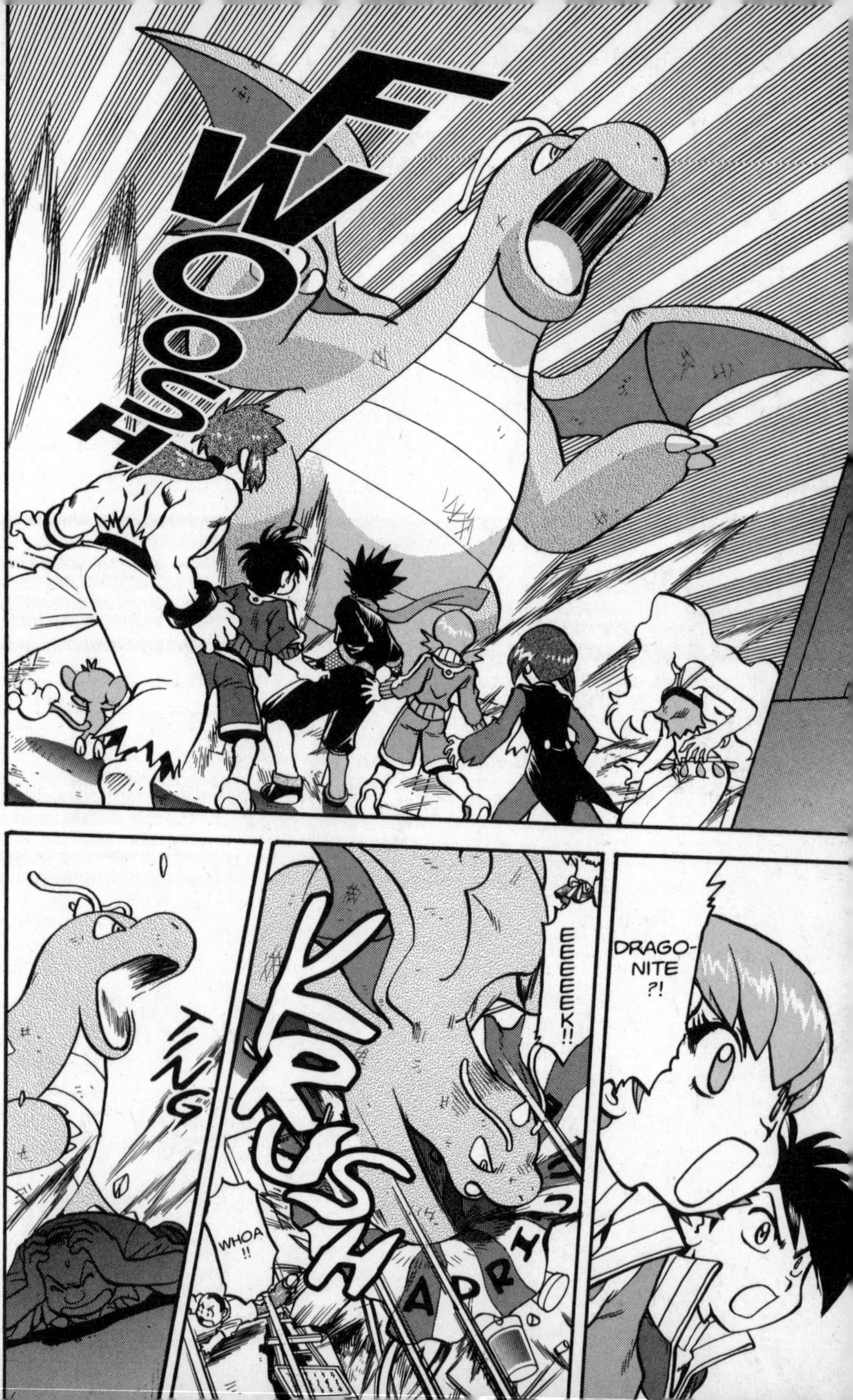
FWOOSH
DRAGO-NITE ?!
EEEEEK!!
KRUSH
WHOA !!
TING

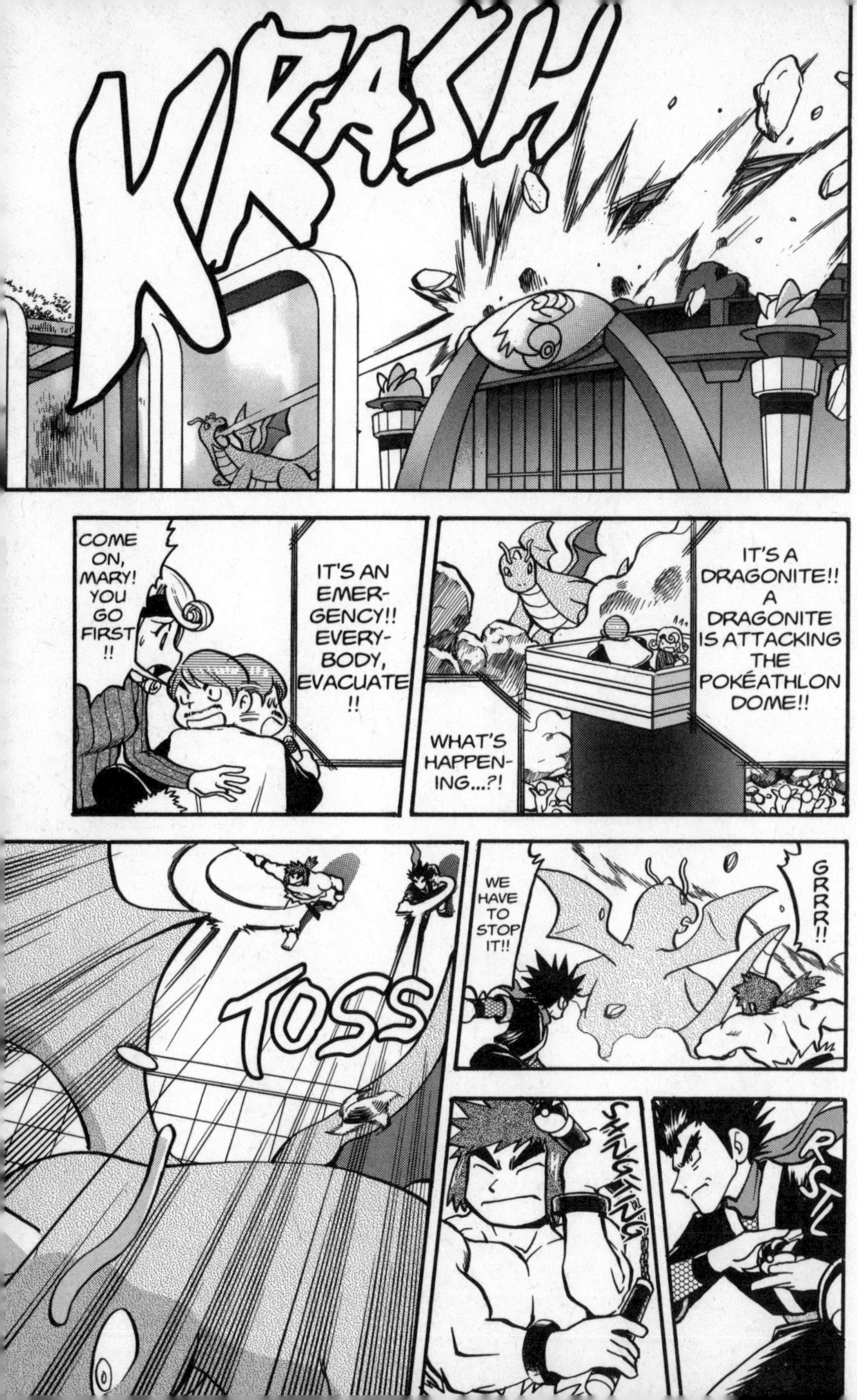
KRASH
IT'S A DRAGONITE!! A DRAGONITE IS ATTACKING THE POKÉATHLON DOME!!
WHAT'S HAPPENING...?!
IT'S AN EMERGENCY!! EVERYBODY, EVACUATE!!
COME ON, MARY! YOU GO FIRST!!
GRRR!!
WE HAVE TO STOP IT!!
RSTL
SHING-TING
TOSS

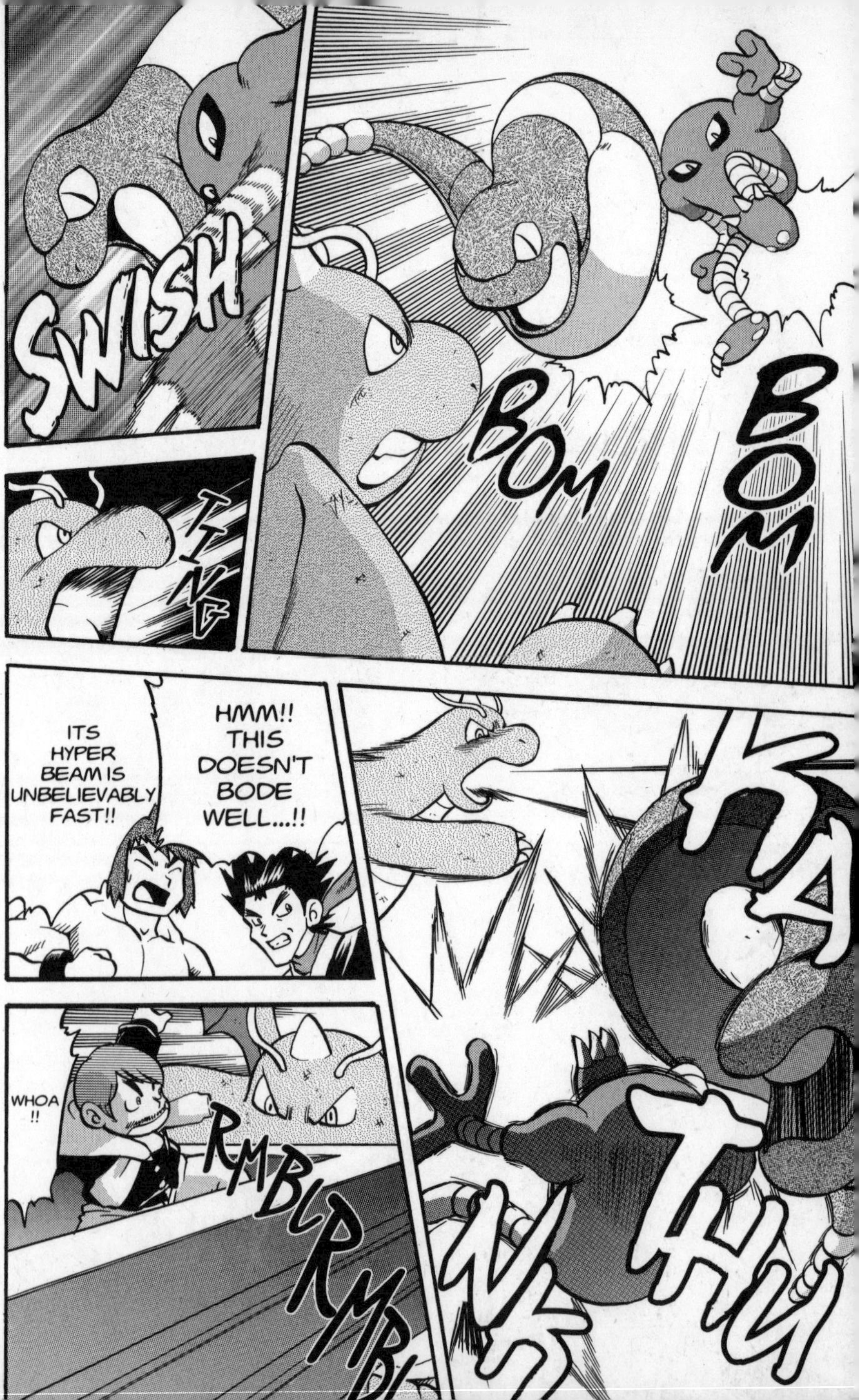
BOM
BOM
SWISH
TING
KATHUNK
HMM!! THIS DOESN'T BODE WELL...!!
ITS HYPER BEAM IS UNBELIEVABLY FAST!!
WHOA!!
RMBLRMBL

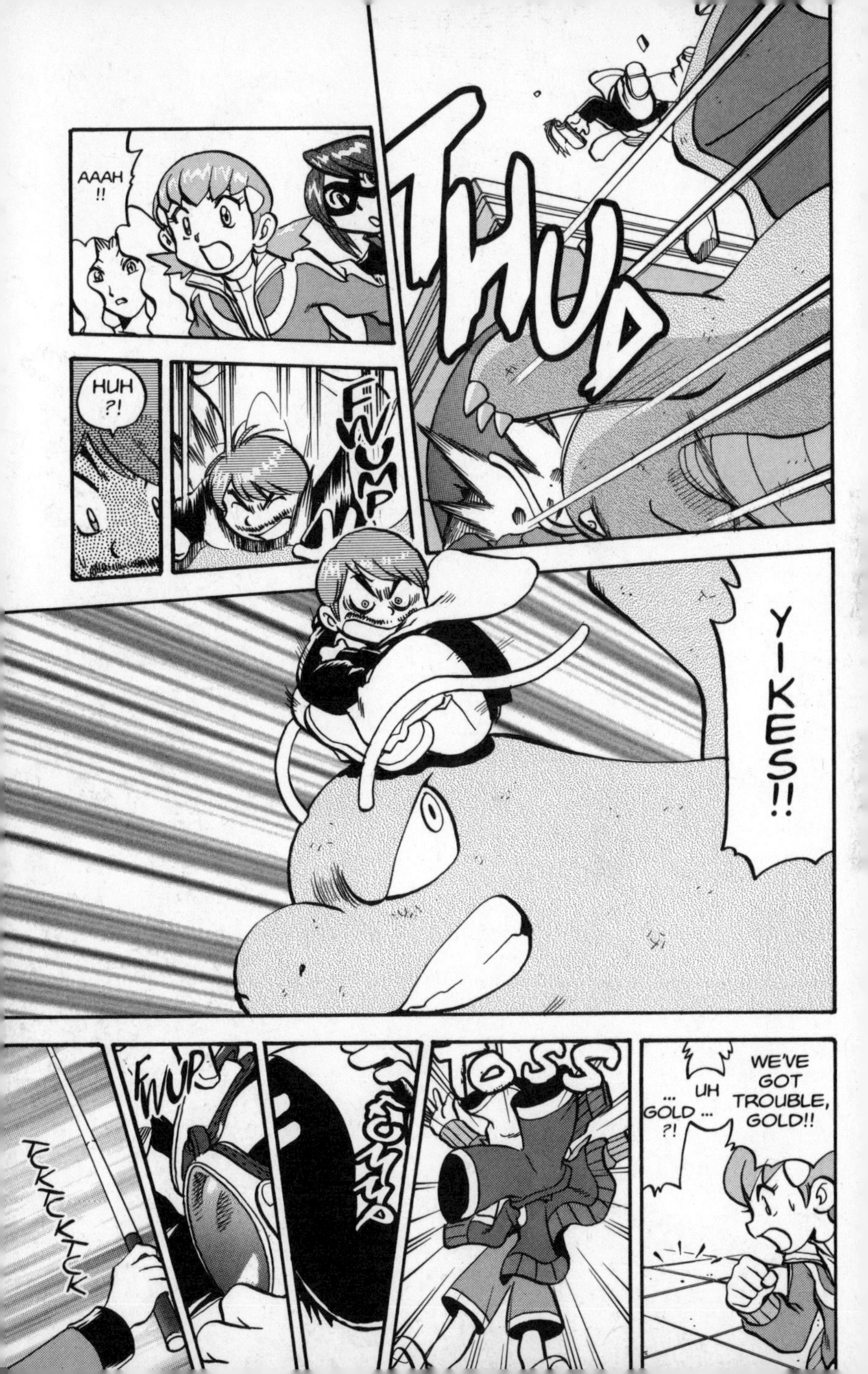
THUD
AAAH !!
FWUMP
HUH ?!
YIKES!!
WE'VE GOT TROUBLE, GOLD!!
UH ...
... GOLD ?!
TOSS
FOMMP
FWUP
TCKTCKTCK

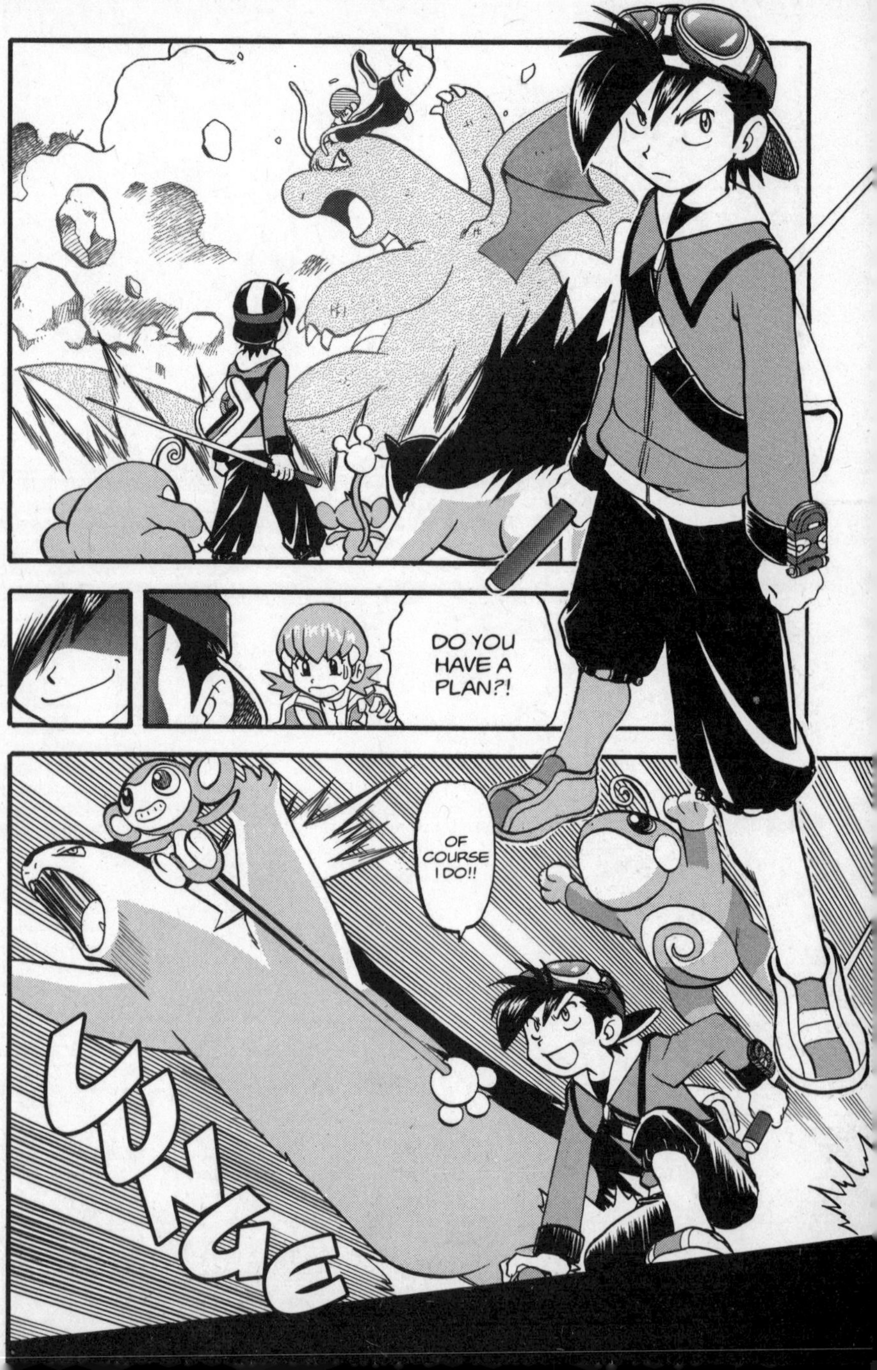
DO YOU HAVE A PLAN?!
OF COURSE I DO!!

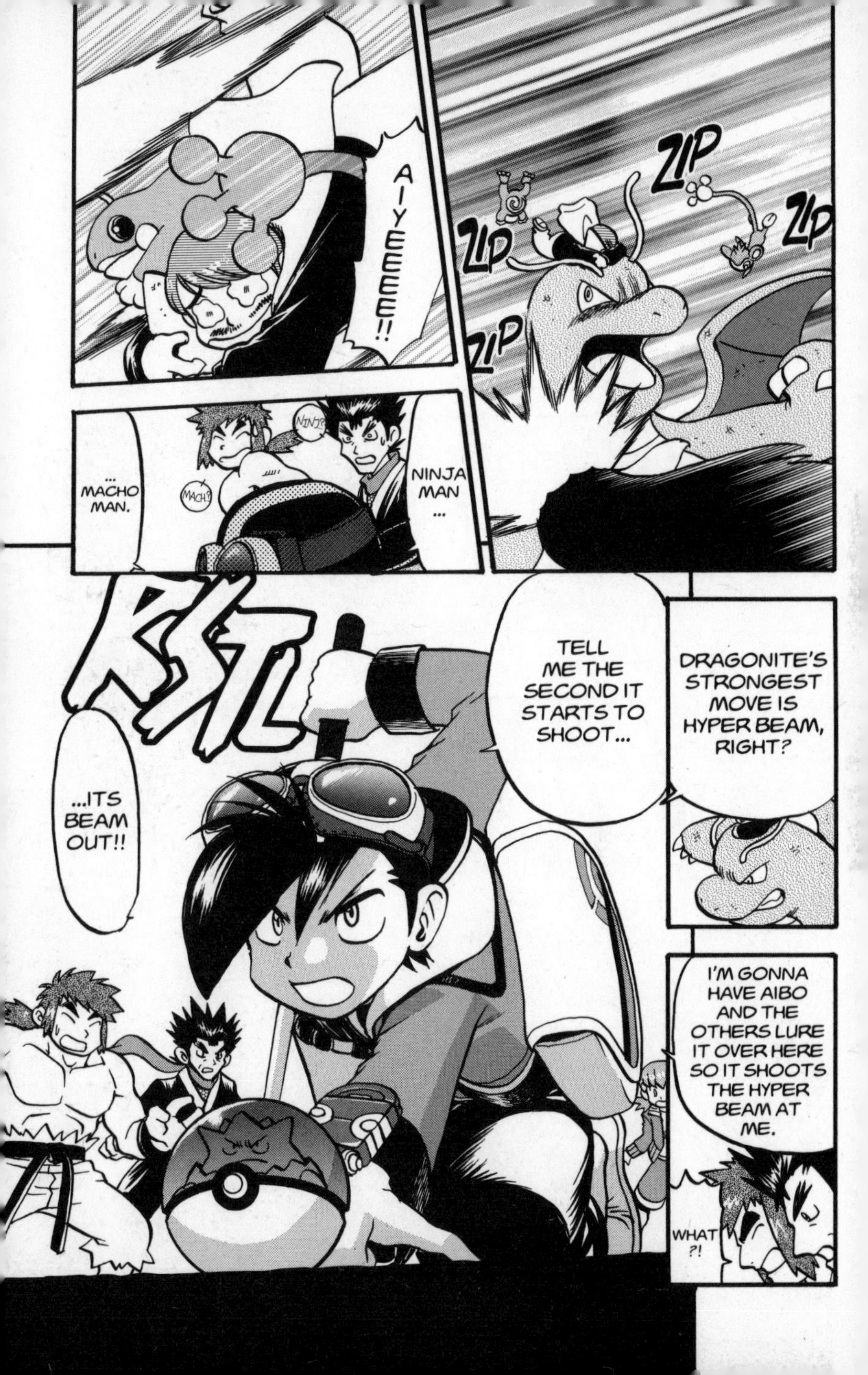
ZIP
ZIP
ZIP
ZIP
AIYEEEEE!!
NINJA MAN ...
NINJ?
MACH?
... MACHO MAN.
DRAGONITE'S STRONGEST MOVE IS HYPER BEAM, RIGHT?
I'M GONNA HAVE AIBO AND THE OTHERS LURE IT OVER HERE SO IT SHOOTS THE HYPER BEAM AT ME.
WHAT?!
TELL ME THE SECOND IT STARTS TO SHOOT...
...ITS BEAM OUT!!

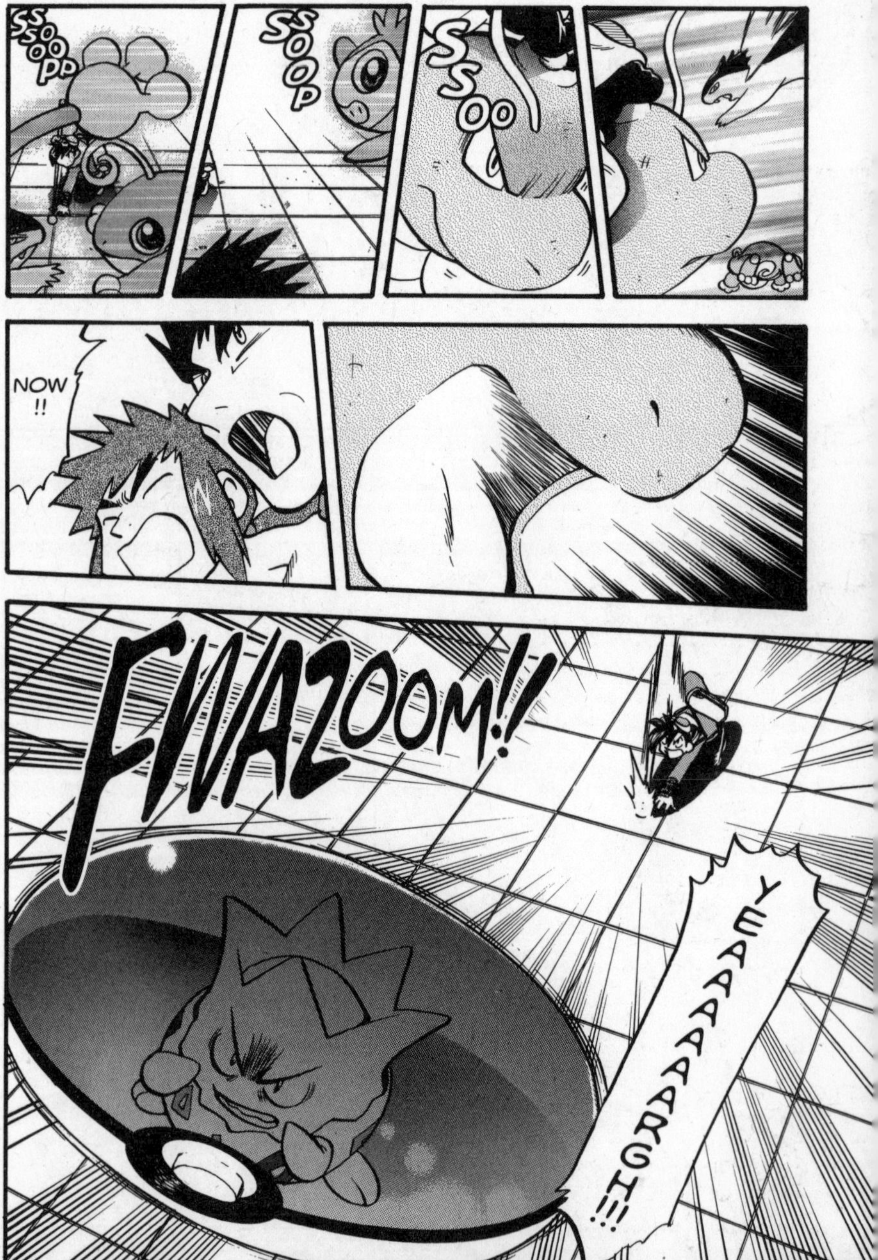
SSOO
SSOOP
SSOOPP
NOW !!
FWAZOOM!!
YEAAAAAARGH!!!

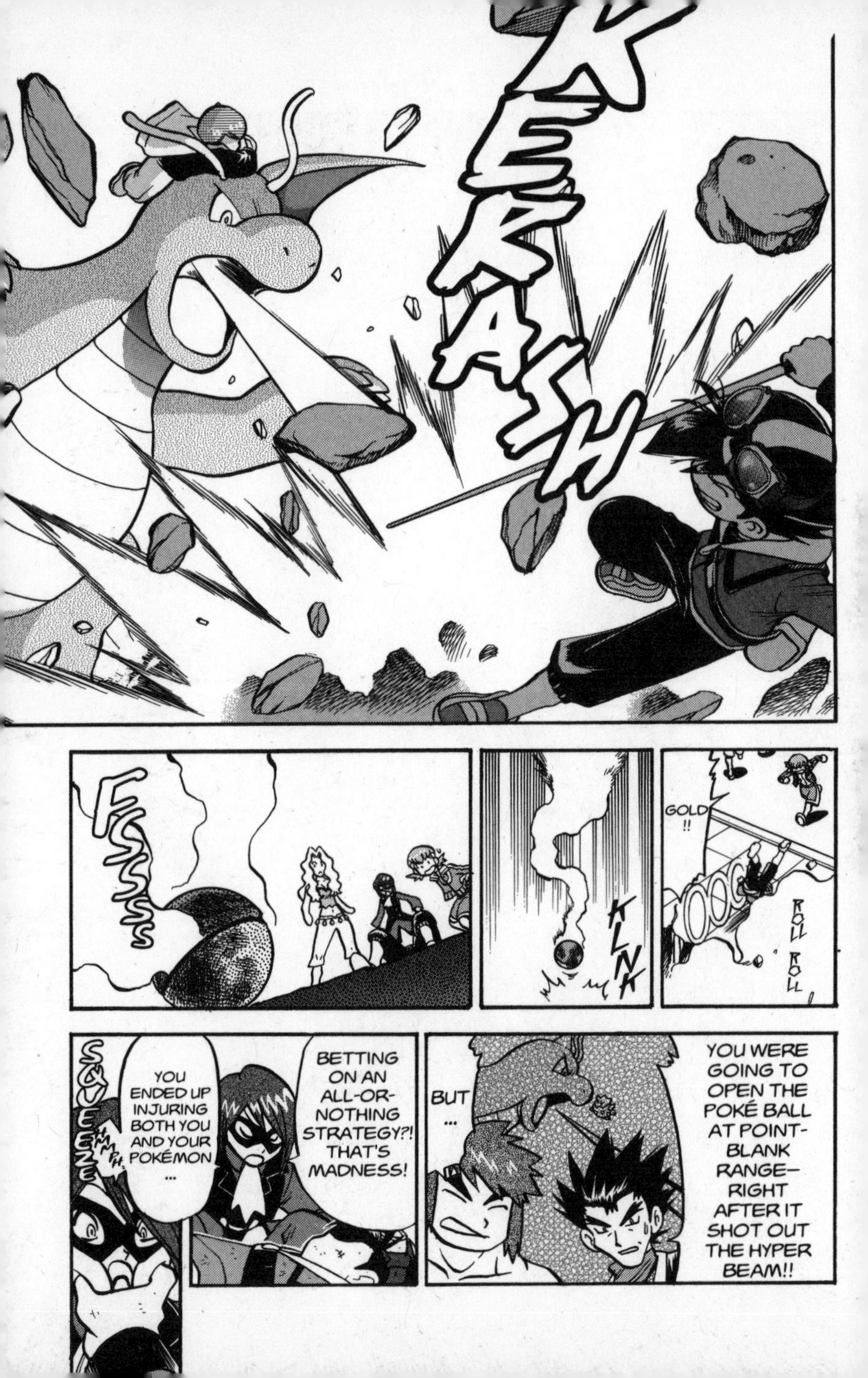
KERASH
GOLD!!
ROLL ROLL
KLNK
FSSSS
YOU WERE GOING TO OPEN THE POKÉ BALL AT POINT-BLANK RANGE—RIGHT AFTER IT SHOT OUT THE HYPER BEAM!!
BUT...
BETTING ON AN ALL-OR-NOTHING STRATEGY?! THAT'S MADNESS!
YOU ENDED UP INJURING BOTH YOU AND YOUR POKÉMON...
HMMPH
SQUEEZE

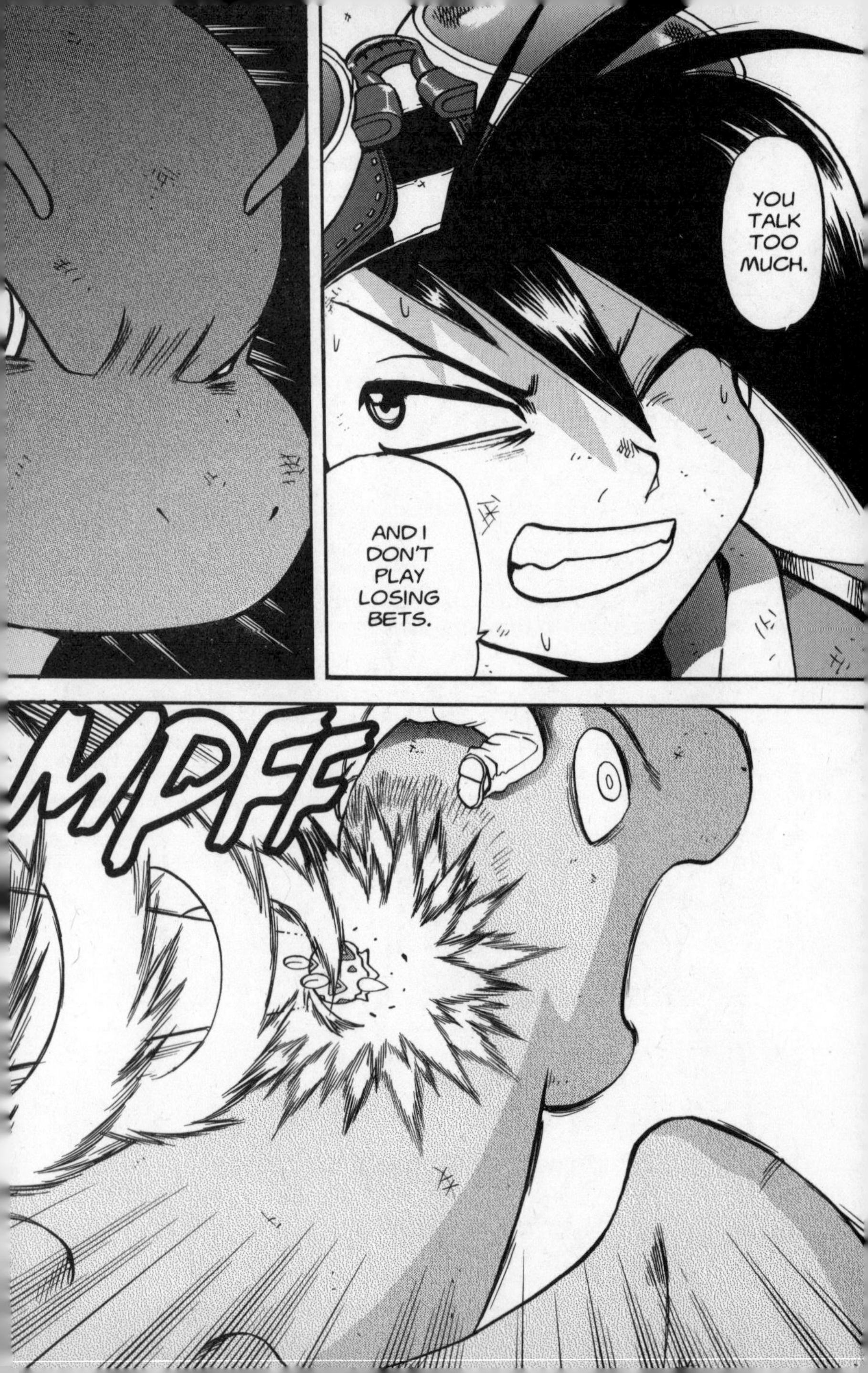
YOU TALK TOO MUCH.
AND I DON'T PLAY LOSING BETS.
MPFF

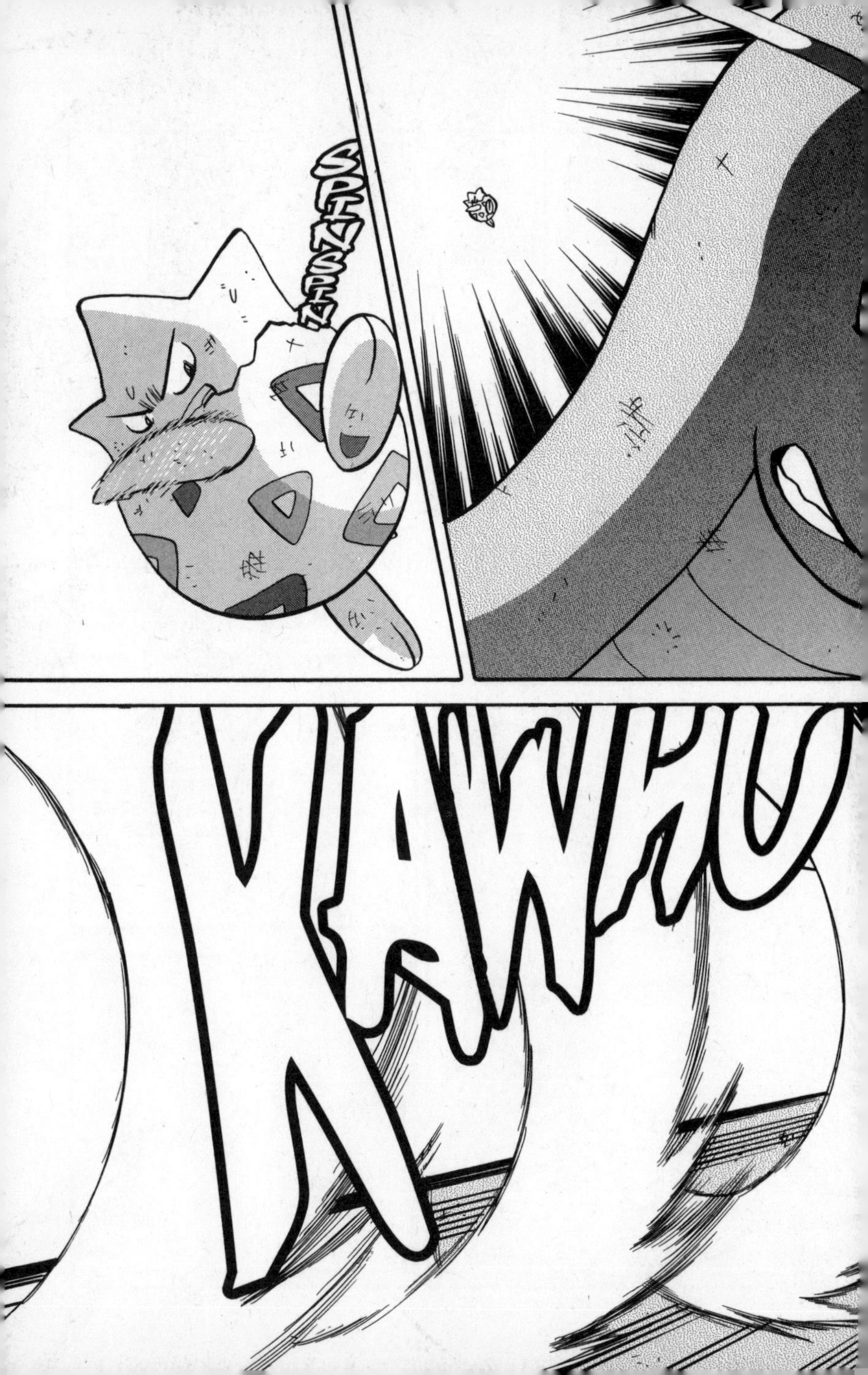
SPINSPIN
KAWHU

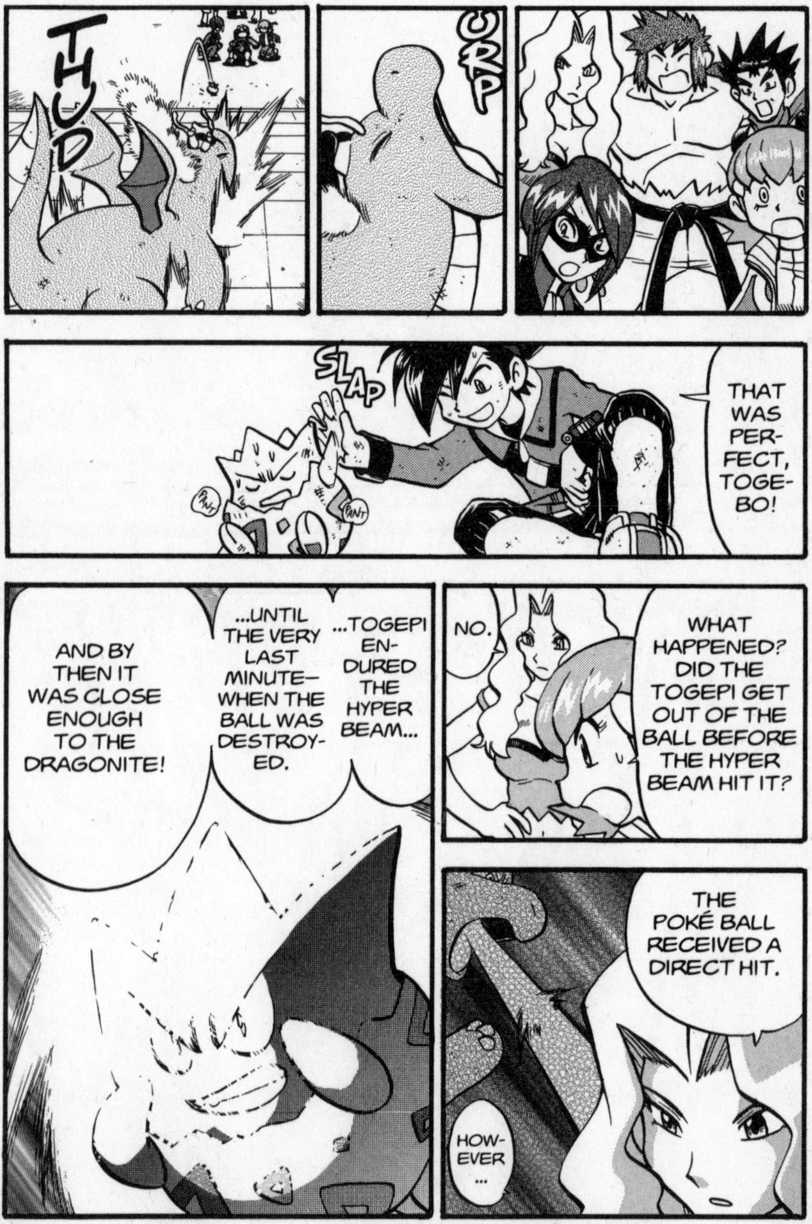
URP
THUD
THAT WAS PERFECT, TOGEBO!
SLAP
PANT
PANT
WHAT HAPPENED? DID THE TOGEPI GET OUT OF THE BALL BEFORE THE HYPER BEAM HIT IT?
NO.
THE POKÉ BALL RECEIVED A DIRECT HIT.
HOWEVER...
...TOGEPI ENDURED THE HYPER BEAM...
...UNTIL THE VERY LAST MINUTE—WHEN THE BALL WAS DESTROYED.
AND BY THEN IT WAS CLOSE ENOUGH TO THE DRAGONITE!

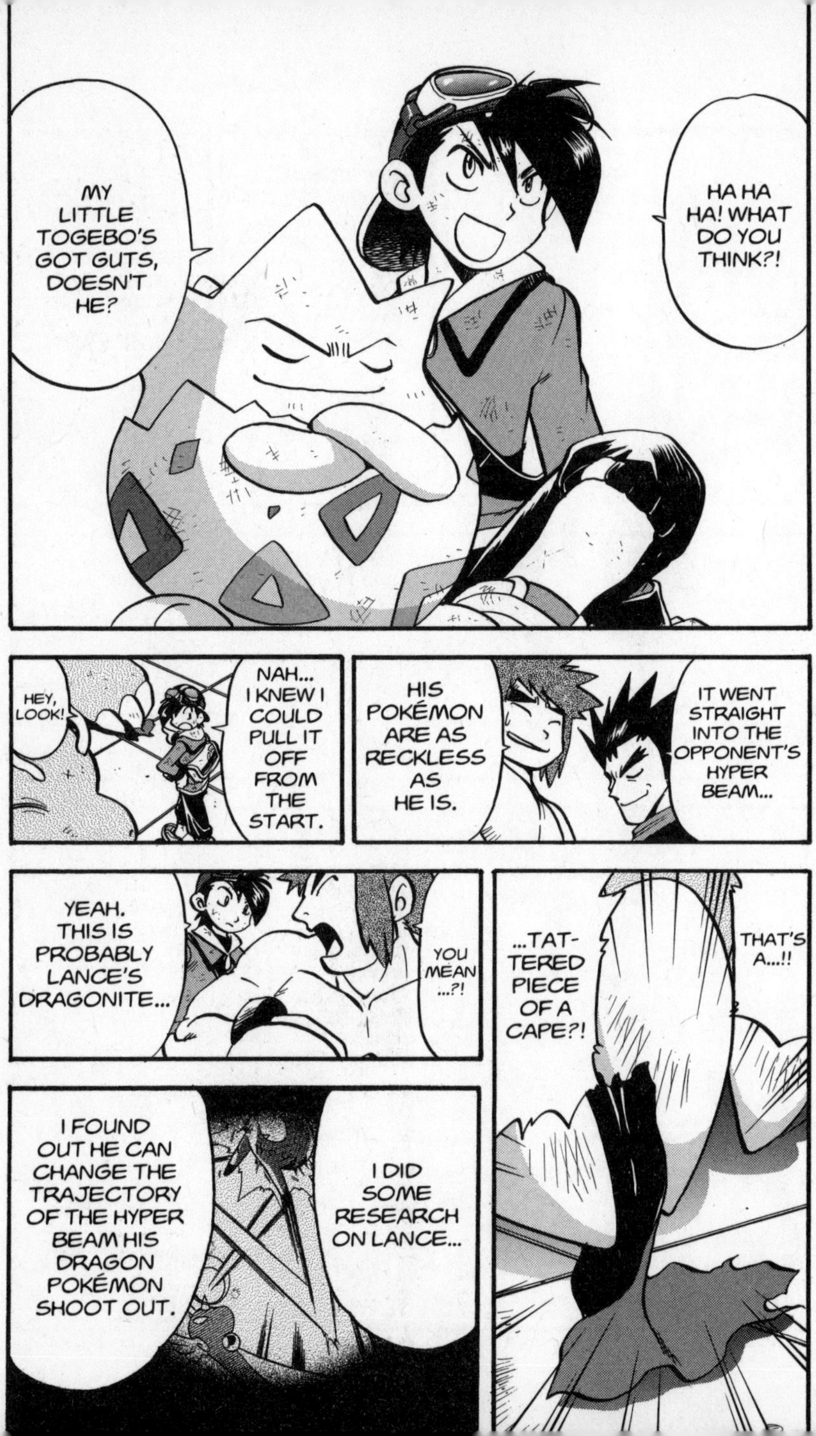
HA HA HA! WHAT DO YOU THINK?!
MY LITTLE TOGEBO'S GOT GUTS, DOESN'T HE?
IT WENT STRAIGHT INTO THE OPPONENT'S HYPER BEAM...
HIS POKÉMON ARE AS RECKLESS AS HE IS.
NAH... I KNEW I COULD PULL IT OFF FROM THE START.
HEY, LOOK!
THAT'S A...!!
...TAT-TERED PIECE OF A CAPE?!
YOU MEAN ...?!
YEAH. THIS IS PROBABLY LANCE'S DRAGONITE...
I DID SOME RESEARCH ON LANCE...
I FOUND OUT HE CAN CHANGE THE TRAJECTORY OF THE HYPER BEAM HIS DRAGON POKÉMON SHOOT OUT.

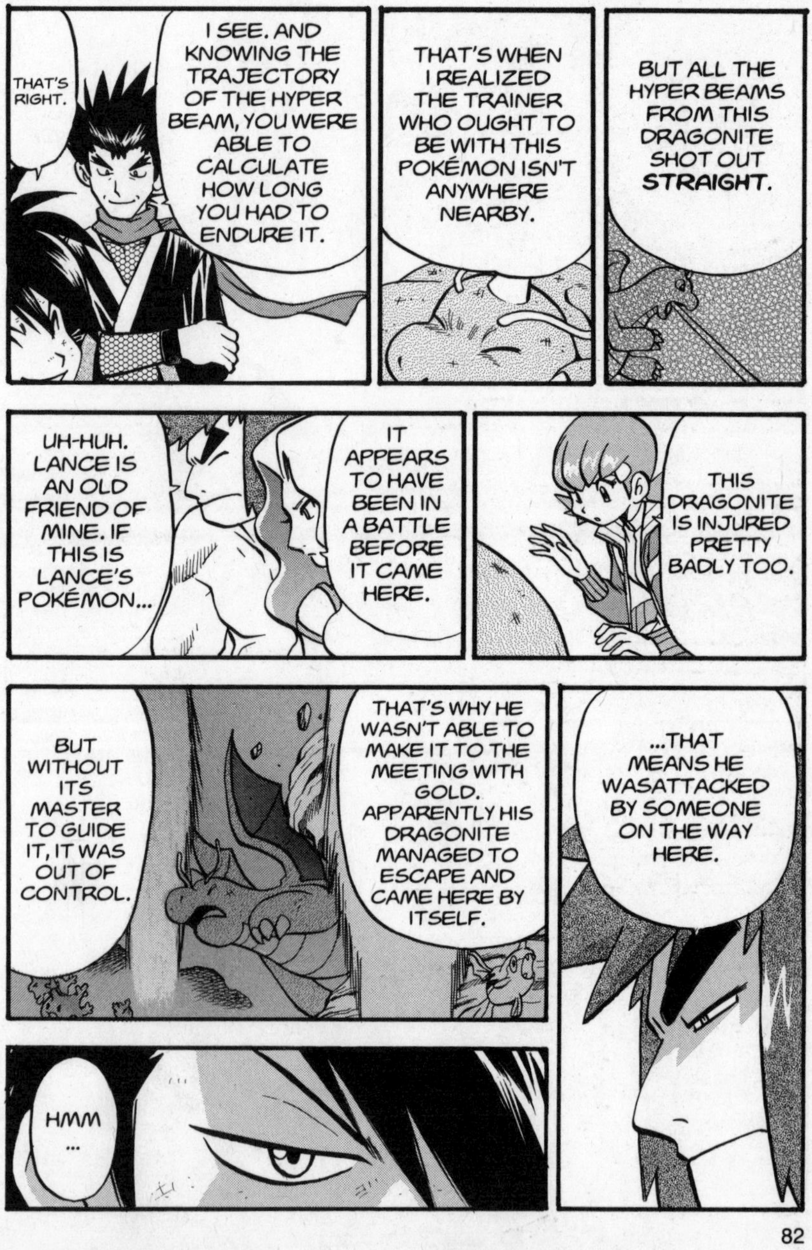

BUT ALL THE HYPER BEAMS FROM THIS DRAGONITE SHOT OUT **STRAIGHT**.
THAT'S WHEN I REALIZED THE TRAINER WHO OUGHT TO BE WITH THIS POKÉMON ISN'T ANYWHERE NEARBY.
I SEE. AND KNOWING THE TRAJECTORY OF THE HYPER BEAM, YOU WERE ABLE TO CALCULATE HOW LONG YOU HAD TO ENDURE IT.
THAT'S RIGHT.
THIS DRAGONITE IS INJURED PRETTY BADLY TOO.
IT APPEARS TO HAVE BEEN IN A BATTLE BEFORE IT CAME HERE.
UH-HUH. LANCE IS AN OLD FRIEND OF MINE. IF THIS IS LANCE'S POKÉMON...
...THAT MEANS HE WASATTACKED BY SOMEONE ON THE WAY HERE.
THAT'S WHY HE WASN'T ABLE TO MAKE IT TO THE MEETING WITH GOLD. APPARENTLY HIS DRAGONITE MANAGED TO ESCAPE AND CAME HERE BY ITSELF.
BUT WITHOUT ITS MASTER TO GUIDE IT, IT WAS OUT OF CONTROL.
HMM ...

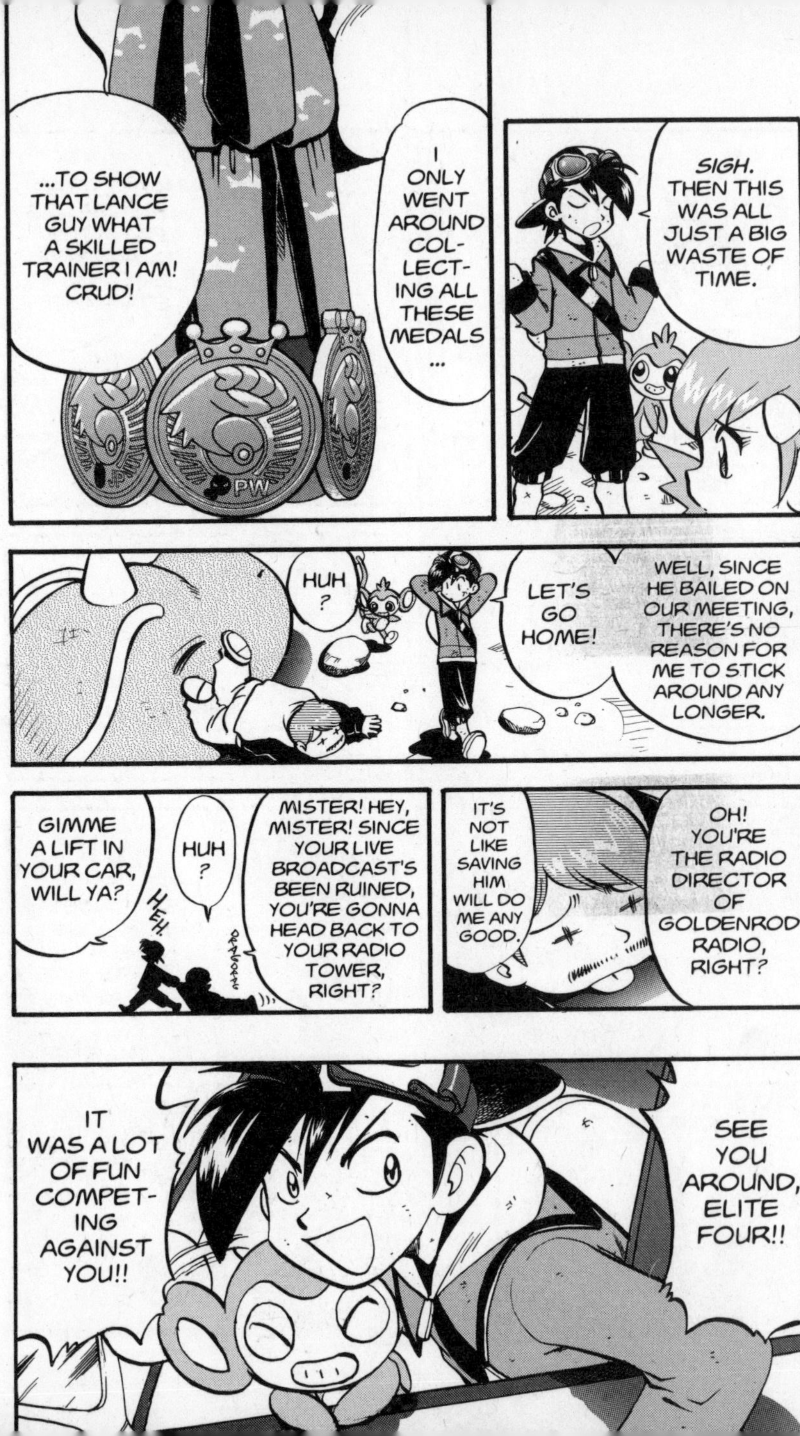
SIGH. THEN THIS WAS ALL JUST A BIG WASTE OF TIME.
I ONLY WENT AROUND COL-LECT-ING ALL THESE MEDALS ...
...TO SHOW THAT LANCE GUY WHAT A SKILLED TRAINER I AM! CRUD!
WELL, SINCE HE BAILED ON OUR MEETING, THERE'S NO REASON FOR ME TO STICK AROUND ANY LONGER.
LET'S GO HOME!
HUH?
OH! YOU'RE THE RADIO DIRECTOR OF GOLDENROD RADIO, RIGHT?
IT'S NOT LIKE SAVING HIM WILL DO ME ANY GOOD.
MISTER! HEY, MISTER! SINCE YOUR LIVE BROADCAST'S BEEN RUINED, YOU'RE GONNA HEAD BACK TO YOUR RADIO TOWER, RIGHT?
HUH?
GIMME A LIFT IN YOUR CAR, WILL YA?
HEH.
SEE YOU AROUND, ELITE FOUR!!
IT WAS A LOT OF FUN COMPET-ING AGAINST YOU!!

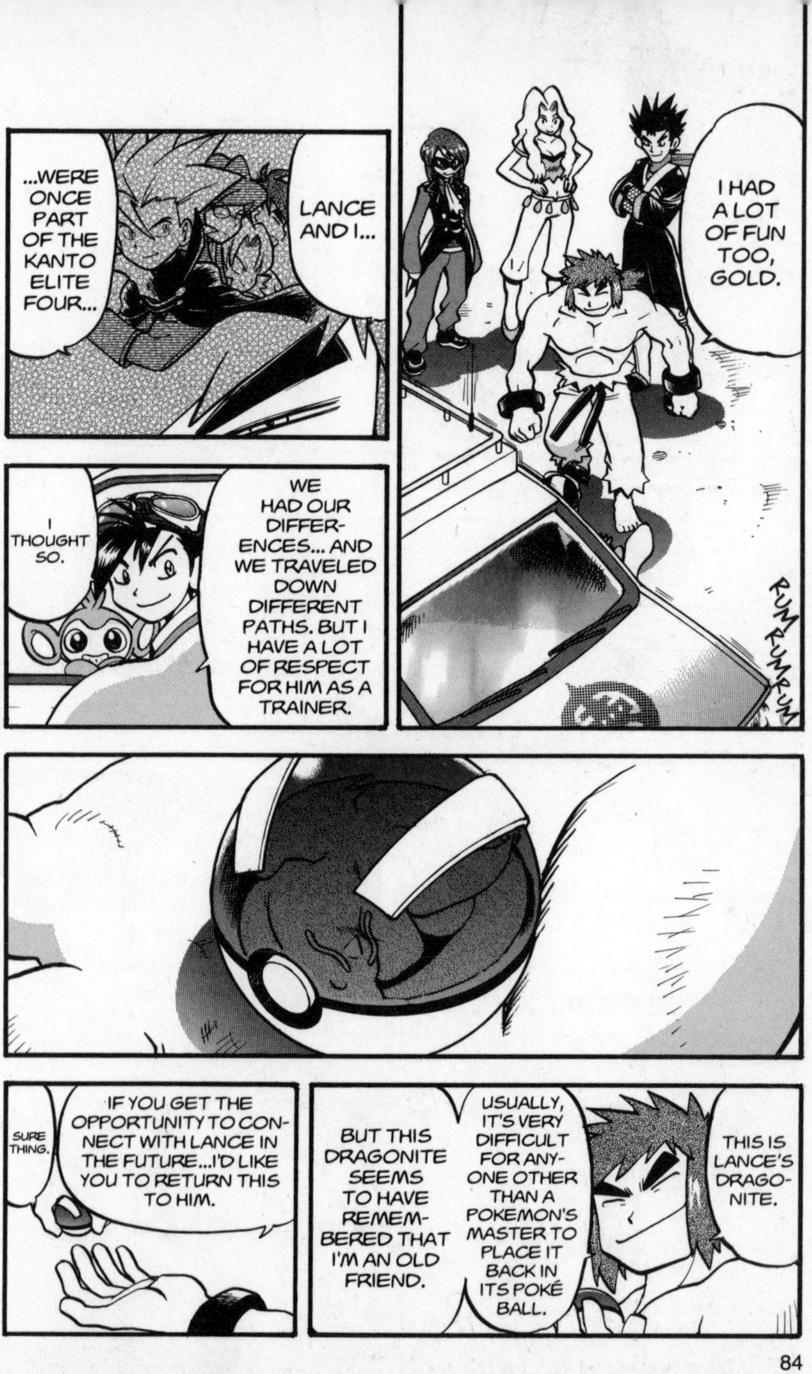
I HAD A LOT OF FUN TOO, GOLD.
RUM RUM RUM
LANCE AND I...
...WERE ONCE PART OF THE KANTO ELITE FOUR...
WE HAD OUR DIFFER-ENCES... AND WE TRAVELED DOWN DIFFERENT PATHS. BUT I HAVE A LOT OF RESPECT FOR HIM AS A TRAINER.
I THOUGHT SO.
THIS IS LANCE'S DRAGO-NITE.
USUALLY, IT'S VERY DIFFICULT FOR ANY-ONE OTHER THAN A POKEMON'S MASTER TO PLACE IT BACK IN ITS POKÉ BALL.
BUT THIS DRAGONITE SEEMS TO HAVE REMEM-BERED THAT I'M AN OLD FRIEND.
IF YOU GET THE OPPORTUNITY TO CON-NECT WITH LANCE IN THE FUTURE...I'D LIKE YOU TO RETURN THIS TO HIM.
SURE THING.

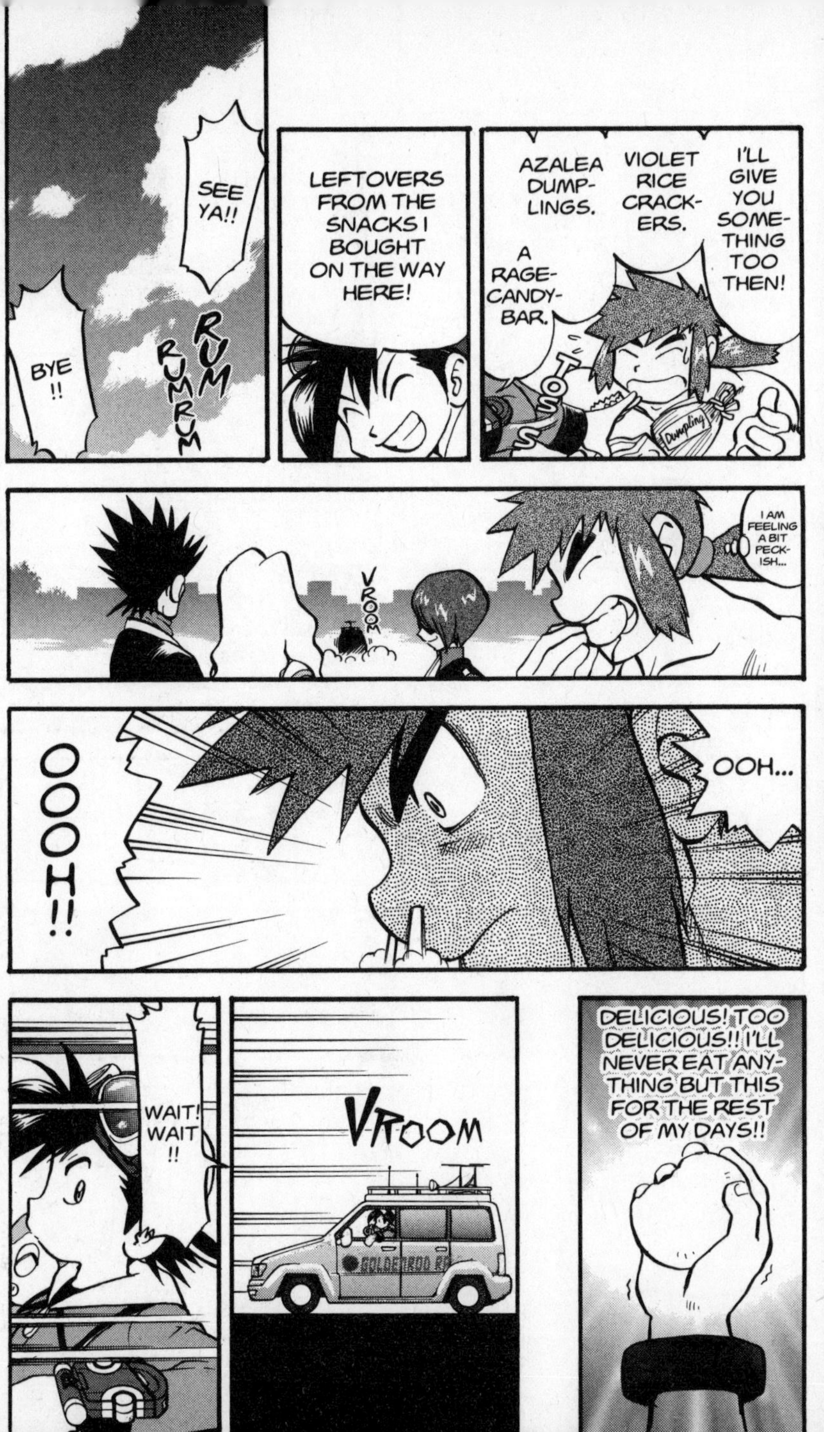
I'LL GIVE YOU SOMETHING TOO THEN!
VIOLET RICE CRACKERS.
AZALEA DUMPLINGS.
A RAGE-CANDY-BAR.
TOSS
Dumpling
LEFTOVERS FROM THE SNACKS I BOUGHT ON THE WAY HERE!
SEE YA!!
RUM RUMRUMRUM
BYE !!
I AM FEELING A BIT PECKISH...
VROOM
OOH...
OOOOH!!
DELICIOUS! TOO DELICIOUS!! I'LL NEVER EAT ANYTHING BUT THIS FOR THE REST OF MY DAYS!!
VROOM
WAIT! WAIT !!

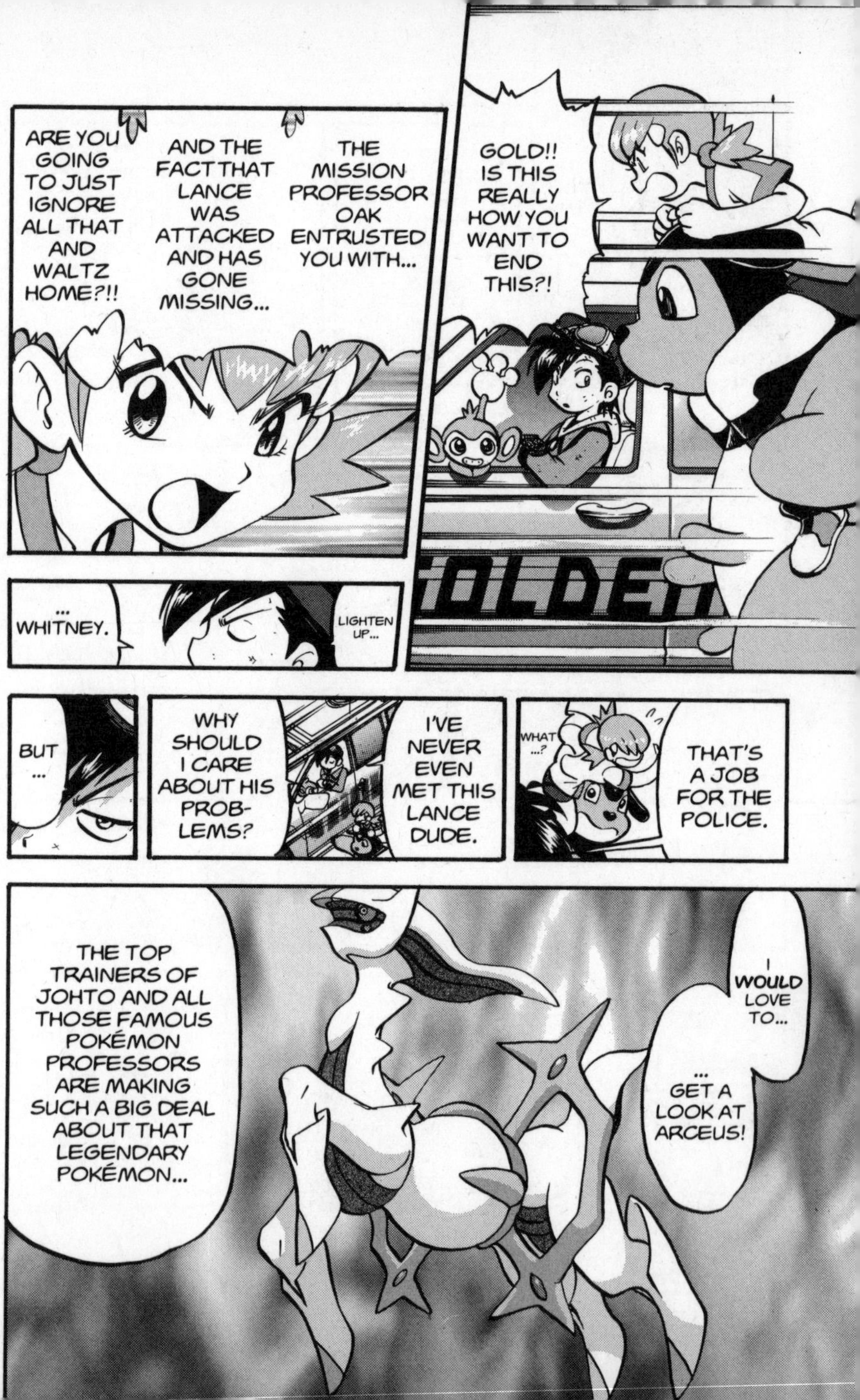
GOLD!! IS THIS REALLY HOW YOU WANT TO END THIS?!
THE MISSION PROFESSOR OAK ENTRUSTED YOU WITH...
AND THE FACT THAT LANCE WAS ATTACKED AND HAS GONE MISSING...
ARE YOU GOING TO JUST IGNORE ALL THAT AND WALTZ HOME?!!
LIGHTEN UP...
... WHITNEY.
THAT'S A JOB FOR THE POLICE.
WHAT ...?
I'VE NEVER EVEN MET THIS LANCE DUDE.
WHY SHOULD I CARE ABOUT HIS PROBLEMS?
BUT ...
THE TOP TRAINERS OF JOHTO AND ALL THOSE FAMOUS POKÉMON PROFESSORS ARE MAKING SUCH A BIG DEAL ABOUT THAT LEGENDARY POKÉMON...
I **WOULD** LOVE TO...
... GET A LOOK AT ARCEUS!

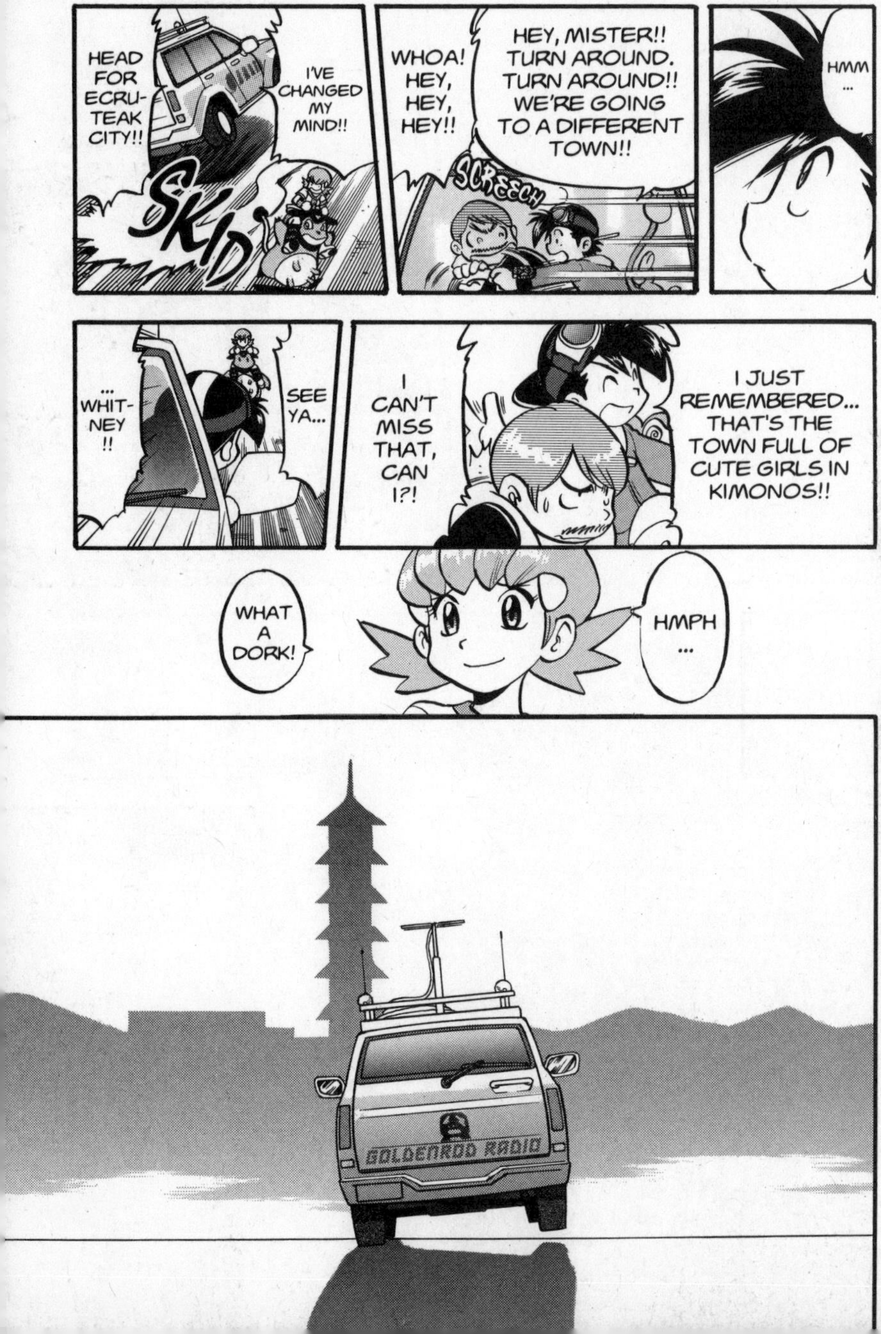
HMM ...
HEY, MISTER!! TURN AROUND. TURN AROUND!! WE'RE GOING TO A DIFFERENT TOWN!!
WHOA! HEY, HEY, HEY!!
SCREECH
I'VE CHANGED MY MIND!!
HEAD FOR ECRU-TEAK CITY!!
SKID
I JUST REMEMBERED... THAT'S THE TOWN FULL OF CUTE GIRLS IN KIMONOS!!
I CAN'T MISS THAT, CAN I?!
SEE YA...
... WHIT-NEY !!
HMPH ...
WHAT A DORK!
GOLDENROD RADIO

Adventure 4

DEALING WITH A KOFFING FIT

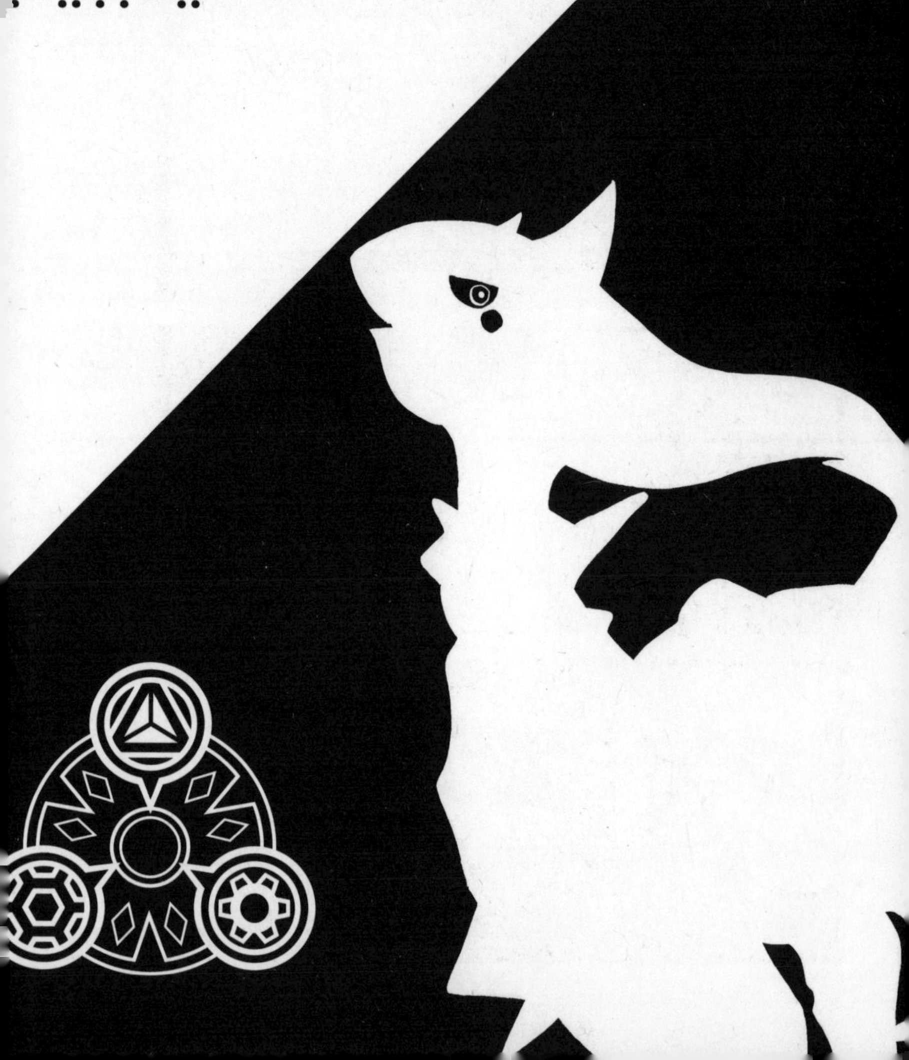

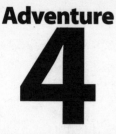

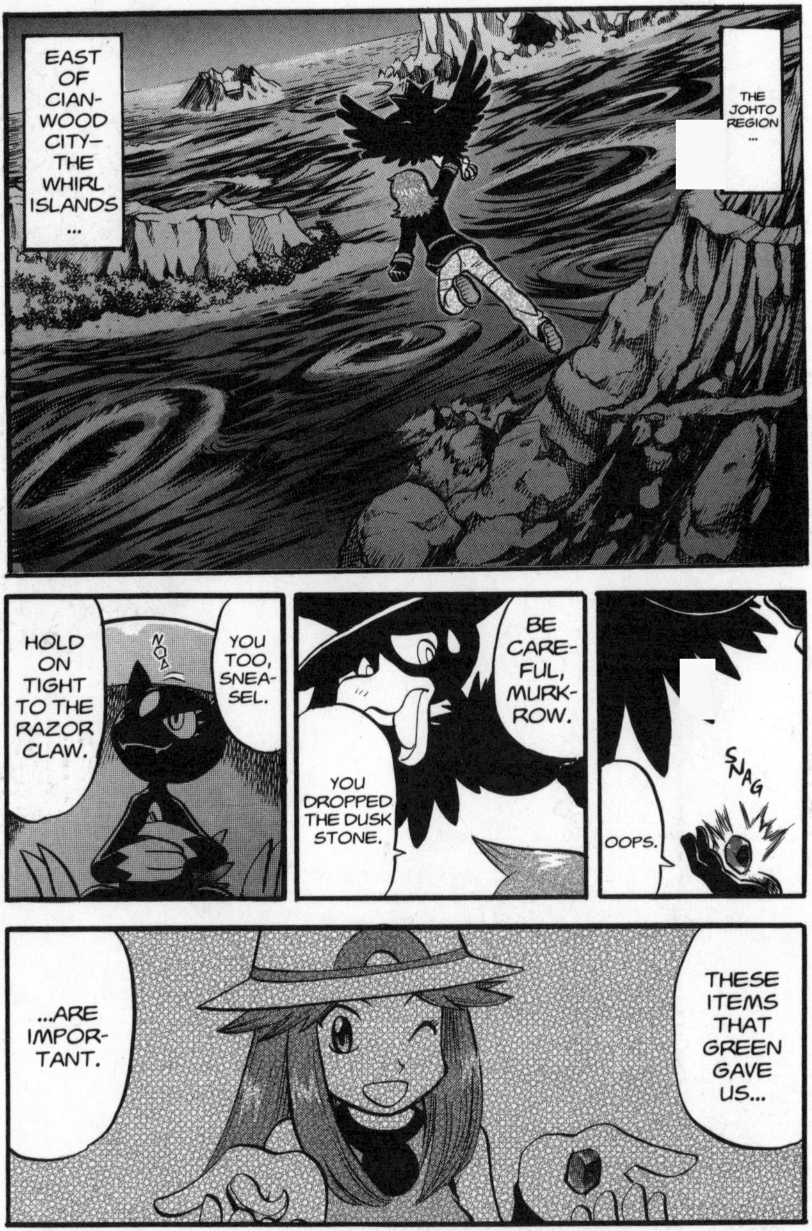
THE JOHTO REGION ...
EAST OF CIANWOOD CITY—THE WHIRL ISLANDS ...
SNAG
OOPS.
BE CAREFUL, MURKROW.
YOU DROPPED THE DUSK STONE.
YOU TOO, SNEASEL.
HOLD ON TIGHT TO THE RAZOR CLAW.
THESE ITEMS THAT GREEN GAVE US...
...ARE IMPORTANT.

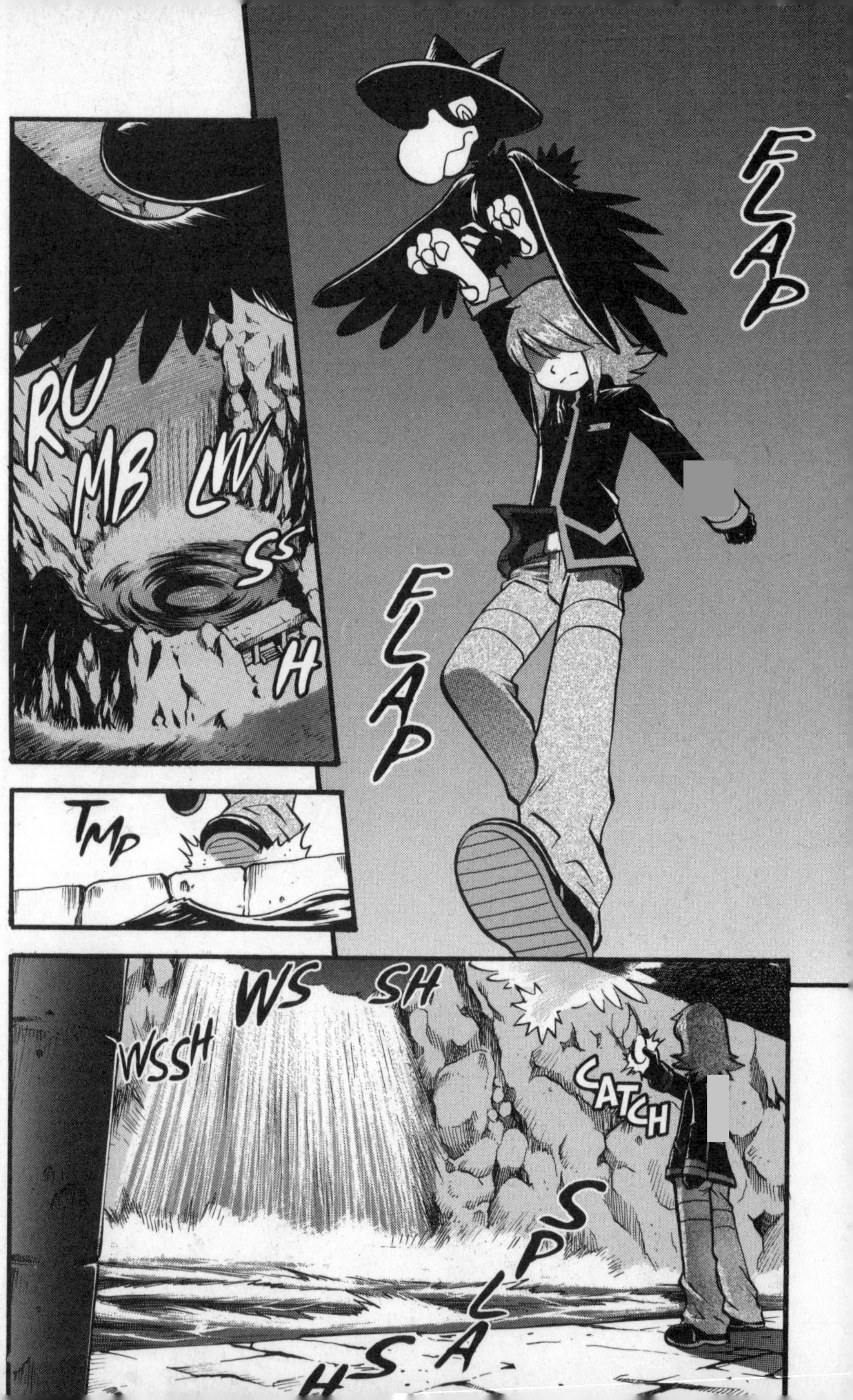
FLAP
FLAP
RUMBLWSSH
TMP
CATCH
SH
WS
WSSH
SPLASH

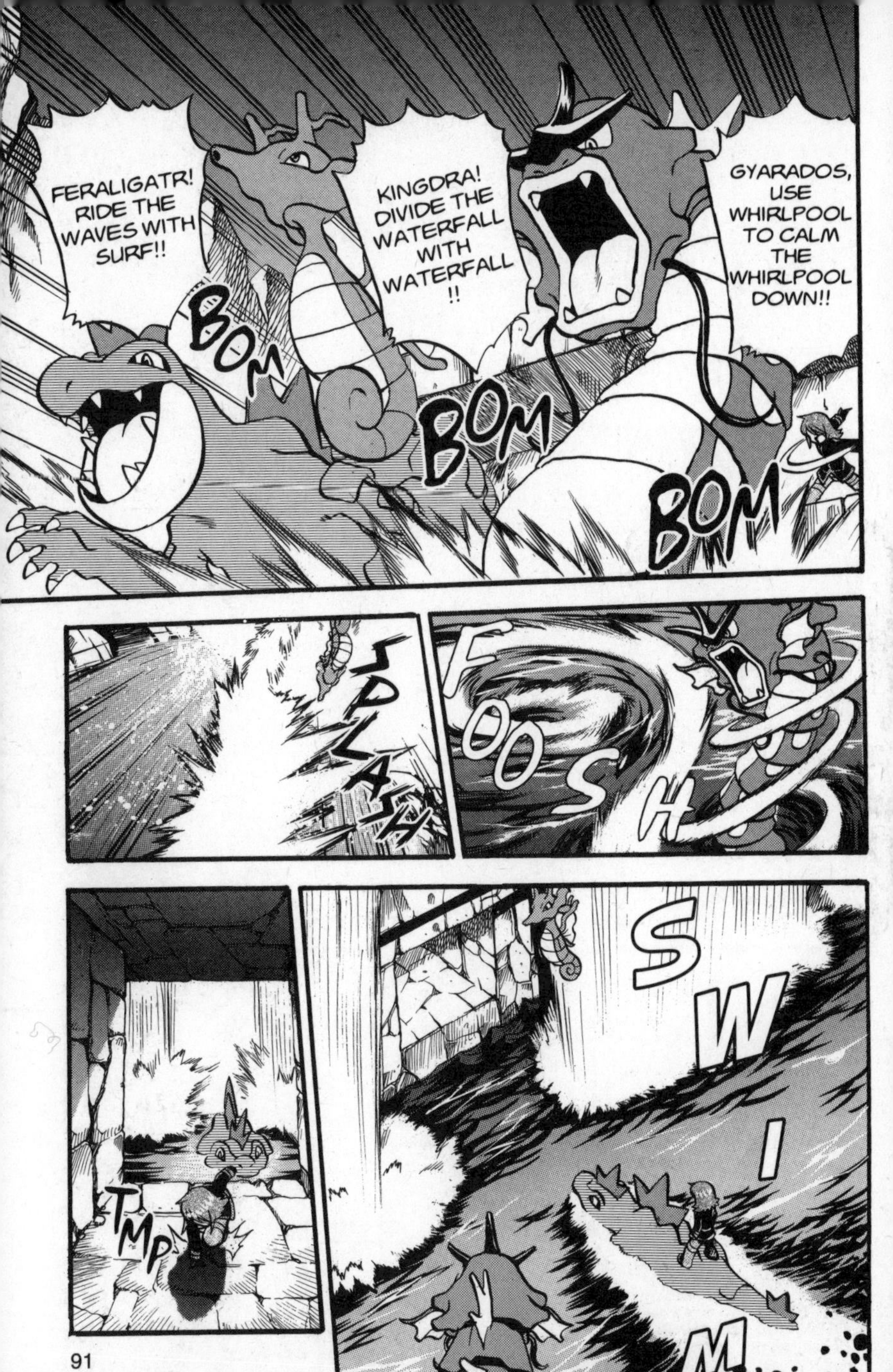
GYARADOS, USE WHIRLPOOL TO CALM THE WHIRLPOOL DOWN!!
KINGDRA! DIVIDE THE WATERFALL WITH WATERFALL!!
FERALIGATR! RIDE THE WAVES WITH SURF!!
BOM
BOM
BOM
FOOOSH
SPLASH
SWIM
TMP

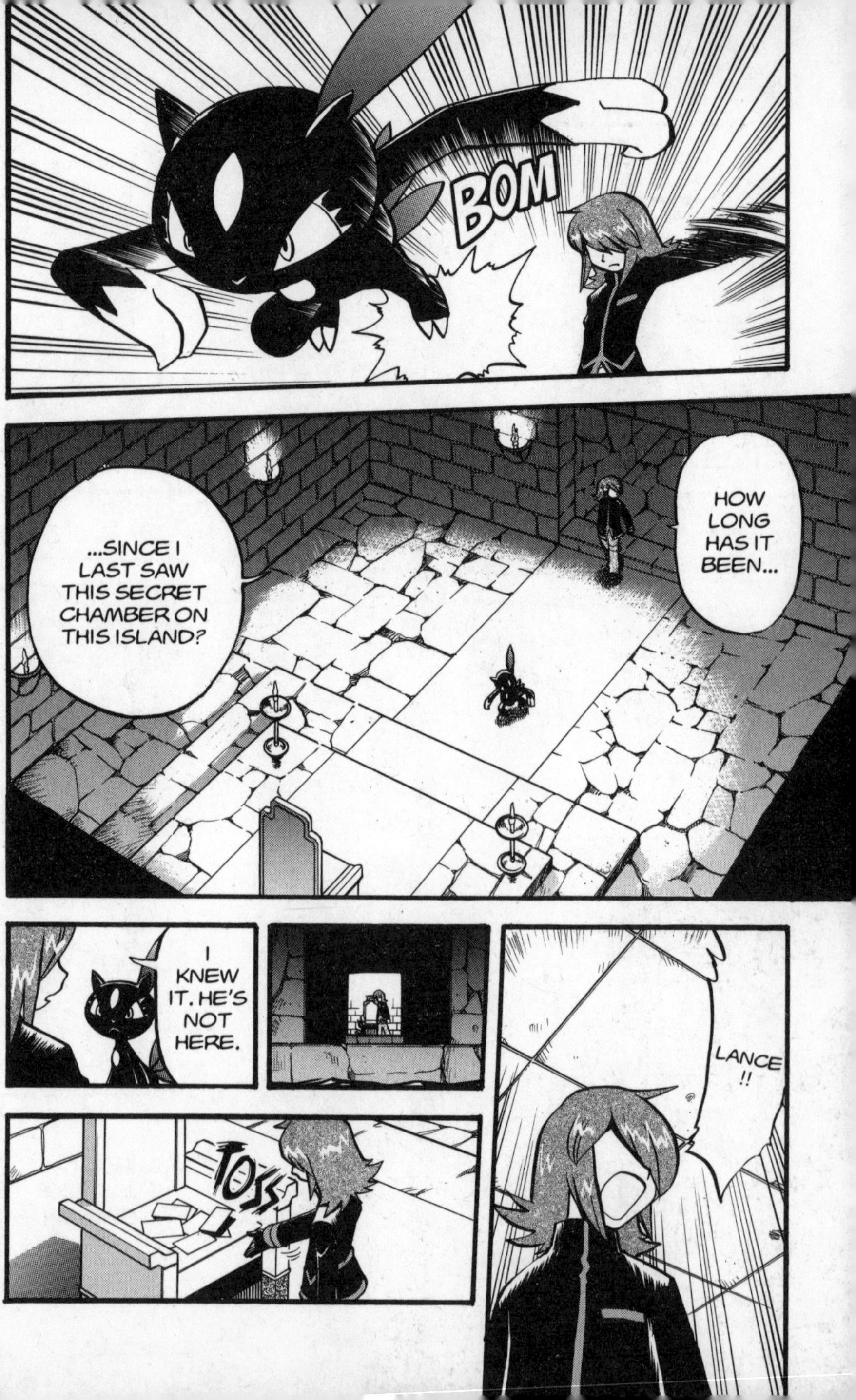
BOM
HOW LONG HAS IT BEEN...
...SINCE I LAST SAW THIS SECRET CHAMBER ON THIS ISLAND?
LANCE!!
I KNEW IT. HE'S NOT HERE.
TOSS

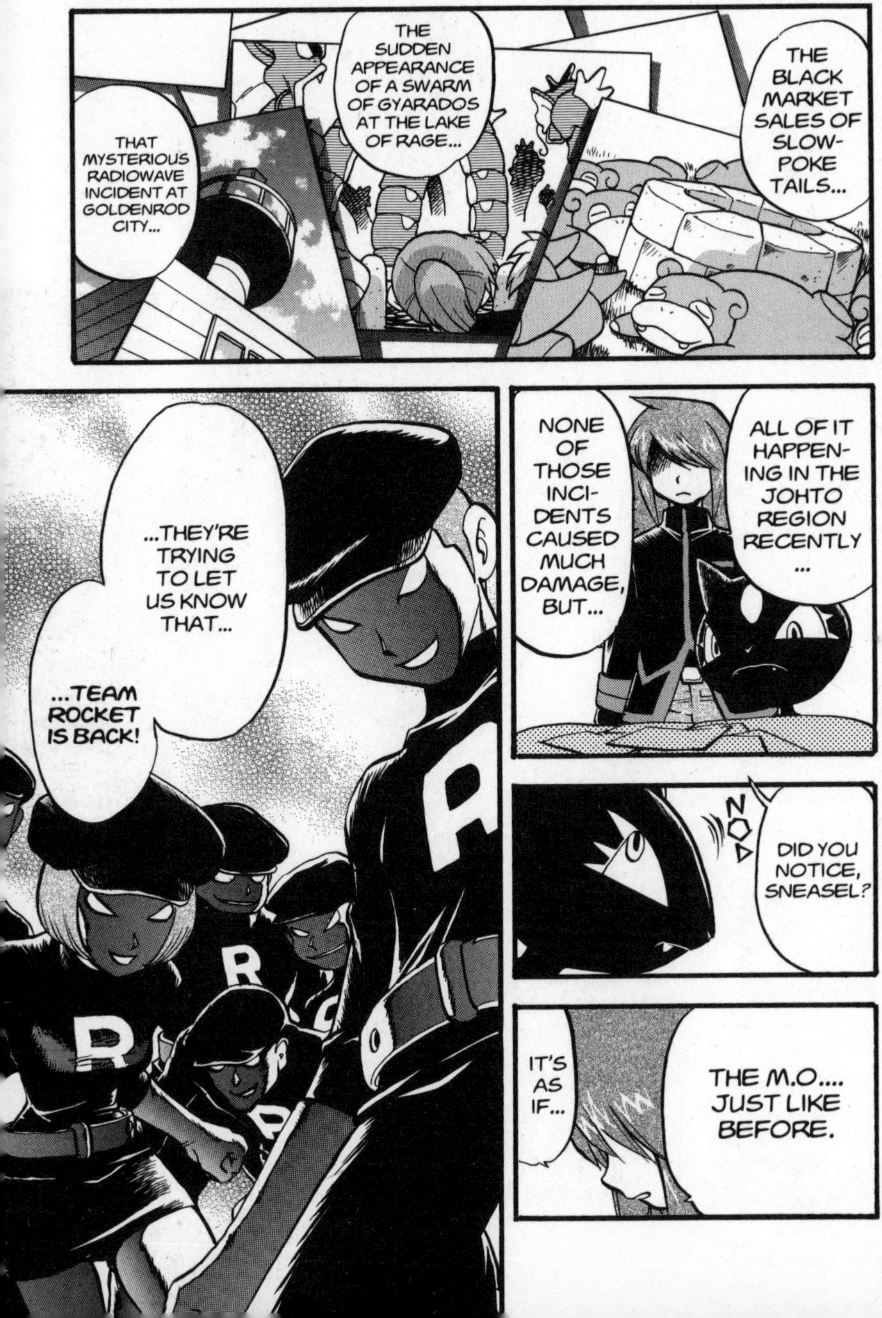
THE BLACK MARKET SALES OF SLOW-POKE TAILS...
THE SUDDEN APPEARANCE OF A SWARM OF GYARADOS AT THE LAKE OF RAGE...
THAT MYSTERIOUS RADIOWAVE INCIDENT AT GOLDENROD CITY...
ALL OF IT HAPPEN-ING IN THE JOHTO REGION RECENTLY ...
NONE OF THOSE INCI-DENTS CAUSED MUCH DAMAGE, BUT...
NOD
DID YOU NOTICE, SNEASEL?
THE M.O.... JUST LIKE BEFORE.
IT'S AS IF...
...THEY'RE TRYING TO LET US KNOW THAT...
...TEAM ROCKET IS BACK!

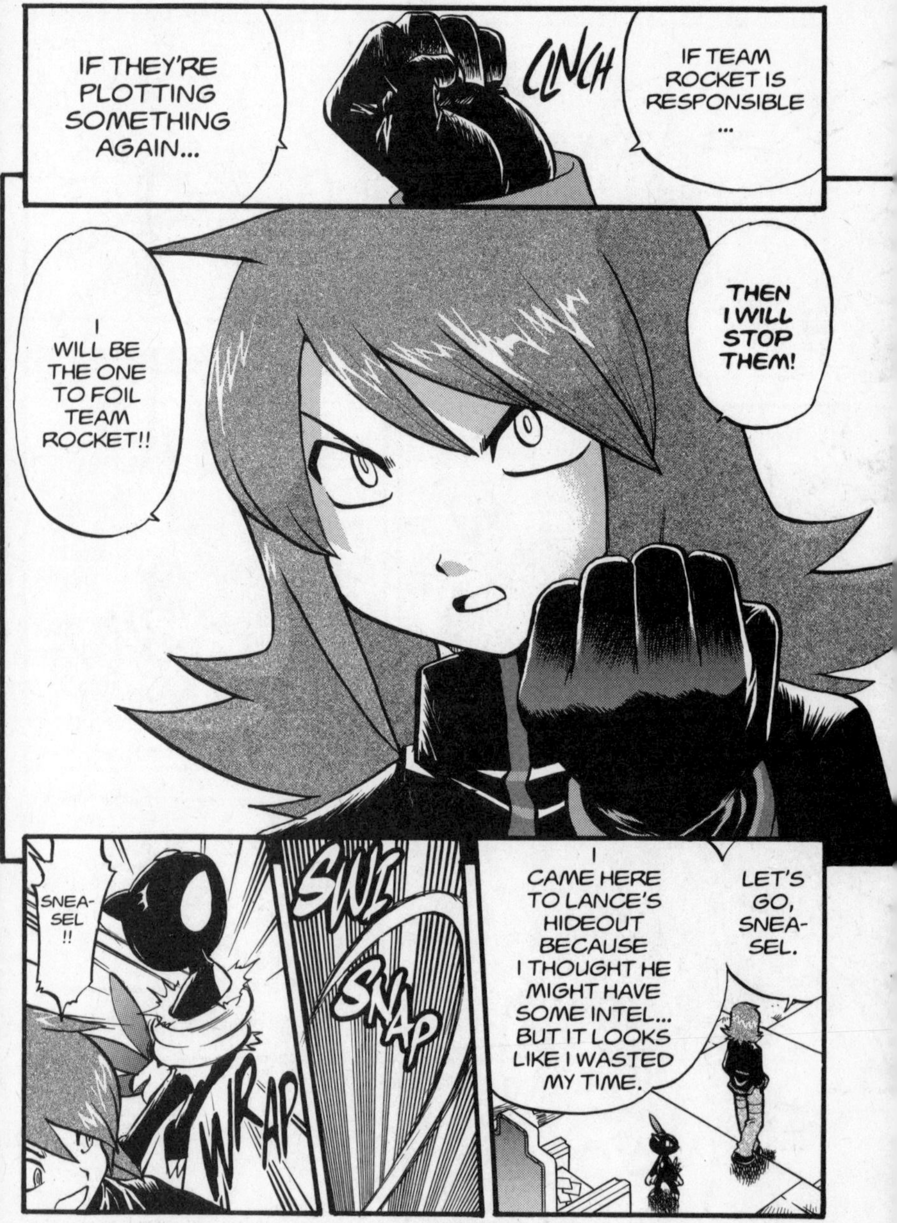
IF TEAM ROCKET IS RESPONSIBLE ...
CLINCH
IF THEY'RE PLOTTING SOMETHING AGAIN...
THEN I WILL STOP THEM!
I WILL BE THE ONE TO FOIL TEAM ROCKET!!
LET'S GO, SNEA-SEL.
I CAME HERE TO LANCE'S HIDEOUT BECAUSE I THOUGHT HE MIGHT HAVE SOME INTEL... BUT IT LOOKS LIKE I WASTED MY TIME.
SWI
SNAP
SNEA-SEL !!
WRAP

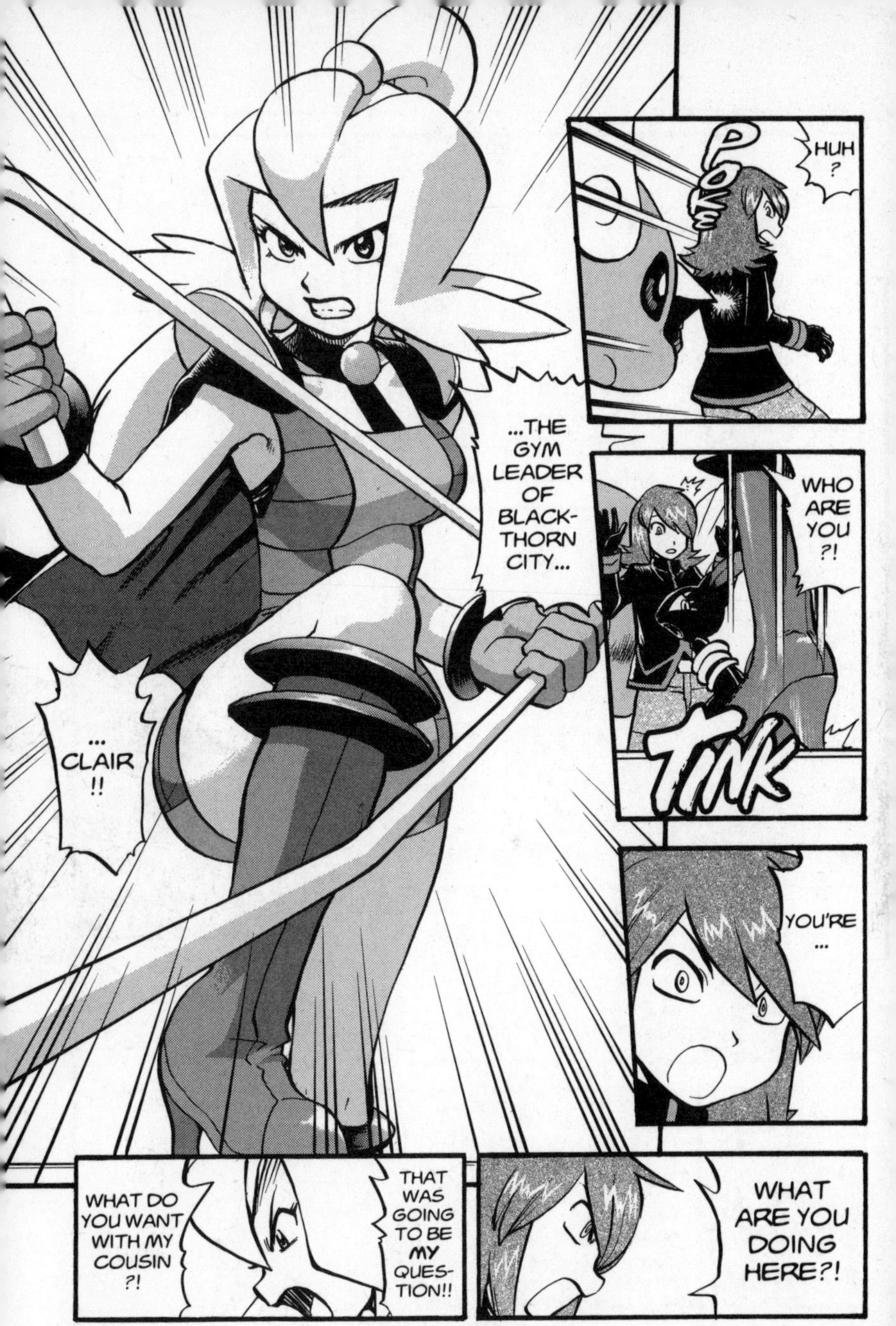
POW
HUH?
WHO ARE YOU?!
TINK
YOU'RE...
...THE GYM LEADER OF BLACKTHORN CITY...
...CLAIR!!
WHAT ARE YOU DOING HERE?!
THAT WAS GOING TO BE **MY** QUESTION!!
WHAT DO YOU WANT WITH MY COUSIN?!

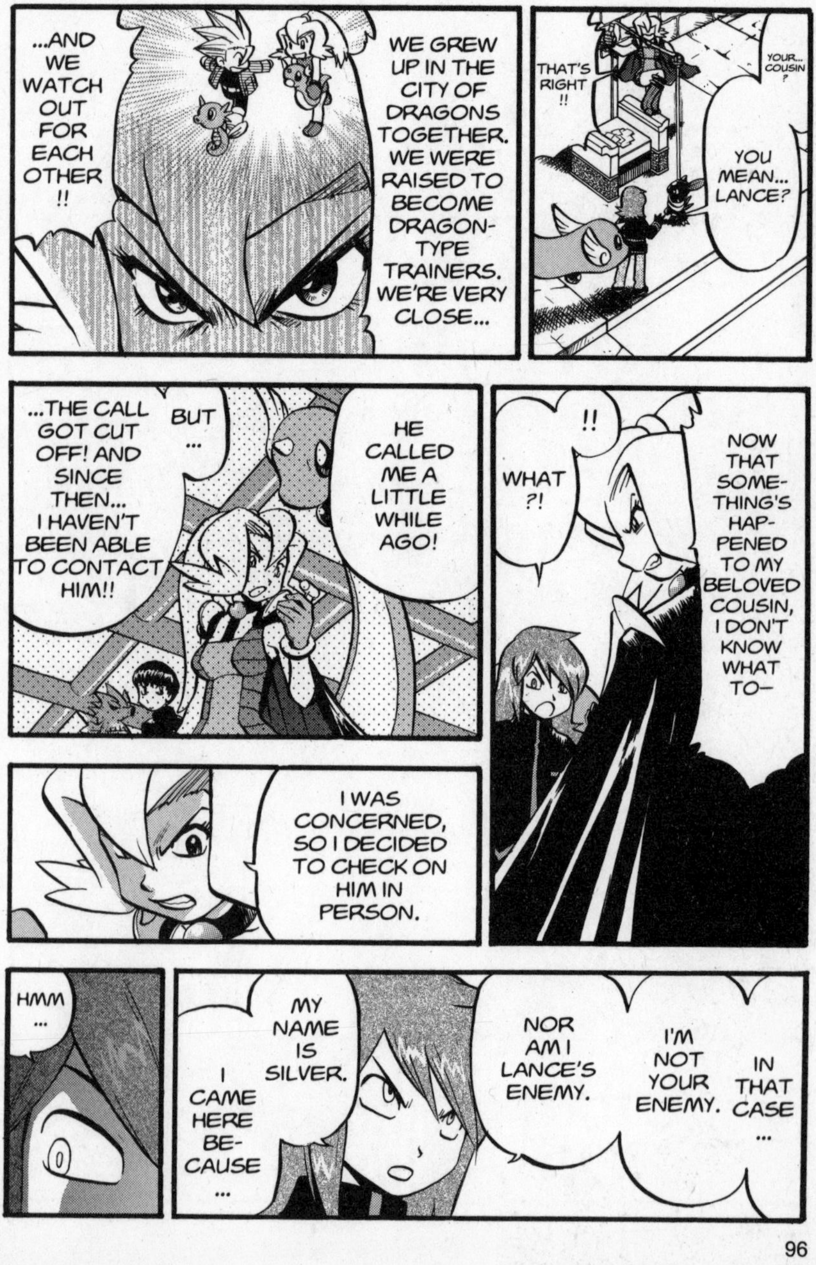
YOUR... COUSIN?
YOU MEAN... LANCE?
THAT'S RIGHT!!
WE GREW UP IN THE CITY OF DRAGONS TOGETHER. WE WERE RAISED TO BECOME DRAGON-TYPE TRAINERS. WE'RE VERY CLOSE...
...AND WE WATCH OUT FOR EACH OTHER!!
NOW THAT SOMETHING'S HAPPENED TO MY BELOVED COUSIN, I DON'T KNOW WHAT TO—
!!
WHAT?!
HE CALLED ME A LITTLE WHILE AGO!
BUT...
...THE CALL GOT CUT OFF! AND SINCE THEN... I HAVEN'T BEEN ABLE TO CONTACT HIM!!
I WAS CONCERNED, SO I DECIDED TO CHECK ON HIM IN PERSON.
IN THAT CASE...
I'M NOT YOUR ENEMY.
NOR AM I LANCE'S ENEMY.
MY NAME IS SILVER.
I CAME HERE BECAUSE...
HMM...

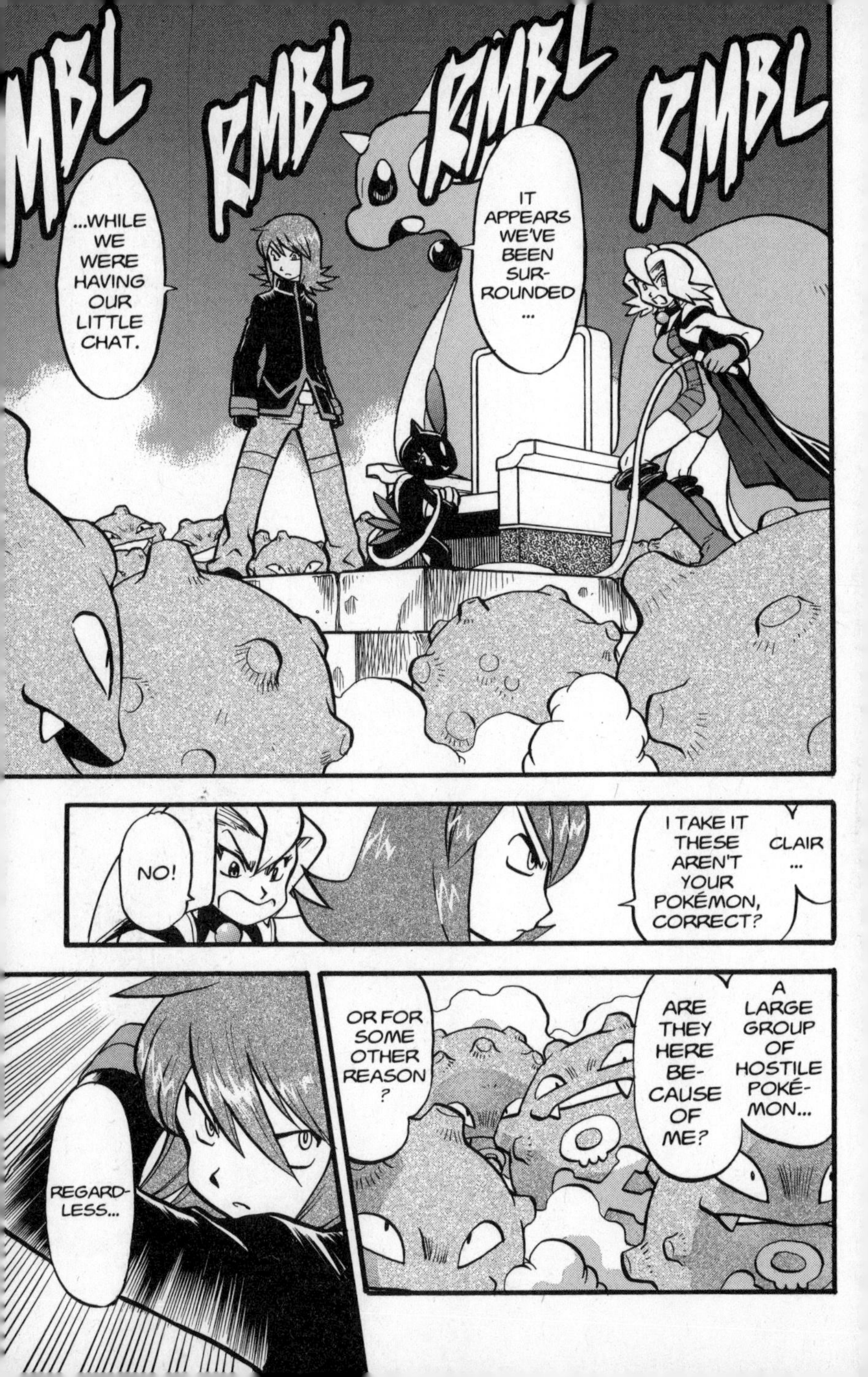
RMBL
RMBL
RMBL
MBL
IT APPEARS WE'VE BEEN SUR-ROUNDED...
...WHILE WE WERE HAVING OUR LITTLE CHAT.
CLAIR...
I TAKE IT THESE AREN'T YOUR POKÉMON, CORRECT?
NO!
A LARGE GROUP OF HOSTILE POKÉ-MON...
ARE THEY HERE BE-CAUSE OF ME?
OR FOR SOME OTHER REASON?
REGARD-LESS...

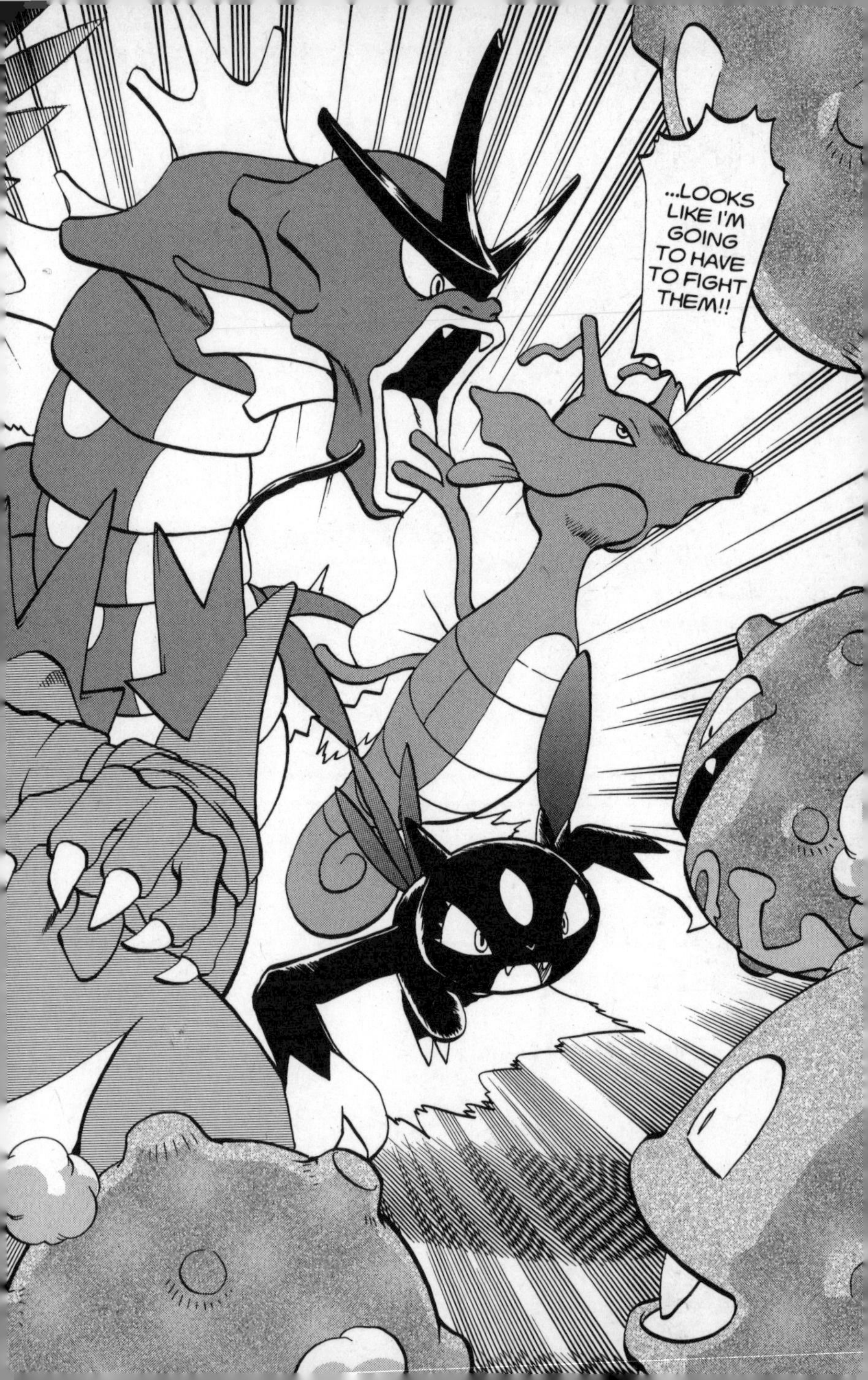
...LOOKS LIKE I'M GOING TO HAVE TO FIGHT THEM!!

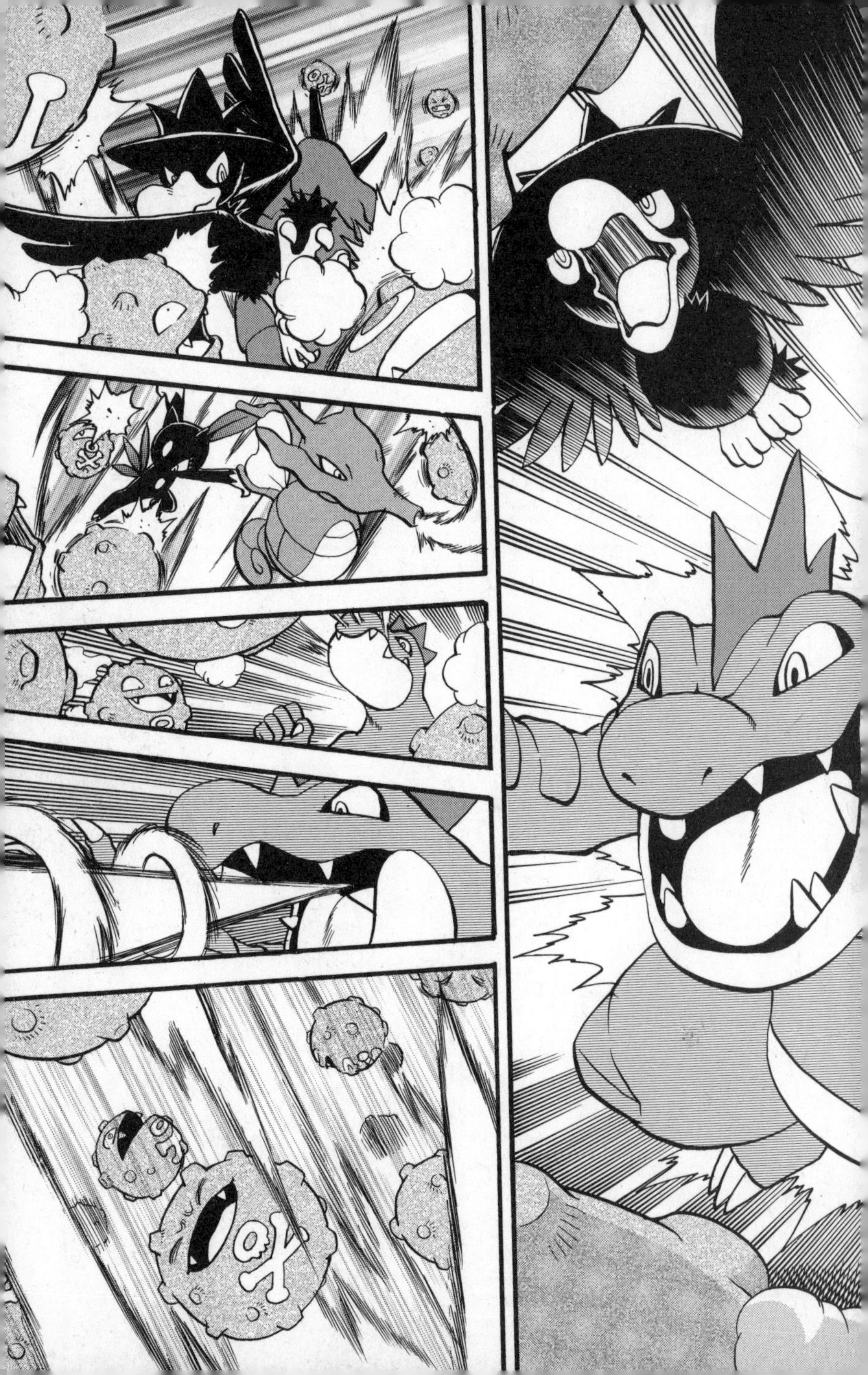

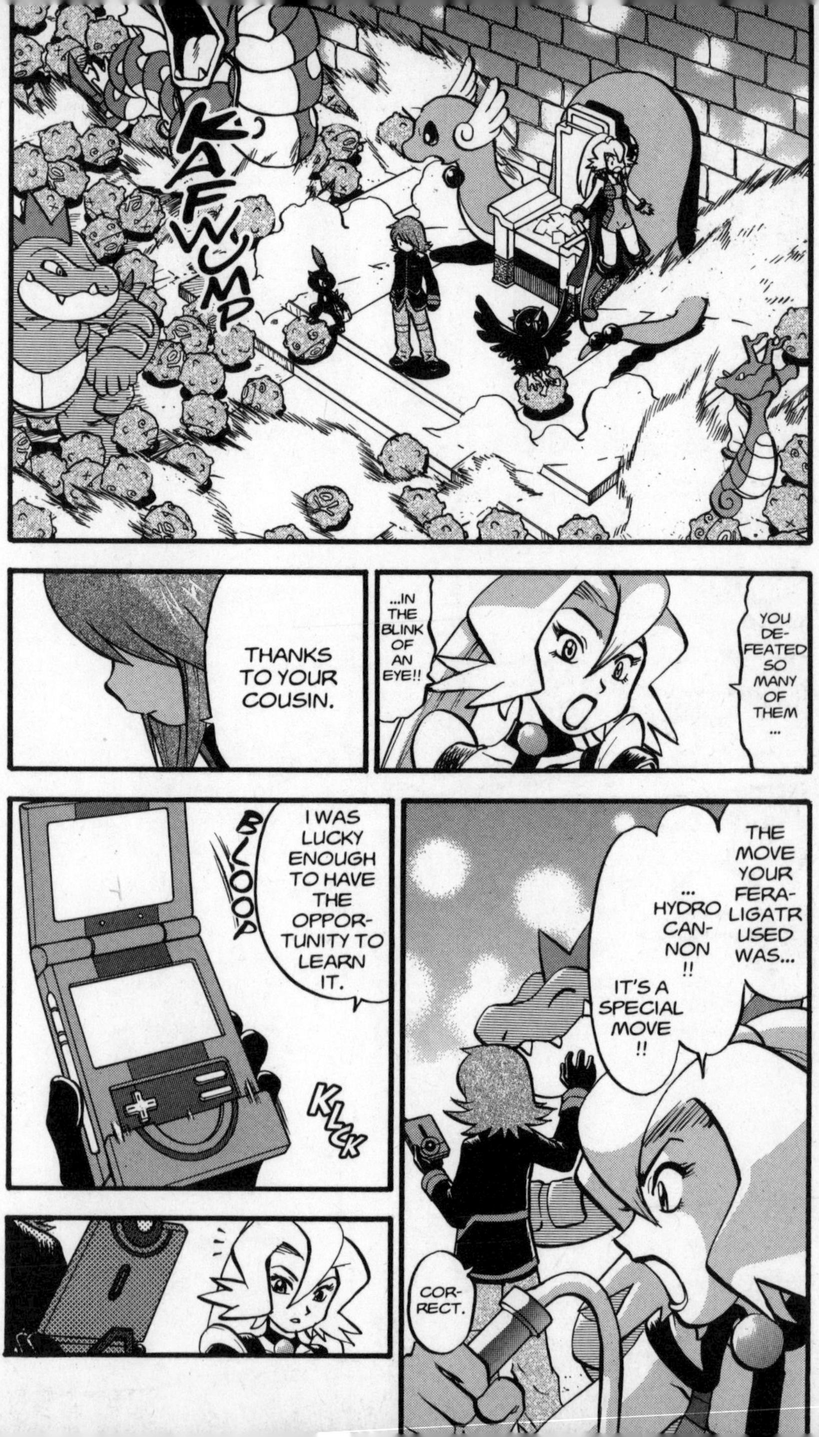
KA-FWUMP
YOU DEFEATED SO MANY OF THEM...
...IN THE BLINK OF AN EYE!!
THANKS TO YOUR COUSIN.
THE MOVE YOUR FERALIGATR USED WAS...
...HYDRO CANNON!!
IT'S A SPECIAL MOVE!!
CORRECT.
I WAS LUCKY ENOUGH TO HAVE THE OPPORTUNITY TO LEARN IT.
BLOOP
KLICK

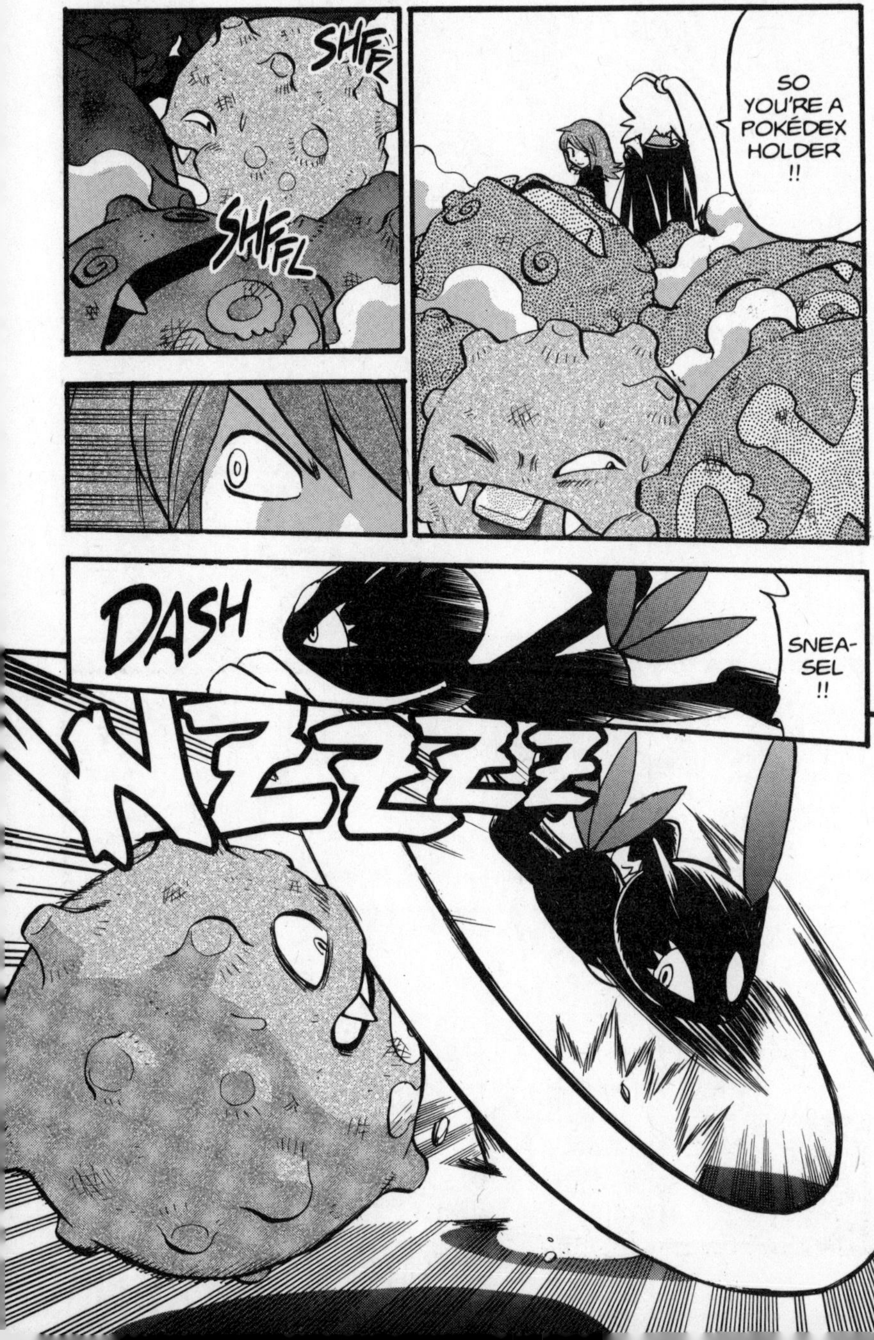
SO YOU'RE A POKÉDEX HOLDER !!
SHFFL
SHFFL
SNEA-SEL !!
DASH
WHZZZZ

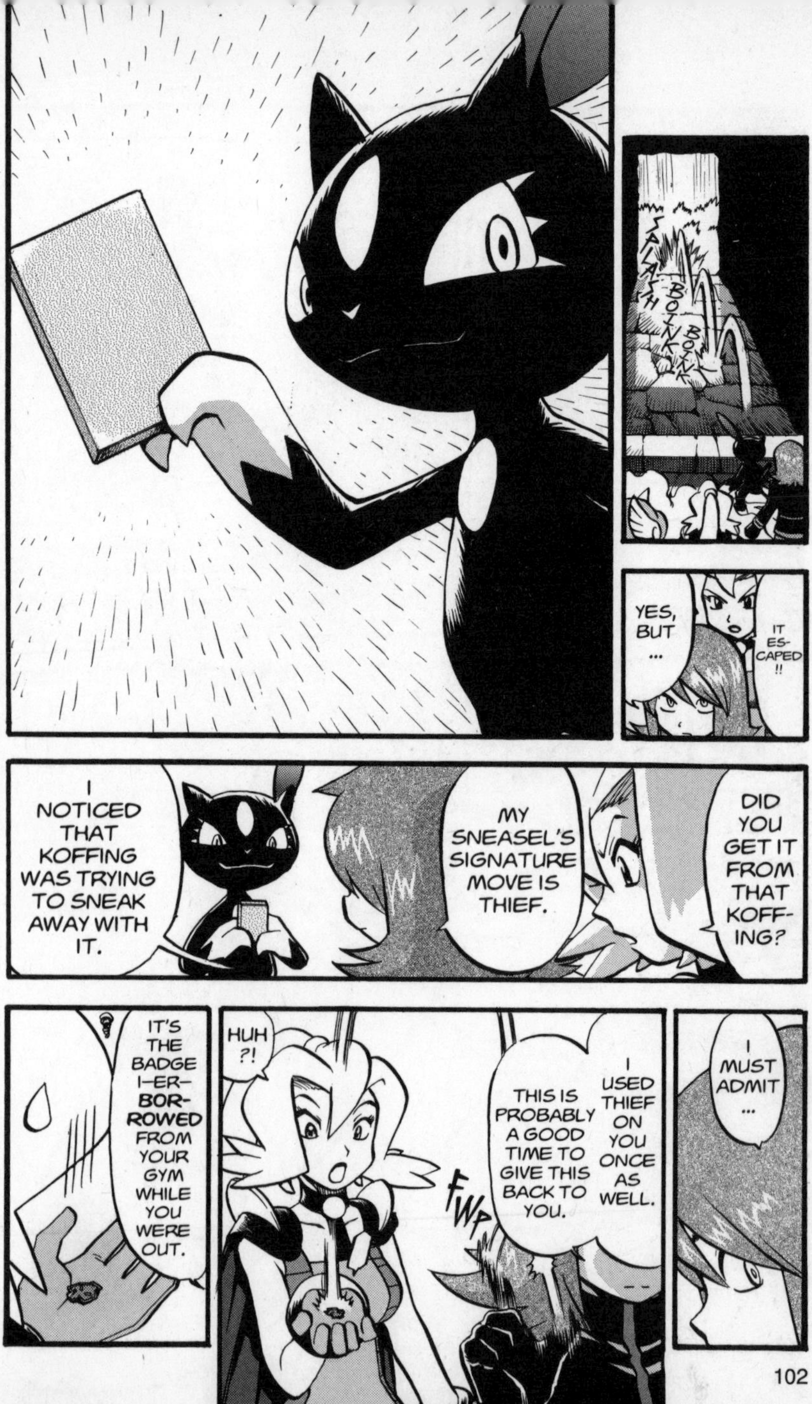

SPLASH
BOINK
BOINK
YES, BUT ...
IT ESCAPED!!
DID YOU GET IT FROM THAT KOFFING?
MY SNEASEL'S SIGNATURE MOVE IS THIEF.
I NOTICED THAT KOFFING WAS TRYING TO SNEAK AWAY WITH IT.
I MUST ADMIT ...
I USED THIEF ON YOU ONCE AS WELL.
THIS IS PROBABLY A GOOD TIME TO GIVE THIS BACK TO YOU.
FWP
HUH?!
IT'S THE BADGE I—ER—**BORROWED** FROM YOUR GYM WHILE YOU WERE OUT.

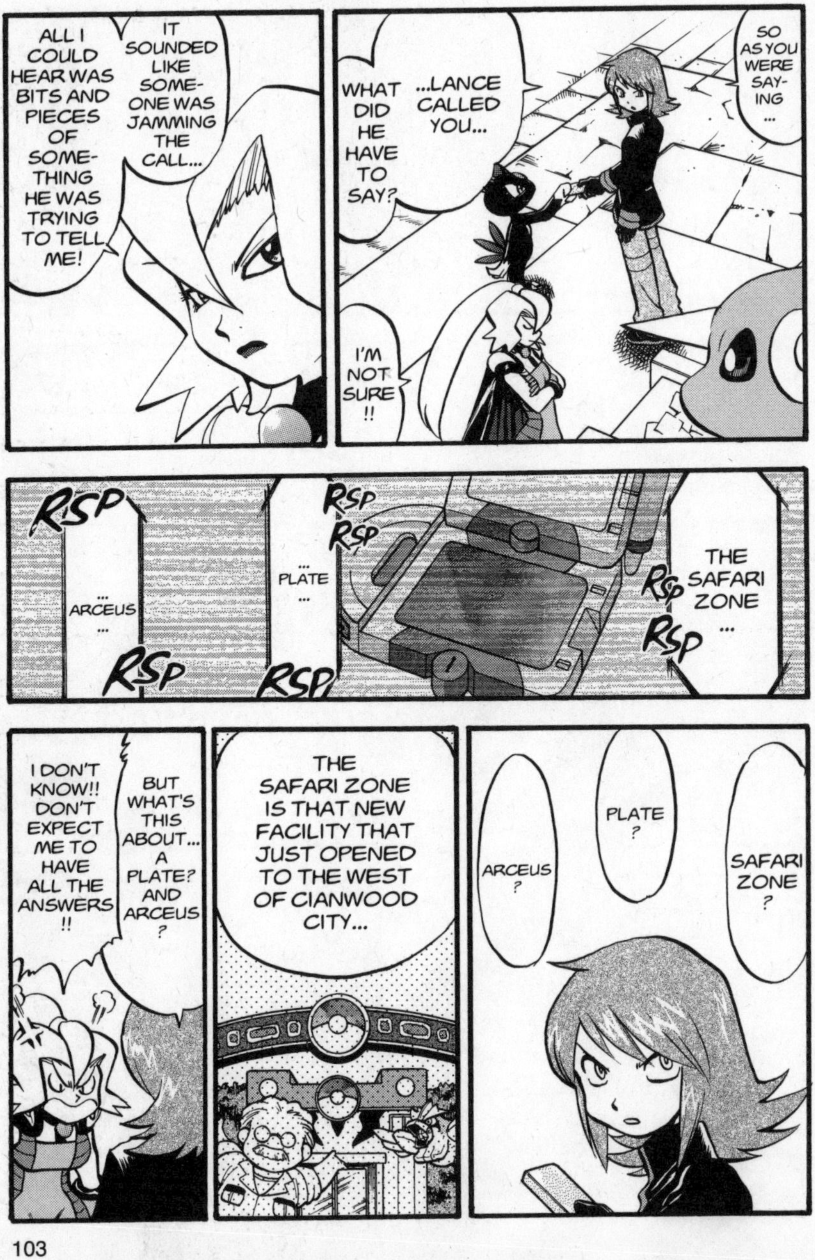
SO AS YOU WERE SAYING...
...LANCE CALLED YOU...
WHAT DID HE HAVE TO SAY?
I'M NOT SURE!!
IT SOUNDED LIKE SOMEONE WAS JAMMING THE CALL...
ALL I COULD HEAR WAS BITS AND PIECES OF SOMETHING HE WAS TRYING TO TELL ME!
RSP
RSP
THE SAFARI ZONE...
RSP
RSP
...PLATE...
RSP
RSP
RSP
...ARCEUS...
RSP
SAFARI ZONE?
PLATE?
ARCEUS?
THE SAFARI ZONE IS THAT NEW FACILITY THAT JUST OPENED TO THE WEST OF CIANWOOD CITY...
BUT WHAT'S THIS ABOUT... A PLATE? AND ARCEUS?
I DON'T KNOW!! DON'T EXPECT ME TO HAVE ALL THE ANSWERS!!

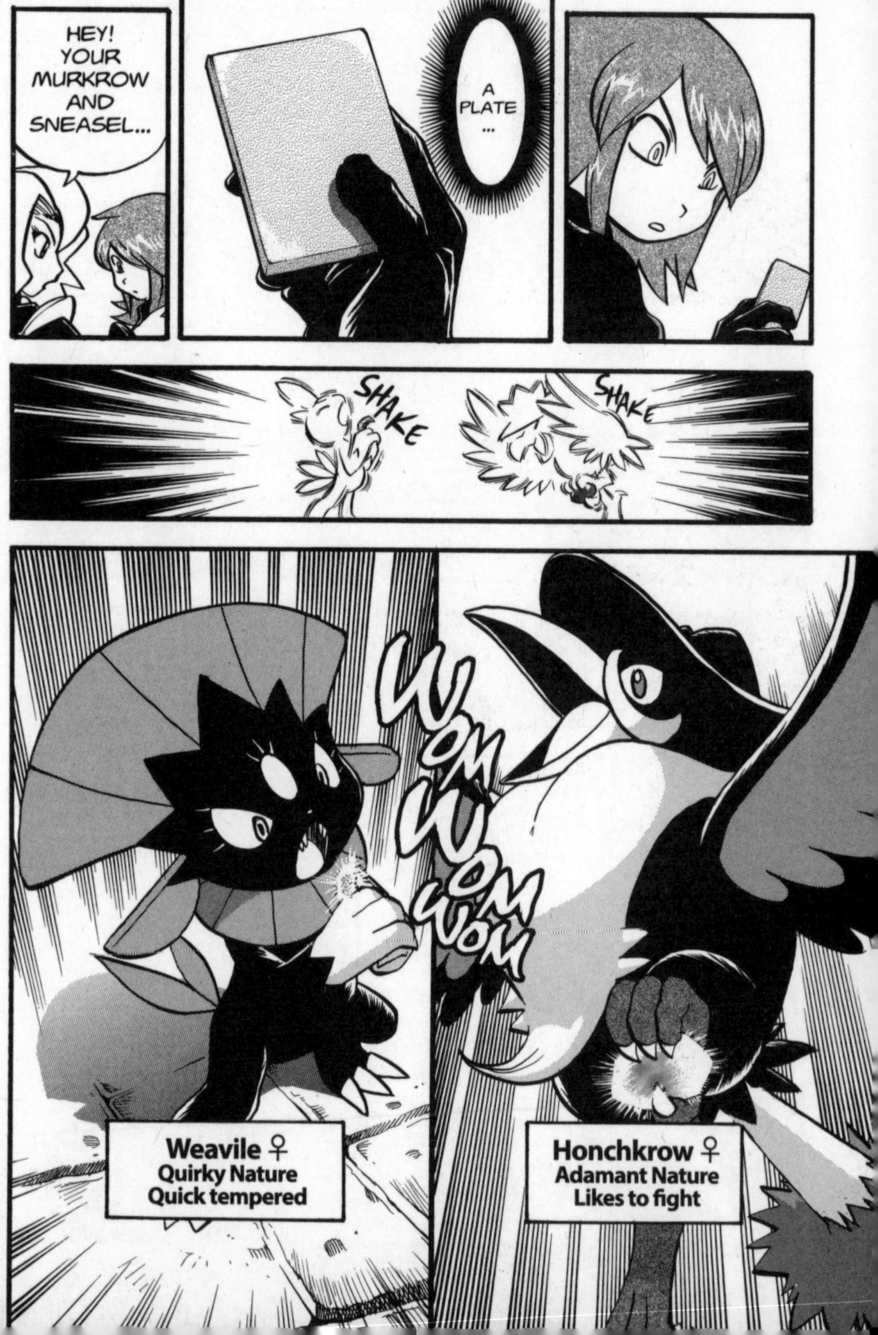
A PLATE ...
HEY! YOUR MURKROW AND SNEASEL...
SHAKE
SHAKE
WOM WOM WOM WOM
Honchkrow ♀
Adamant Nature
Likes to fight
Weavile ♀
Quirky Nature
Quick tempered

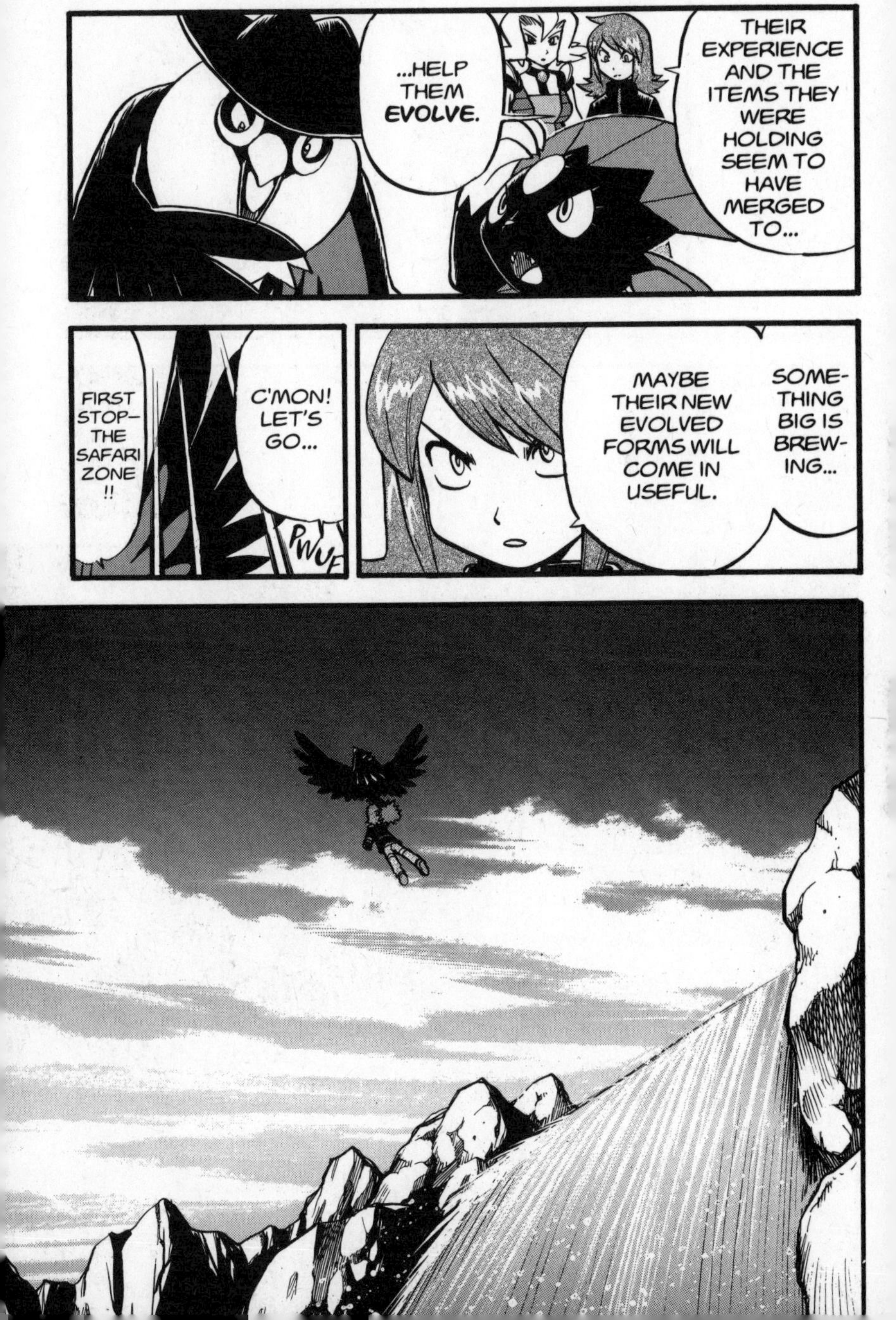
THEIR EXPERIENCE AND THE ITEMS THEY WERE HOLDING SEEM TO HAVE MERGED TO...
...HELP THEM EVOLVE.
SOMETHING BIG IS BREWING...
MAYBE THEIR NEW EVOLVED FORMS WILL COME IN USEFUL.
C'MON! LET'S GO...
PWUF
FIRST STOP—THE SAFARI ZONE!!

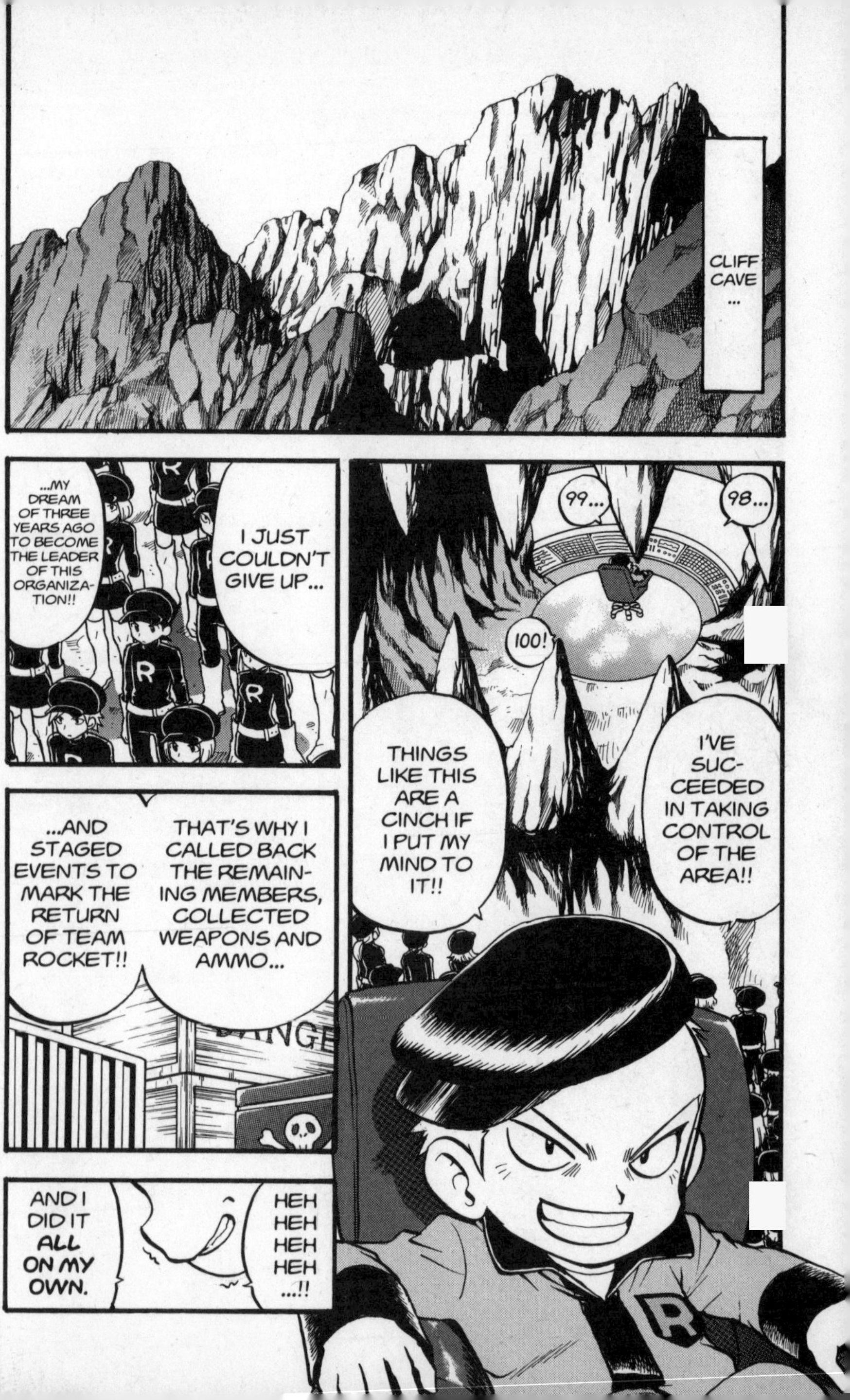
CLIFF CAVE ...
98...
99...
100!
I'VE SUCCEEDED IN TAKING CONTROL OF THE AREA!!
THINGS LIKE THIS ARE A CINCH IF I PUT MY MIND TO IT!!
I JUST COULDN'T GIVE UP...
...MY DREAM OF THREE YEARS AGO TO BECOME THE LEADER OF THIS ORGANIZATION!!
THAT'S WHY I CALLED BACK THE REMAINING MEMBERS, COLLECTED WEAPONS AND AMMO...
...AND STAGED EVENTS TO MARK THE RETURN OF TEAM ROCKET!!
HEH HEH HEH HEH ...!!
AND I DID IT **ALL** ON MY OWN.

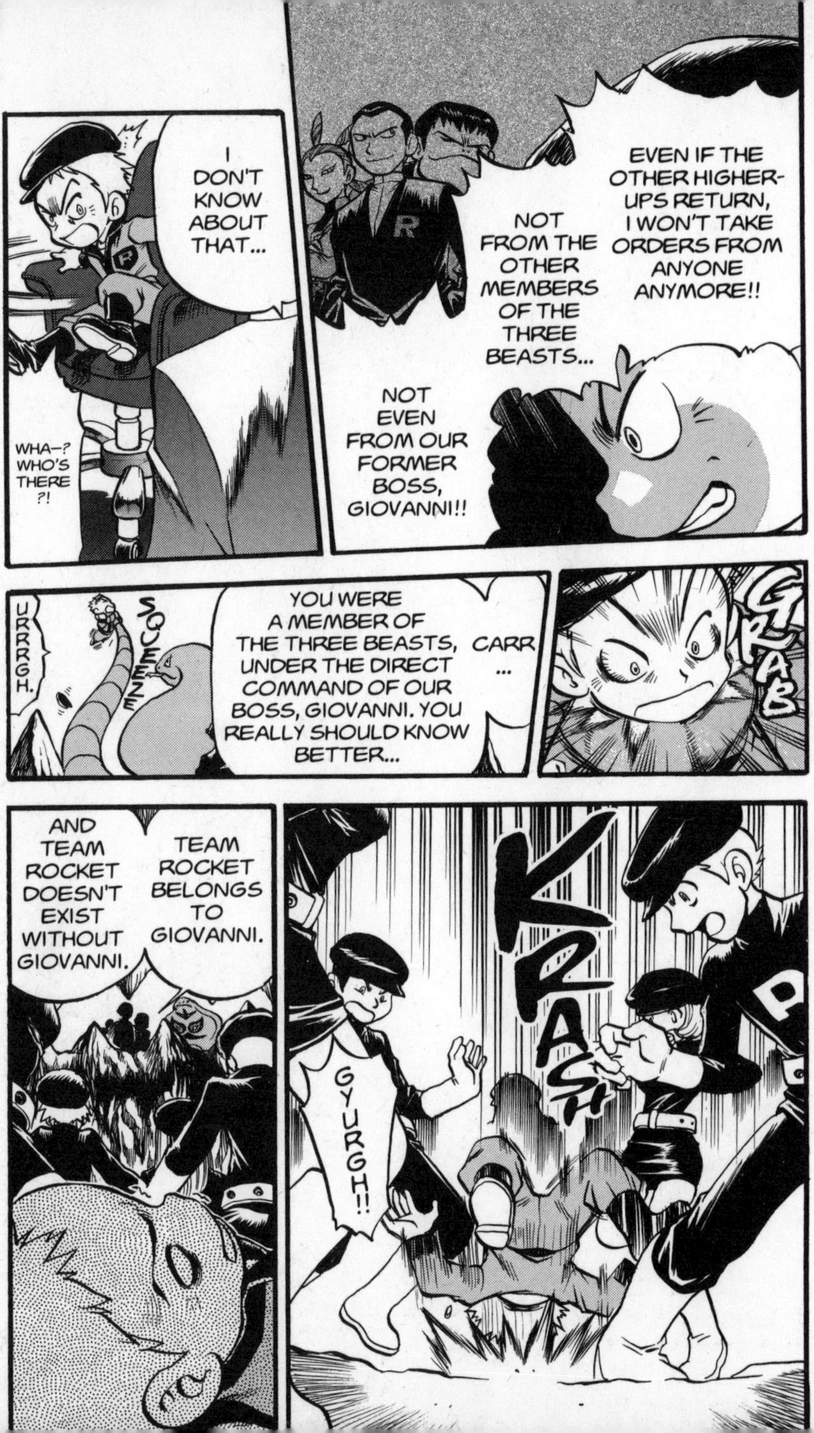
EVEN IF THE OTHER HIGHER-UPS RETURN, I WON'T TAKE ORDERS FROM ANYONE ANYMORE!!
NOT FROM THE OTHER MEMBERS OF THE THREE BEASTS...
NOT EVEN FROM OUR FORMER BOSS, GIOVANNI!!
I DON'T KNOW ABOUT THAT...
WHA-? WHO'S THERE?!
GRAB
CARR...
YOU WERE A MEMBER OF THE THREE BEASTS, UNDER THE DIRECT COMMAND OF OUR BOSS, GIOVANNI. YOU REALLY SHOULD KNOW BETTER...
SQUEEZE
URRRGH.
KRASH!!
GYURGH!!
TEAM ROCKET BELONGS TO GIOVANNI.
AND TEAM ROCKET DOESN'T EXIST WITHOUT GIOVANNI.

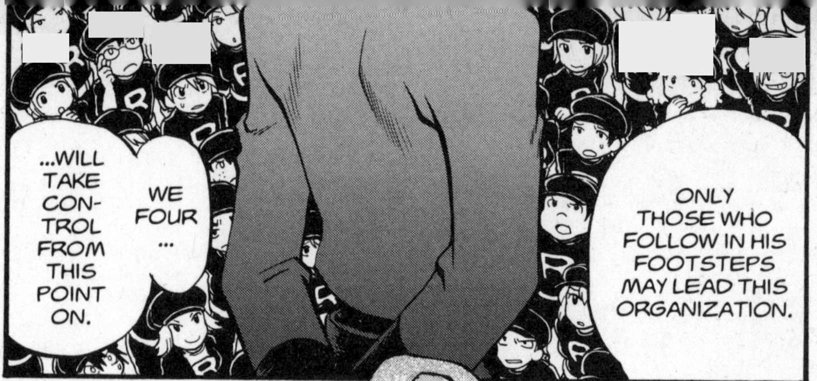
ONLY THOSE WHO FOLLOW IN HIS FOOTSTEPS MAY LEAD THIS ORGANIZATION.
WE FOUR ...
...WILL TAKE CON-TROL FROM THIS POINT ON.

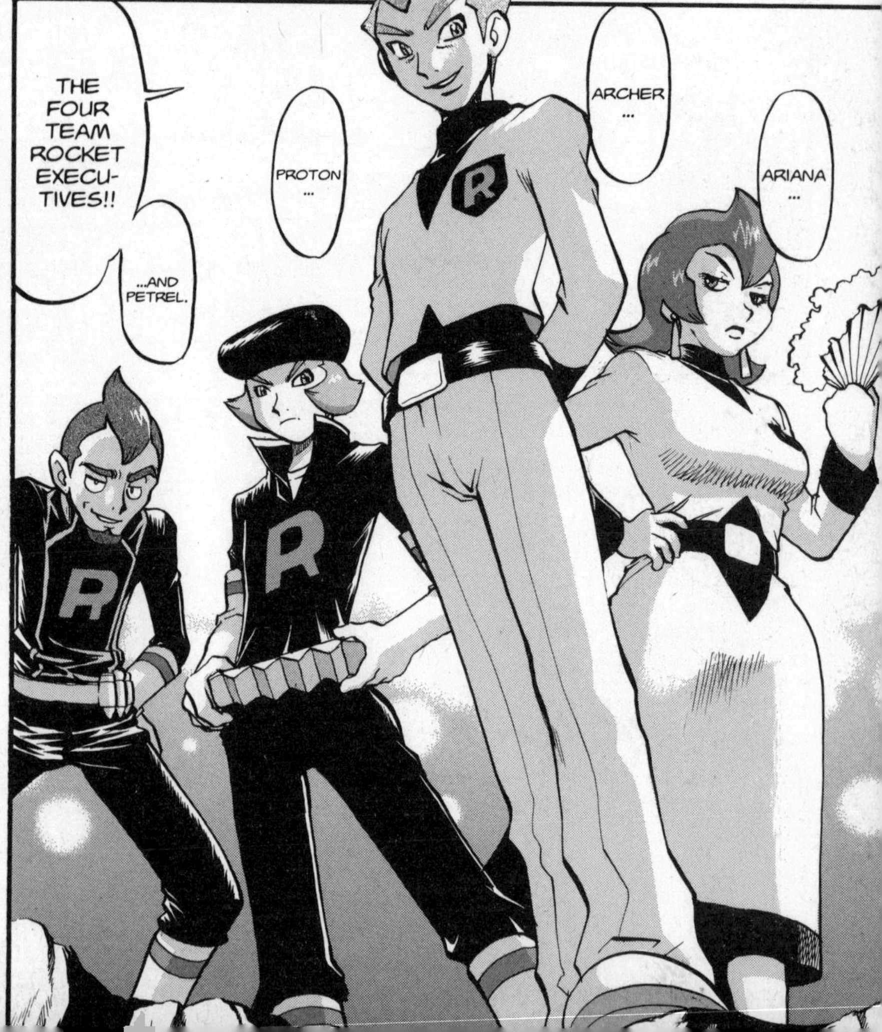
ARCHER ...
ARIANA ...
PROTON ...
...AND PETREL.
THE FOUR TEAM ROCKET EXECU-TIVES!!

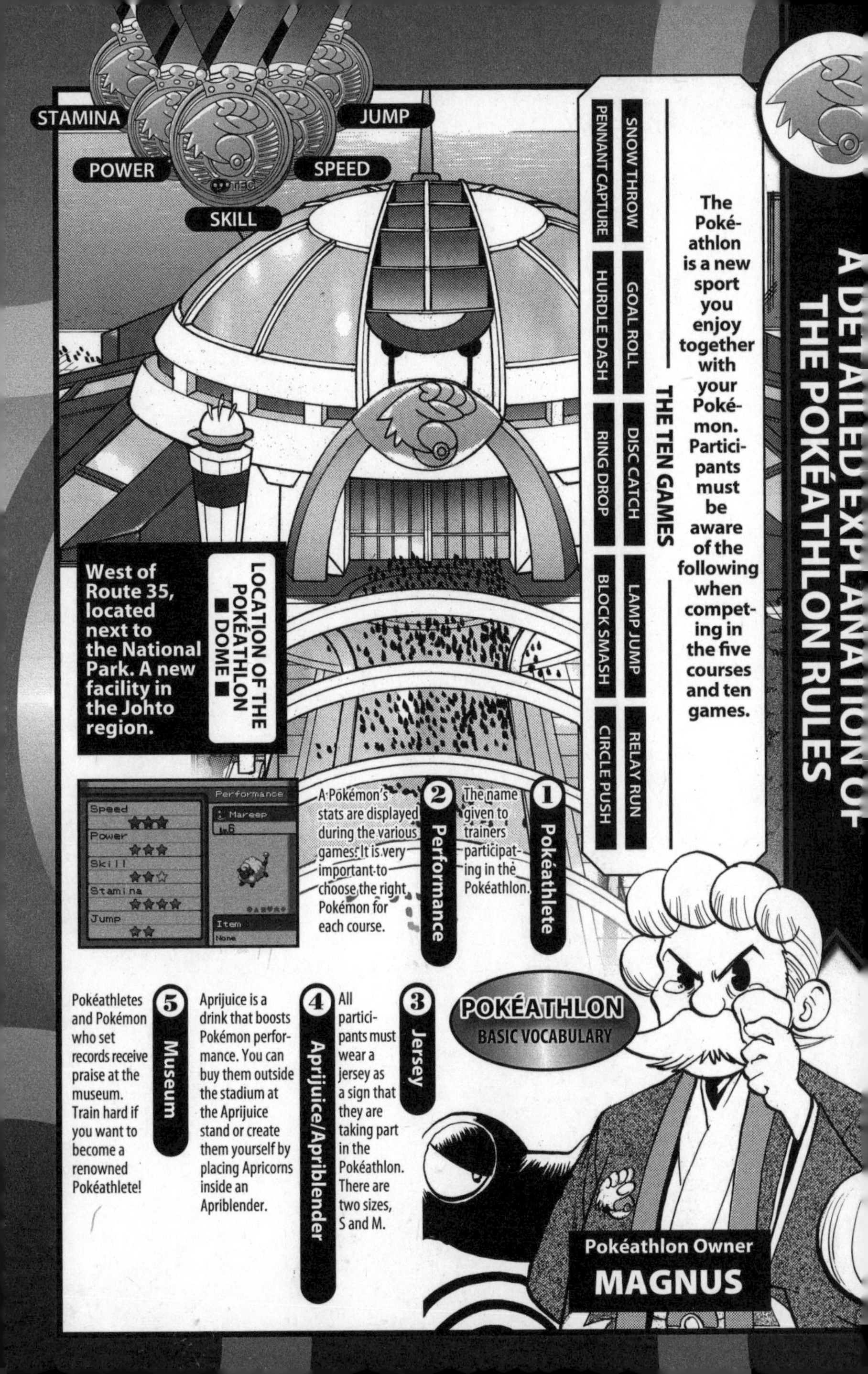
A DETAILED EXPLANATION OF THE POKÉATHLON RULES
The Pokéathlon is a new sport you enjoy together with your Pokémon. Participants must be aware of the following when competing in the five courses and ten games.
THE TEN GAMES
SNOW THROW
GOAL ROLL
DISC CATCH
LAMP JUMP
RELAY RUN
PENNANT CAPTURE
HURDLE DASH
RING DROP
BLOCK SMASH
CIRCLE PUSH
STAMINA
JUMP
POWER
SPEED
SKILL
LOCATION OF THE POKÉATHLON ■ DOME ■
West of Route 35, located next to the National Park. A new facility in the Johto region.
POKÉATHLON BASIC VOCABULARY
1 Pokéathlete
The name given to trainers participating in the Pokéathlon.
2 Performance
A Pokémon's stats are displayed during the various games. It is very important to choose the right Pokémon for each course.
Performance
Speed
Power
Skill
Stamina
Jump
Mareep
Item
None
3 Jersey
All participants must wear a jersey as a sign that they are taking part in the Pokéathlon. There are two sizes, S and M.
4 Aprijuice/Apriblender
Aprijuice is a drink that boosts Pokémon performance. You can buy them outside the stadium at the Aprijuice stand or create them yourself by placing Apricorns inside an Apriblender.
5 Museum
Pokéathletes and Pokémon who set records receive praise at the museum. Train hard if you want to become a renowned Pokéathlete!
Pokéathlon Owner
MAGNUS

Adventure 5

WEAVILE WOBBLES BUT IT WON'T FALL DOWN

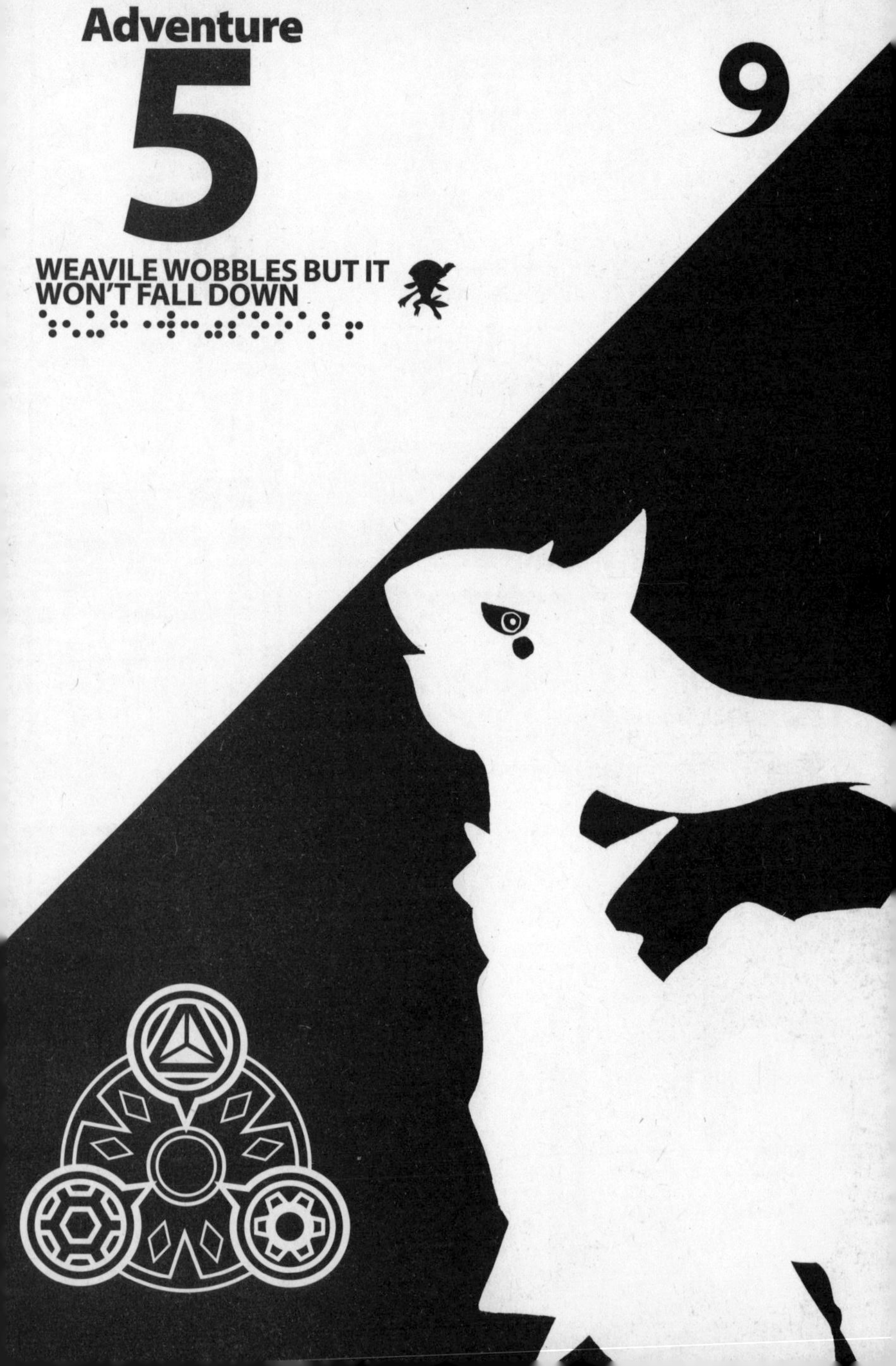

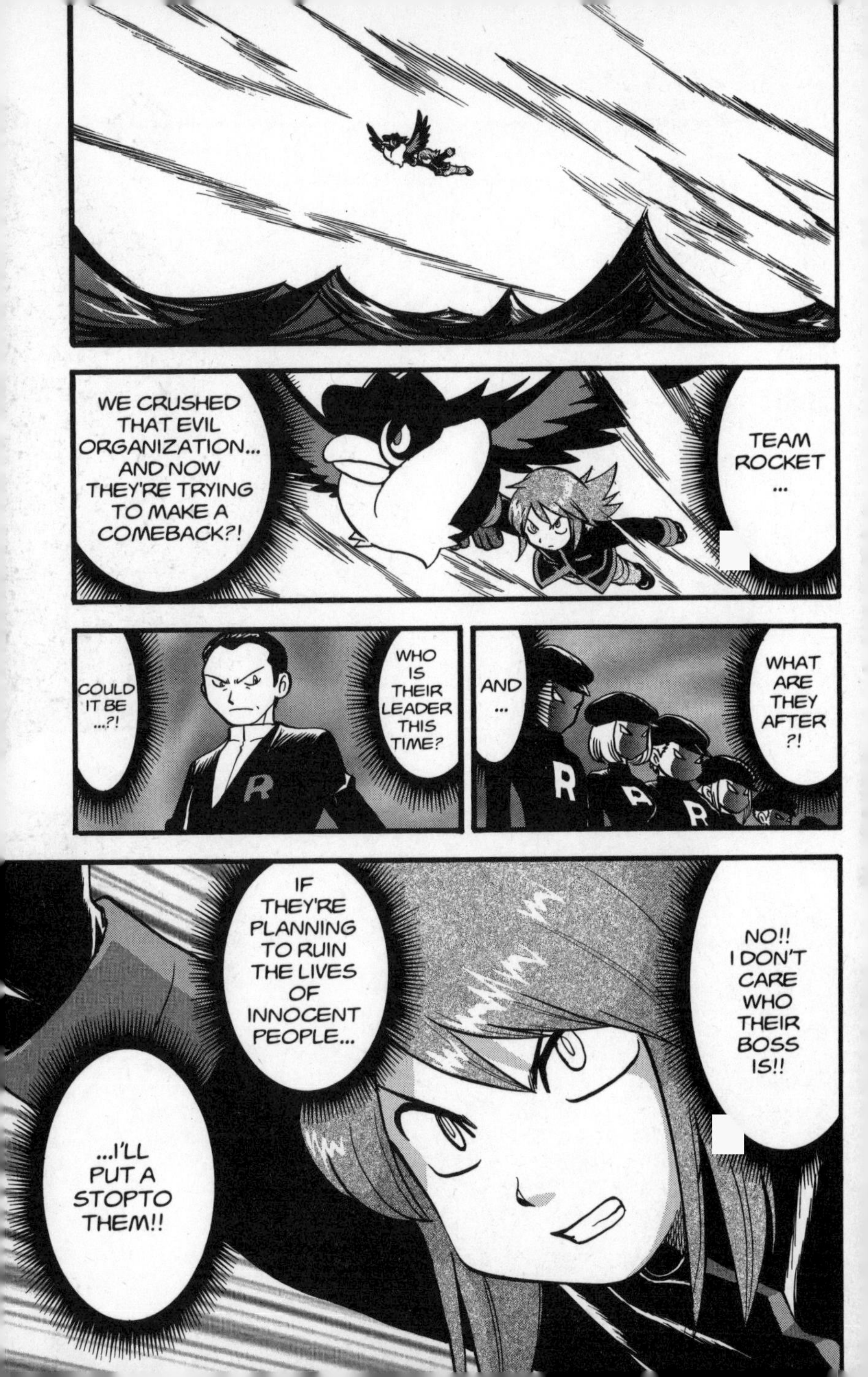
TEAM ROCKET ...
WE CRUSHED THAT EVIL ORGANIZATION... AND NOW THEY'RE TRYING TO MAKE A COMEBACK?!
WHAT ARE THEY AFTER ?!
AND ...
WHO IS THEIR LEADER THIS TIME?
COULD IT BE ...?!
NO!! I DON'T CARE WHO THEIR BOSS IS!!
IF THEY'RE PLANNING TO RUIN THE LIVES OF INNOCENT PEOPLE...
...I'LL PUT A STOPTO THEM!!

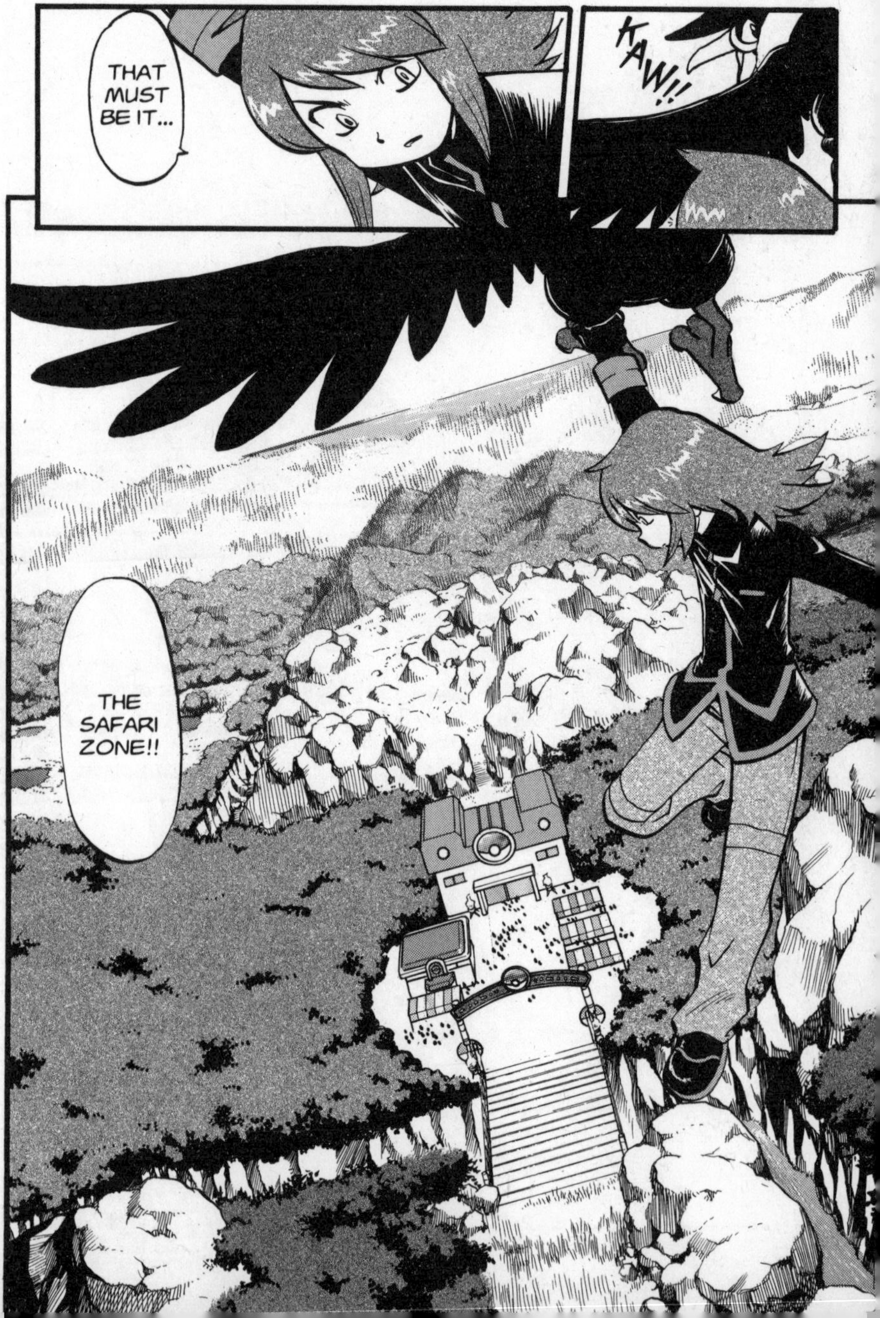
KAW!!
THAT MUST BE IT...
THE SAFARI ZONE!!

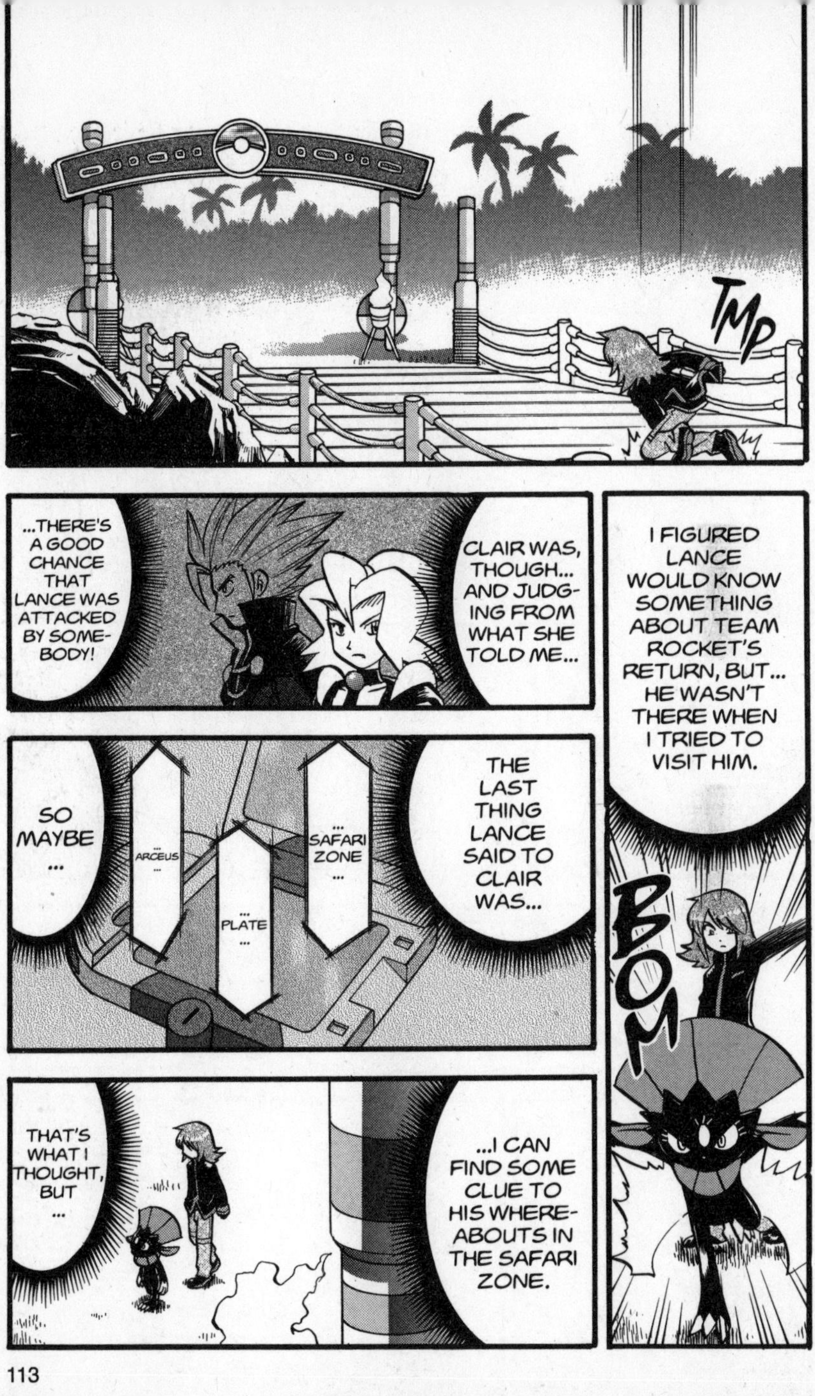
TMP
I FIGURED LANCE WOULD KNOW SOMETHING ABOUT TEAM ROCKET'S RETURN, BUT... HE WASN'T THERE WHEN I TRIED TO VISIT HIM.
BOM
CLAIR WAS, THOUGH... AND JUDG-ING FROM WHAT SHE TOLD ME...
...THERE'S A GOOD CHANCE THAT LANCE WAS ATTACKED BY SOME-BODY!
THE LAST THING LANCE SAID TO CLAIR WAS...
... SAFARI ZONE ...
... PLATE ...
... ARCEUS ...
SO MAYBE ...
...I CAN FIND SOME CLUE TO HIS WHERE-ABOUTS IN THE SAFARI ZONE.
THAT'S WHAT I THOUGHT, BUT ...

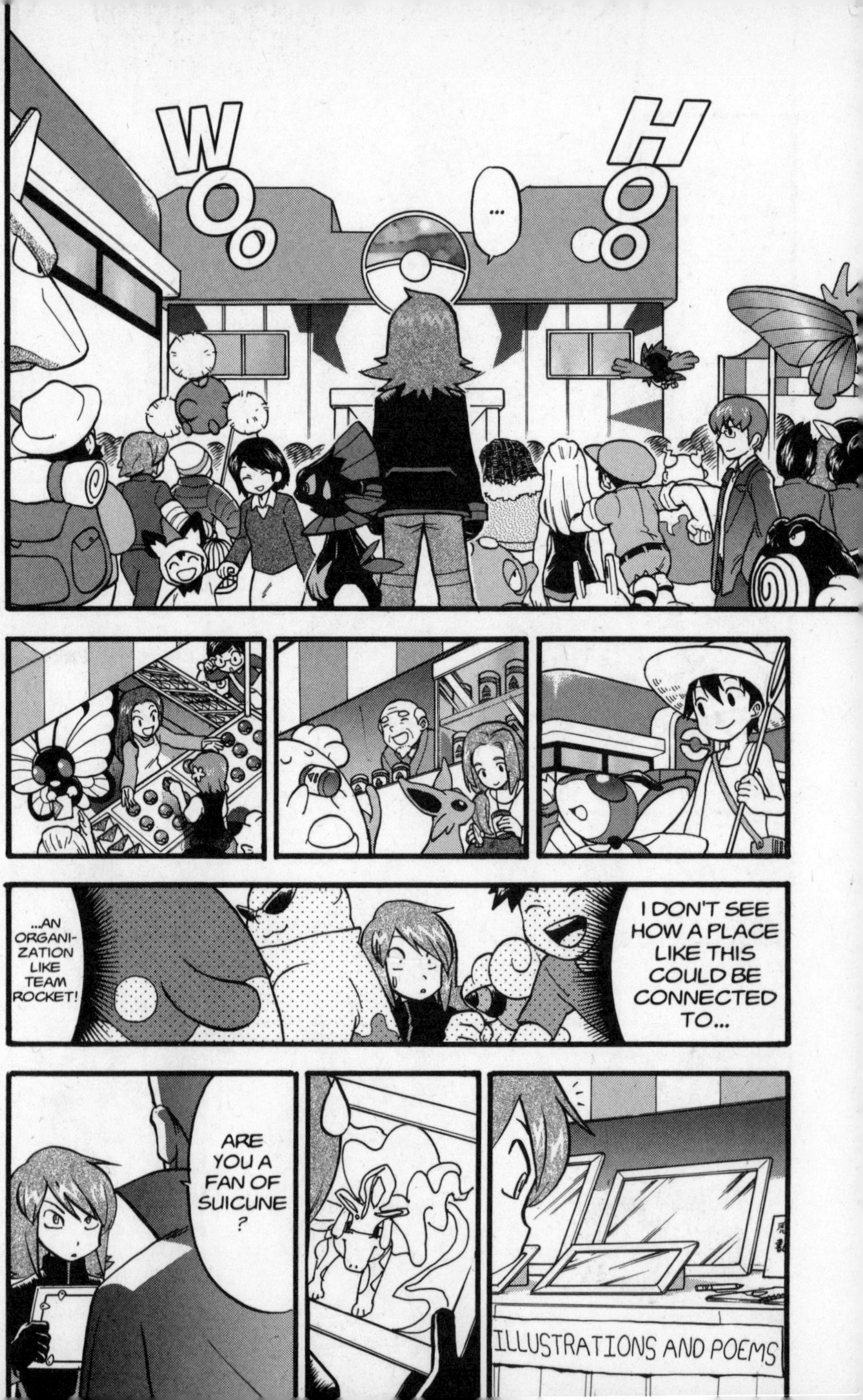
WOO HOO
...
I DON'T SEE HOW A PLACE LIKE THIS COULD BE CONNECTED TO...
...AN ORGANIZATION LIKE TEAM ROCKET!
ILLUSTRATIONS AND POEMS
ARE YOU A FAN OF SUICUNE?

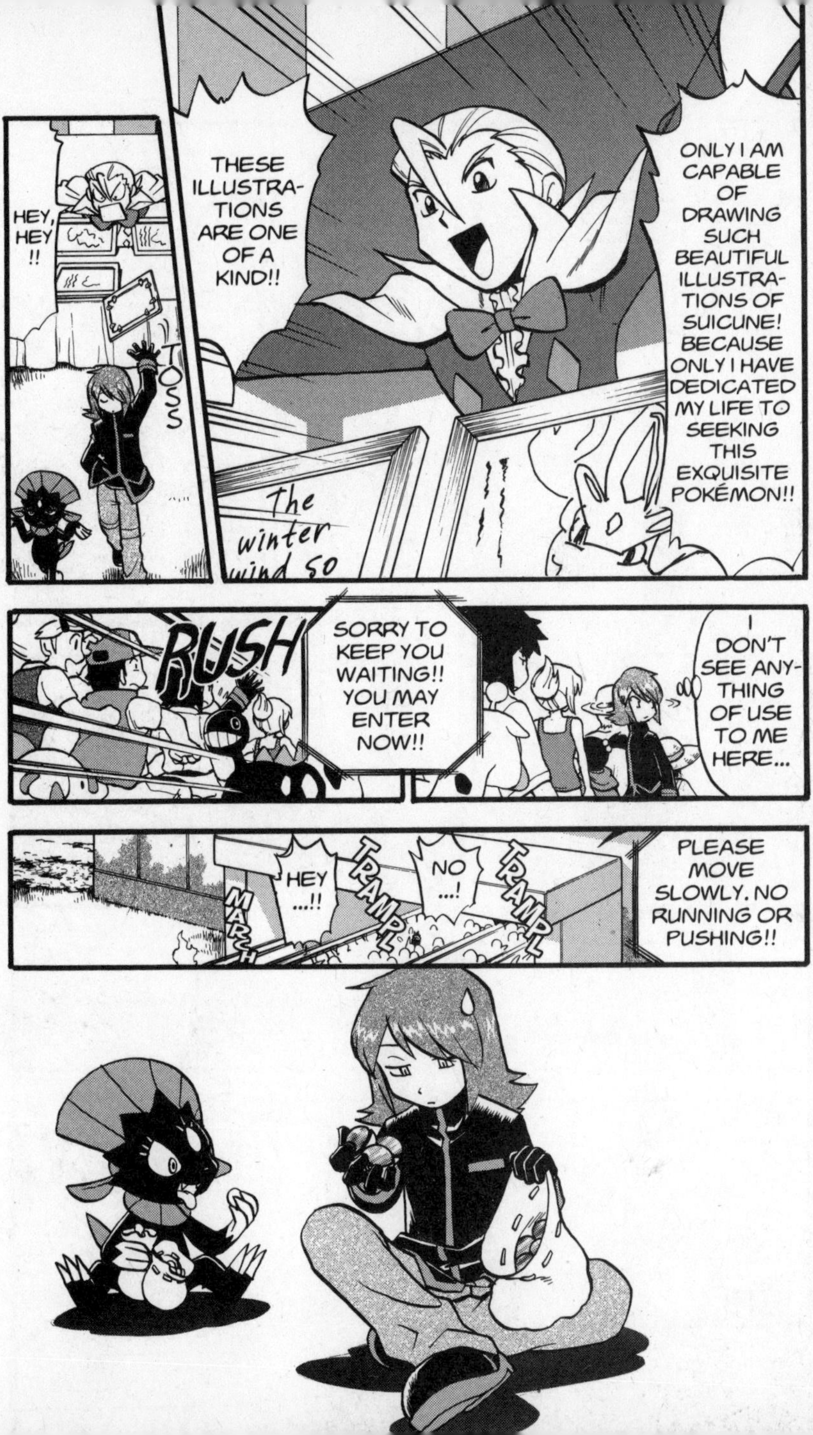
ONLY I AM CAPABLE OF DRAWING SUCH BEAUTIFUL ILLUSTRATIONS OF SUICUNE! BECAUSE ONLY I HAVE DEDICATED MY LIFE TO SEEKING THIS EXQUISITE POKÉMON!!
THESE ILLUSTRATIONS ARE ONE OF A KIND!!
The winter wind so
TOSS
HEY, HEY !!
I DON'T SEE ANYTHING OF USE TO ME HERE...
SORRY TO KEEP YOU WAITING!! YOU MAY ENTER NOW!!
RUSH
PLEASE MOVE SLOWLY. NO RUNNING OR PUSHING!!
TRAMPL
NO ...!
TRAMPL
HEY ...!!
MARCH

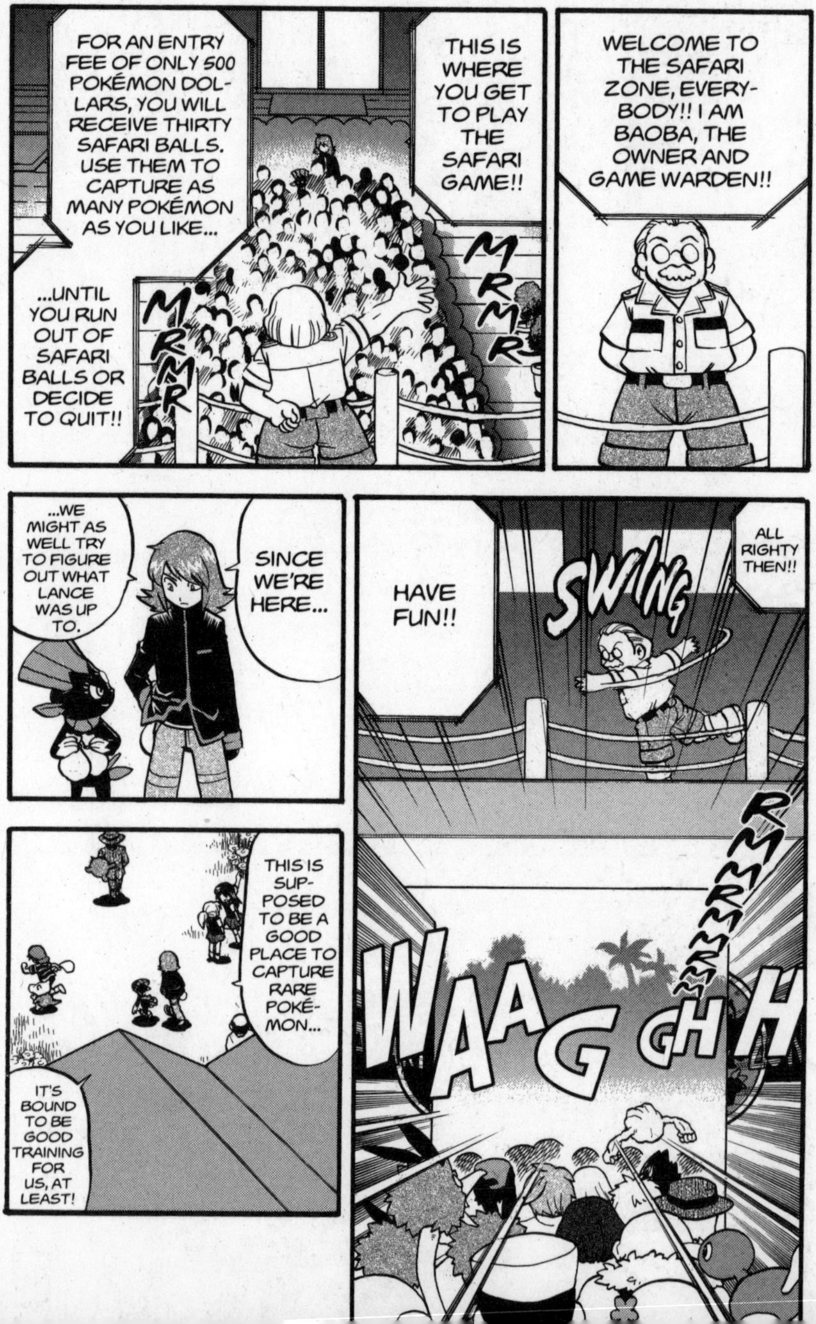
WELCOME TO THE SAFARI ZONE, EVERYBODY!! I AM BAOBA, THE OWNER AND GAME WARDEN!!
THIS IS WHERE YOU GET TO PLAY THE SAFARI GAME!!
MRMR
FOR AN ENTRY FEE OF ONLY 500 POKÉMON DOLLARS, YOU WILL RECEIVE THIRTY SAFARI BALLS. USE THEM TO CAPTURE AS MANY POKÉMON AS YOU LIKE...
...UNTIL YOU RUN OUT OF SAFARI BALLS OR DECIDE TO QUIT!!
MRMR
ALL RIGHTY THEN!!
SWING
HAVE FUN!!
WAAGHH
SINCE WE'RE HERE...
...WE MIGHT AS WELL TRY TO FIGURE OUT WHAT LANCE WAS UP TO.
THIS IS SUPPOSED TO BE A GOOD PLACE TO CAPTURE RARE POKÉMON...
IT'S BOUND TO BE GOOD TRAINING FOR US, AT LEAST!

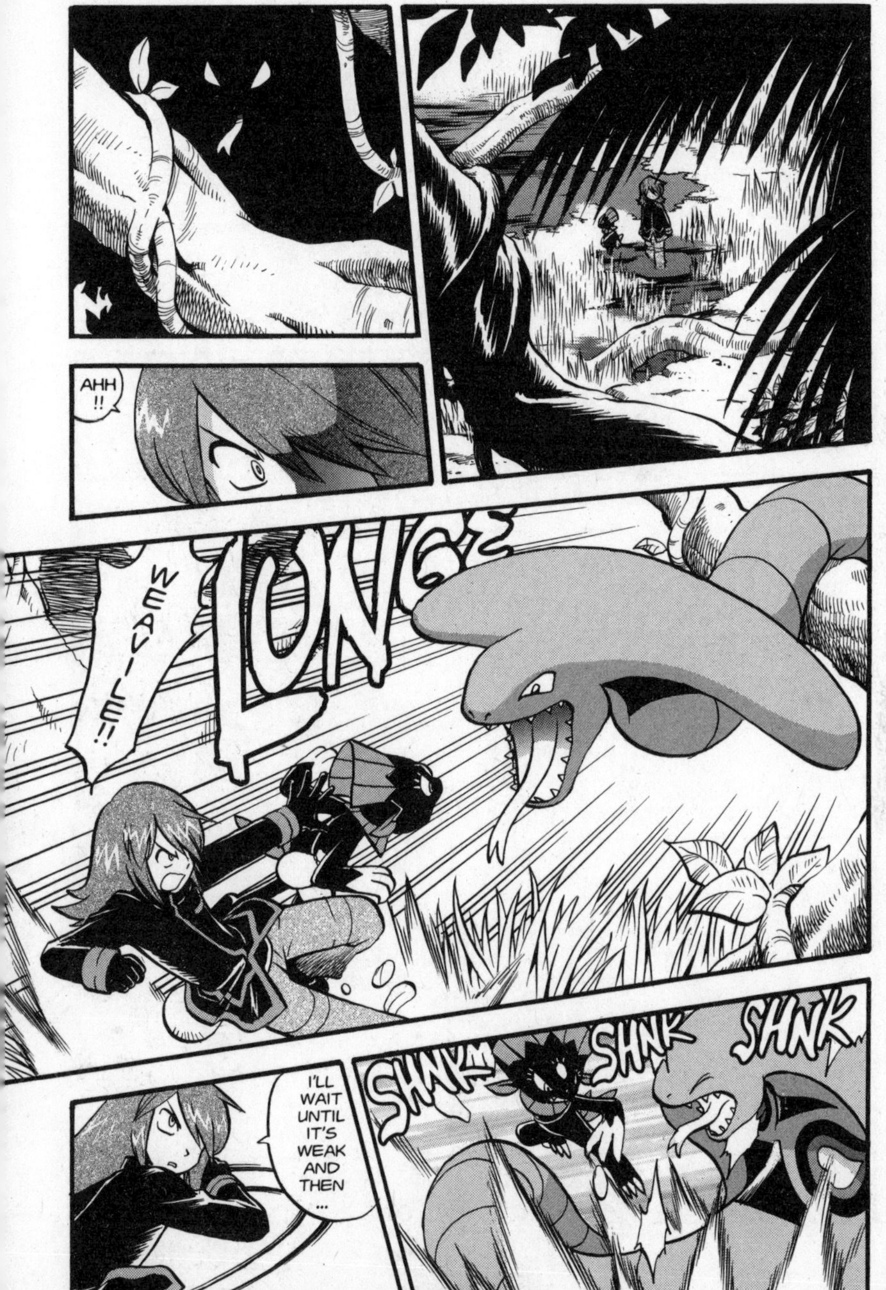
AHH !!
LUNGE
WEAVILE!!
SHNK SHNK SHNK
I'LL WAIT UNTIL IT'S WEAK AND THEN ...

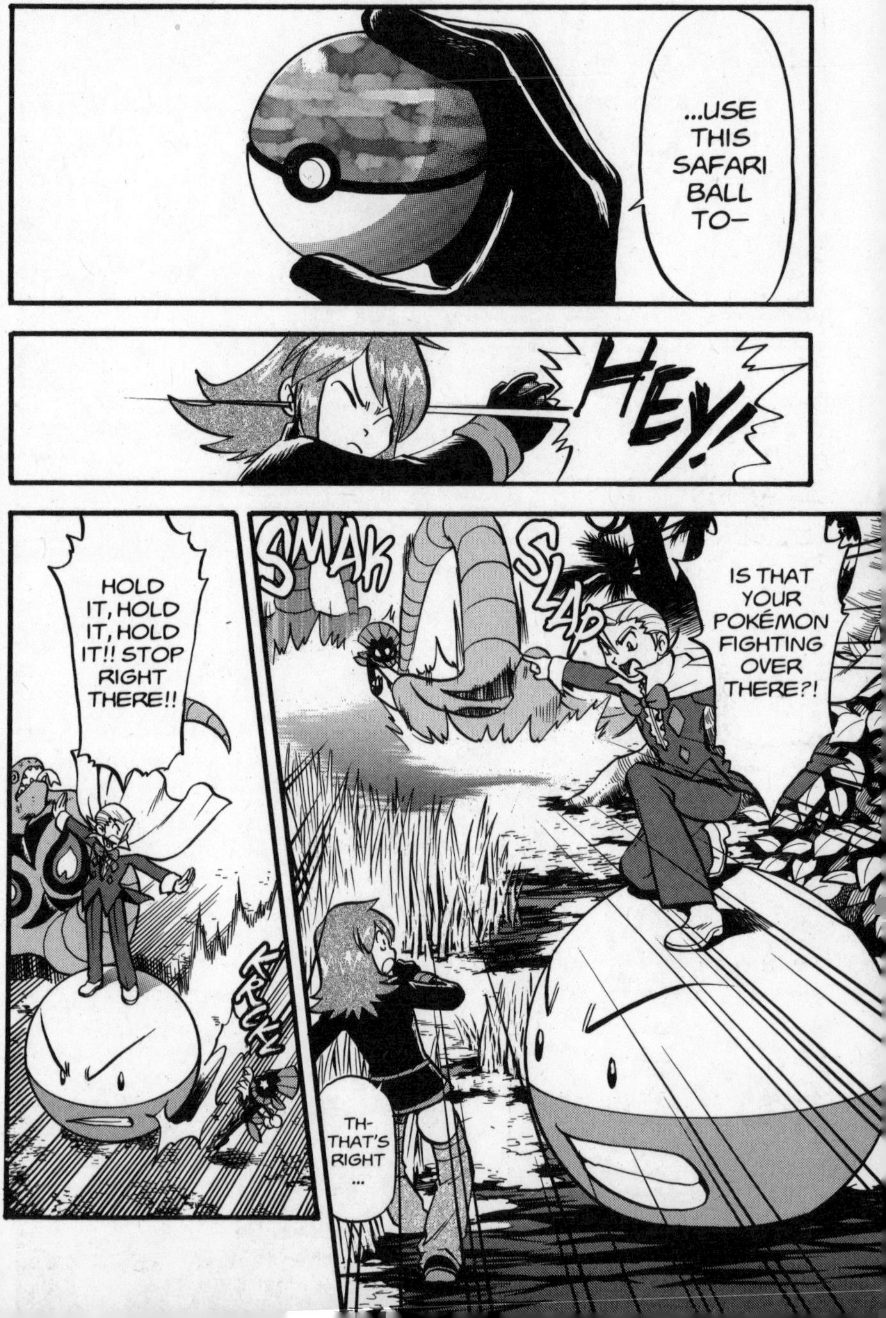
...USE THIS SAFARI BALL TO—
HEY!
SMAK
SLAP
IS THAT YOUR POKÉMON FIGHTING OVER THERE?!
TH-THAT'S RIGHT ...
HOLD IT, HOLD IT, HOLD IT!! STOP RIGHT THERE!!
KRICK

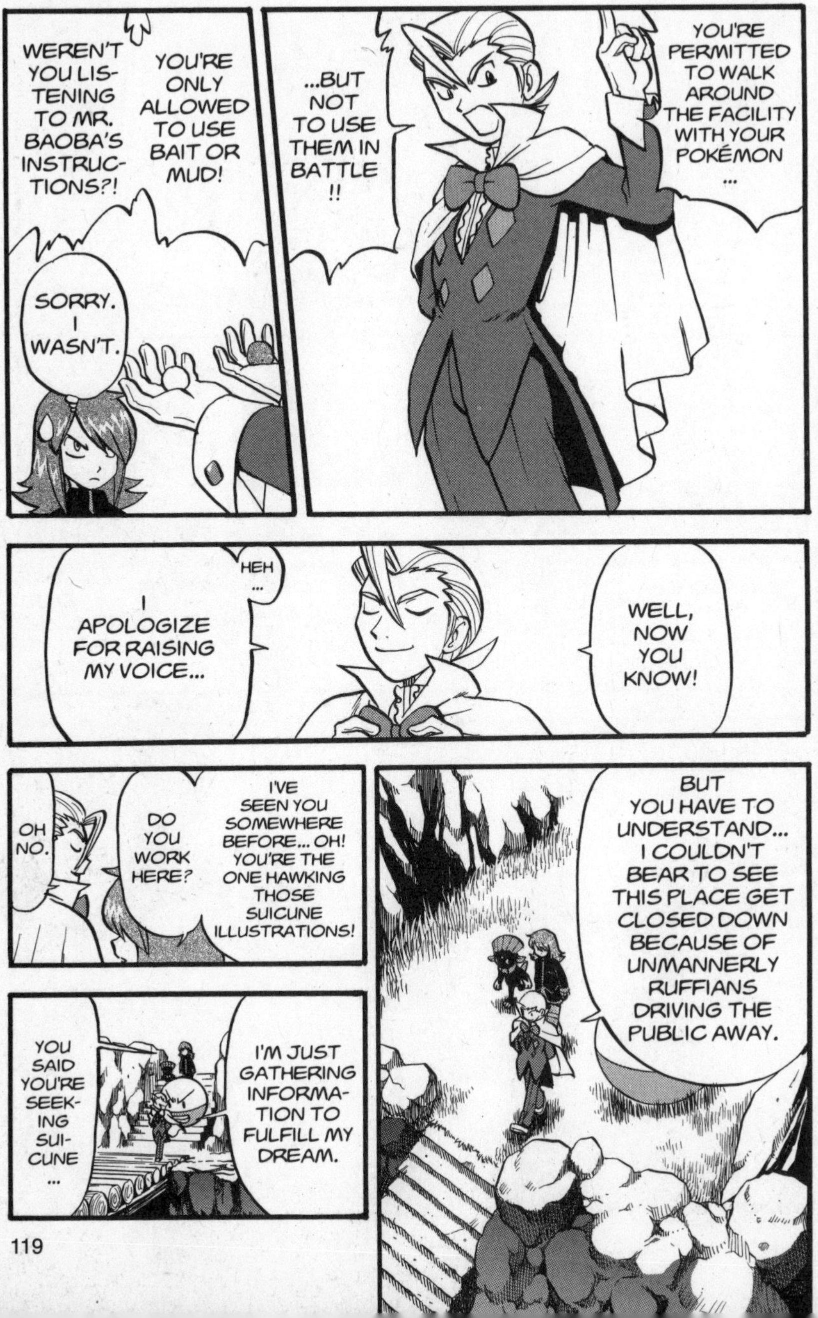
YOU'RE PERMITTED TO WALK AROUND THE FACILITY WITH YOUR POKÉMON ...
...BUT NOT TO USE THEM IN BATTLE !!
YOU'RE ONLY ALLOWED TO USE BAIT OR MUD!
WEREN'T YOU LIS-TENING TO MR. BAOBA'S INSTRUC-TIONS?!
SORRY. I WASN'T.
WELL, NOW YOU KNOW!
HEH ...
I APOLOGIZE FOR RAISING MY VOICE...
BUT YOU HAVE TO UNDERSTAND... I COULDN'T BEAR TO SEE THIS PLACE GET CLOSED DOWN BECAUSE OF UNMANNERLY RUFFIANS DRIVING THE PUBLIC AWAY.
I'VE SEEN YOU SOMEWHERE BEFORE... OH! YOU'RE THE ONE HAWKING THOSE SUICUNE ILLUSTRATIONS!
DO YOU WORK HERE?
OH NO.
I'M JUST GATHERING INFORMA-TION TO FULFILL MY DREAM.
YOU SAID YOU'RE SEEK-ING SUI-CUNE ...

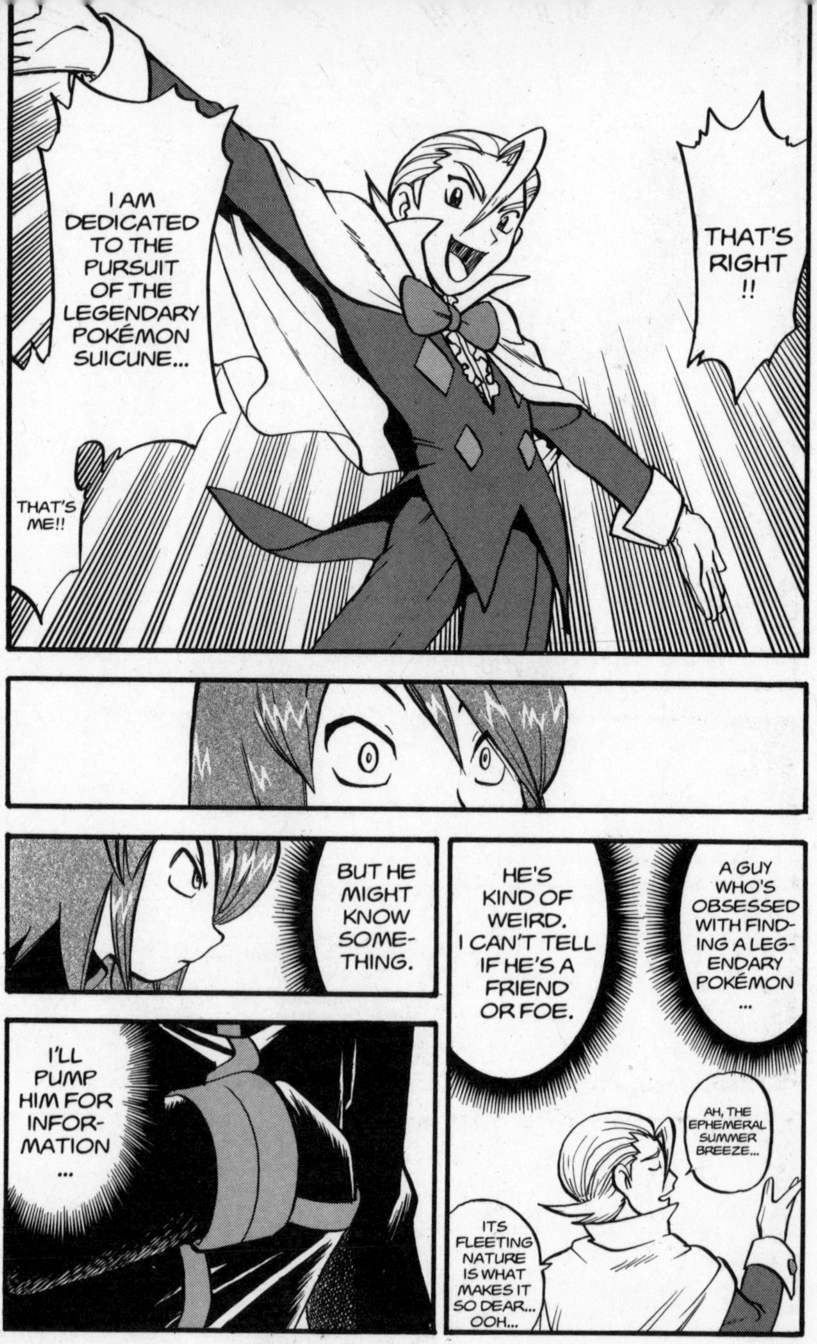
THAT'S RIGHT!!
I AM DEDICATED TO THE PURSUIT OF THE LEGENDARY POKÉMON SUICUNE...
THAT'S ME!!
A GUY WHO'S OBSESSED WITH FINDING A LEGENDARY POKÉMON...
HE'S KIND OF WEIRD. I CAN'T TELL IF HE'S A FRIEND OR FOE.
AH, THE EPHEMERAL SUMMER BREEZE...
ITS FLEETING NATURE IS WHAT MAKES IT SO DEAR... OOH...
BUT HE MIGHT KNOW SOMETHING.
I'LL PUMP HIM FOR INFORMATION...

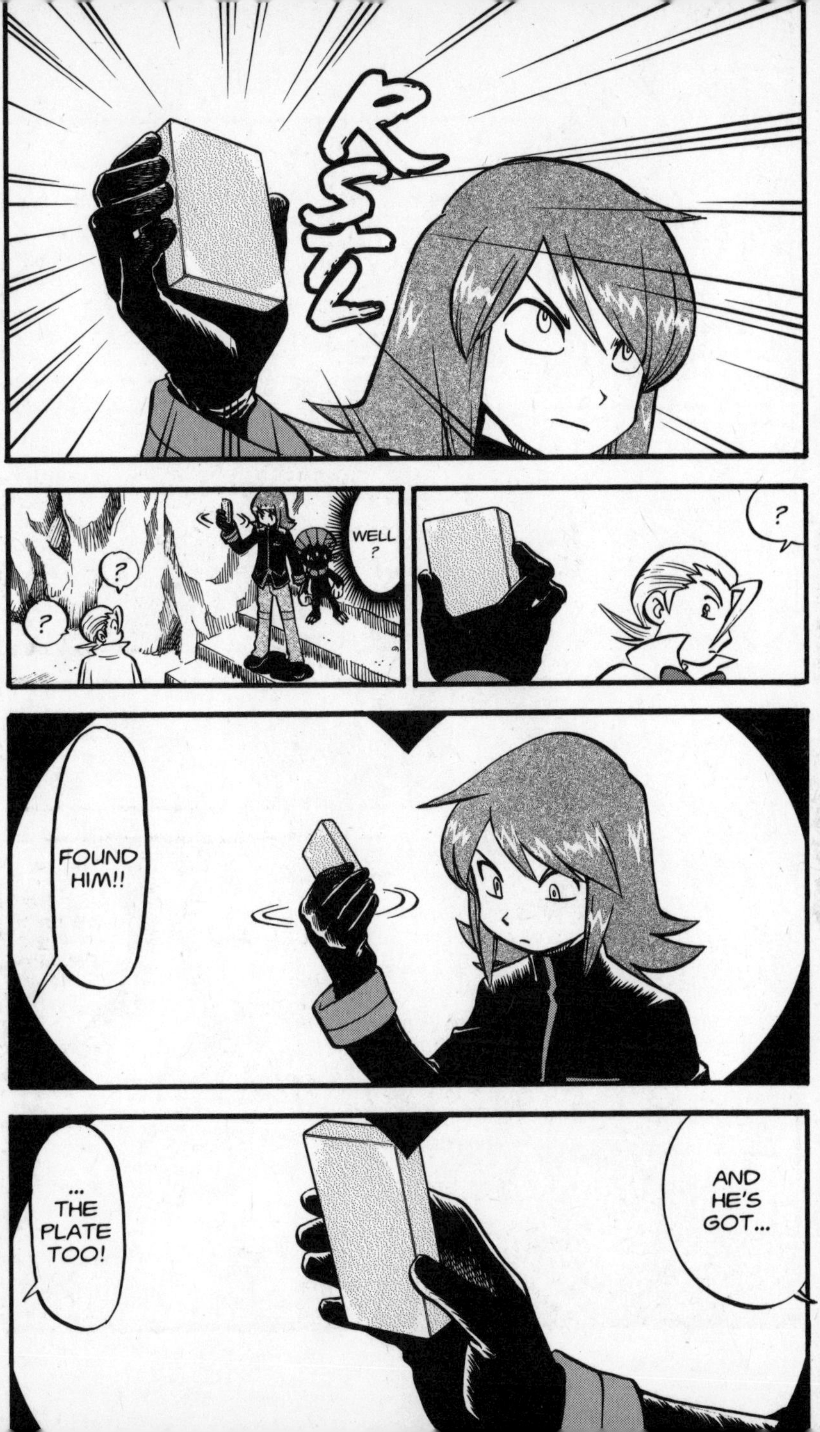
RSTL
?
WELL?
?
?
FOUND HIM!!
AND HE'S GOT...
...THE PLATE TOO!

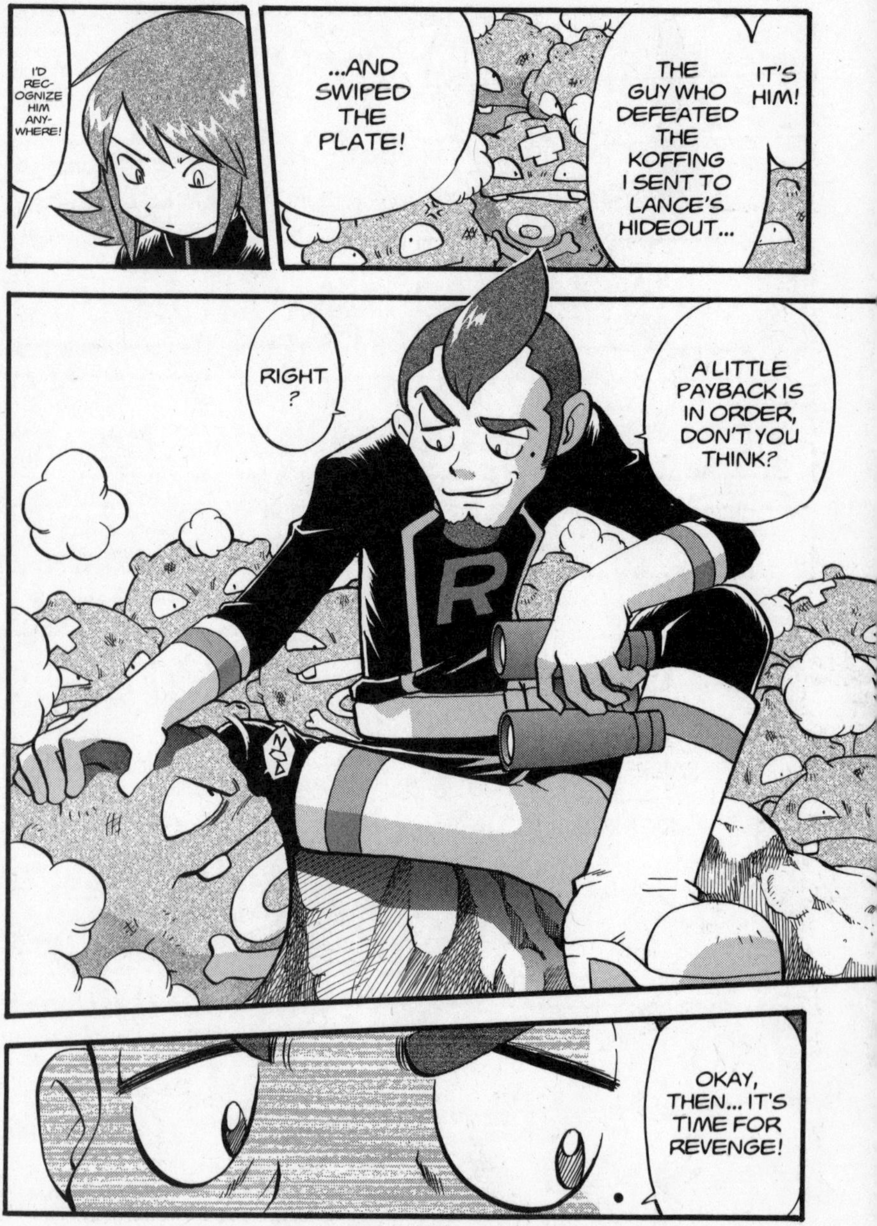
IT'S HIM!
THE GUY WHO DEFEATED THE KOFFING I SENT TO LANCE'S HIDEOUT...
...AND SWIPED THE PLATE!
I'D RECOGNIZE HIM ANYWHERE!
A LITTLE PAYBACK IS IN ORDER, DON'T YOU THINK?
RIGHT?
OKAY, THEN... IT'S TIME FOR REVENGE!

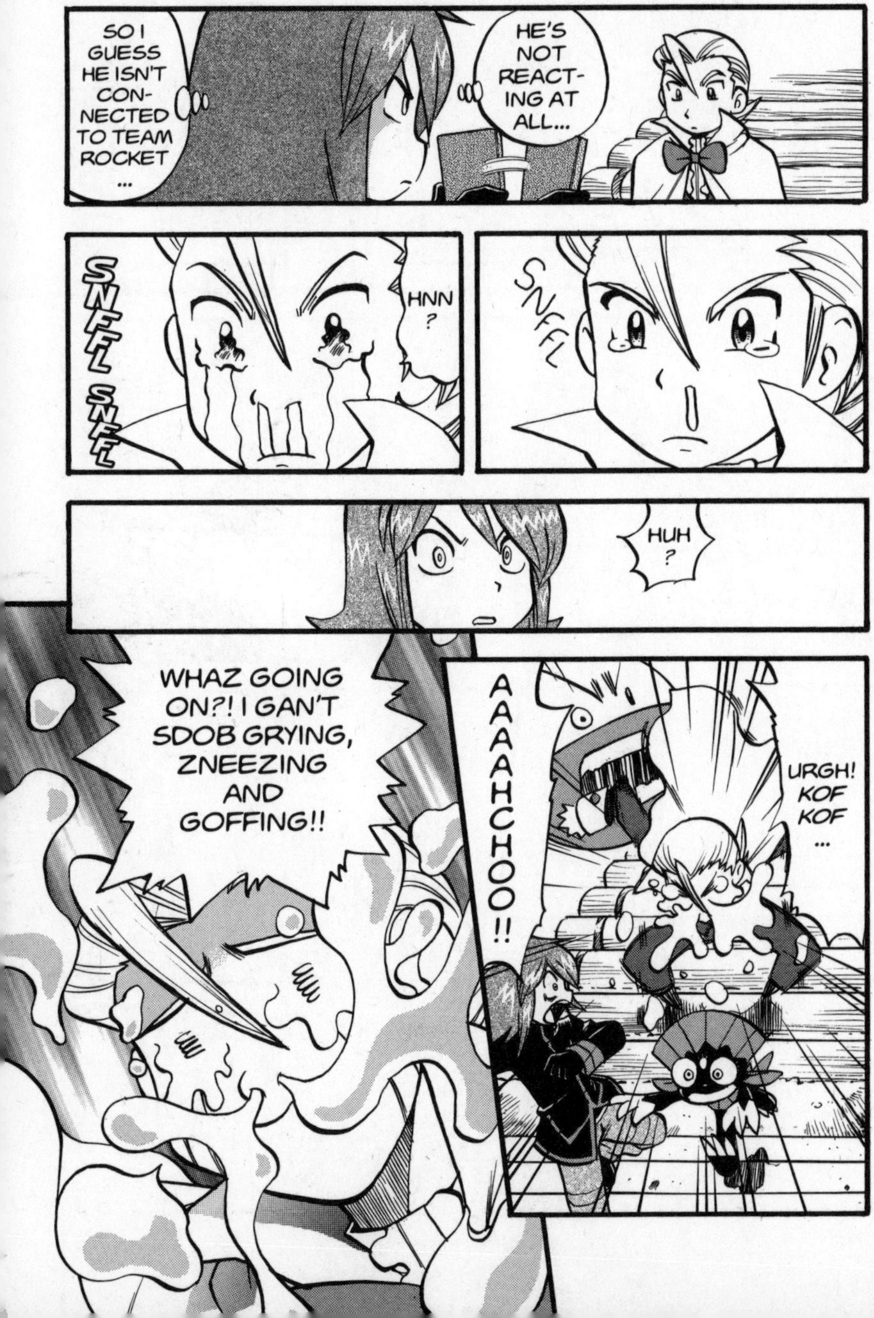
HE'S NOT REACT-ING AT ALL...
SO I GUESS HE ISN'T CON-NECTED TO TEAM ROCKET ...
SNFFL
HNN ?
SNFFL SNFFL
HUH ?
AAAAHCHOO!!
URGH! KOF KOF ...
WHAZ GOING ON?! I GAN'T SDOB GRYING, ZNEEZING AND GOFFING!!

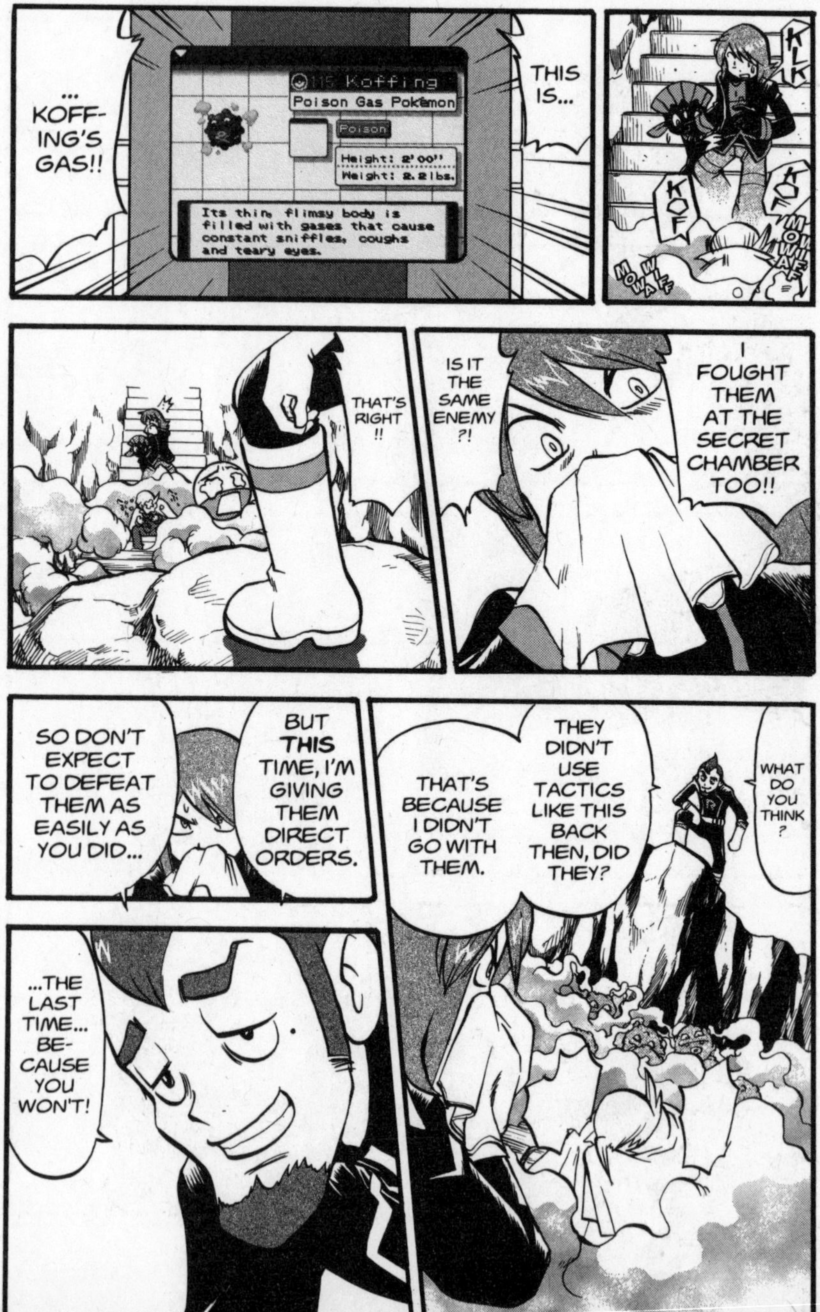
KLK
KOF
KOF
THIS IS...
...KOFF-ING'S GAS!!
115 Koffing
Poison Gas Pokémon
Poison
Height: 2'00"
Weight: 2.2 lbs.
Its thin, flimsy body is filled with gases that cause constant sniffles, coughs and teary eyes.
I FOUGHT THEM AT THE SECRET CHAMBER TOO!!
IS IT THE SAME ENEMY?!
THAT'S RIGHT!!
WHAT DO YOU THINK?
THEY DIDN'T USE TACTICS LIKE THIS BACK THEN, DID THEY?
THAT'S BECAUSE I DIDN'T GO WITH THEM.
BUT THIS TIME, I'M GIVING THEM DIRECT ORDERS.
SO DON'T EXPECT TO DEFEAT THEM AS EASILY AS YOU DID...
...THE LAST TIME... BE-CAUSE YOU WON'T!

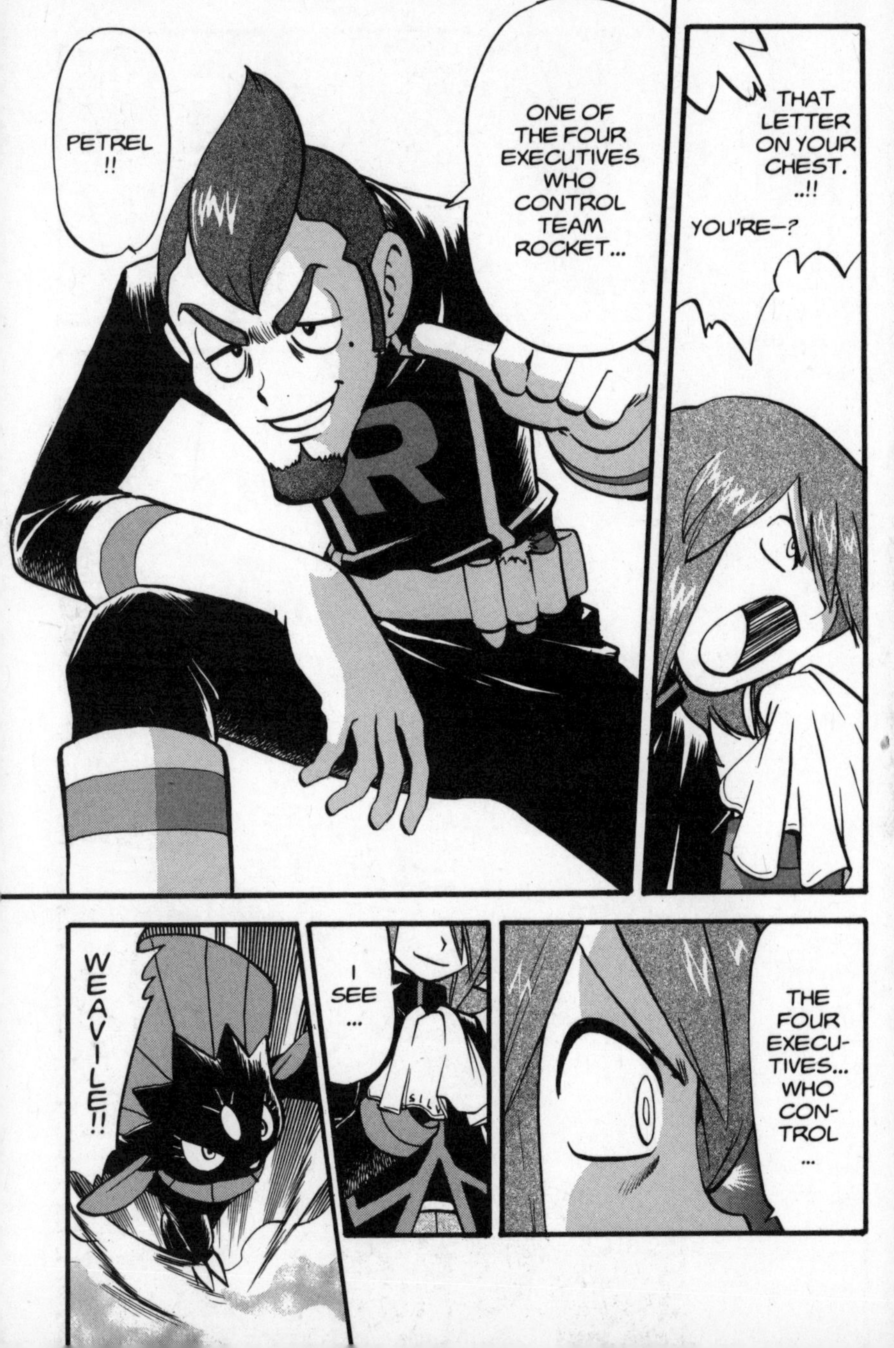
THAT LETTER ON YOUR CHEST. ..!!
YOU'RE–?
ONE OF THE FOUR EXECUTIVES WHO CONTROL TEAM ROCKET...
PETREL !!
THE FOUR EXECU-TIVES... WHO CON-TROL ...
I SEE ...
WEAVILE!!

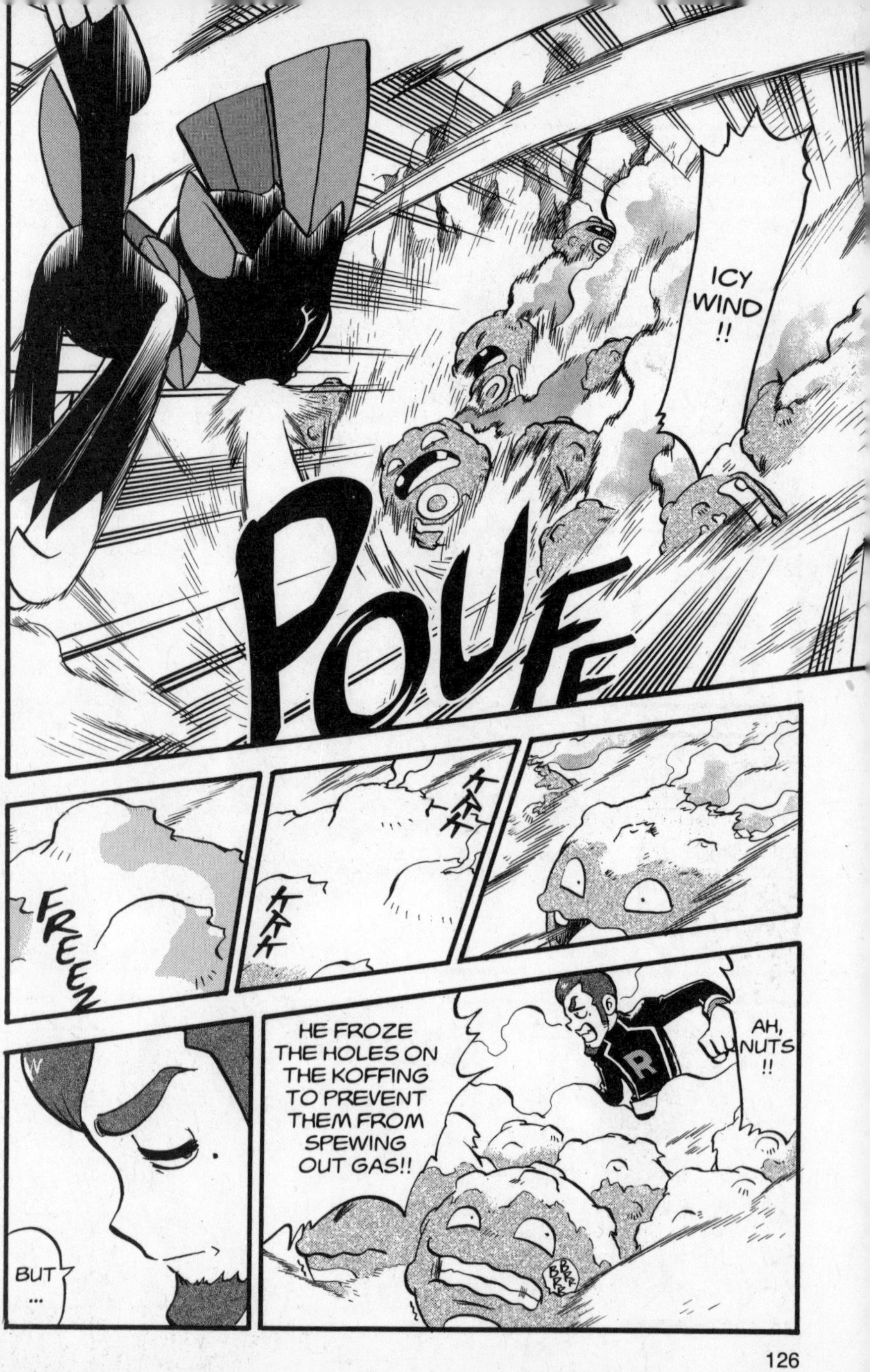
ICY WIND!!
POUF
FREEZ
AH, NUTS!!
HE FROZE THE HOLES ON THE KOFFING TO PREVENT THEM FROM SPEWING OUT GAS!!
BUT...

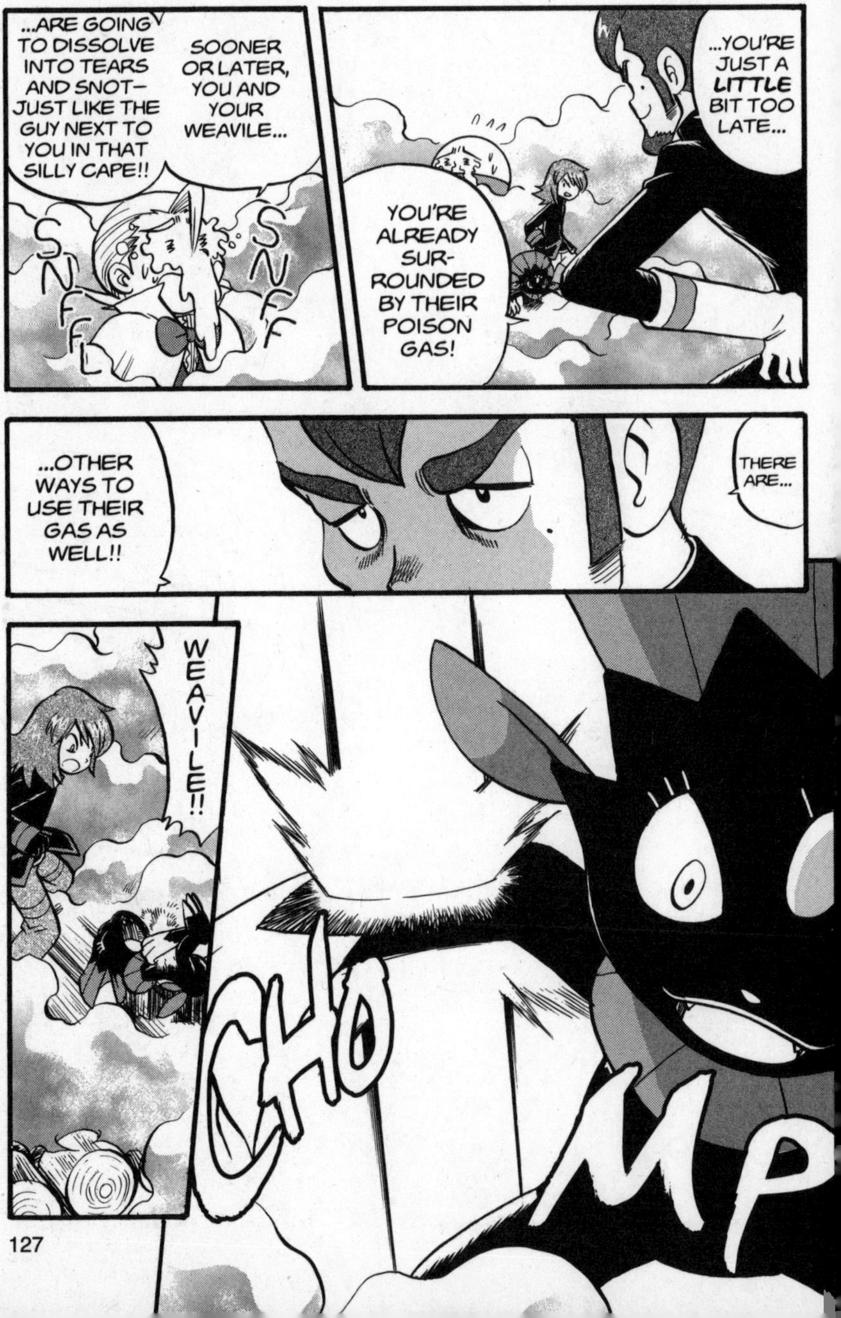
...YOU'RE JUST A LITTLE BIT TOO LATE...
YOU'RE ALREADY SUR-ROUNDED BY THEIR POISON GAS!
SOONER OR LATER, YOU AND YOUR WEAVILE...
...ARE GOING TO DISSOLVE INTO TEARS AND SNOT—JUST LIKE THE GUY NEXT TO YOU IN THAT SILLY CAPE!!
SNFF
SNFFL
THERE ARE...
...OTHER WAYS TO USE THEIR GAS AS WELL!!
CHOMP
WEAVILE!!

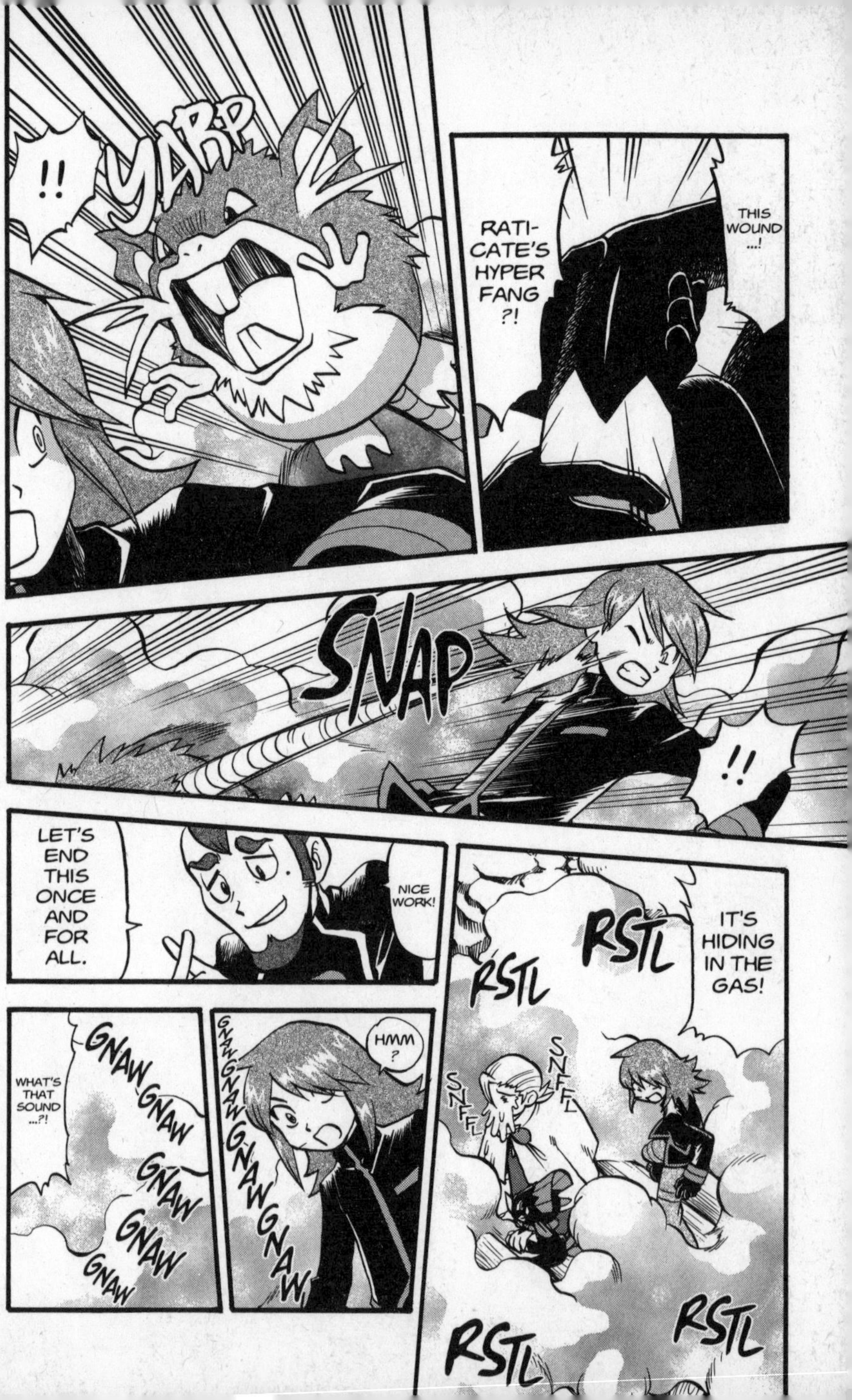

THIS WOUND ...!
RATI-CATE'S HYPER FANG ?!
YARP
!!
SNAP
!!
IT'S HIDING IN THE GAS!
RSTL
RSTL
SNFFL
SNFFL
RSTL
RSTL
LET'S END THIS ONCE AND FOR ALL.
NICE WORK!
HMM ?
GNAW GNAW GNAW GNAW GNAW
WHAT'S THAT SOUND ...?!
GNAW GNAW GNAW GNAW GNAW

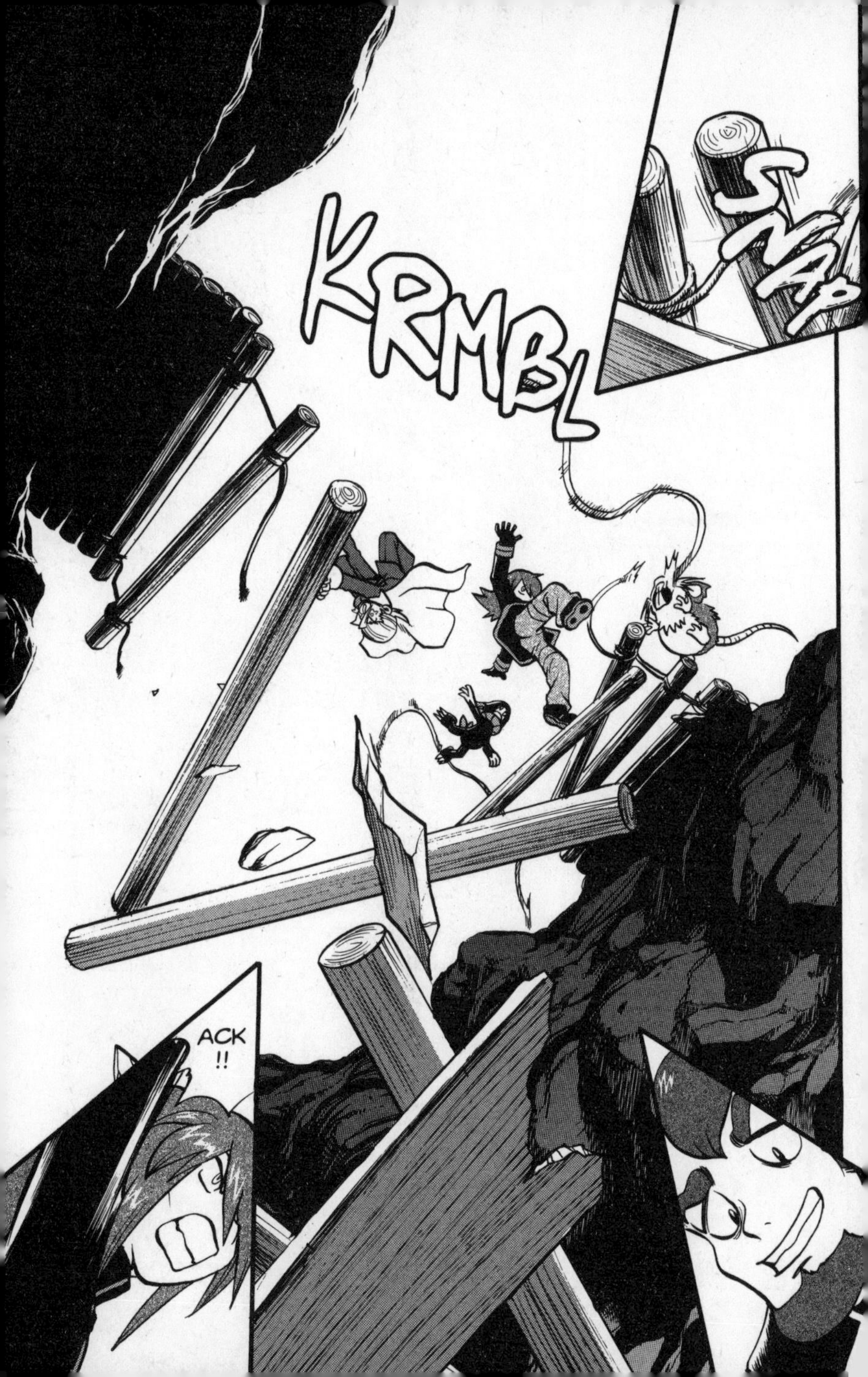
SNAP
KRMBL
ACK !!

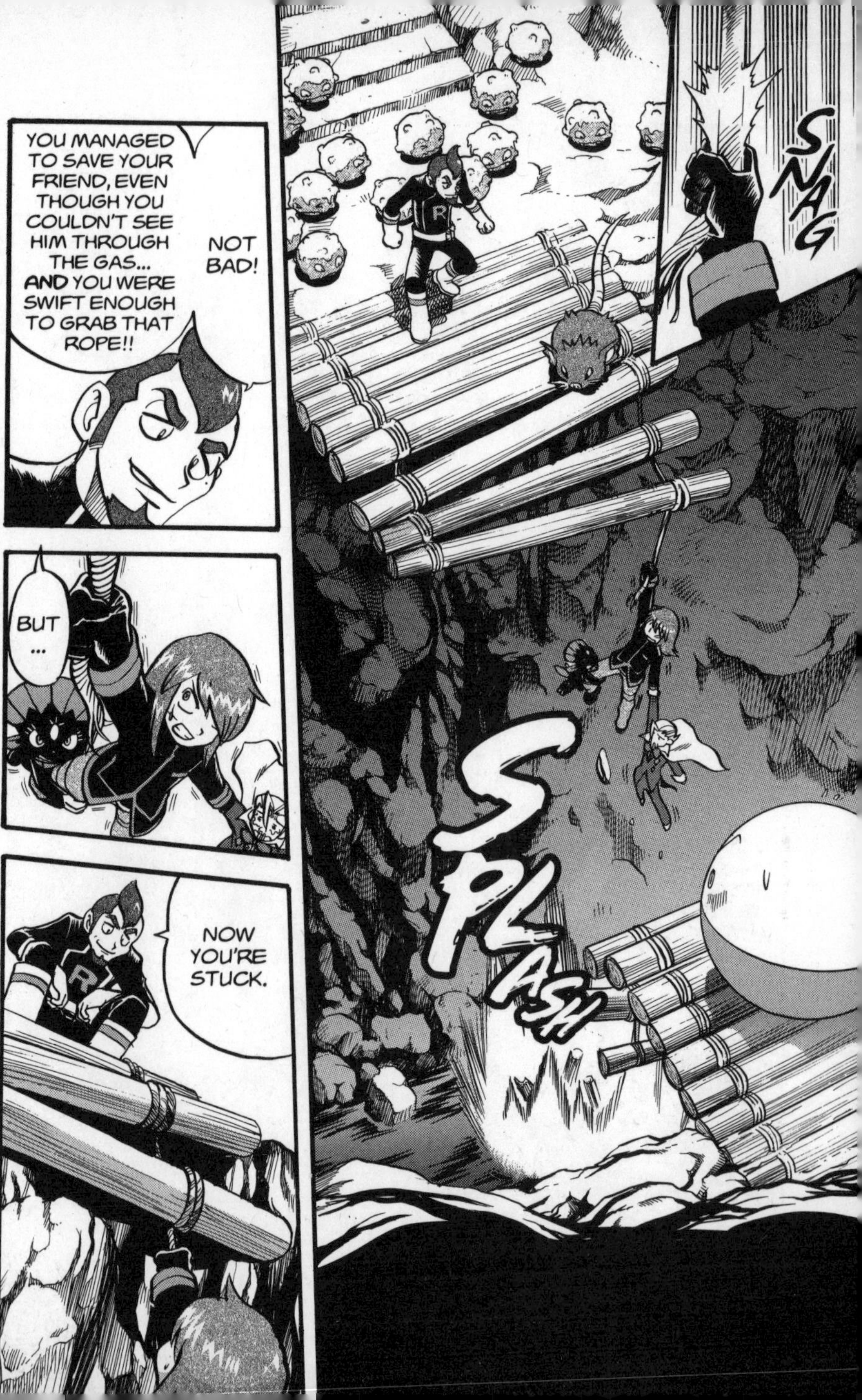
SNAG
SPLASH
YOU MANAGED TO SAVE YOUR FRIEND, EVEN THOUGH YOU COULDN'T SEE HIM THROUGH THE GAS... **AND** YOU WERE SWIFT ENOUGH TO GRAB THAT ROPE!!
NOT BAD!
BUT ...
NOW YOU'RE STUCK.

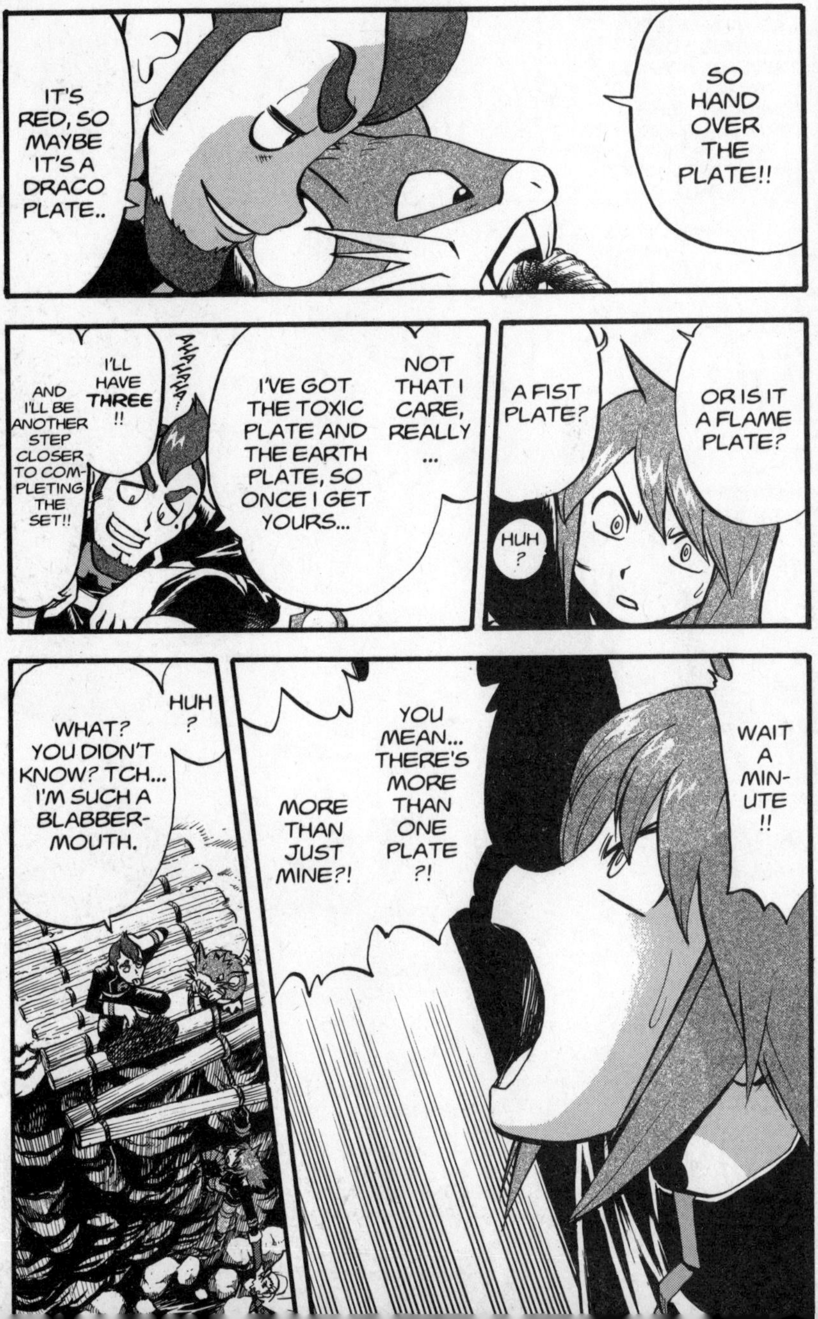
SO HAND OVER THE PLATE!!
IT'S RED, SO MAYBE IT'S A DRACO PLATE..
OR IS IT A FLAME PLATE?
A FIST PLATE?
HUH?
NOT THAT I CARE, REALLY...
I'VE GOT THE TOXIC PLATE AND THE EARTH PLATE, SO ONCE I GET YOURS...
I'LL HAVE THREE!!
AND I'LL BE ANOTHER STEP CLOSER TO COMPLETING THE SET!!
WAIT A MINUTE!!
YOU MEAN... THERE'S MORE THAN ONE PLATE?!
MORE THAN JUST MINE?!
HUH?
WHAT? YOU DIDN'T KNOW? TCH... I'M SUCH A BLABBERMOUTH.

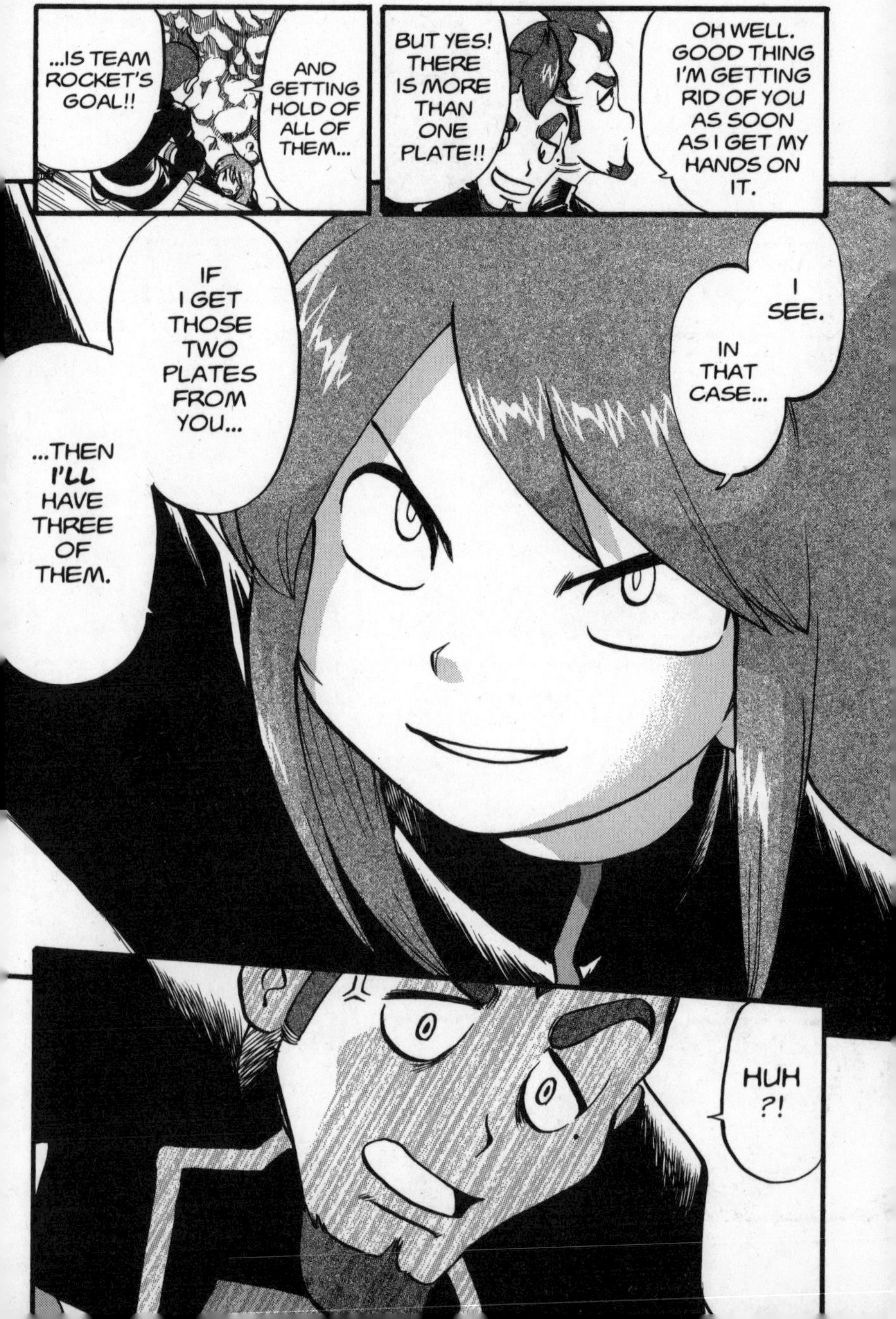
OH WELL. GOOD THING I'M GETTING RID OF YOU AS SOON AS I GET MY HANDS ON IT.
BUT YES! THERE IS MORE THAN ONE PLATE!!
AND GETTING HOLD OF ALL OF THEM...
...IS TEAM ROCKET'S GOAL!!
I SEE.
IN THAT CASE...
IF I GET THOSE TWO PLATES FROM YOU...
...THEN **I'LL** HAVE THREE OF THEM.
HUH?!

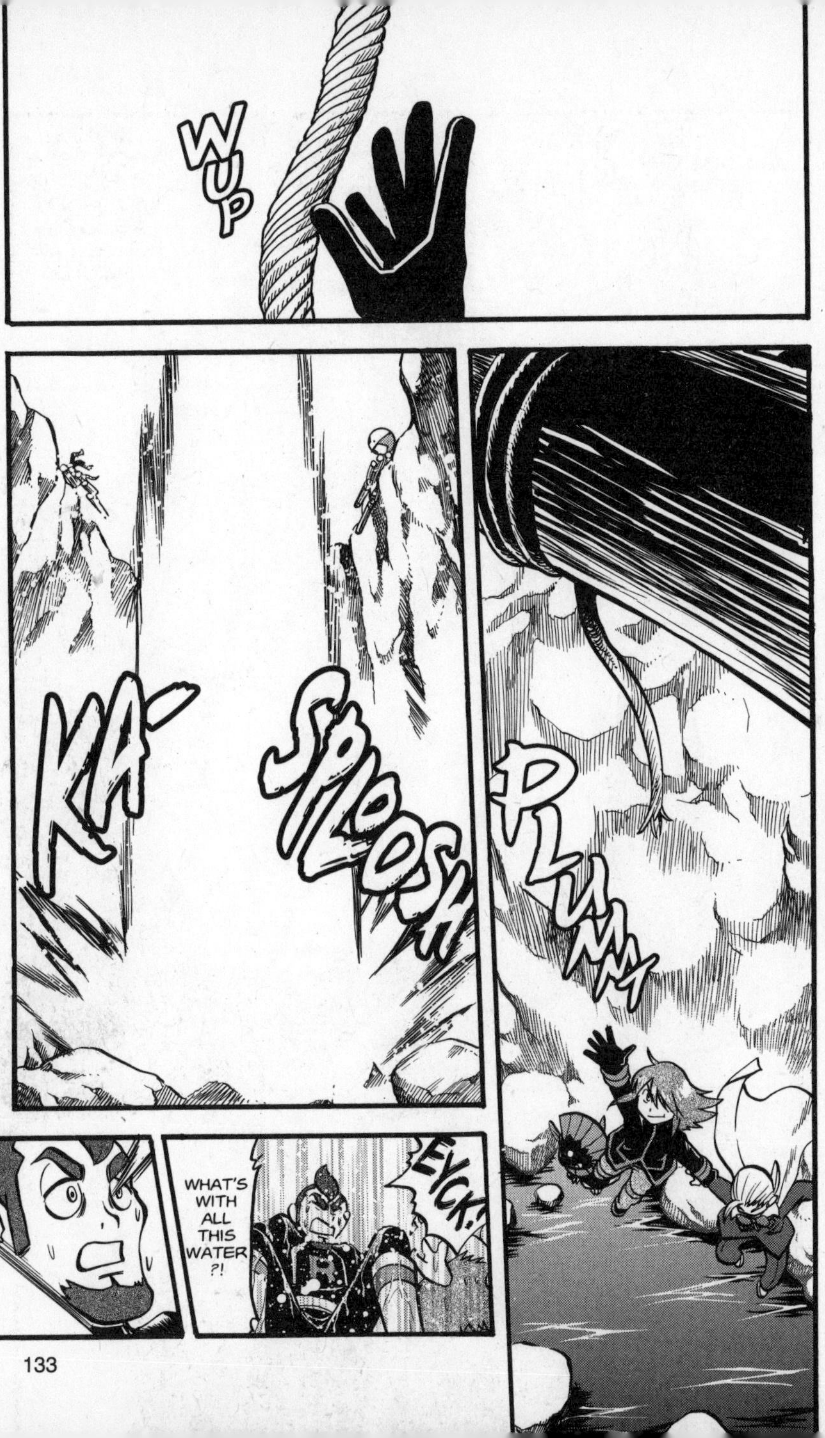
WUP
PLUNNN
KA-
SPLOOSH
EYCK!
WHAT'S WITH ALL THIS WATER?!

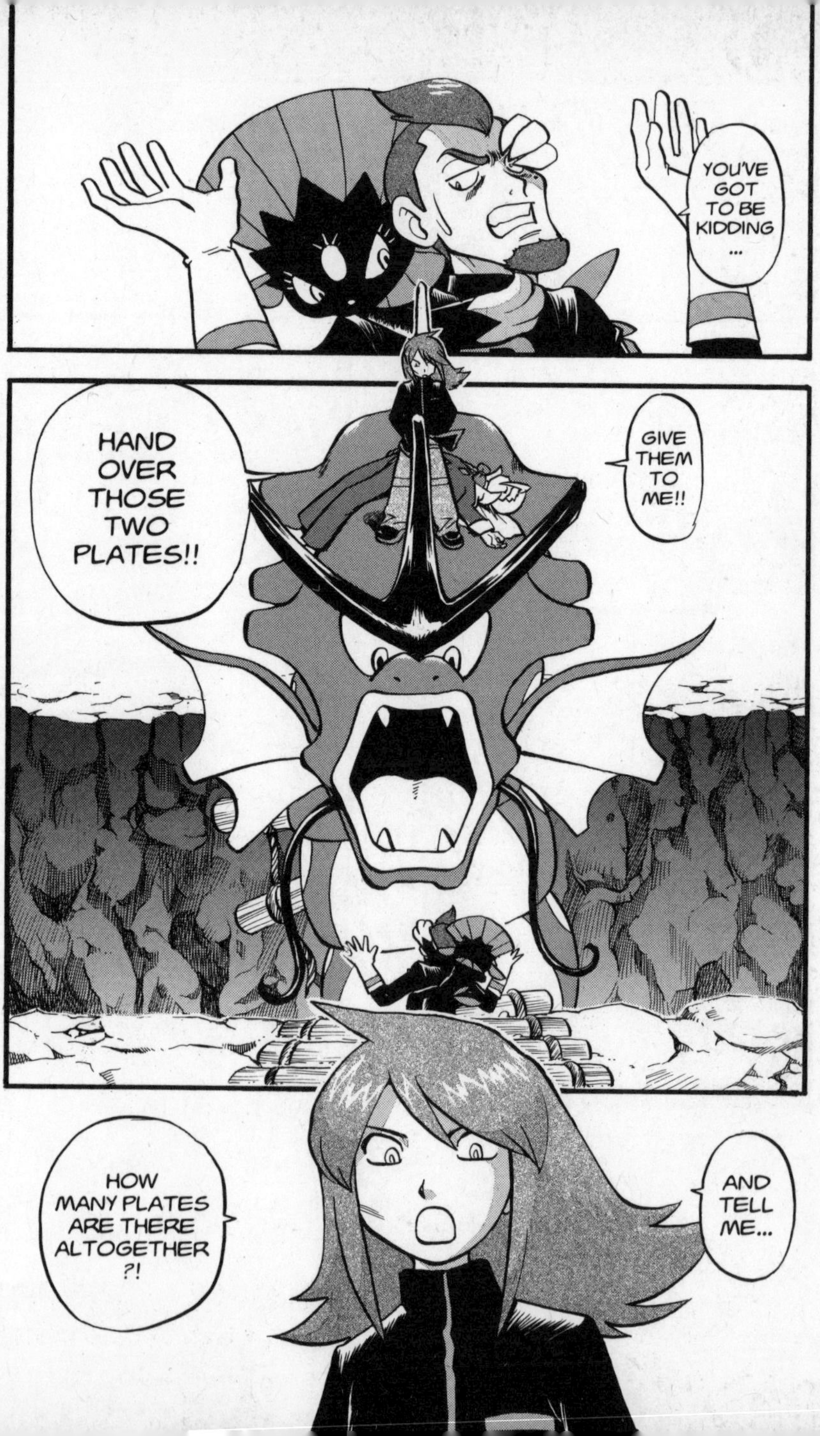
YOU'VE GOT TO BE KIDDING...
GIVE THEM TO ME!!
HAND OVER THOSE TWO PLATES!!
AND TELL ME...
HOW MANY PLATES ARE THERE ALTOGETHER?!

A DETAILED EXPLANATION OF THE POKÉATHLON RULES

SKILL COURSE

SNOW THROW | GOAL ROLL | PENNANT CAPTURE

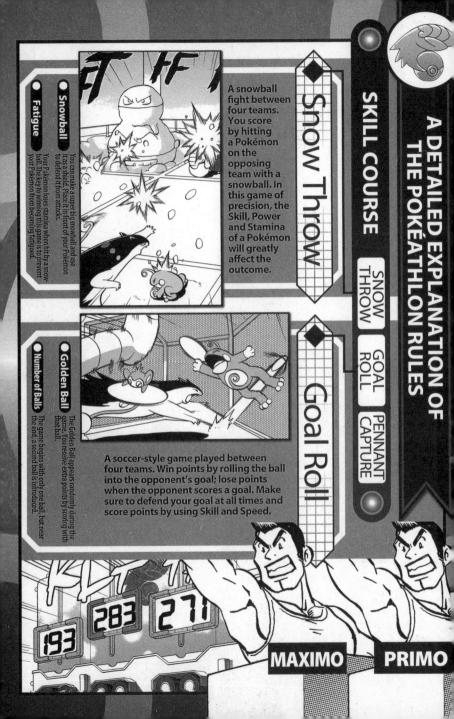

Snow Throw

A snowball fight between four teams. You score by hitting a Pokémon on the opposing team with a snowball. In this game of precision, the Skill, Power and Stamina of a Pokémon will greatly affect the outcome.

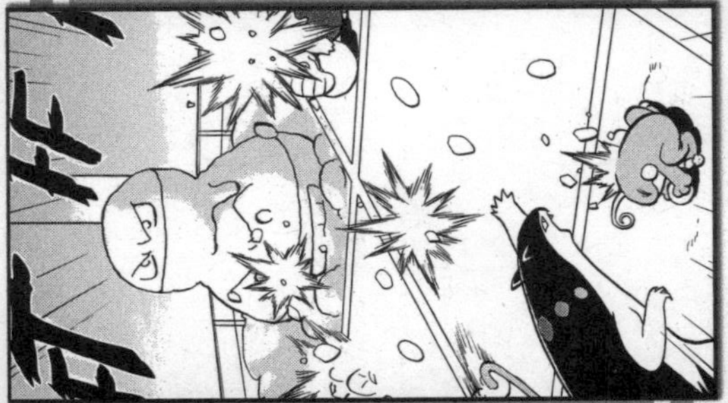

- **Snowball** You can make a super big snowball and use it as a shield. Place it in front of your Pokémon to defend it from attacks.
- **Fatigue** Your Pokémon loses stamina when hit by a snowball. The key to winning this game is to prevent your Pokémon from becoming fatigued.

Goal Roll

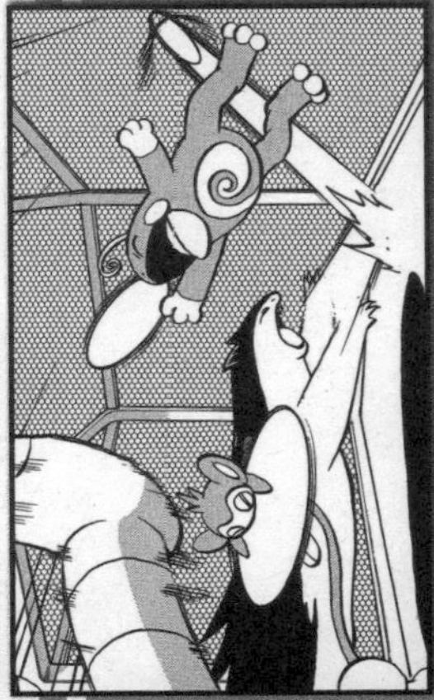

A soccer-style game played between four teams. Win points by rolling the ball into the opponent's goal; lose points when the opponent scores a goal. Make sure to defend your goal at all times and score points by using Skill and Speed.

- **Golden Ball** The Golden Ball appears randomly during the game. You receive extra points by scoring with that ball.
- **Number of Balls** The game begins with only one ball, but near the end, a second ball is introduced.

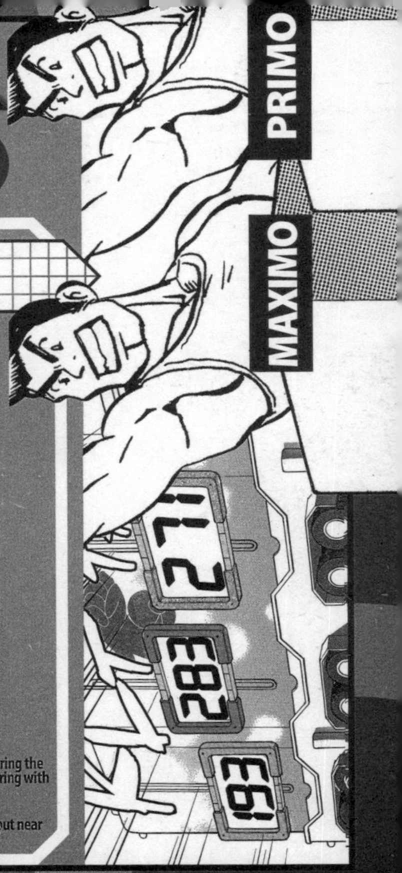
PRIMO
MAXIMO
193
283

Adventure
6
9

FORTUNATELY FOR FERALIGATR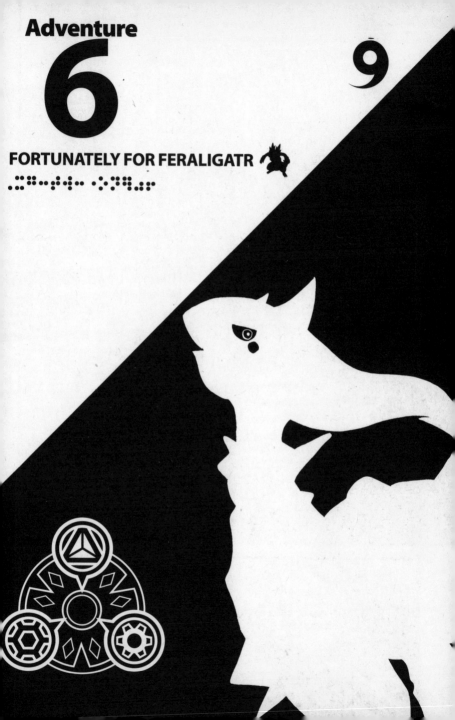

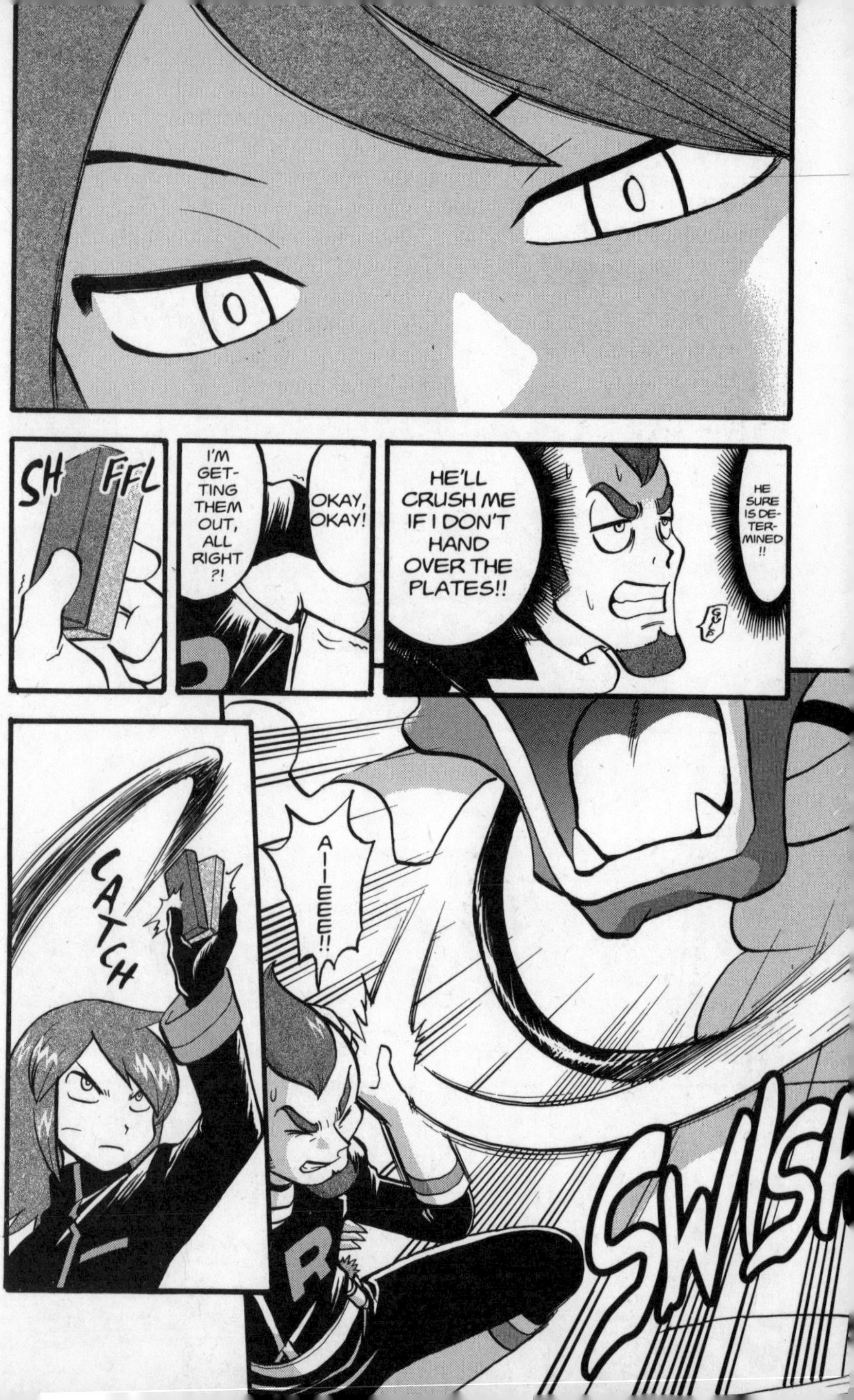
HE SURE IS DE-TERMINED!!
HE'LL CRUSH ME IF I DON'T HAND OVER THE PLATES!!
GULP
OKAY, OKAY!
I'M GET-TING THEM OUT, ALL RIGHT?!
SHFFL
SWISH
AIIEEE!!
CATCH

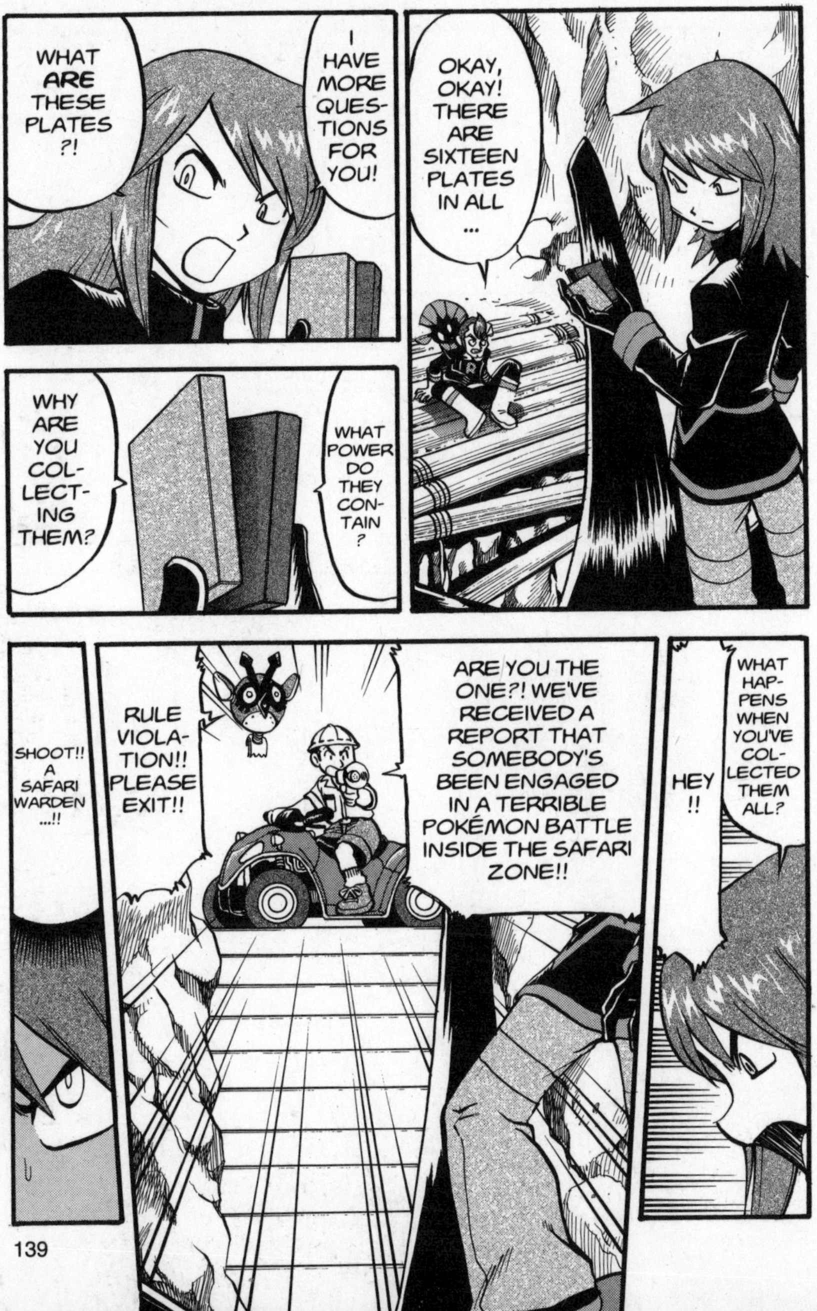
OKAY, OKAY! THERE ARE SIXTEEN PLATES IN ALL ...
I HAVE MORE QUESTIONS FOR YOU!
WHAT **ARE** THESE PLATES?!
WHAT POWER DO THEY CONTAIN?
WHY ARE YOU COLLECTING THEM?
WHAT HAPPENS WHEN YOU'VE COLLECTED THEM ALL?
HEY!!
ARE YOU THE ONE?! WE'VE RECEIVED A REPORT THAT SOMEBODY'S BEEN ENGAGED IN A TERRIBLE POKÉMON BATTLE INSIDE THE SAFARI ZONE!!
RULE VIOLATION!! PLEASE EXIT!!
SHOOT!! A SAFARI WARDEN ...!!

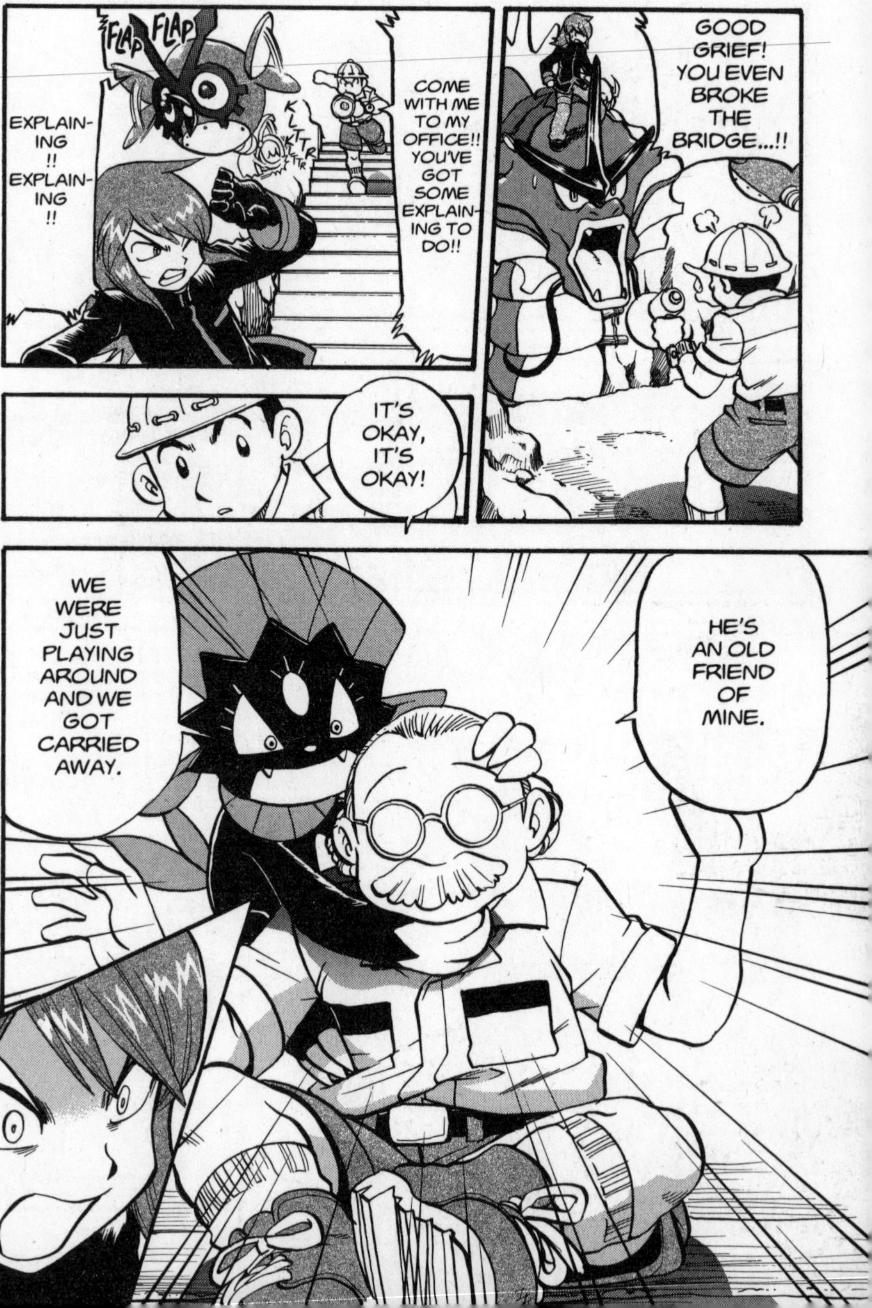
GOOD GRIEF! YOU EVEN BROKE THE BRIDGE...!!
COME WITH ME TO MY OFFICE!! YOU'VE GOT SOME EXPLAINING TO DO!!
FLAP FLAP
EXPLAINING!! EXPLAINING!!
IT'S OKAY, IT'S OKAY!
HE'S AN OLD FRIEND OF MINE.
WE WERE JUST PLAYING AROUND AND WE GOT CARRIED AWAY.

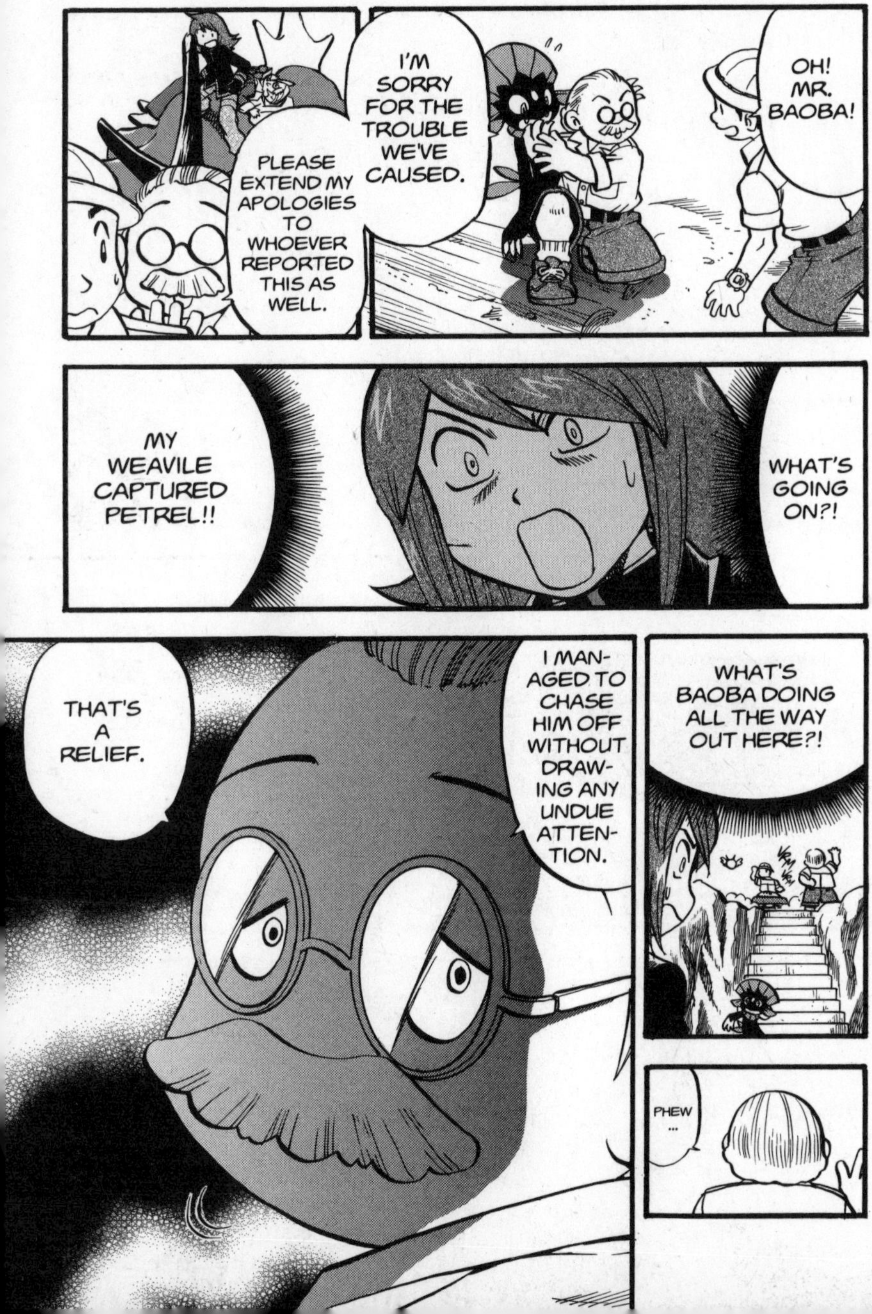
OH! MR. BAOBA!
I'M SORRY FOR THE TROUBLE WE'VE CAUSED.
PLEASE EXTEND MY APOLOGIES TO WHOEVER REPORTED THIS AS WELL.
WHAT'S GOING ON?!
MY WEAVILE CAPTURED PETREL!!
WHAT'S BAOBA DOING ALL THE WAY OUT HERE?!
PHEW...
I MAN-AGED TO CHASE HIM OFF WITHOUT DRAW-ING ANY UNDUE ATTEN-TION.
THAT'S A RELIEF.

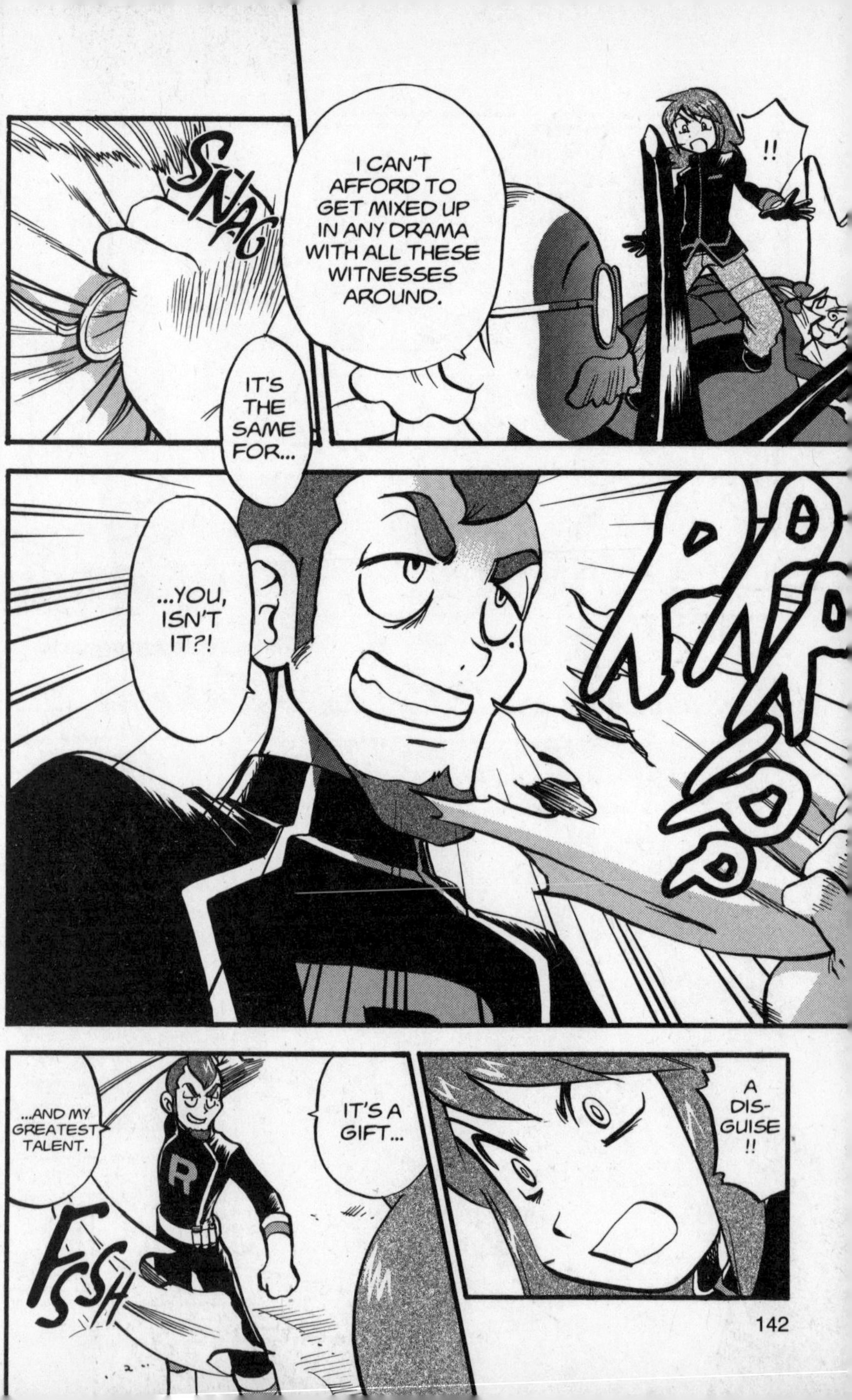
!!
I CAN'T AFFORD TO GET MIXED UP IN ANY DRAMA WITH ALL THESE WITNESSES AROUND.
SNAG
IT'S THE SAME FOR...
...YOU, ISN'T IT?!
A DIS-GUISE!!
IT'S A GIFT...
...AND MY GREATEST TALENT.
FSH

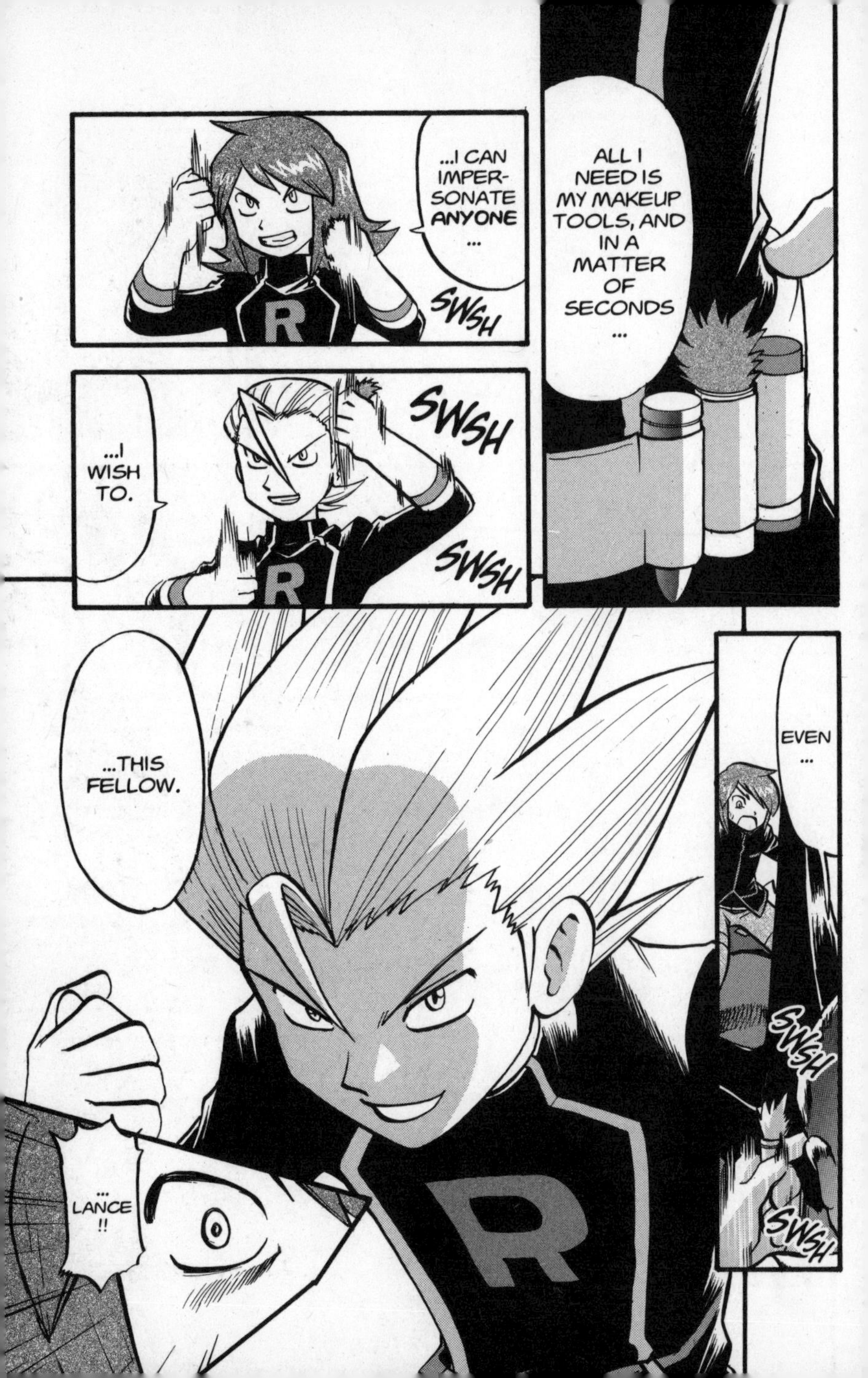
ALL I NEED IS MY MAKEUP TOOLS, AND IN A MATTER OF SECONDS ...
...I CAN IMPERSONATE ANYONE ...
SWSH
...I WISH TO.
SWSH
SWSH
EVEN ...
SWSH
SWSH
...THIS FELLOW.
... LANCE !!

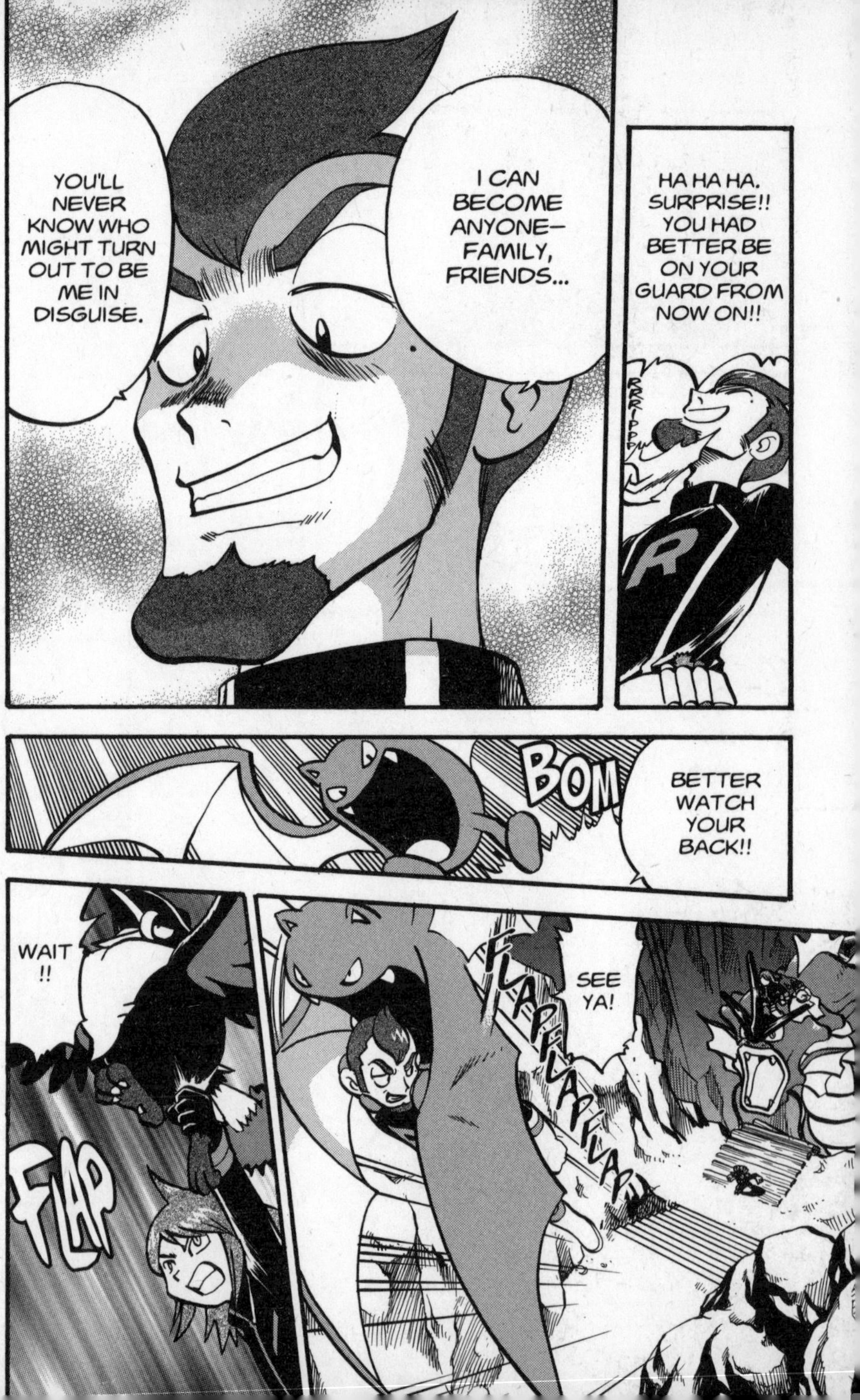
HA HA HA. SURPRISE!! YOU HAD BETTER BE ON YOUR GUARD FROM NOW ON!!
RRRIPPP
I CAN BECOME ANYONE— FAMILY, FRIENDS...
YOU'LL NEVER KNOW WHO MIGHT TURN OUT TO BE ME IN DISGUISE.
BETTER WATCH YOUR BACK!!
BOM
SEE YA!
FLAPFLAPFLAP
WAIT !!
FLAP

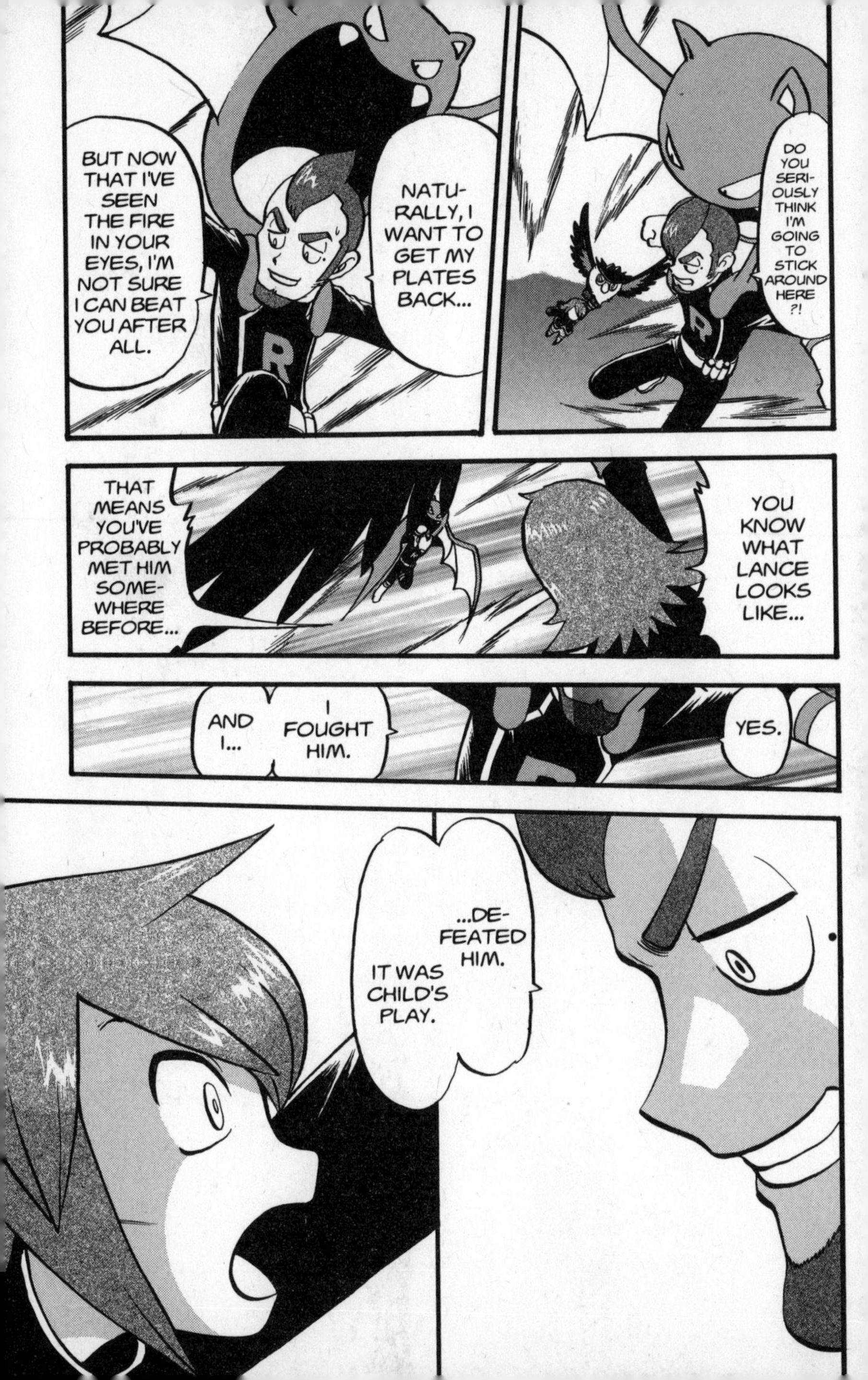
DO YOU SERI-OUSLY THINK I'M GOING TO STICK AROUND HERE ?!
NATU-RALLY, I WANT TO GET MY PLATES BACK...
BUT NOW THAT I'VE SEEN THE FIRE IN YOUR EYES, I'M NOT SURE I CAN BEAT YOU AFTER ALL.
YOU KNOW WHAT LANCE LOOKS LIKE...
THAT MEANS YOU'VE PROBABLY MET HIM SOME-WHERE BEFORE...
YES.
I FOUGHT HIM.
AND I...
...DE-FEATED HIM.
IT WAS CHILD'S PLAY.

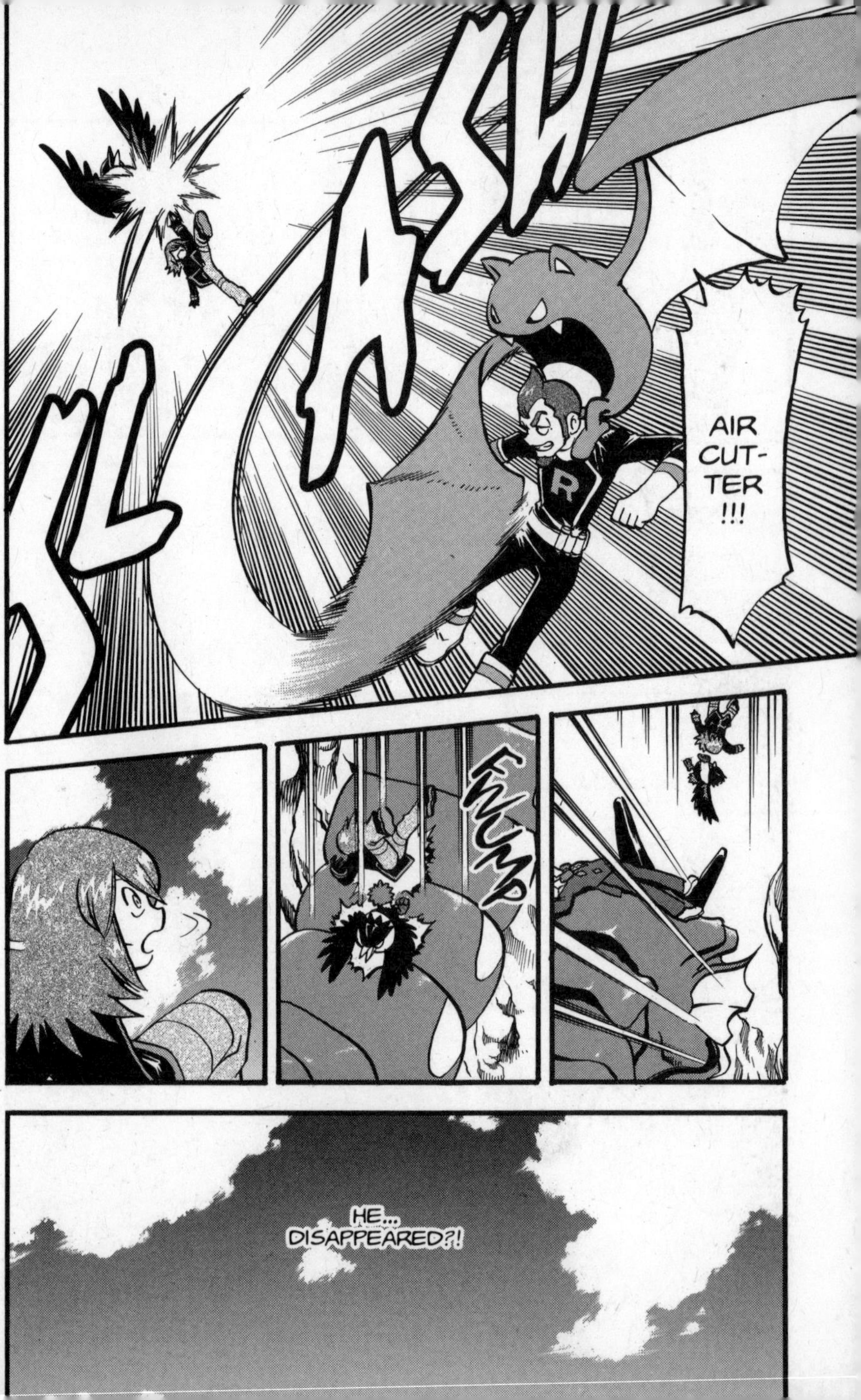
LASH
AIR CUT-TER!!!
FWUMP
HE... DISAPPEARED?!

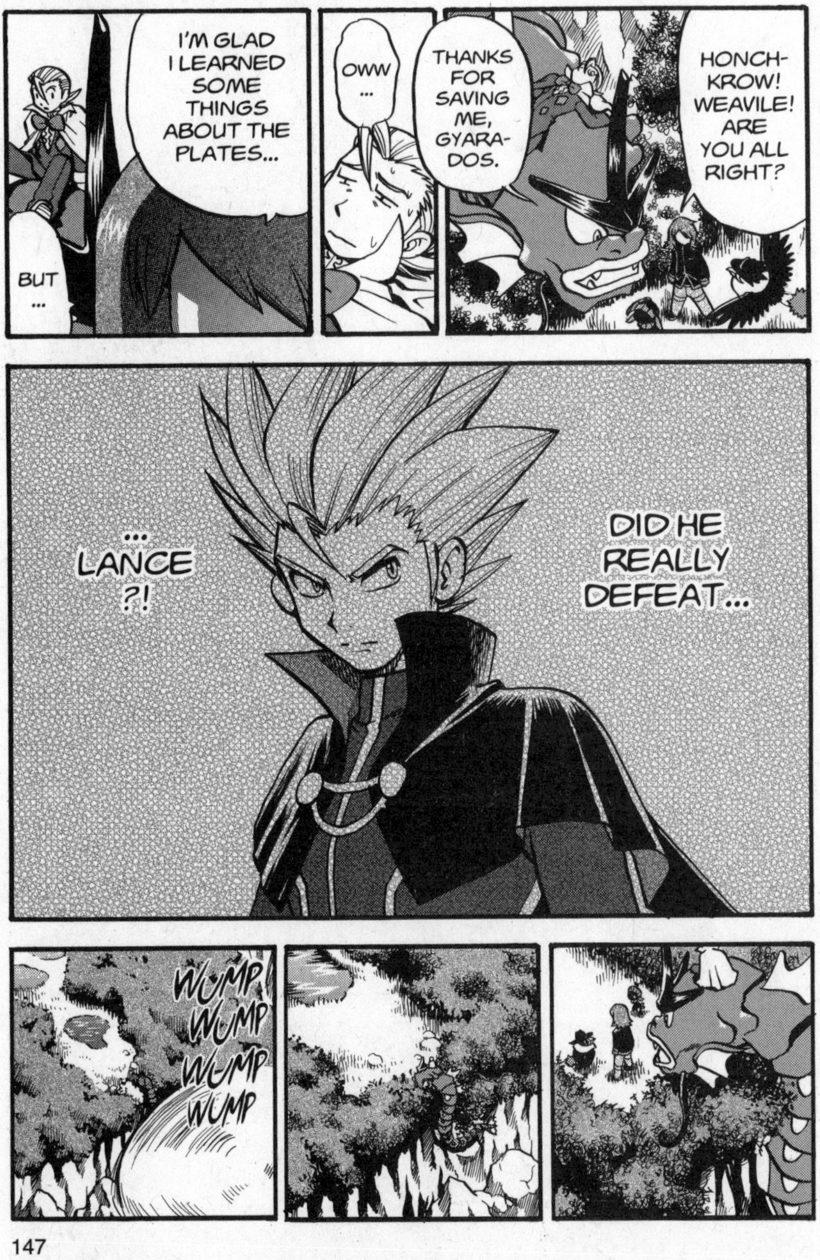
HONCH-KROW! WEAVILE! ARE YOU ALL RIGHT?
THANKS FOR SAVING ME, GYARADOS.
OWW ...
I'M GLAD I LEARNED SOME THINGS ABOUT THE PLATES...
BUT ...
DID HE REALLY DEFEAT...
... LANCE ?!
WUMP WUMP WUMP WUMP

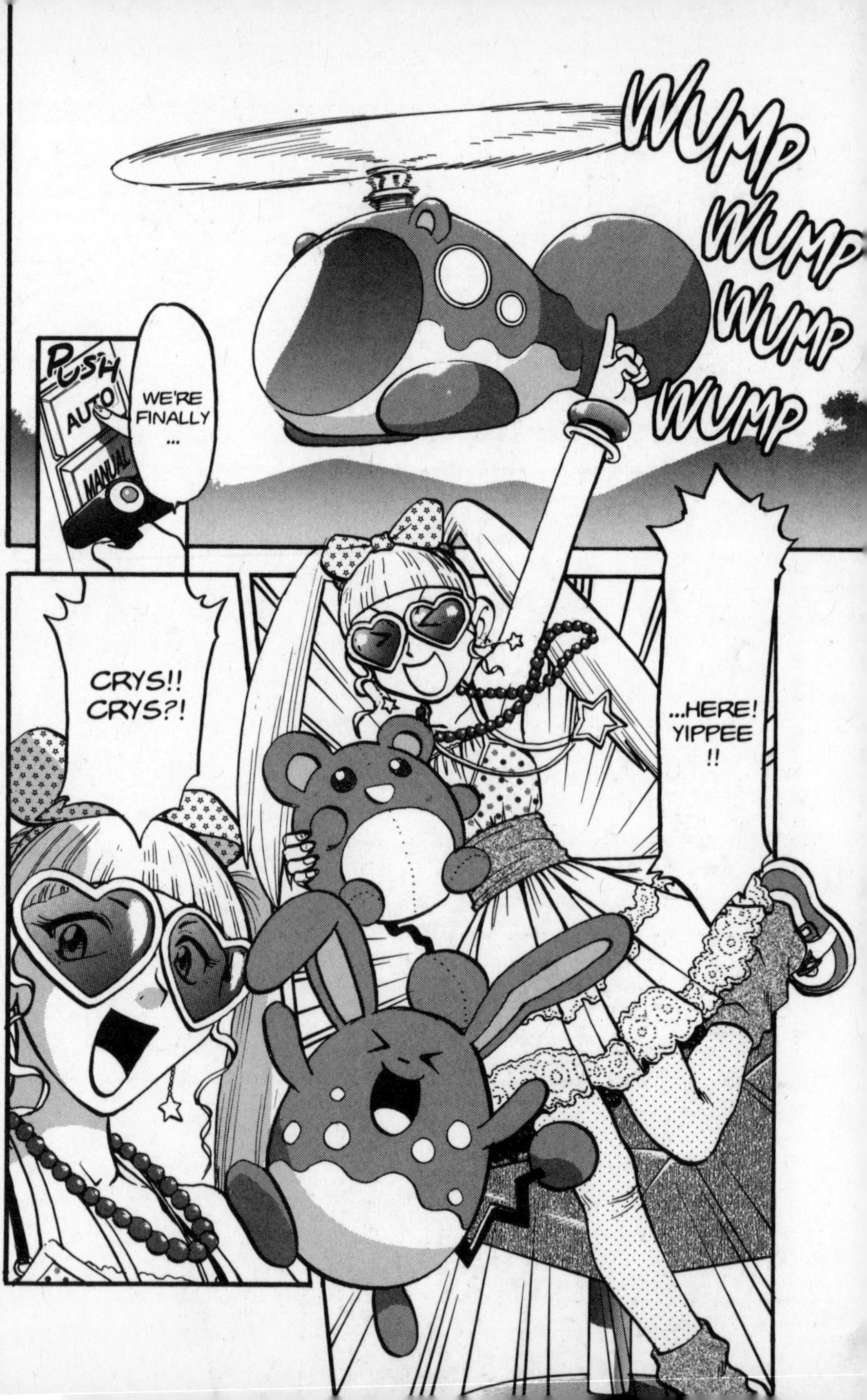
WUMP WUMP WUMP WUMP
PUSH
AUTO
MANUAL
WE'RE FINALLY ...
...HERE! YIPPEE !!
CRYS!! CRYS?!

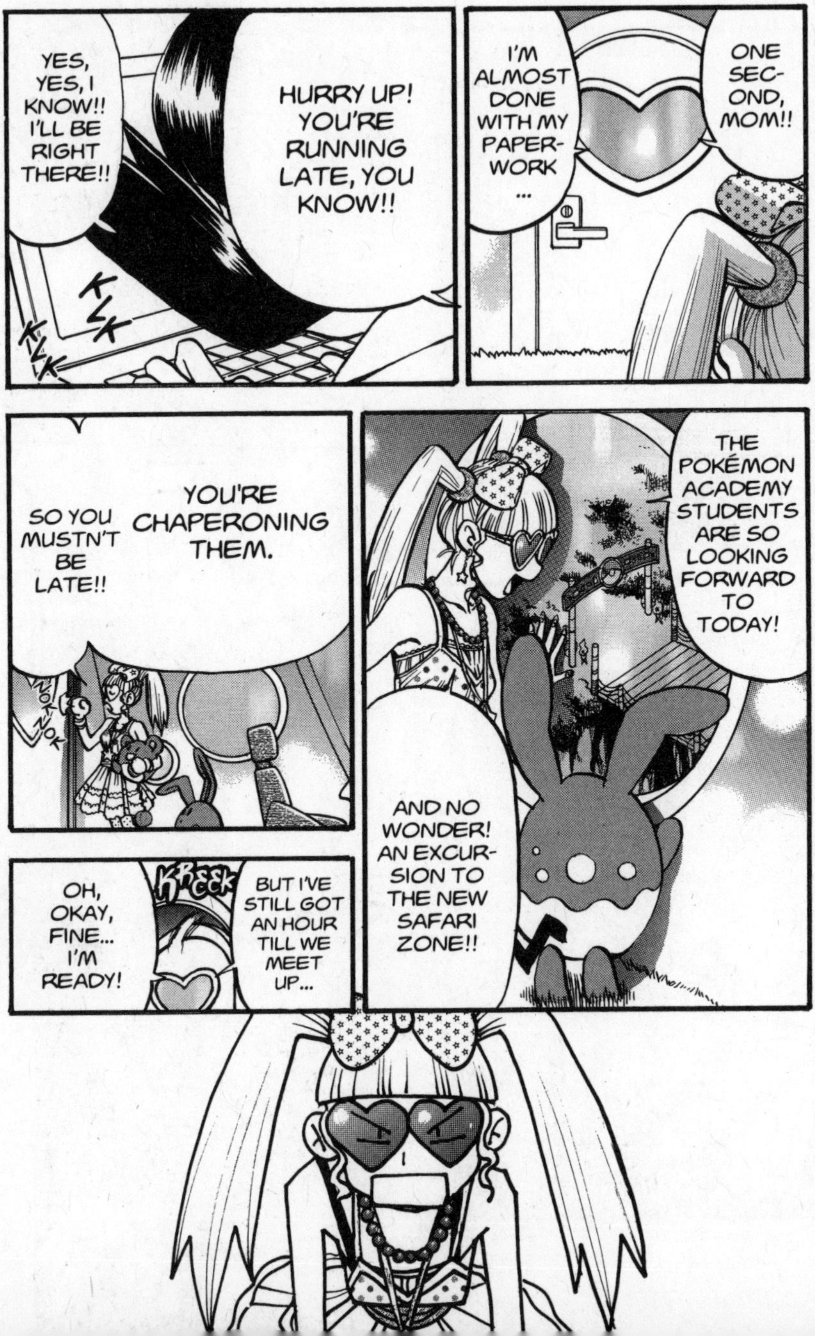
ONE SEC-OND, MOM!!
I'M ALMOST DONE WITH MY PAPER-WORK ...
HURRY UP! YOU'RE RUNNING LATE, YOU KNOW!!
YES, YES, I KNOW!! I'LL BE RIGHT THERE!!
KLIK KLIK
THE POKÉMON ACADEMY STUDENTS ARE SO LOOKING FORWARD TO TODAY!
AND NO WONDER! AN EXCUR-SION TO THE NEW SAFARI ZONE!!
YOU'RE CHAPERONING THEM.
SO YOU MUSTN'T BE LATE!!
NOK NOK
KREEK
BUT I'VE STILL GOT AN HOUR TILL WE MEET UP...
OH, OKAY, FINE... I'M READY!

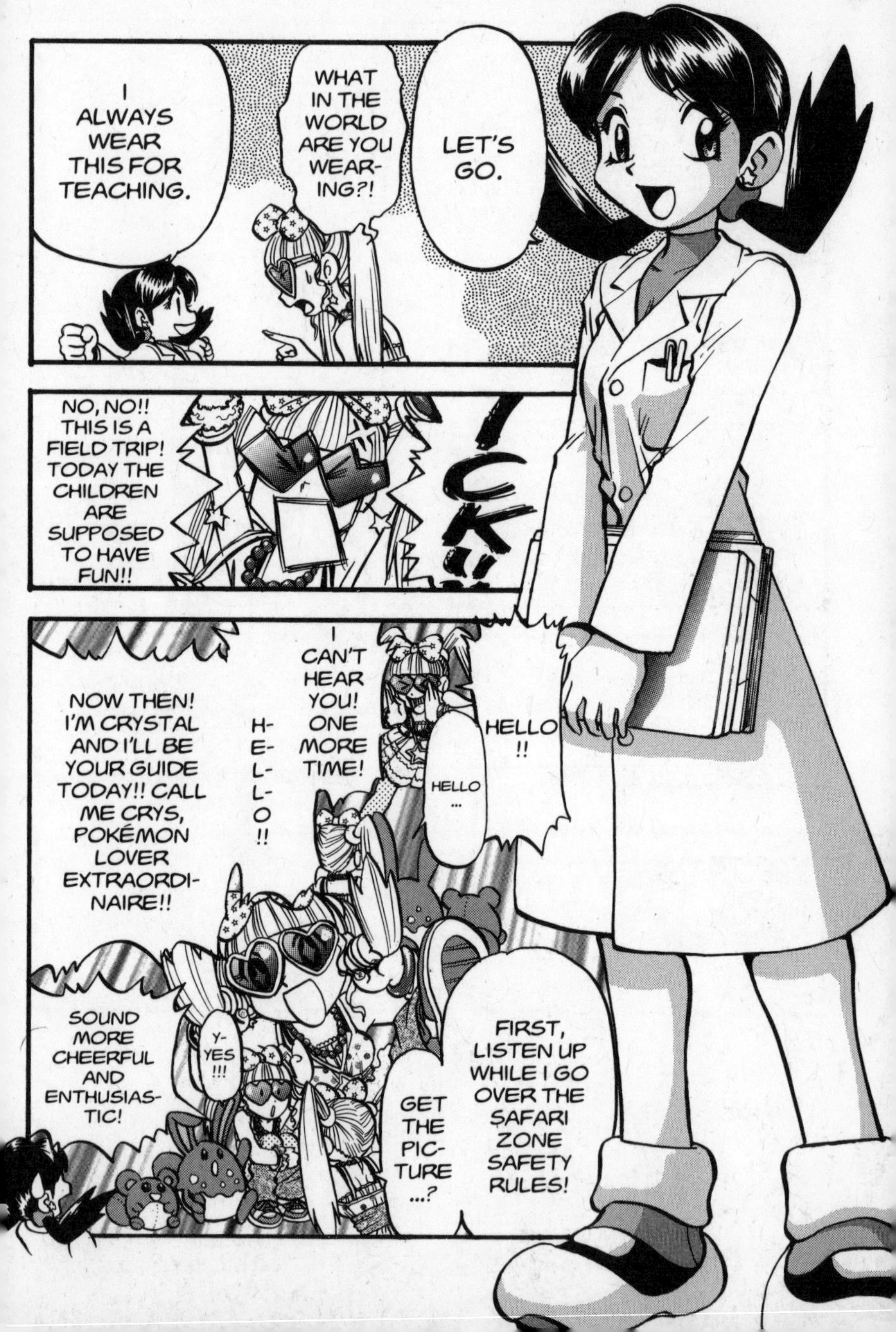
LET'S GO.
WHAT IN THE WORLD ARE YOU WEAR-ING?!
I ALWAYS WEAR THIS FOR TEACHING.
NO, NO!! THIS IS A FIELD TRIP! TODAY THE CHILDREN ARE SUPPOSED TO HAVE FUN!!
HELLO !!
HELLO ...
I CAN'T HEAR YOU! ONE MORE TIME!
H-E-L-L-O !!
NOW THEN! I'M CRYSTAL AND I'LL BE YOUR GUIDE TODAY!! CALL ME CRYS, POKÉMON LOVER EXTRAORDI-NAIRE!!
FIRST, LISTEN UP WHILE I GO OVER THE SAFARI ZONE SAFETY RULES!
GET THE PIC-TURE ...?
Y-YES !!!
SOUND MORE CHEERFUL AND ENTHUSIAS-TIC!

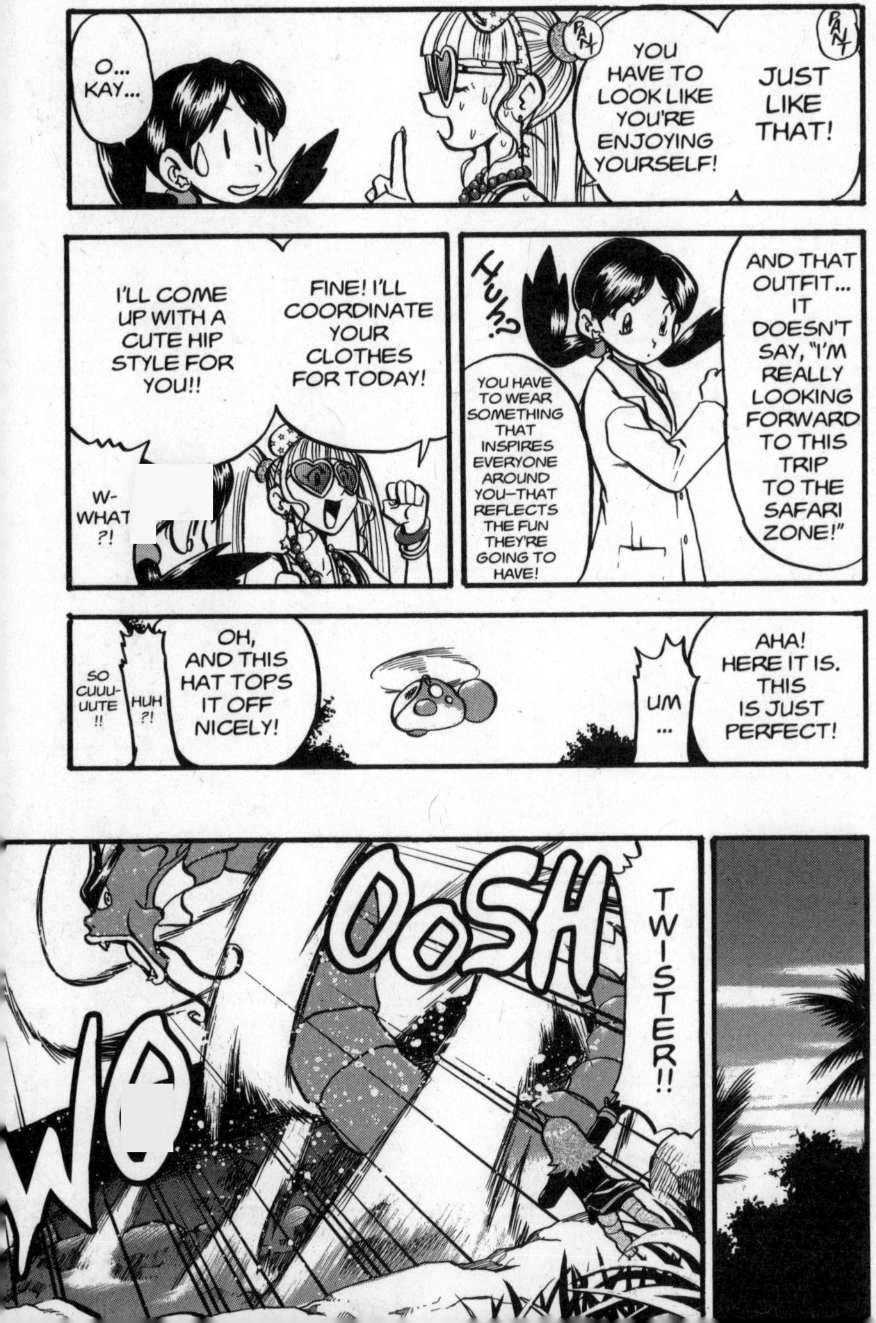
PANT
JUST LIKE THAT!
PANT
YOU HAVE TO LOOK LIKE YOU'RE ENJOYING YOURSELF!
O... KAY...
AND THAT OUTFIT... IT DOESN'T SAY, “I'M REALLY LOOKING FORWARD TO THIS TRIP TO THE SAFARI ZONE!”
YOU HAVE TO WEAR SOMETHING THAT INSPIRES EVERYONE AROUND YOU—THAT REFLECTS THE FUN THEY'RE GOING TO HAVE!
HUH?
FINE! I'LL COORDINATE YOUR CLOTHES FOR TODAY!
I'LL COME UP WITH A CUTE HIP STYLE FOR YOU!!
W-WHAT ?!
AHA! HERE IT IS. THIS IS JUST PERFECT!
UM ...
OH, AND THIS HAT TOPS IT OFF NICELY!
HUH ?!
SO CUUUUUTE !!
TWISTER!!
WO
OOSH

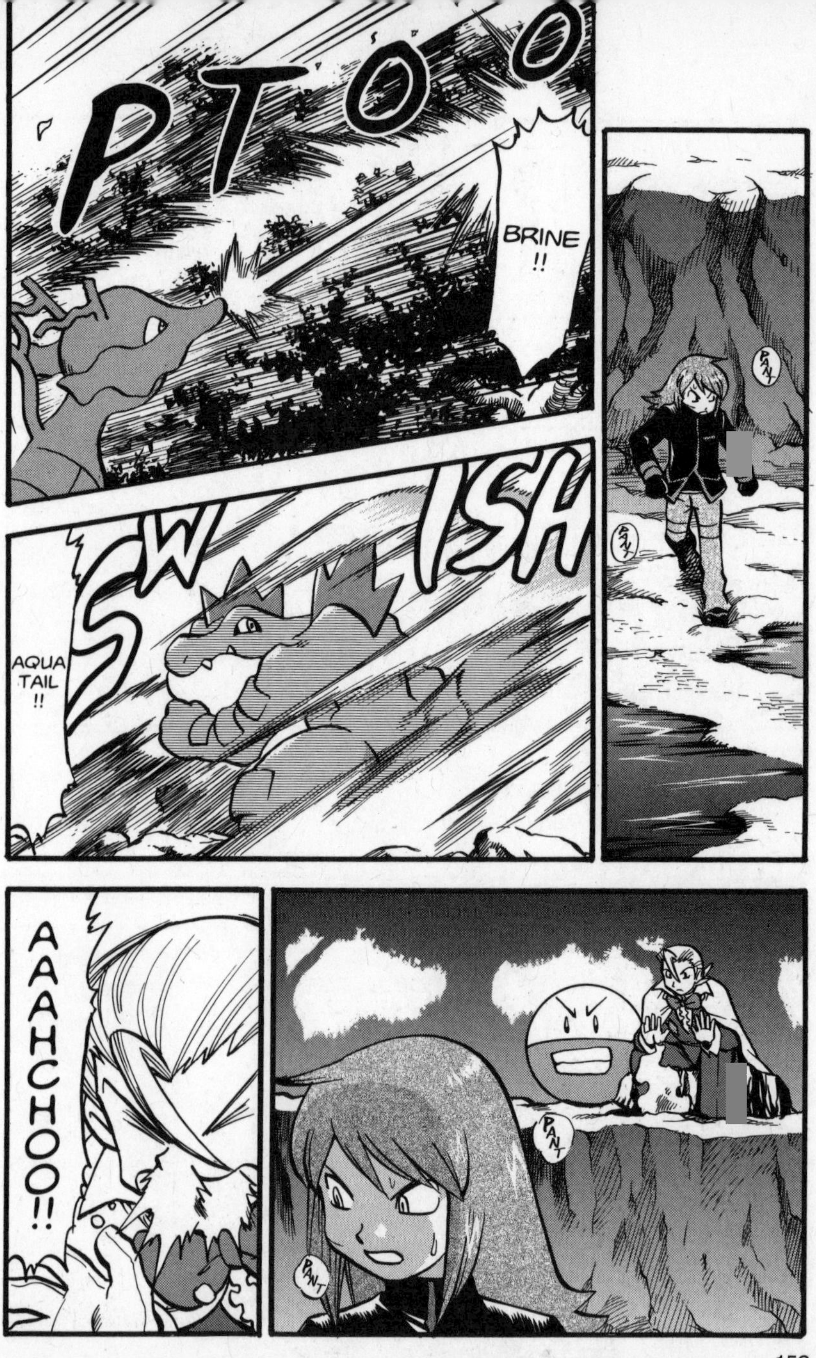
PANT
PANT
PTOOO
BRINE!!
SWISH
AQUA TAIL!!
PANT
PANT
AAAHCHOO!!

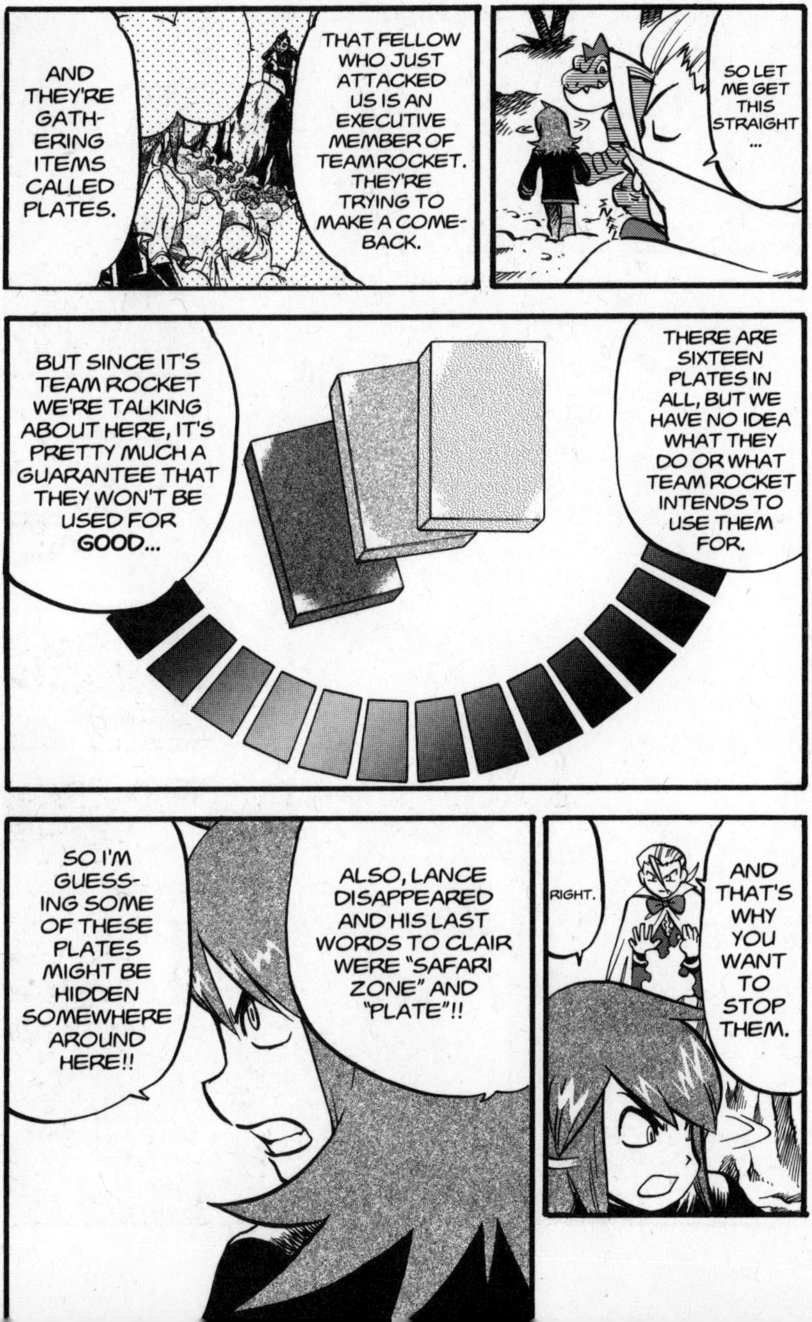
SO LET ME GET THIS STRAIGHT...
THAT FELLOW WHO JUST ATTACKED US IS AN EXECUTIVE MEMBER OF TEAM ROCKET. THEY'RE TRYING TO MAKE A COME-BACK.
AND THEY'RE GATH-ERING ITEMS CALLED PLATES.
THERE ARE SIXTEEN PLATES IN ALL, BUT WE HAVE NO IDEA WHAT THEY DO OR WHAT TEAM ROCKET INTENDS TO USE THEM FOR.
BUT SINCE IT'S TEAM ROCKET WE'RE TALKING ABOUT HERE, IT'S PRETTY MUCH A GUARANTEE THAT THEY WON'T BE USED FOR GOOD...
AND THAT'S WHY YOU WANT TO STOP THEM.
RIGHT.
ALSO, LANCE DISAPPEARED AND HIS LAST WORDS TO CLAIR WERE "SAFARI ZONE" AND "PLATE"!!
SO I'M GUESS-ING SOME OF THESE PLATES MIGHT BE HIDDEN SOMEWHERE AROUND HERE!!

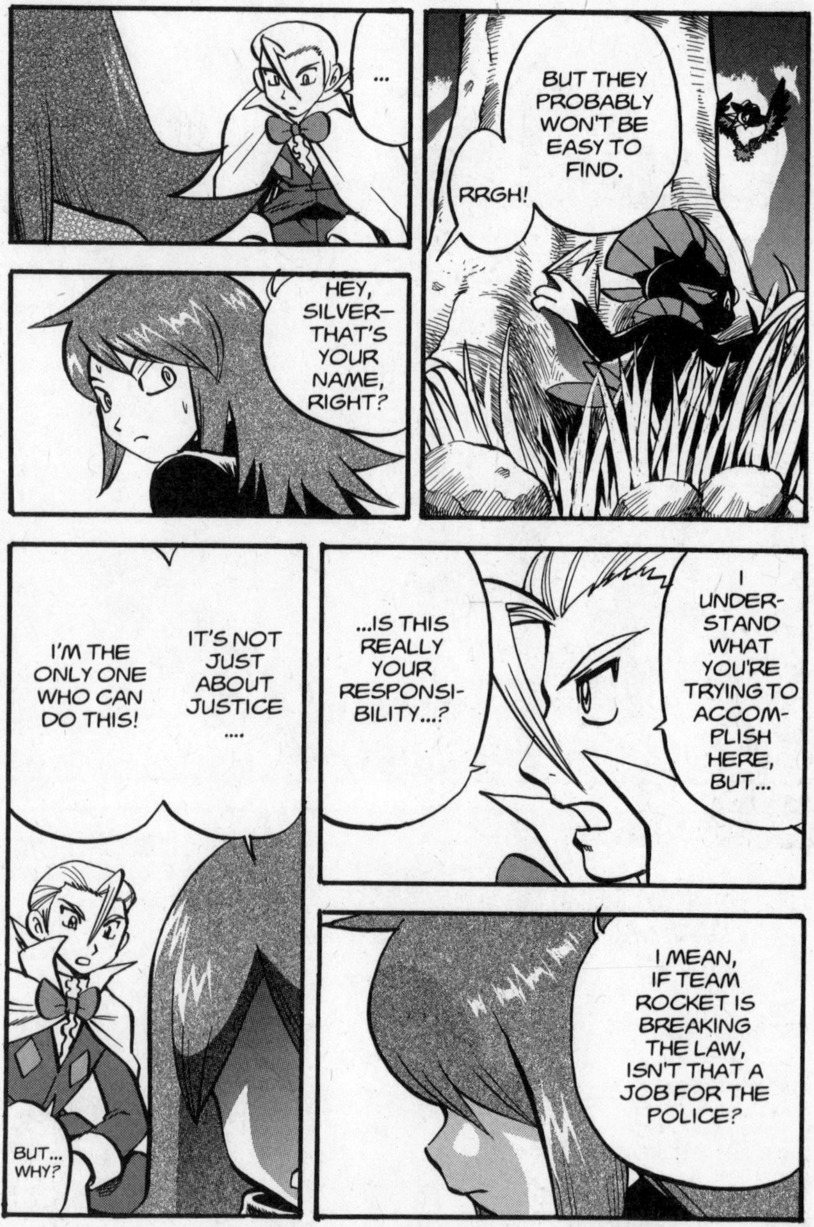
BUT THEY PROBABLY WON'T BE EASY TO FIND.
RRGH!
...
HEY, SILVER—THAT'S YOUR NAME, RIGHT?
I UNDER-STAND WHAT YOU'RE TRYING TO ACCOM-PLISH HERE, BUT...
...IS THIS REALLY YOUR RESPONSI-BILITY...?
I MEAN, IF TEAM ROCKET IS BREAKING THE LAW, ISN'T THAT A JOB FOR THE POLICE?
BUT... WHY?
IT'S NOT JUST ABOUT JUSTICE ....
I'M THE ONLY ONE WHO CAN DO THIS!

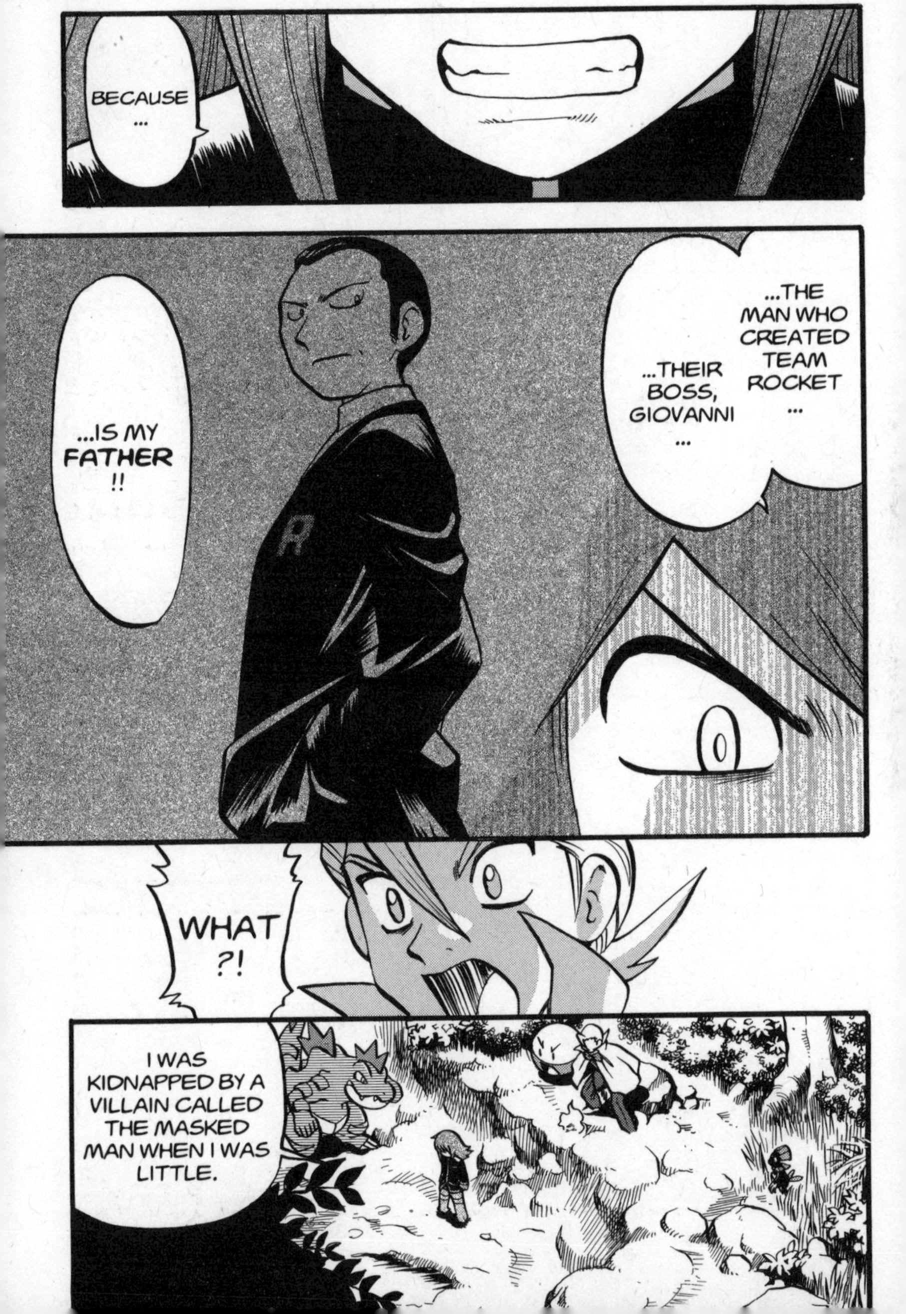
BECAUSE ...
...THE MAN WHO CREATED TEAM ROCKET ...
...THEIR BOSS, GIOVANNI ...
...IS MY FATHER !!
WHAT ?!
I WAS KIDNAPPED BY A VILLAIN CALLED THE MASKED MAN WHEN I WAS LITTLE.

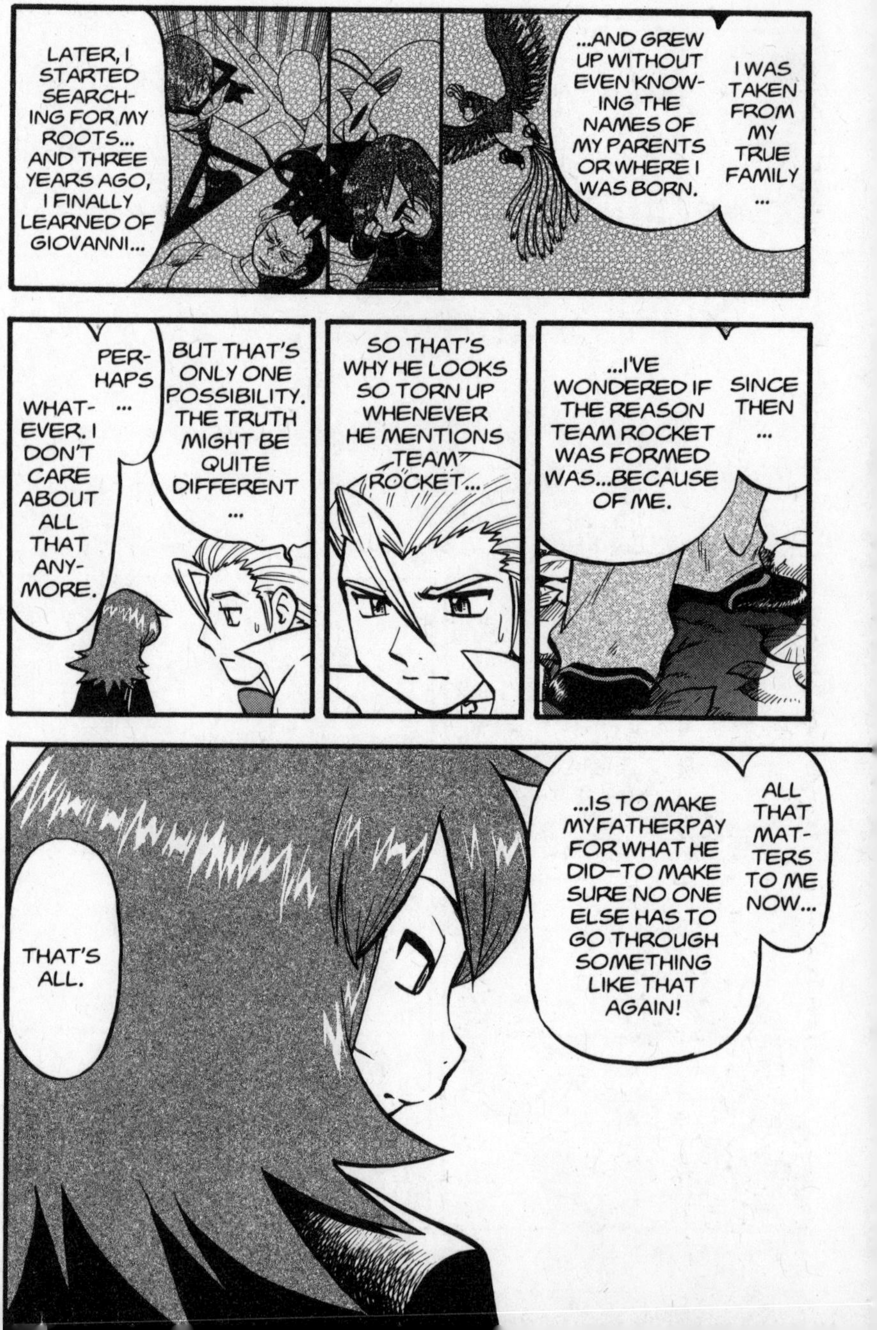
I WAS TAKEN FROM MY TRUE FAMILY...
...AND GREW UP WITHOUT EVEN KNOWING THE NAMES OF MY PARENTS OR WHERE I WAS BORN.
LATER, I STARTED SEARCHING FOR MY ROOTS... AND THREE YEARS AGO, I FINALLY LEARNED OF GIOVANNI...
SINCE THEN...
...I'VE WONDERED IF THE REASON TEAM ROCKET WAS FORMED WAS...BECAUSE OF ME.
SO THAT'S WHY HE LOOKS SO TORN UP WHENEVER HE MENTIONS TEAM ROCKET...
BUT THAT'S ONLY ONE POSSIBILITY. THE TRUTH MIGHT BE QUITE DIFFERENT...
PERHAPS...
WHATEVER. I DON'T CARE ABOUT ALL THAT ANYMORE.
ALL THAT MATTERS TO ME NOW...
...IS TO MAKE MY FATHER PAY FOR WHAT HE DID—TO MAKE SURE NO ONE ELSE HAS TO GO THROUGH SOMETHING LIKE THAT AGAIN!
THAT'S ALL.

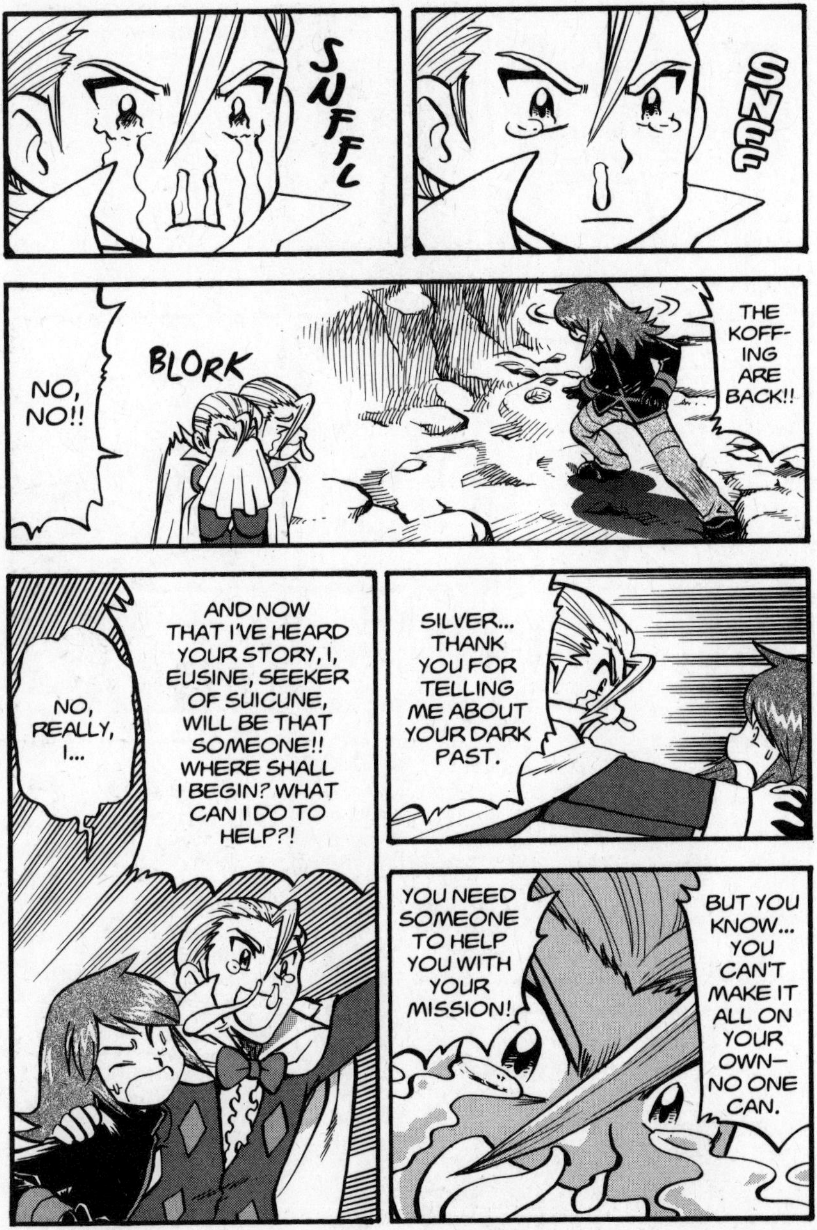
SNFF
SNFFL
THE KOFF-ING ARE BACK!!
BLORK
NO, NO!!
SILVER... THANK YOU FOR TELLING ME ABOUT YOUR DARK PAST.
BUT YOU KNOW... YOU CAN'T MAKE IT ALL ON YOUR OWN—NO ONE CAN.
YOU NEED SOMEONE TO HELP YOU WITH YOUR MISSION!
AND NOW THAT I'VE HEARD YOUR STORY, I, EUSINE, SEEKER OF SUICUNE, WILL BE THAT SOMEONE!! WHERE SHALL I BEGIN? WHAT CAN I DO TO HELP?!
NO, REALLY, I...

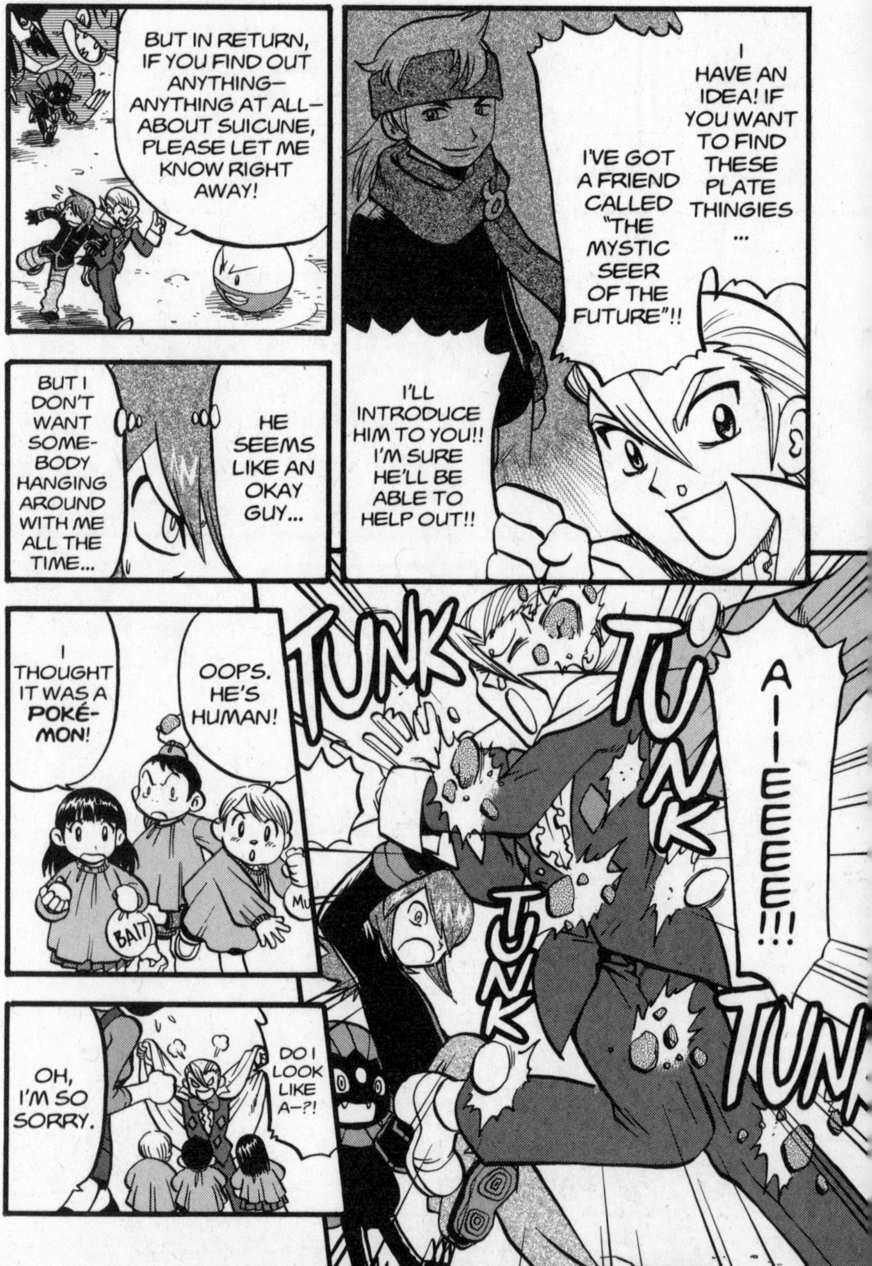
I HAVE AN IDEA! IF YOU WANT TO FIND THESE PLATE THINGIES...
I'VE GOT A FRIEND CALLED "THE MYSTIC SEER OF THE FUTURE"!!
I'LL INTRODUCE HIM TO YOU!! I'M SURE HE'LL BE ABLE TO HELP OUT!!
BUT IN RETURN, IF YOU FIND OUT ANYTHING—ANYTHING AT ALL—ABOUT SUICUNE, PLEASE LET ME KNOW RIGHT AWAY!
HE SEEMS LIKE AN OKAY GUY...
BUT I DON'T WANT SOMEBODY HANGING AROUND WITH ME ALL THE TIME...
A-IIEEEE!!!
TUNK
TUNK
TUNK
TUNK
OOPS. HE'S HUMAN!
I THOUGHT IT WAS A POKÉMON!
BAIT
MU
DO I LOOK LIKE A–?!
OH, I'M SO SORRY.

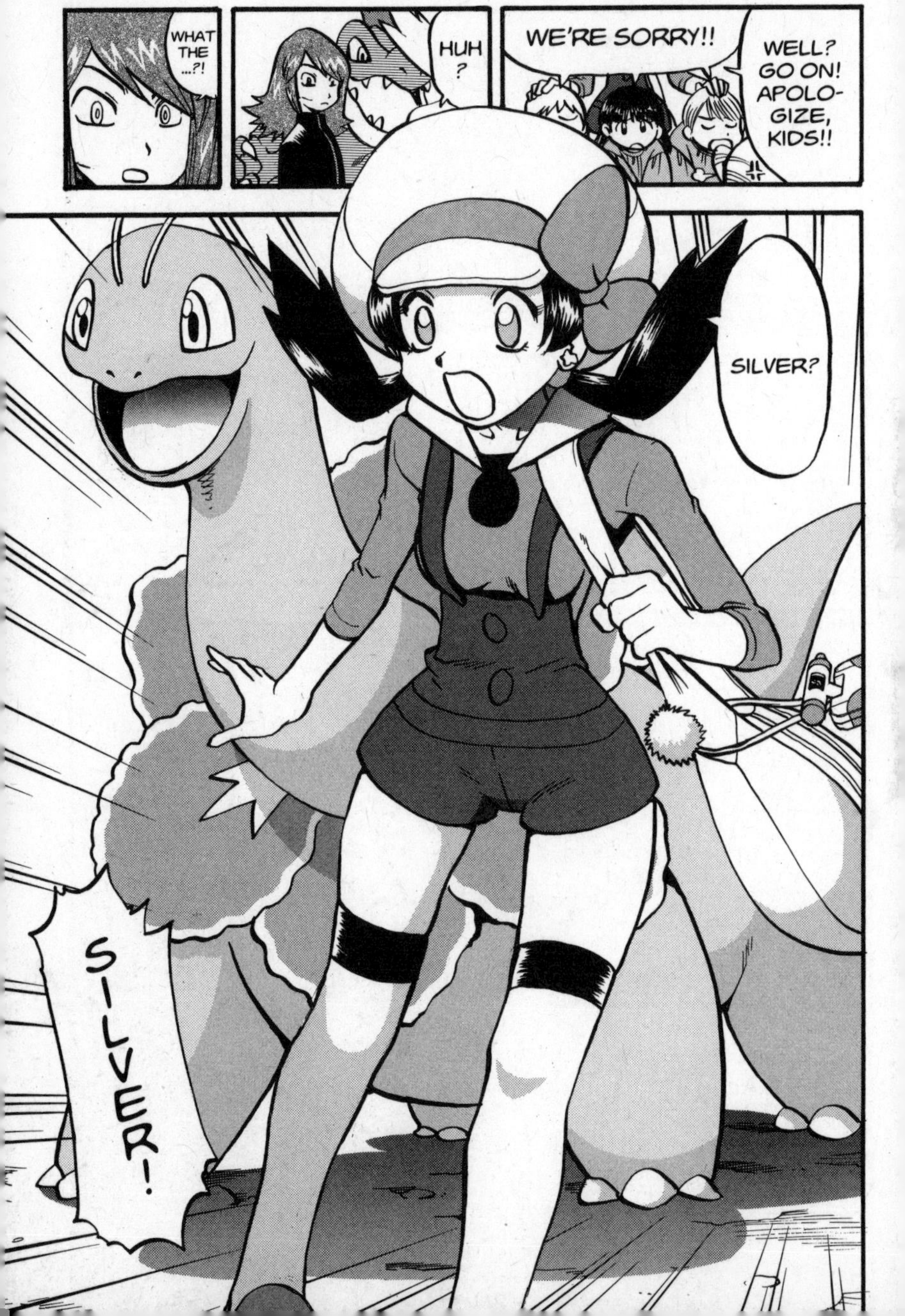
WELL? GO ON! APOLO-GIZE, KIDS!!
WE'RE SORRY!!
HUH ?
WHAT THE ...?!
SILVER?
SILVER!

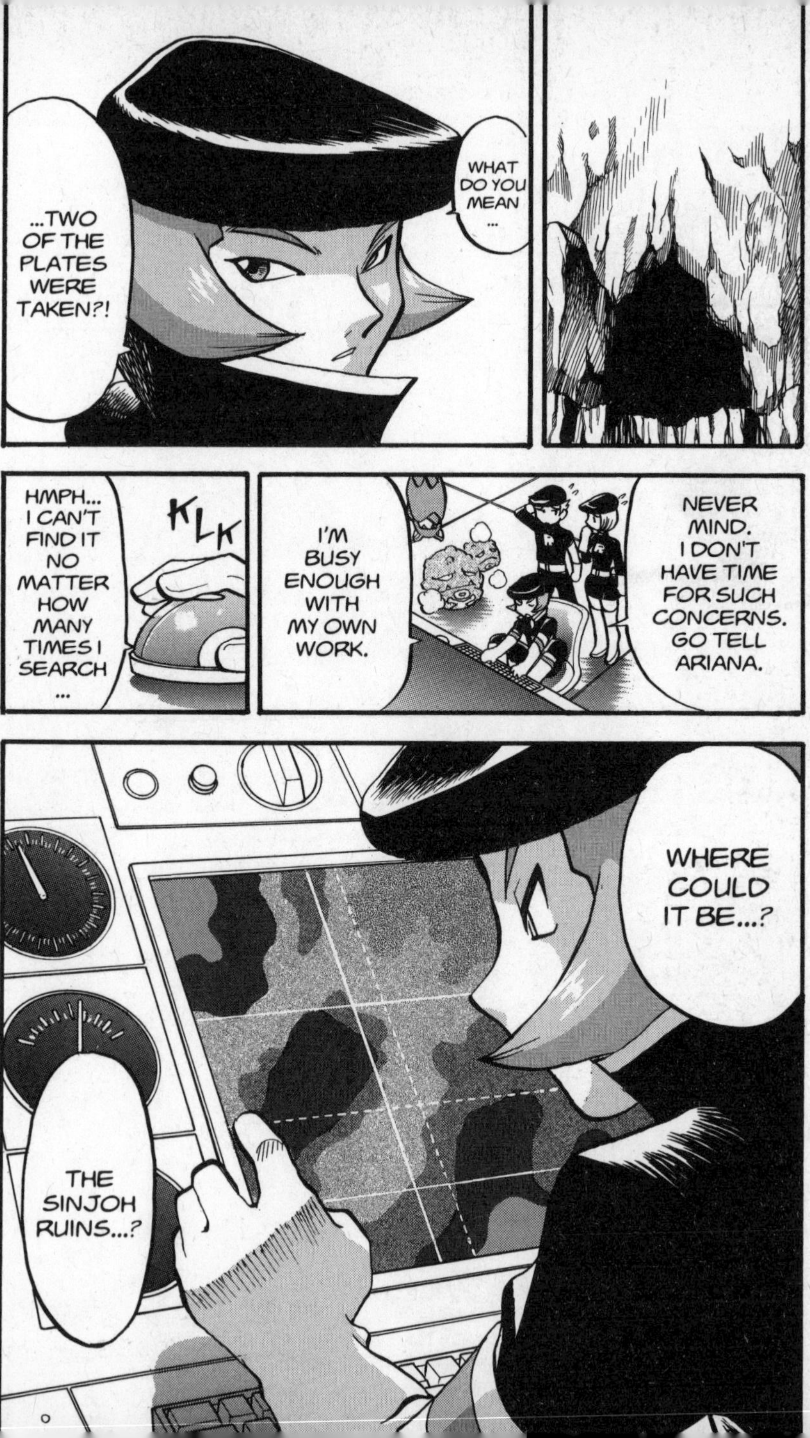
WHAT DO YOU MEAN ...
...TWO OF THE PLATES WERE TAKEN?!
NEVER MIND. I DON'T HAVE TIME FOR SUCH CONCERNS. GO TELL ARIANA.
I'M BUSY ENOUGH WITH MY OWN WORK.
KLK
HMPH... I CAN'T FIND IT NO MATTER HOW MANY TIMES I SEARCH ...
WHERE COULD IT BE...?
THE SINJOH RUINS...?

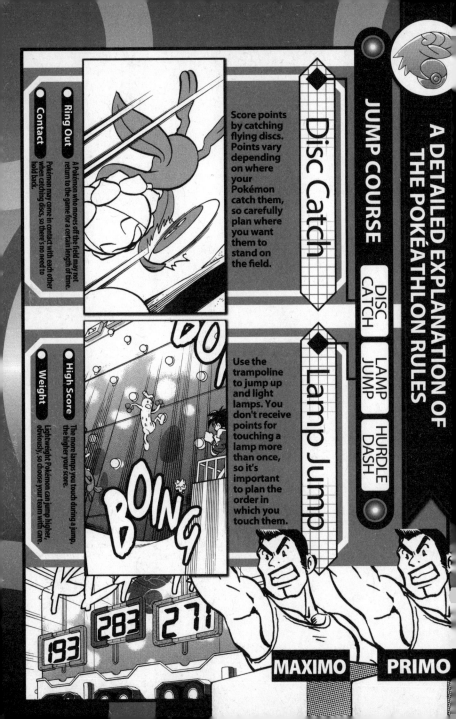

A DETAILED EXPLANATION OF THE POKÉATHLON RULES

JUMP COURSE

DISC CATCH | LAMP JUMP | HURDLE DASH

Disc Catch

Score points by catching flying discs. Points vary depending on where your Pokémon catch them, so carefully plan where you want them to stand on the field.

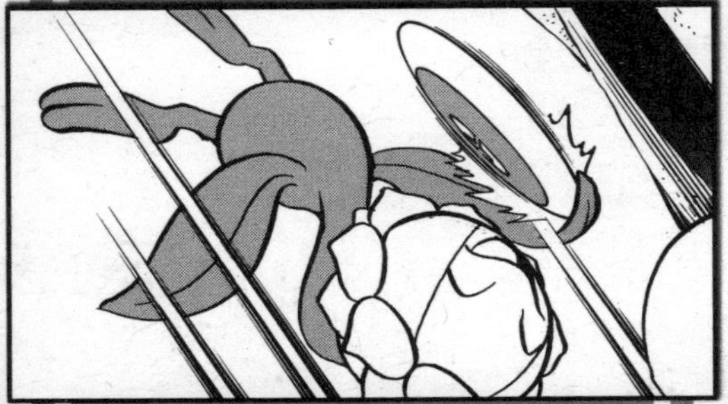

- **Ring Out** A Pokémon who moves off the field may not return to the game for a certain length of time.
- **Contact** Pokémon may come in contact with each other when catching discs, so there's no need to hold back.

Lamp Jump

Use the trampoline to jump up and light lamps. You don't receive points for touching a lamp more than once, so it's important to plan the order in which you touch them.

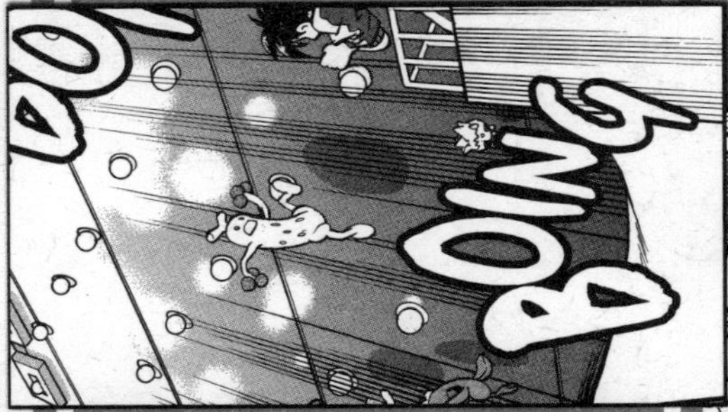
BOING

- **High Score** The more lamps you touch during a jump, the higher your score.
- **Weight** Lightweight Pokémon can jump higher, obviously, so choose your team with care.

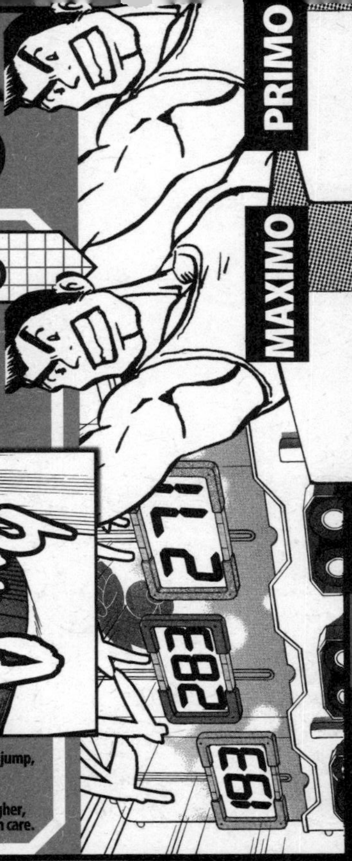
PRIMO
MAXIMO
277
283
193

Adventure 79

PLEASED AS PUNCH WITH PARASECT

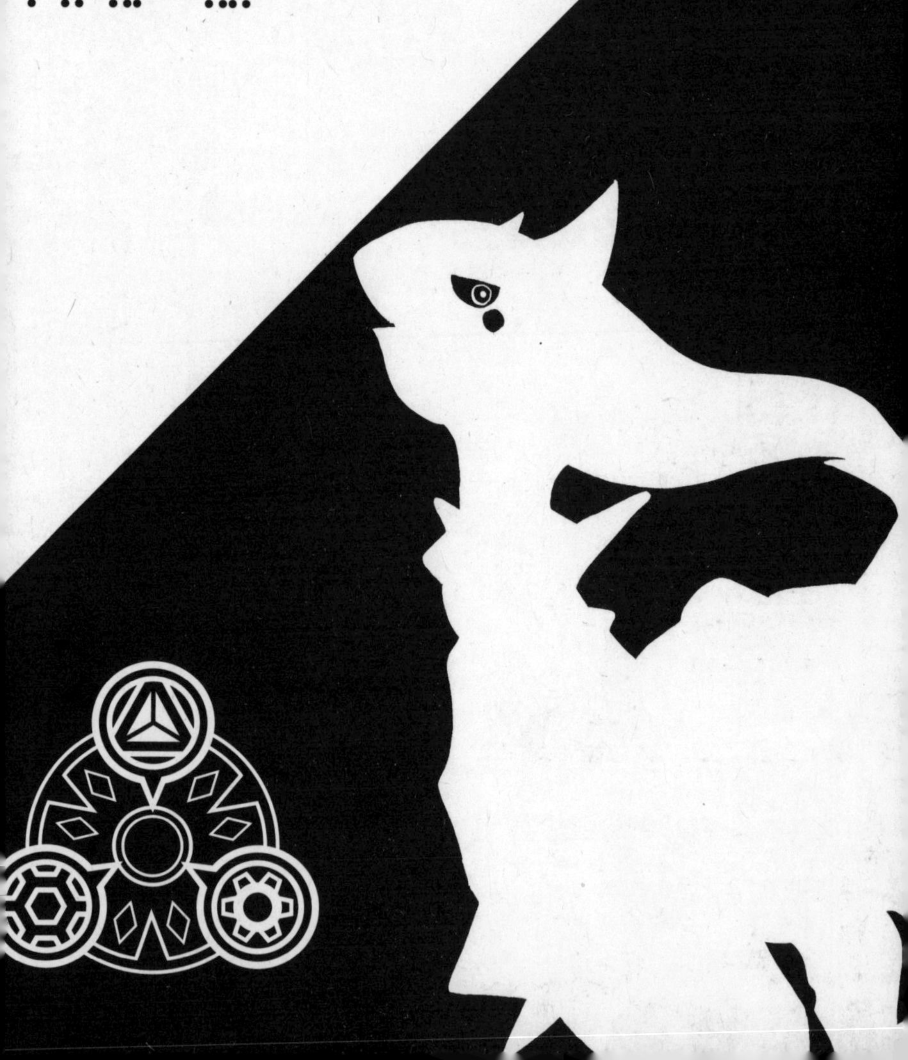

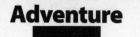

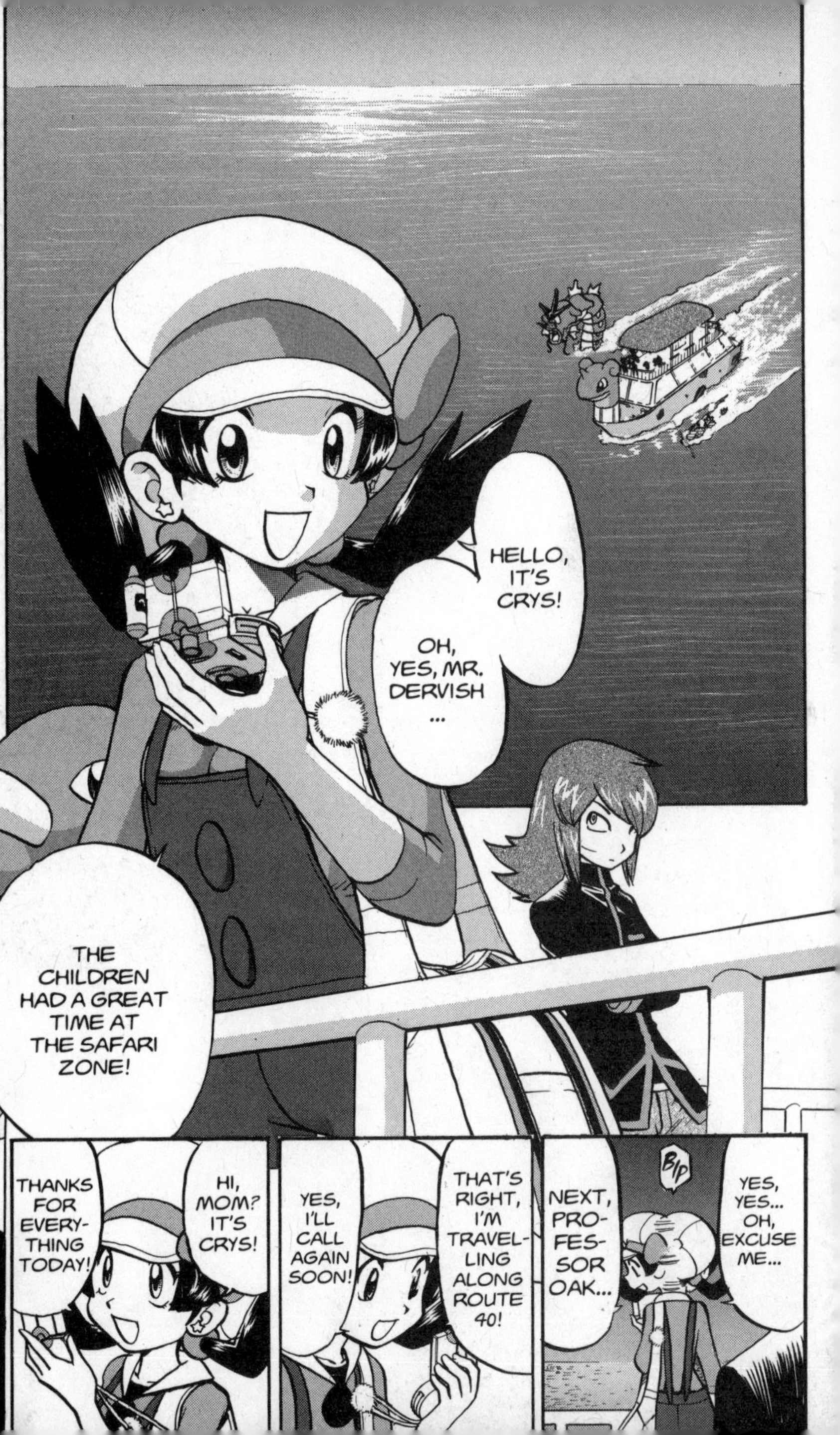
HELLO, IT'S CRYS!
OH, YES, MR. DERVISH ...
THE CHILDREN HAD A GREAT TIME AT THE SAFARI ZONE!
YES, YES... OH, EXCUSE ME...
BIP
NEXT, PROFESSOR OAK...
THAT'S RIGHT, I'M TRAVELLING ALONG ROUTE 40!
YES, I'LL CALL AGAIN SOON!
HI, MOM? IT'S CRYS!
THANKS FOR EVERYTHING TODAY!

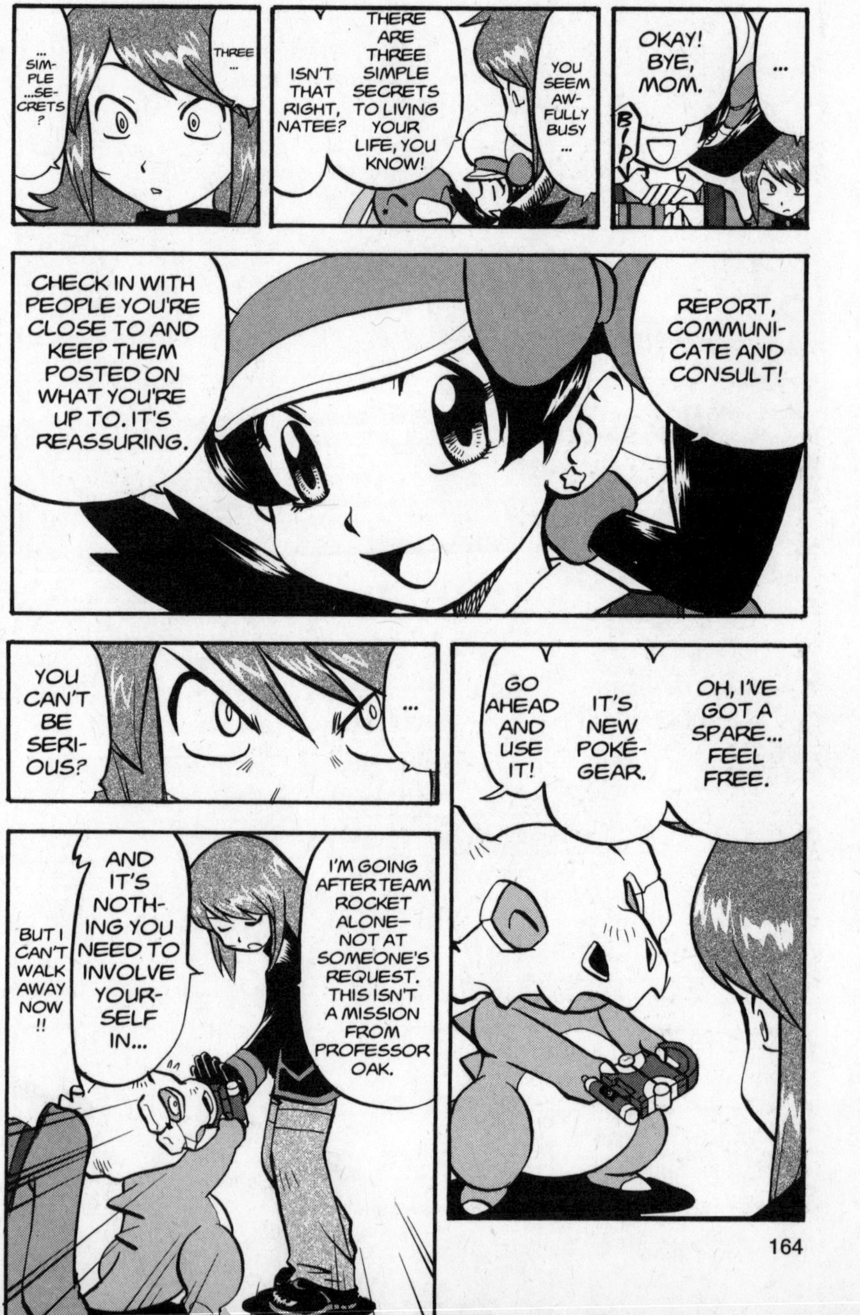
...
OKAY! BYE, MOM.
BIP
YOU SEEM AWFULLY BUSY...
THERE ARE THREE SIMPLE SECRETS TO LIVING YOUR LIFE, YOU KNOW!
ISN'T THAT RIGHT, NATEE?
THREE...
...SIMPLE ...SECRETS?
REPORT, COMMUNICATE AND CONSULT!
CHECK IN WITH PEOPLE YOU'RE CLOSE TO AND KEEP THEM POSTED ON WHAT YOU'RE UP TO. IT'S REASSURING.
OH, I'VE GOT A SPARE... FEEL FREE.
IT'S NEW POKÉGEAR.
GO AHEAD AND USE IT!
...
YOU CAN'T BE SERIOUS?
I'M GOING AFTER TEAM ROCKET ALONE—NOT AT SOMEONE'S REQUEST. THIS ISN'T A MISSION FROM PROFESSOR OAK.
AND IT'S NOTHING YOU NEED TO INVOLVE YOURSELF IN...
BUT I CAN'T WALK AWAY NOW!!

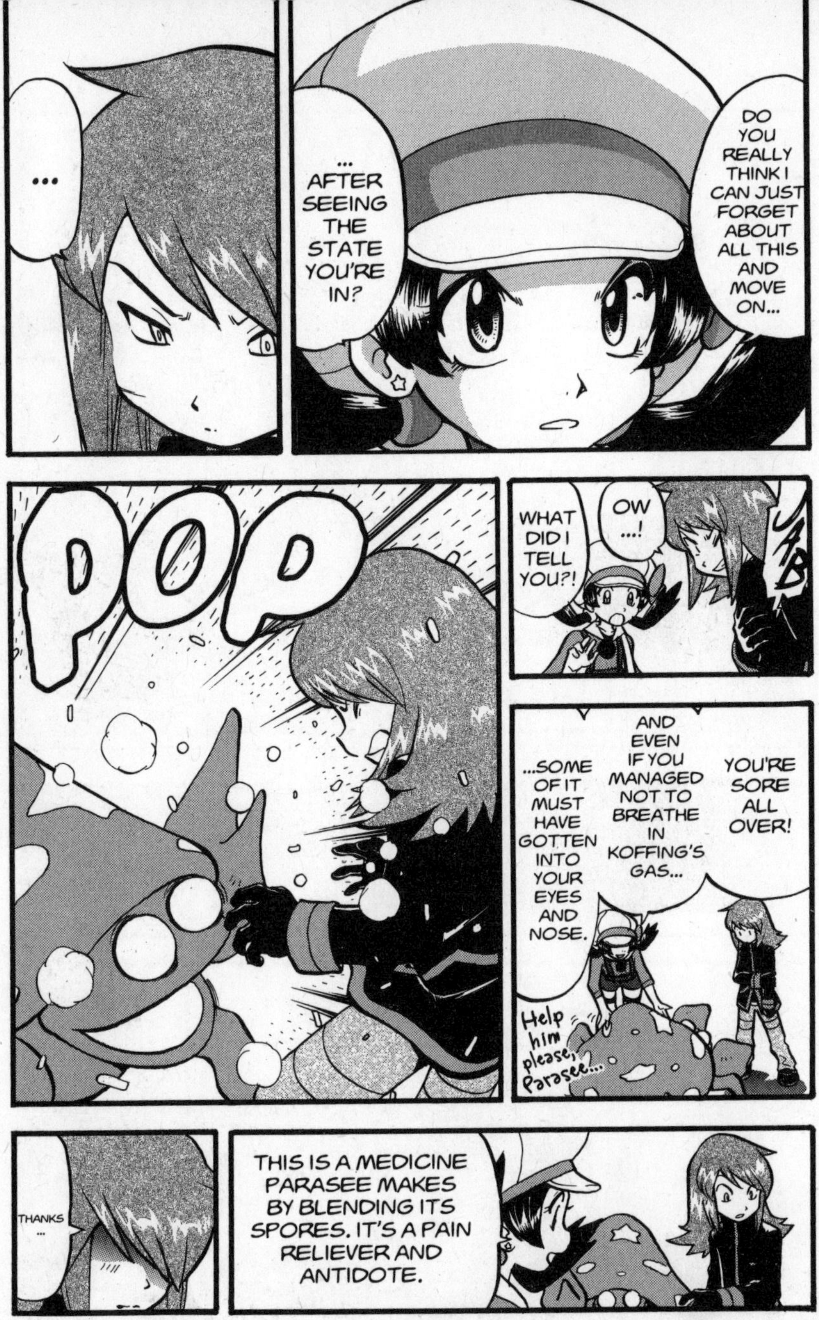
DO YOU REALLY THINK I CAN JUST FORGET ABOUT ALL THIS AND MOVE ON...
... AFTER SEEING THE STATE YOU'RE IN?
...
OW ...!
WHAT DID I TELL YOU?!
JAB
YOU'RE SORE ALL OVER!
AND EVEN IF YOU MANAGED NOT TO BREATHE IN KOFFING'S GAS...
...SOME OF IT MUST HAVE GOTTEN INTO YOUR EYES AND NOSE.
Help him please, Parasee...
POP
THIS IS A MEDICINE PARASEE MAKES BY BLENDING ITS SPORES. IT'S A PAIN RELIEVER AND ANTIDOTE.
THANKS ...

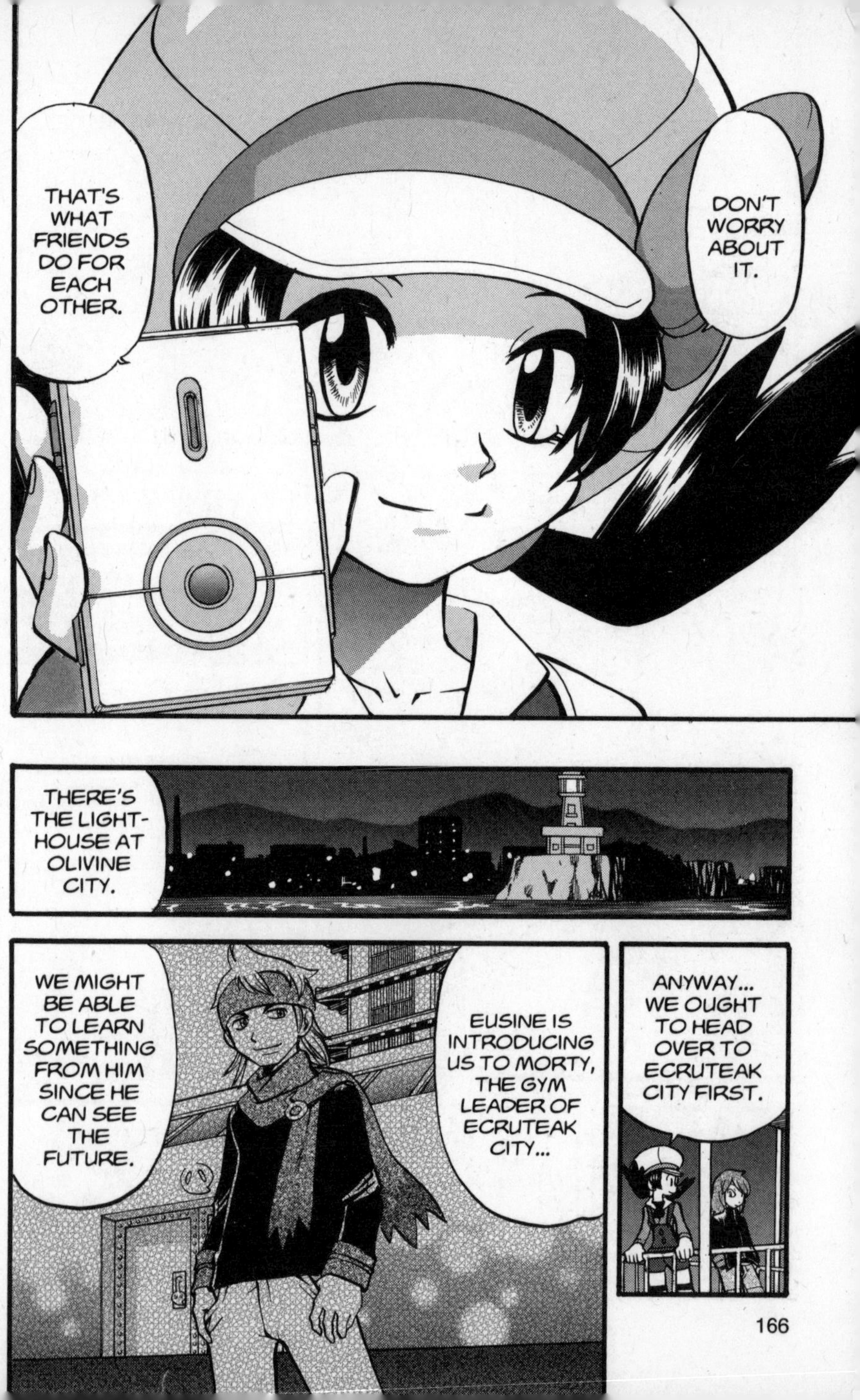
DON'T WORRY ABOUT IT.
THAT'S WHAT FRIENDS DO FOR EACH OTHER.
THERE'S THE LIGHT-HOUSE AT OLIVINE CITY.
ANYWAY... WE OUGHT TO HEAD OVER TO ECRUTEAK CITY FIRST.
EUSINE IS INTRODUCING US TO MORTY, THE GYM LEADER OF ECRUTEAK CITY...
WE MIGHT BE ABLE TO LEARN SOMETHING FROM HIM SINCE HE CAN SEE THE FUTURE.

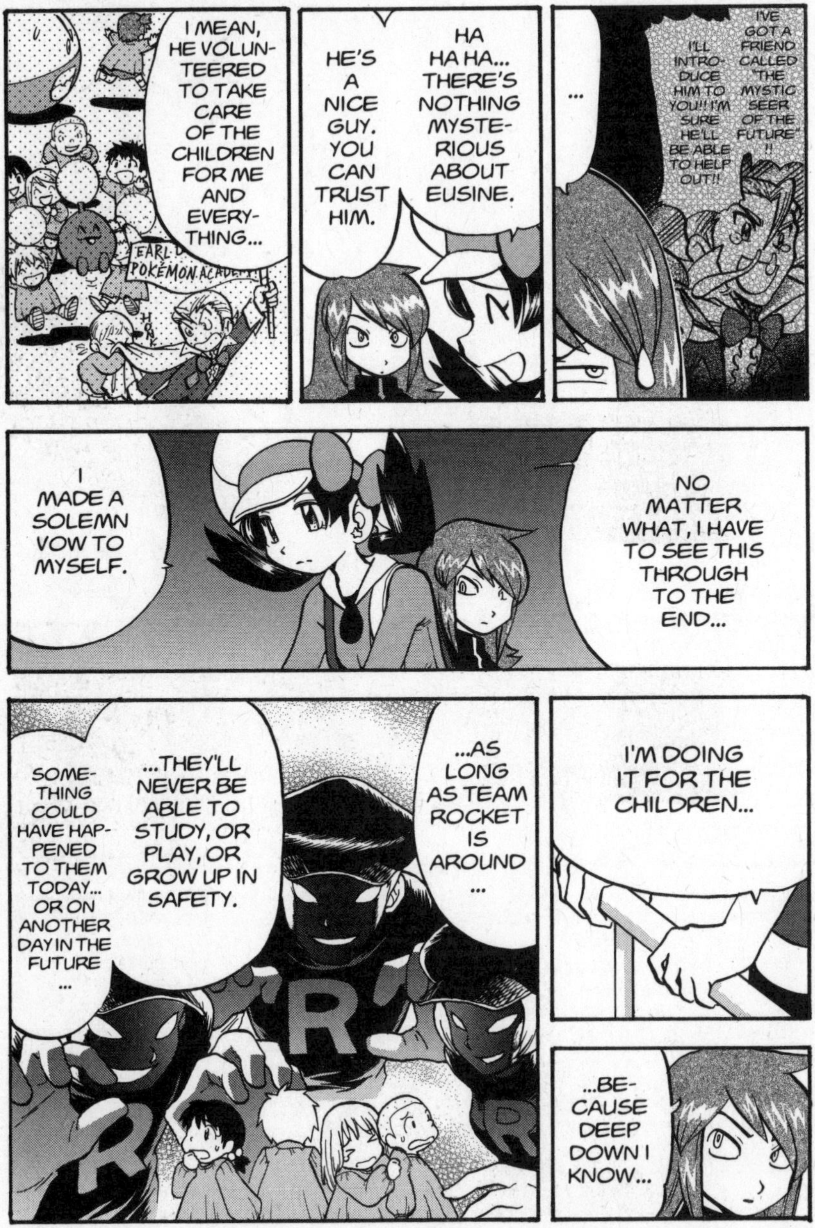
I'VE GOT A FRIEND CALLED "THE MYSTIC SEER OF THE FUTURE"!!
I'LL INTRODUCE HIM TO YOU!! I'M SURE HE'LL BE ABLE TO HELP OUT!!
...
HA HA HA... THERE'S NOTHING MYSTERIOUS ABOUT EUSINE.
HE'S A NICE GUY. YOU CAN TRUST HIM.
I MEAN, HE VOLUNTEERED TO TAKE CARE OF THE CHILDREN FOR ME AND EVERYTHING...
HONK
NO MATTER WHAT, I HAVE TO SEE THIS THROUGH TO THE END...
I MADE A SOLEMN VOW TO MYSELF.
I'M DOING IT FOR THE CHILDREN...
...BECAUSE DEEP DOWN I KNOW...
...AS LONG AS TEAM ROCKET IS AROUND...
...THEY'LL NEVER BE ABLE TO STUDY, OR PLAY, OR GROW UP IN SAFETY.
SOMETHING COULD HAVE HAPPENED TO THEM TODAY... OR ON ANOTHER DAY IN THE FUTURE...

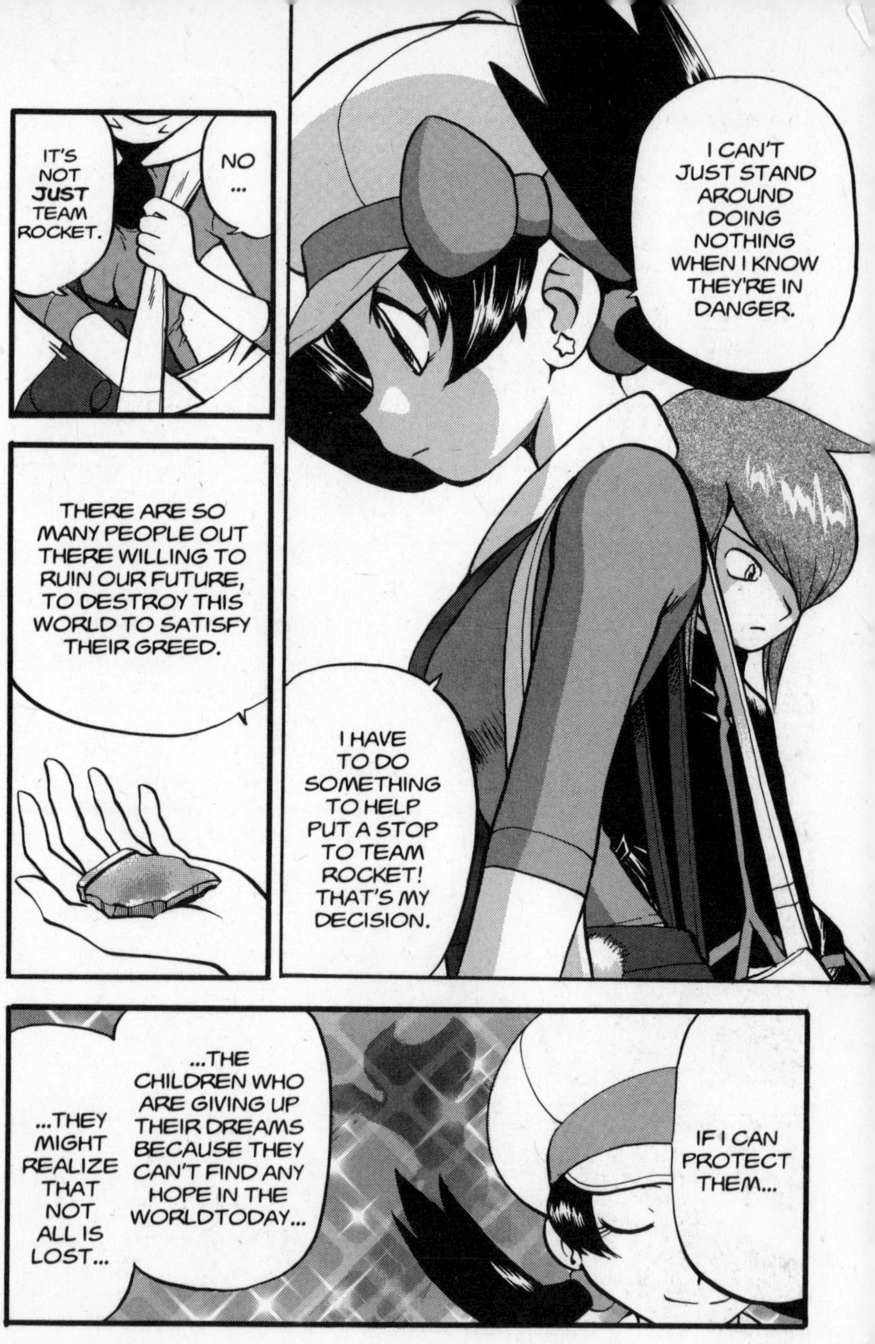
I CAN'T JUST STAND AROUND DOING NOTHING WHEN I KNOW THEY'RE IN DANGER.
I HAVE TO DO SOMETHING TO HELP PUT A STOP TO TEAM ROCKET! THAT'S MY DECISION.
NO ...
IT'S NOT **JUST** TEAM ROCKET.
THERE ARE SO MANY PEOPLE OUT THERE WILLING TO RUIN OUR FUTURE, TO DESTROY THIS WORLD TO SATISFY THEIR GREED.
IF I CAN PROTECT THEM...
...THE CHILDREN WHO ARE GIVING UP THEIR DREAMS BECAUSE THEY CAN'T FIND ANY HOPE IN THE WORLDTODAY...
...THEY MIGHT REALIZE THAT NOT ALL IS LOST...

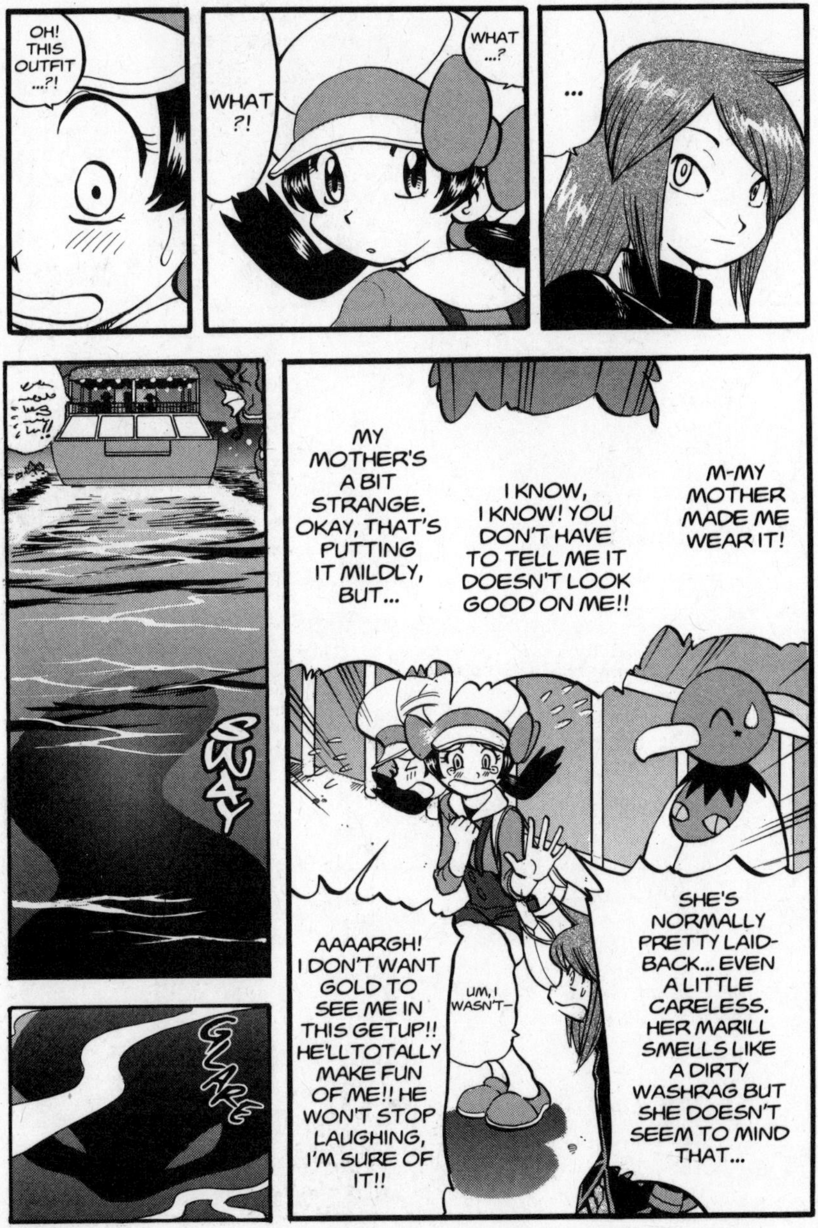
...
WHAT ...?
WHAT ?!
OH! THIS OUTFIT ...?!
M-MY MOTHER MADE ME WEAR IT!
I KNOW, I KNOW! YOU DON'T HAVE TO TELL ME IT DOESN'T LOOK GOOD ON ME!!
MY MOTHER'S A BIT STRANGE. OKAY, THAT'S PUTTING IT MILDLY, BUT...
SHE'S NORMALLY PRETTY LAID-BACK... EVEN A LITTLE CARELESS. HER MARILL SMELLS LIKE A DIRTY WASHRAG BUT SHE DOESN'T SEEM TO MIND THAT...
UM, I WASN'T—
AAAARGH! I DON'T WANT GOLD TO SEE ME IN THIS GETUP!! HE'LL TOTALLY MAKE FUN OF ME!! HE WON'T STOP LAUGHING, I'M SURE OF IT!!
SWAY
GLARE

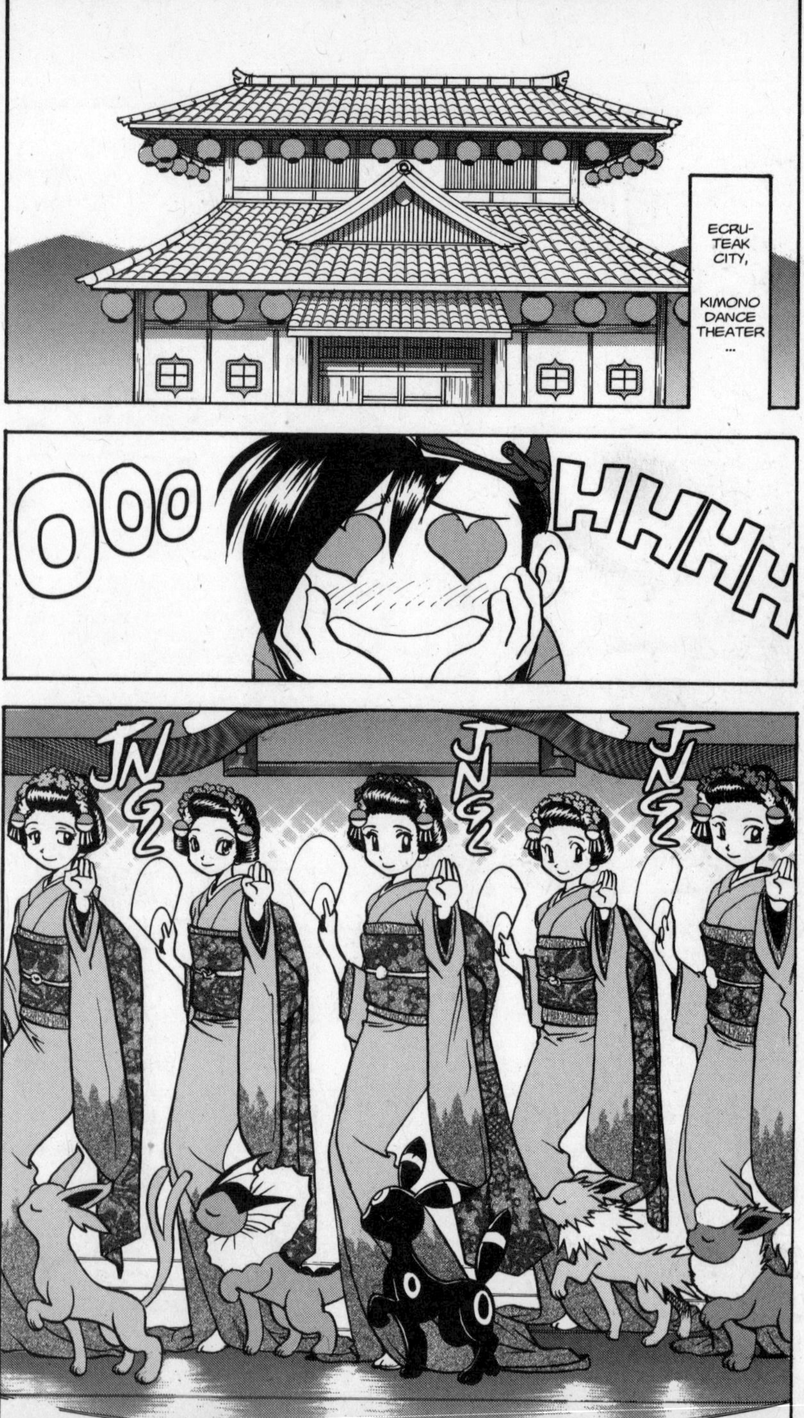
ECRU-TEAK CITY,
KIMONO DANCE THEATER ...
OOOHHHHHH
JNG
JNG
JNG

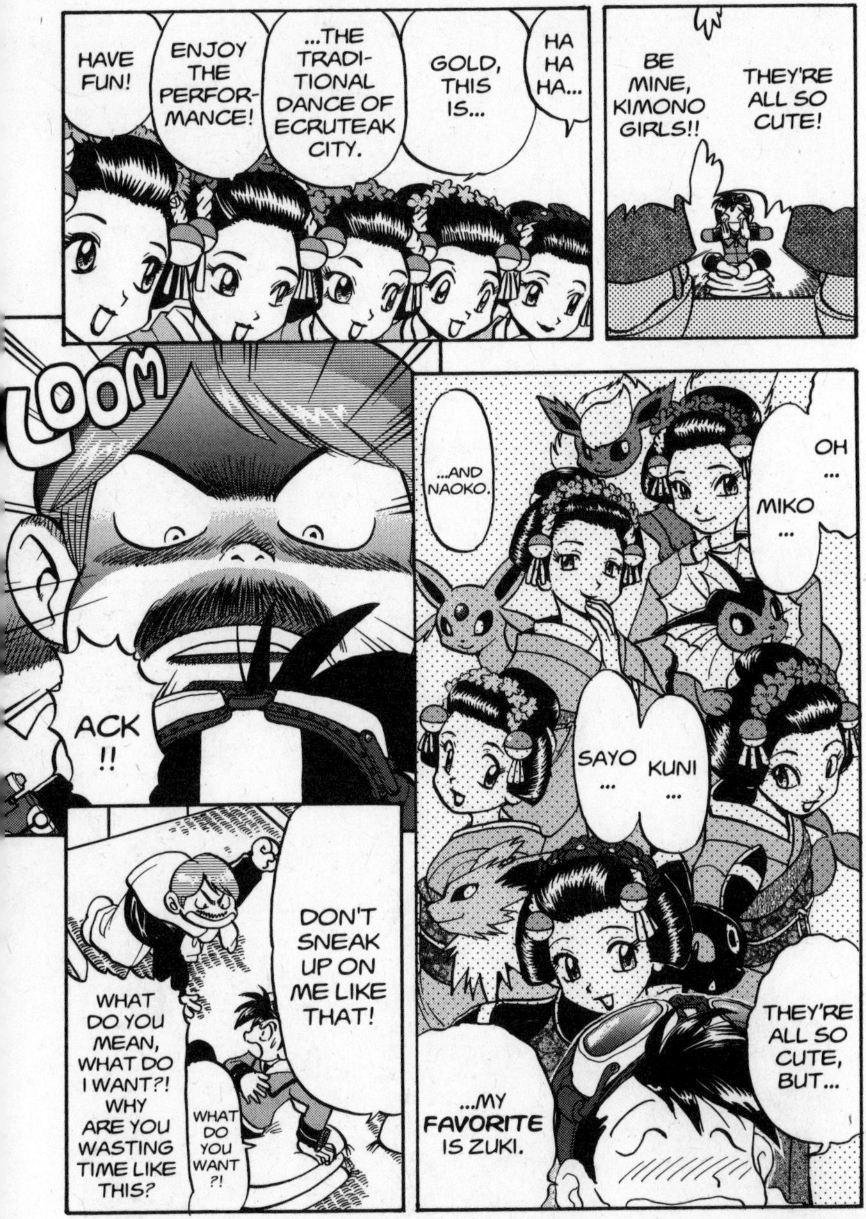
THEY'RE ALL SO CUTE!
BE MINE, KIMONO GIRLS!!
HA HA HA...
GOLD, THIS IS...
...THE TRADI- TIONAL DANCE OF ECRUTEAK CITY.
ENJOY THE PERFOR- MANCE!
HAVE FUN!
OH ... MIKO ...
KUNI ...
SAYO ...
...AND NAOKO.
THEY'RE ALL SO CUTE, BUT...
...MY FAVORITE IS ZUKI.
LOOM
ACK !!
DON'T SNEAK UP ON ME LIKE THAT!
WHAT DO YOU WANT ?!
WHAT DO YOU MEAN, WHAT DO I WANT?! WHY ARE YOU WASTING TIME LIKE THIS?

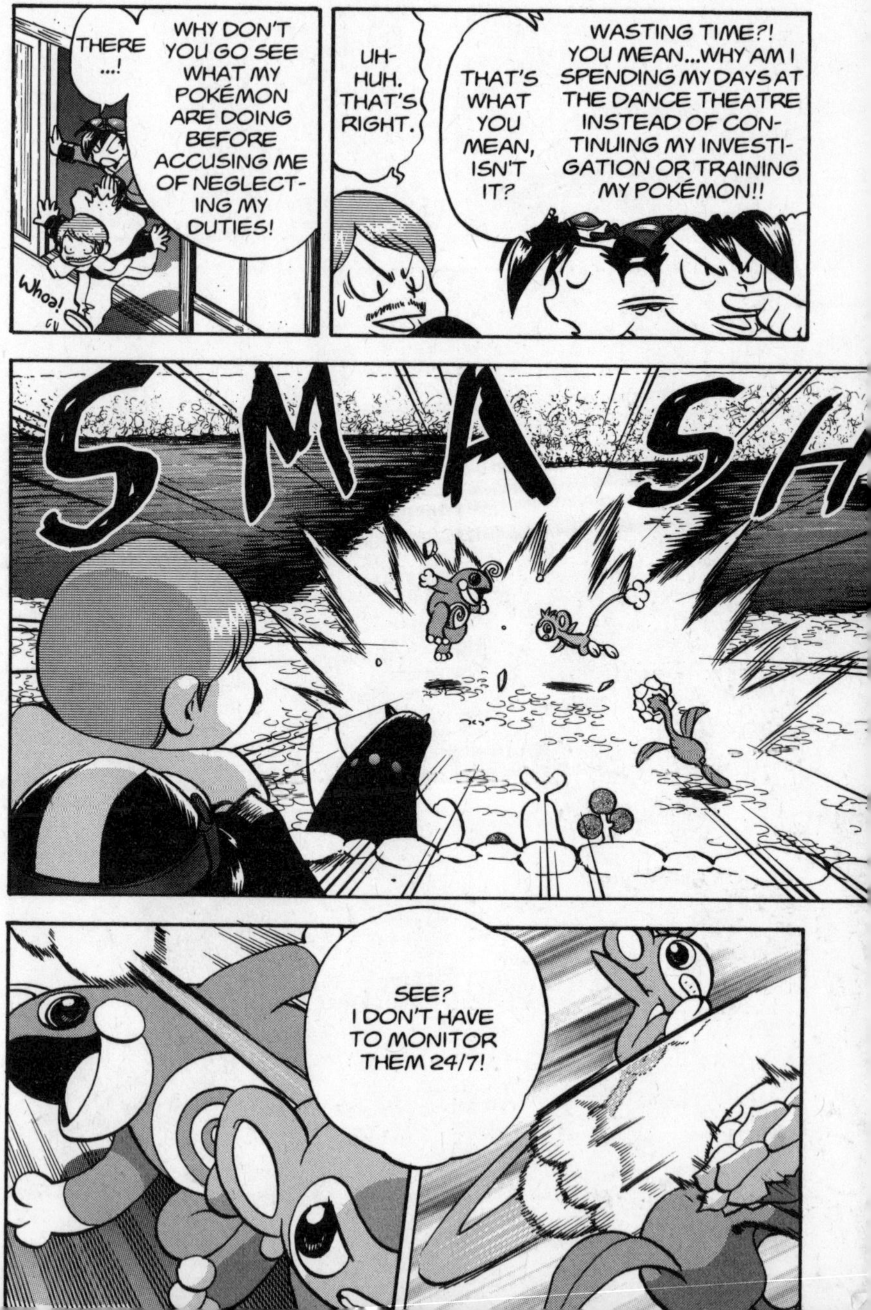
WASTING TIME?! YOU MEAN...WHY AM I SPENDING MY DAYS AT THE DANCE THEATRE INSTEAD OF CONTINUING MY INVESTIGATION OR TRAINING MY POKÉMON!!
THAT'S WHAT YOU MEAN, ISN'T IT?
UH-HUH. THAT'S RIGHT.
WHY DON'T YOU GO SEE WHAT MY POKÉMON ARE DOING BEFORE ACCUSING ME OF NEGLECTING MY DUTIES!
THERE ...!
Whoa!
SMASH
SEE? I DON'T HAVE TO MONITOR THEM 24/7!

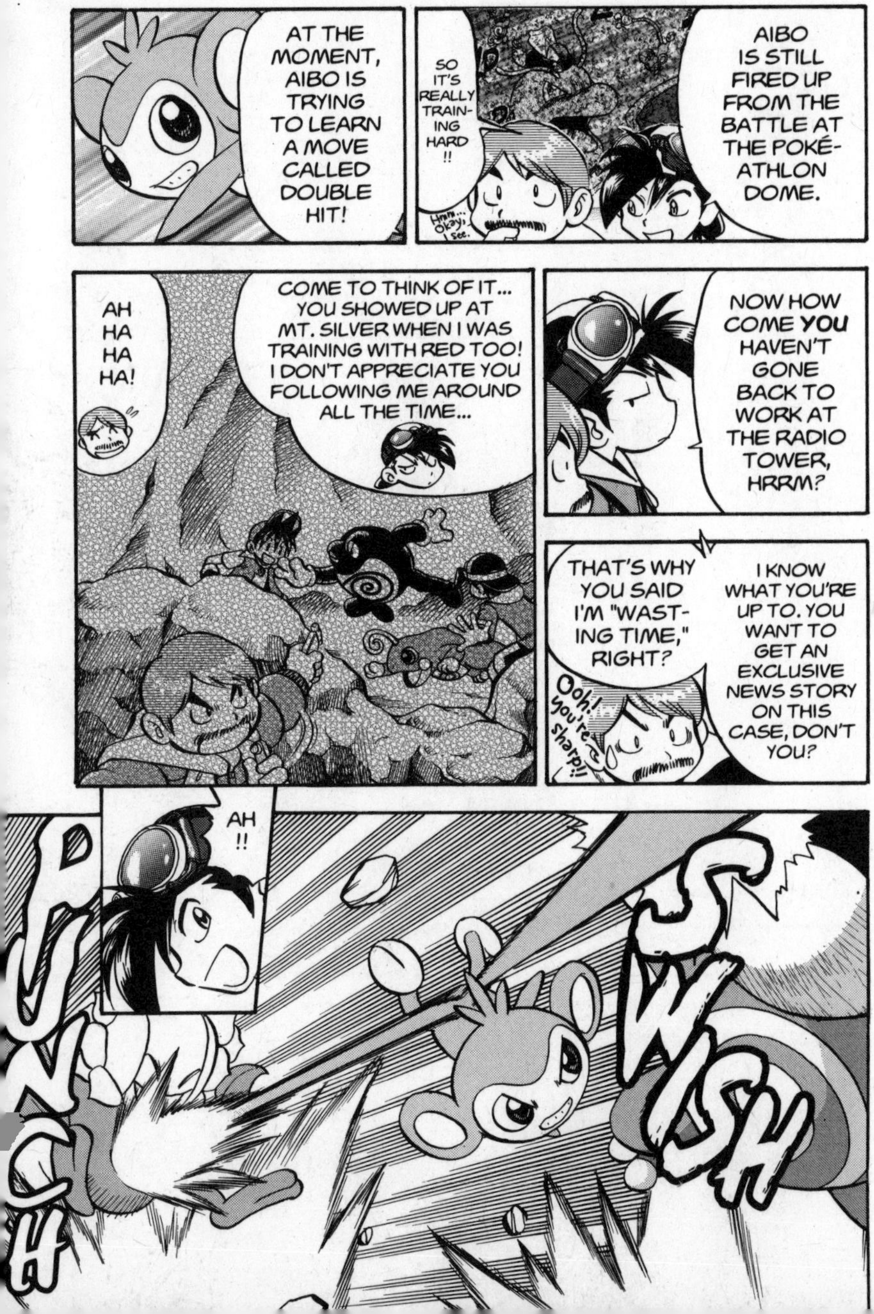
AIBO IS STILL FIRED UP FROM THE BATTLE AT THE POKÉ-ATHLON DOME.
SO IT'S REALLY TRAINING HARD !!
Hmm... Okay, I see.
AT THE MOMENT, AIBO IS TRYING TO LEARN A MOVE CALLED DOUBLE HIT!
NOW HOW COME **YOU** HAVEN'T GONE BACK TO WORK AT THE RADIO TOWER, HRRM?
I KNOW WHAT YOU'RE UP TO. YOU WANT TO GET AN EXCLUSIVE NEWS STORY ON THIS CASE, DON'T YOU?
THAT'S WHY YOU SAID I'M "WASTING TIME," RIGHT?
Ooh! You're sharp!!
COME TO THINK OF IT... YOU SHOWED UP AT MT. SILVER WHEN I WAS TRAINING WITH RED TOO! I DON'T APPRECIATE YOU FOLLOWING ME AROUND ALL THE TIME...
AH HA HA HA!
SWISH
AH !!

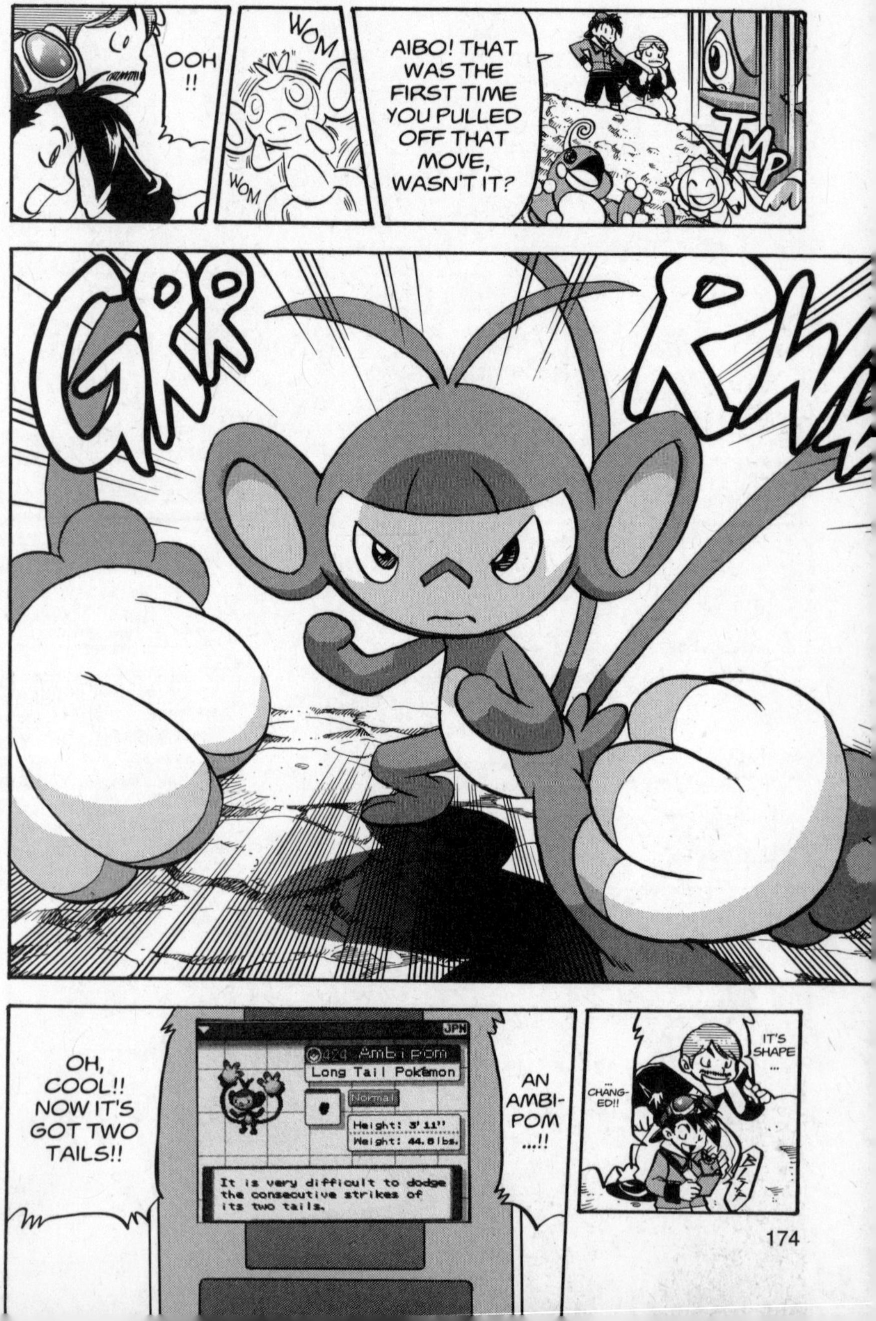
AIBO! THAT WAS THE FIRST TIME YOU PULLED OFF THAT MOVE, WASN'T IT?
TMP
WOM
WOM
OOH!!
GRR
IT'S SHAPE ...
... CHANG-ED!!
AN AMBI-POM ...!!
JPN
424 Ambipom
Long Tail Pokémon
Normal
Height: 3'11''
Weight: 44.8lbs.
It is very difficult to dodge the consecutive strikes of its two tails.
OH, COOL!! NOW IT'S GOT TWO TAILS!!

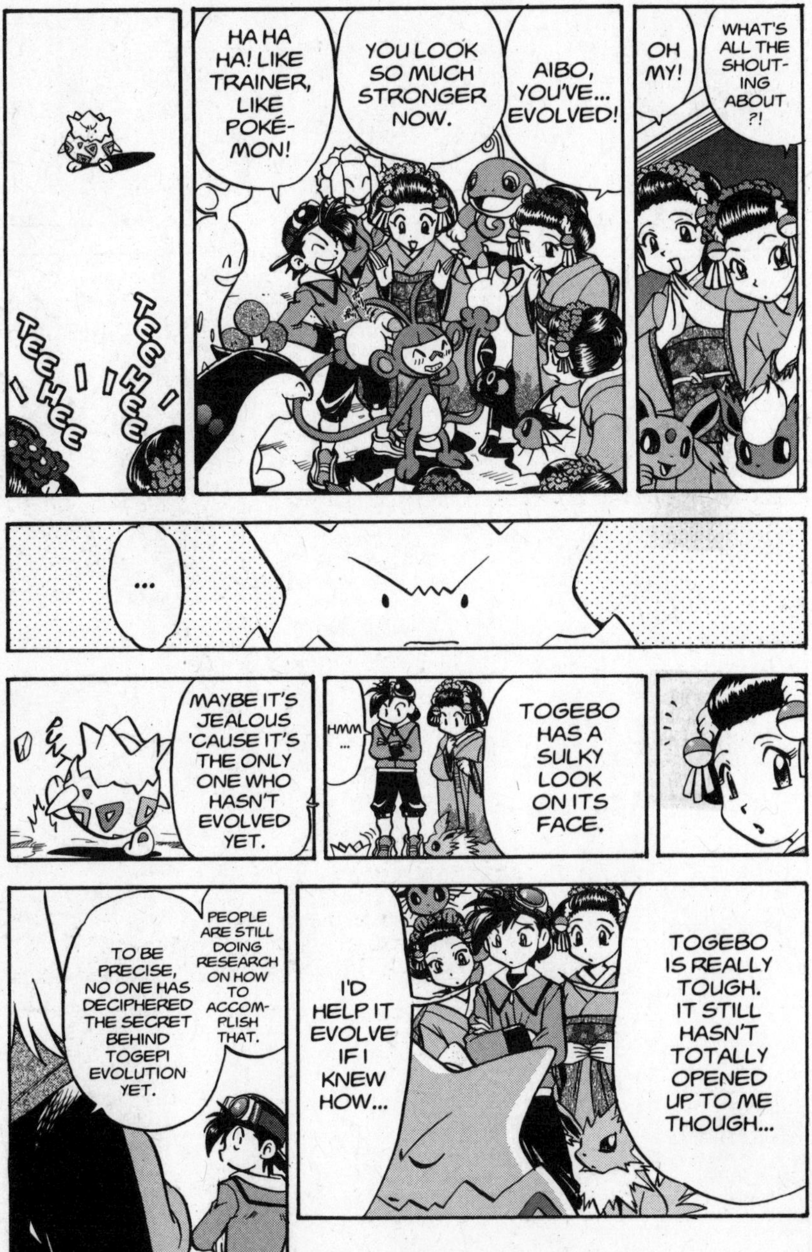
WHAT'S ALL THE SHOUTING ABOUT?!
OH MY!
AIBO, YOU'VE... EVOLVED!
YOU LOOK SO MUCH STRONGER NOW.
HA HA HA! LIKE TRAINER, LIKE POKÉMON!
TEE HEE
TEE HEE
...
TOGEBO HAS A SULKY LOOK ON ITS FACE.
HMM...
MAYBE IT'S JEALOUS 'CAUSE IT'S THE ONLY ONE WHO HASN'T EVOLVED YET.
PUNT
TOGEBO IS REALLY TOUGH. IT STILL HASN'T TOTALLY OPENED UP TO ME THOUGH...
I'D HELP IT EVOLVE IF I KNEW HOW...
PEOPLE ARE STILL DOING RESEARCH ON HOW TO ACCOMPLISH THAT.
TO BE PRECISE, NO ONE HAS DECIPHERED THE SECRET BEHIND TOGEPI EVOLUTION YET.

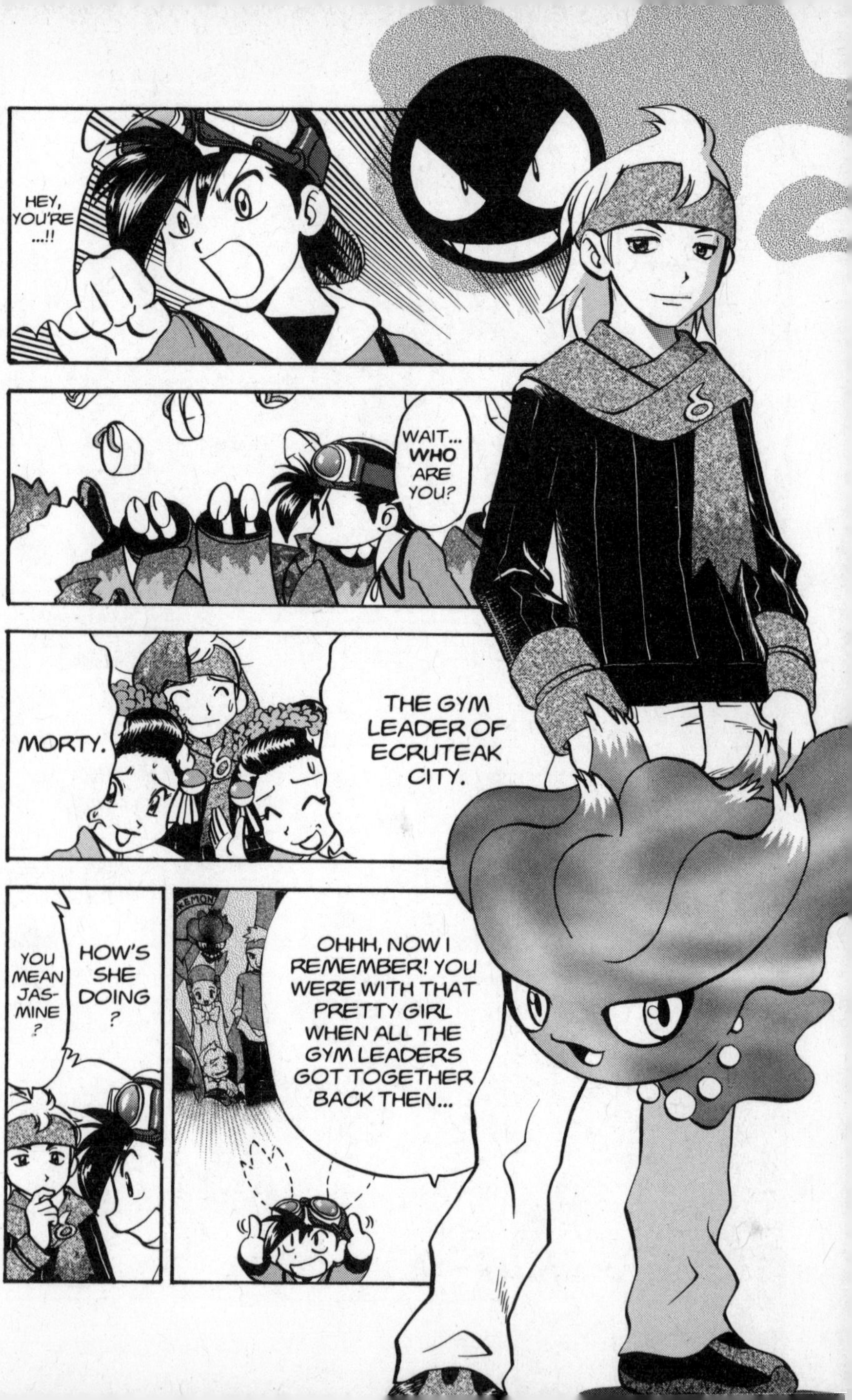
HEY, YOU'RE ...!!
WAIT... WHO ARE YOU?
THE GYM LEADER OF ECRUTEAK CITY.
MORTY.
OHHH, NOW I REMEMBER! YOU WERE WITH THAT PRETTY GIRL WHEN ALL THE GYM LEADERS GOT TOGETHER BACK THEN...
HOW'S SHE DOING?
YOU MEAN JAS-MINE?

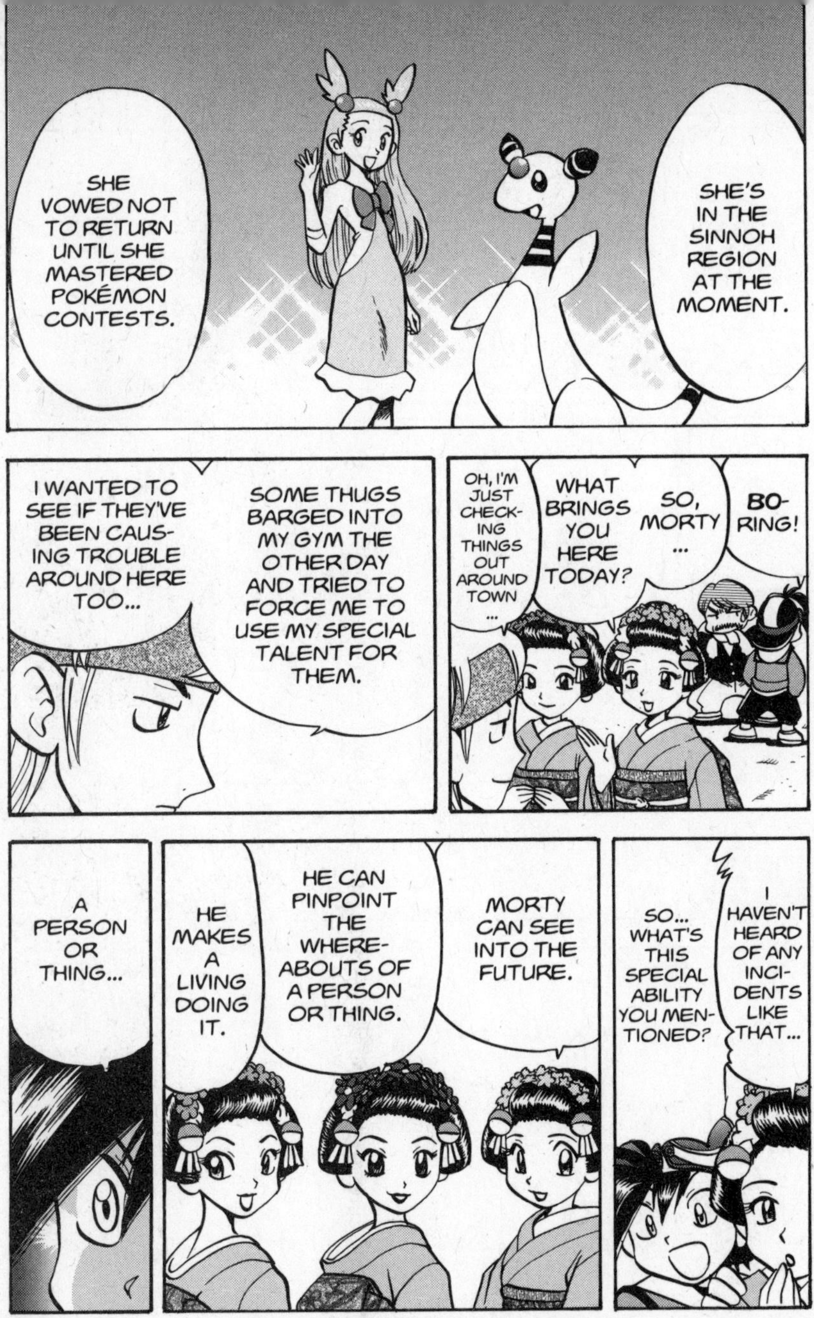
SHE'S IN THE SINNOH REGION AT THE MOMENT.
SHE VOWED NOT TO RETURN UNTIL SHE MASTERED POKÉMON CONTESTS.
BO-RING!
SO, MORTY...
WHAT BRINGS YOU HERE TODAY?
OH, I'M JUST CHECKING THINGS OUT AROUND TOWN...
SOME THUGS BARGED INTO MY GYM THE OTHER DAY AND TRIED TO FORCE ME TO USE MY SPECIAL TALENT FOR THEM.
I WANTED TO SEE IF THEY'VE BEEN CAUSING TROUBLE AROUND HERE TOO...
I HAVEN'T HEARD OF ANY INCIDENTS LIKE THAT...
SO... WHAT'S THIS SPECIAL ABILITY YOU MENTIONED?
MORTY CAN SEE INTO THE FUTURE.
HE CAN PINPOINT THE WHEREABOUTS OF A PERSON OR THING.
HE MAKES A LIVING DOING IT.
A PERSON OR THING...

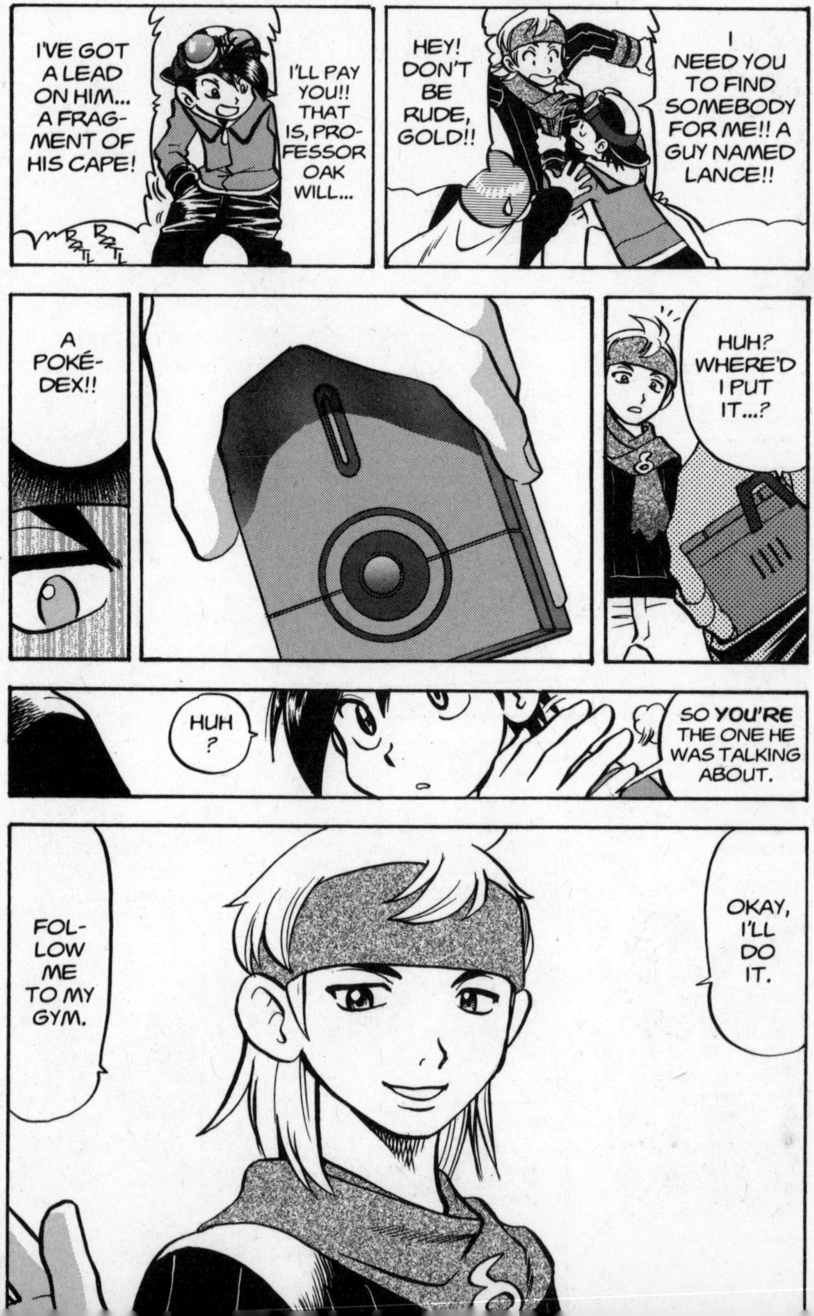
I NEED YOU TO FIND SOMEBODY FOR ME!! A GUY NAMED LANCE!!
HEY! DON'T BE RUDE, GOLD!!
I'LL PAY YOU!! THAT IS, PROFESSOR OAK WILL...
I'VE GOT A LEAD ON HIM... A FRAGMENT OF HIS CAPE!
HUH? WHERE'D I PUT IT...?
A POKÉDEX!!
SO **YOU'RE** THE ONE HE WAS TALKING ABOUT.
HUH?
OKAY, I'LL DO IT.
FOLLOW ME TO MY GYM.

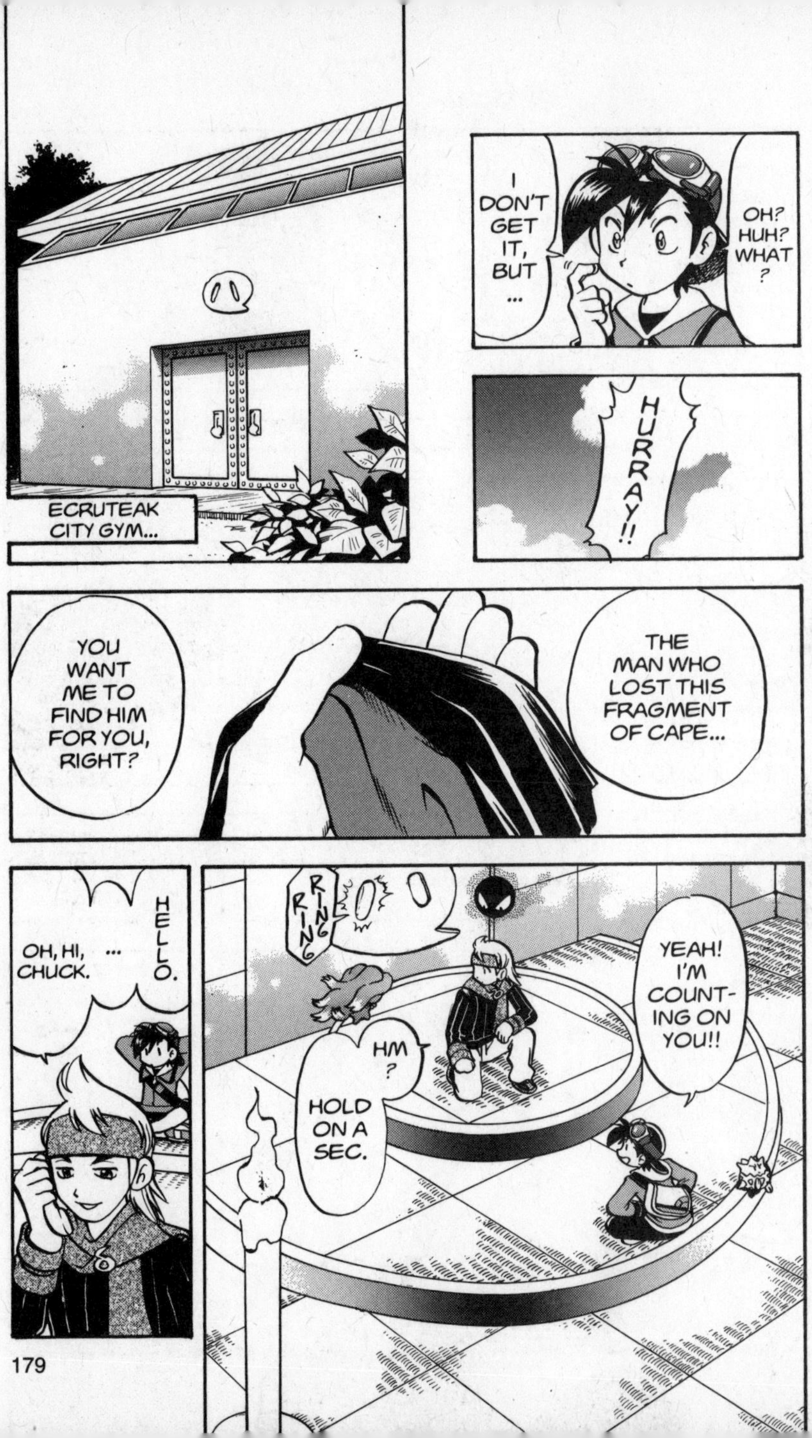
OH? HUH? WHAT?
I DON'T GET IT, BUT...
HURRAY!!
ECRUTEAK CITY GYM...
THE MAN WHO LOST THIS FRAGMENT OF CAPE...
YOU WANT ME TO FIND HIM FOR YOU, RIGHT?
YEAH! I'M COUNTING ON YOU!!
RING RING
HM?
HOLD ON A SEC.
HELLO.
... OH, HI, CHUCK.

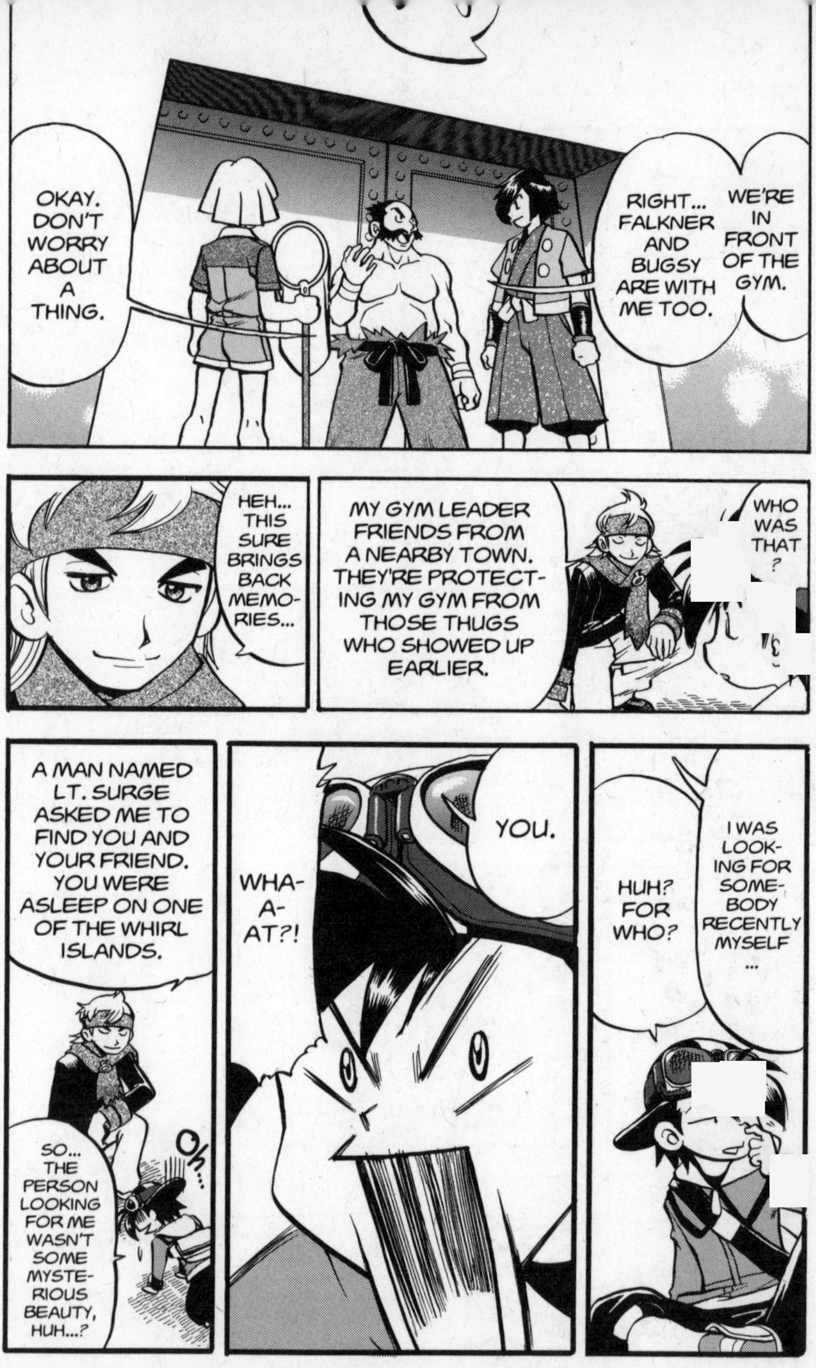

WE'RE IN FRONT OF THE GYM.
RIGHT... FALKNER AND BUGSY ARE WITH ME TOO.
OKAY. DON'T WORRY ABOUT A THING.
WHO WAS THAT?
MY GYM LEADER FRIENDS FROM A NEARBY TOWN. THEY'RE PROTECTING MY GYM FROM THOSE THUGS WHO SHOWED UP EARLIER.
HEH... THIS SURE BRINGS BACK MEMORIES...
I WAS LOOKING FOR SOMEBODY RECENTLY MYSELF...
HUH? FOR WHO?
YOU.
WHA-A-AT?!
A MAN NAMED LT. SURGE ASKED ME TO FIND YOU AND YOUR FRIEND. YOU WERE ASLEEP ON ONE OF THE WHIRL ISLANDS.
SO... THE PERSON LOOKING FOR ME WASN'T SOME MYSTERIOUS BEAUTY, HUH...?

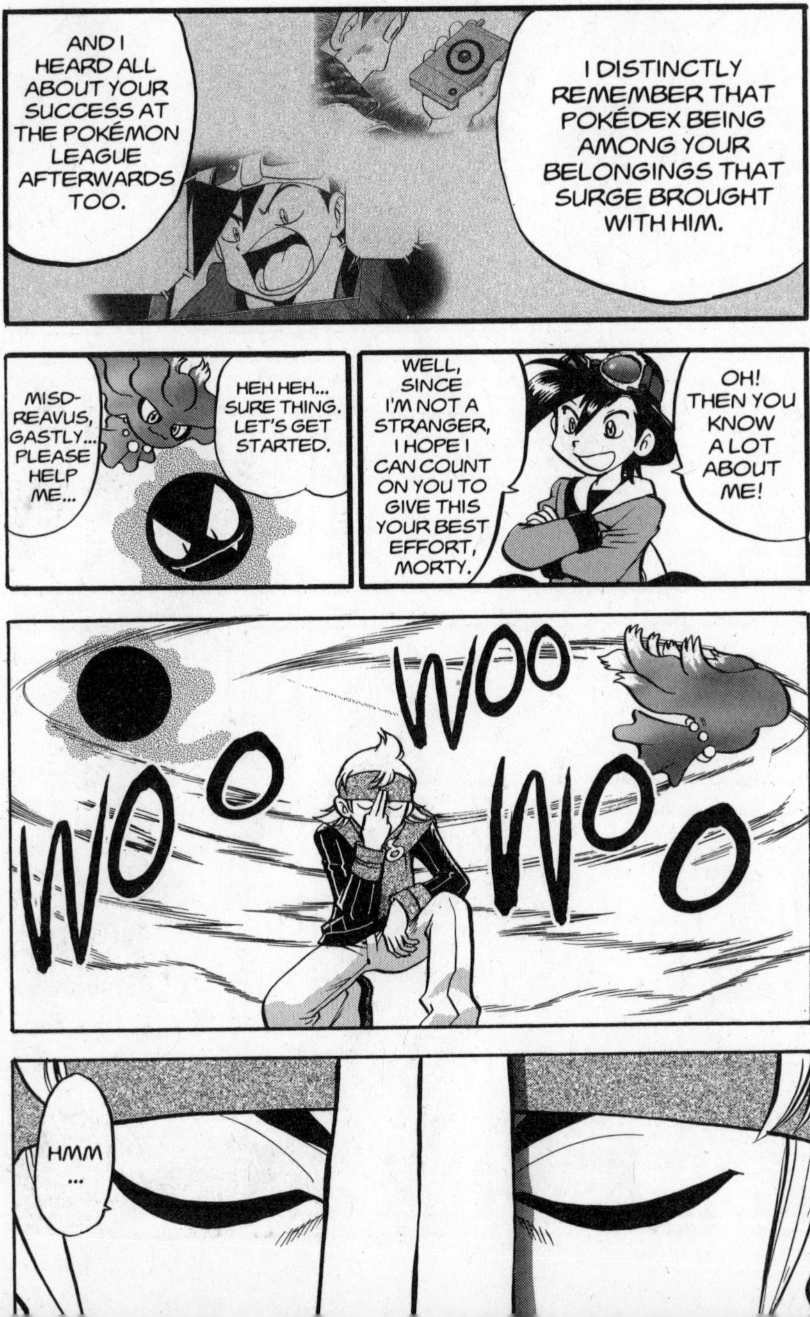
I DISTINCTLY REMEMBER THAT POKÉDEX BEING AMONG YOUR BELONGINGS THAT SURGE BROUGHT WITH HIM.
AND I HEARD ALL ABOUT YOUR SUCCESS AT THE POKÉMON LEAGUE AFTERWARDS TOO.
OH! THEN YOU KNOW A LOT ABOUT ME!
WELL, SINCE I'M NOT A STRANGER, I HOPE I CAN COUNT ON YOU TO GIVE THIS YOUR BEST EFFORT, MORTY.
HEH HEH... SURE THING. LET'S GET STARTED.
MISD-REAVUS, GASTLY... PLEASE HELP ME...
WOO
WOO
WOO
WOO
HMM...

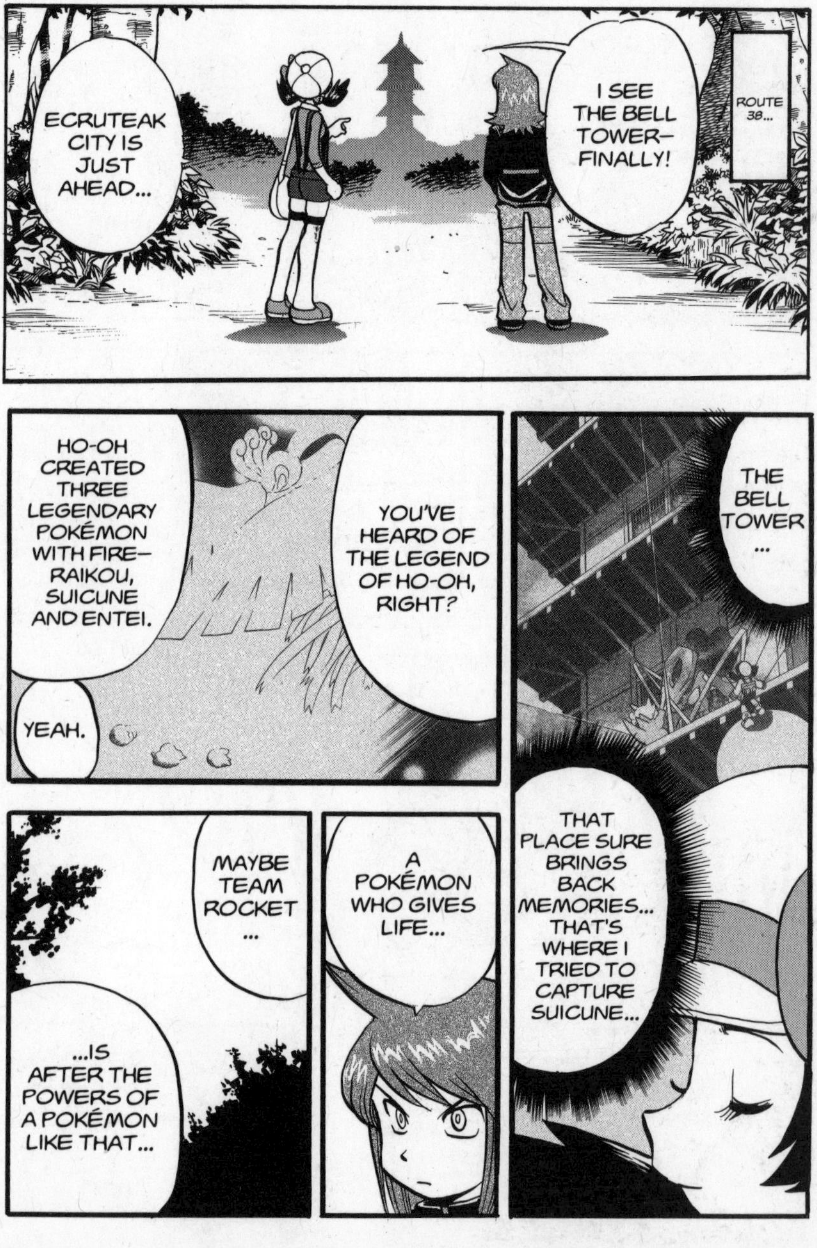
ROUTE 38...
I SEE THE BELL TOWER—FINALLY!
ECRUTEAK CITY IS JUST AHEAD...
THE BELL TOWER ...
THAT PLACE SURE BRINGS BACK MEMORIES... THAT'S WHERE I TRIED TO CAPTURE SUICUNE...
YOU'VE HEARD OF THE LEGEND OF HO-OH, RIGHT?
HO-OH CREATED THREE LEGENDARY POKÉMON WITH FIRE—RAIKOU, SUICUNE AND ENTEI.
YEAH.
A POKÉMON WHO GIVES LIFE...
MAYBE TEAM ROCKET ...
...IS AFTER THE POWERS OF A POKÉMON LIKE THAT...

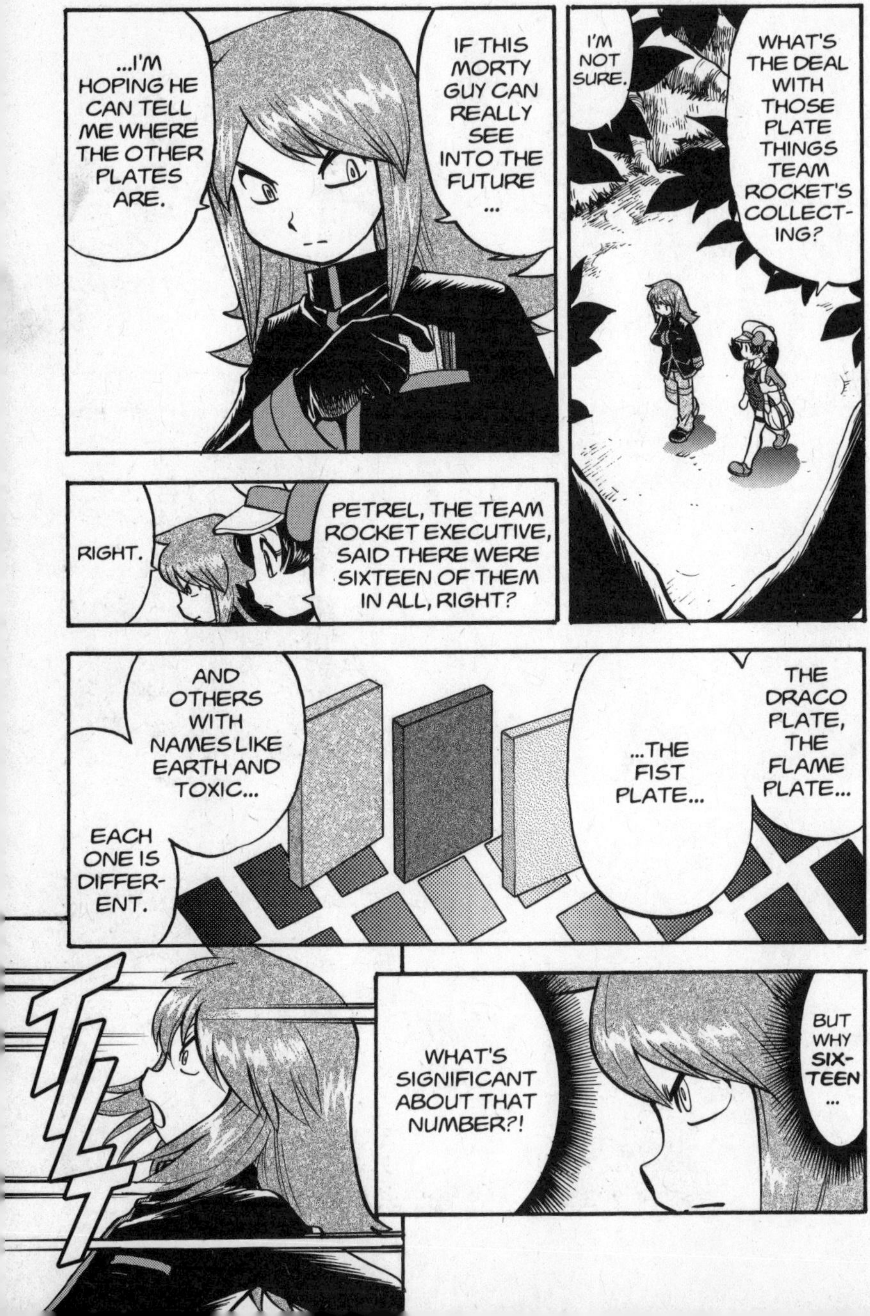
WHAT'S THE DEAL WITH THOSE PLATE THINGS TEAM ROCKET'S COLLECTING?
I'M NOT SURE.
IF THIS MORTY GUY CAN REALLY SEE INTO THE FUTURE ...
...I'M HOPING HE CAN TELL ME WHERE THE OTHER PLATES ARE.
PETREL, THE TEAM ROCKET EXECUTIVE, SAID THERE WERE SIXTEEN OF THEM IN ALL, RIGHT?
RIGHT.
THE DRACO PLATE, THE FLAME PLATE...
...THE FIST PLATE...
AND OTHERS WITH NAMES LIKE EARTH AND TOXIC...
EACH ONE IS DIFFERENT.
BUT WHY **SIXTEEN** ...
WHAT'S SIGNIFICANT ABOUT THAT NUMBER?!
TILT

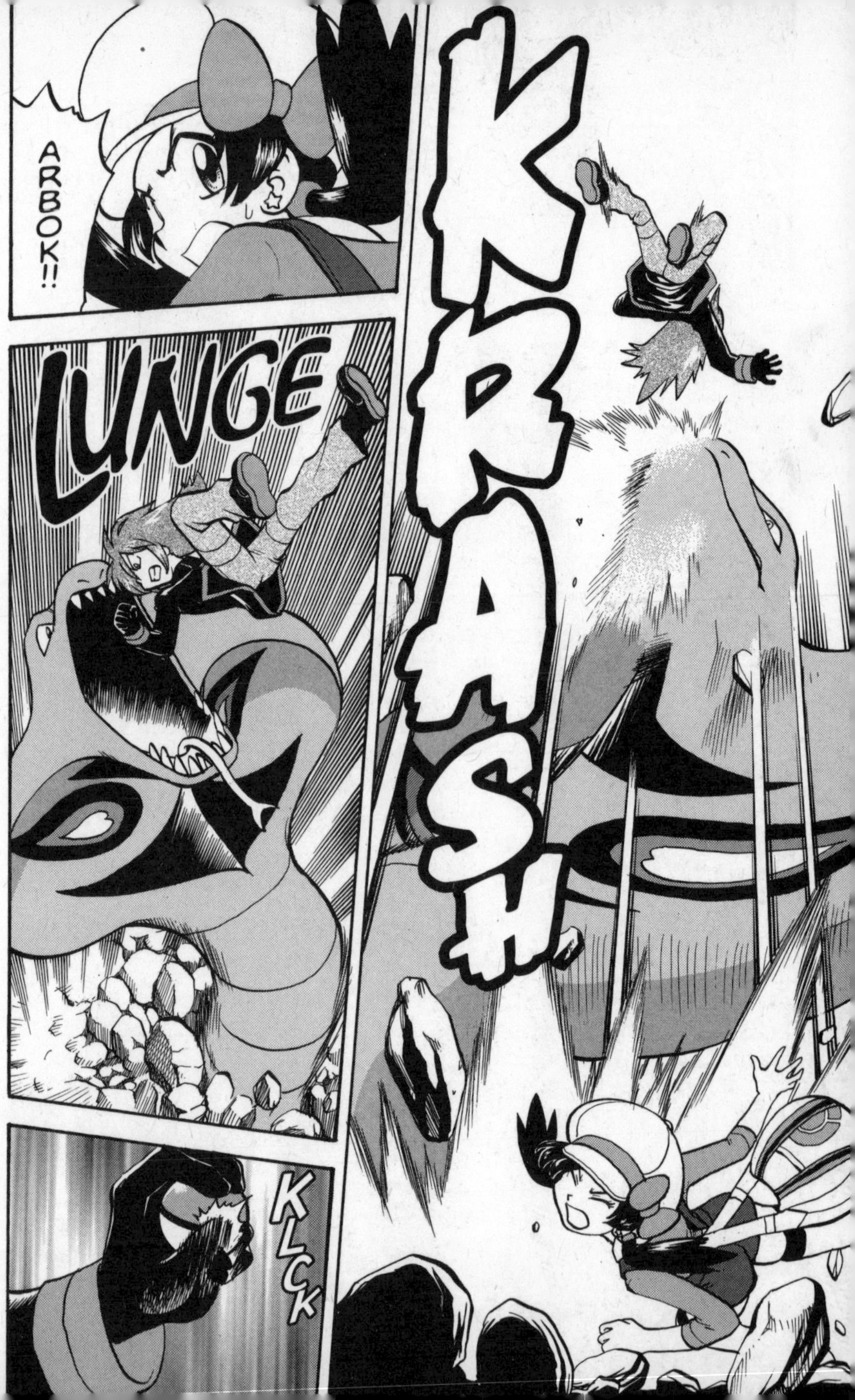
KRASH
ARBOK!!
LUNGE
KLCK

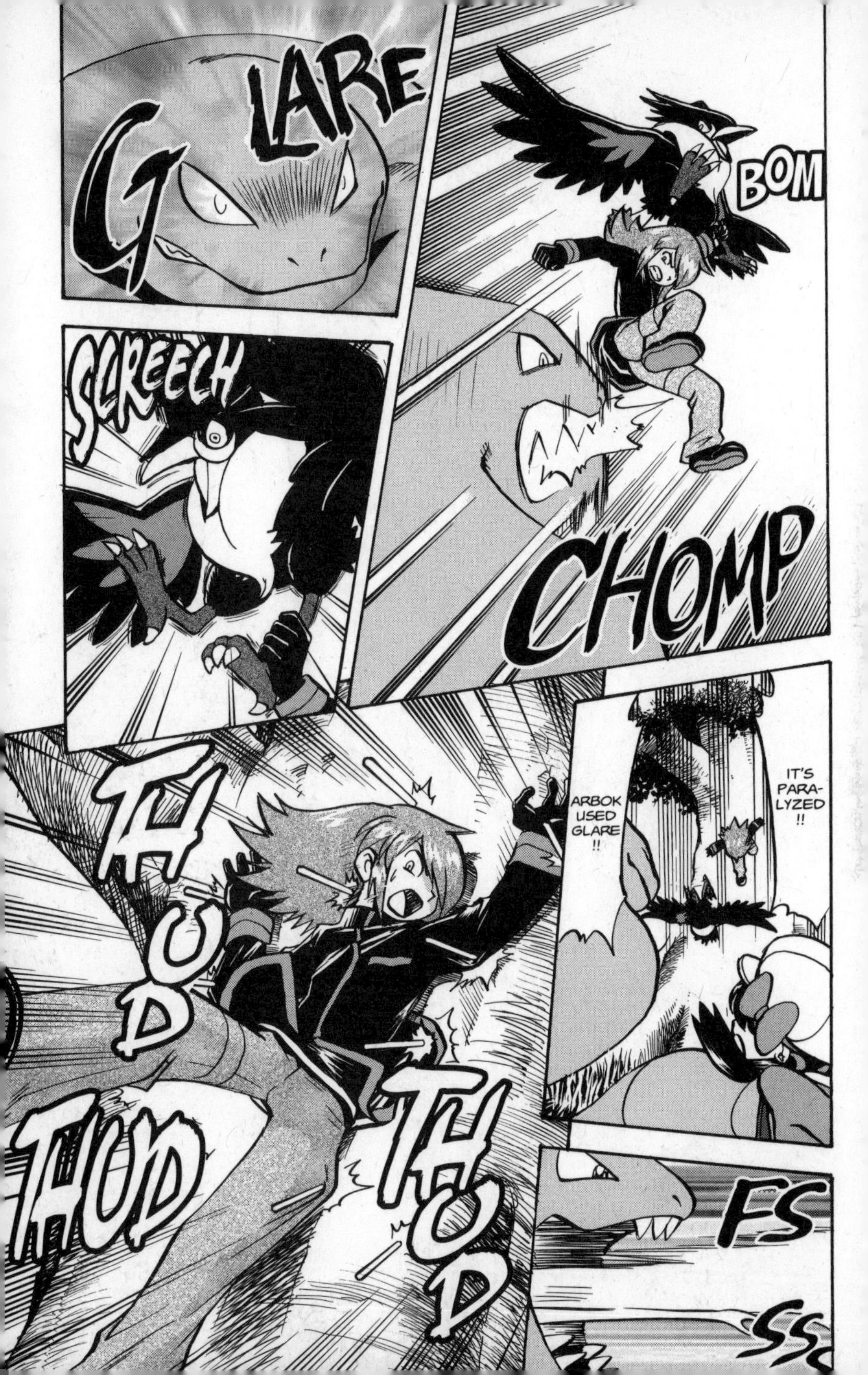
BOM
CHOMP
GLARE
SCREECH
IT'S PARA-LYZED!!
ARBOK USED GLARE!!
FSSS
THUD
THUD
THUD

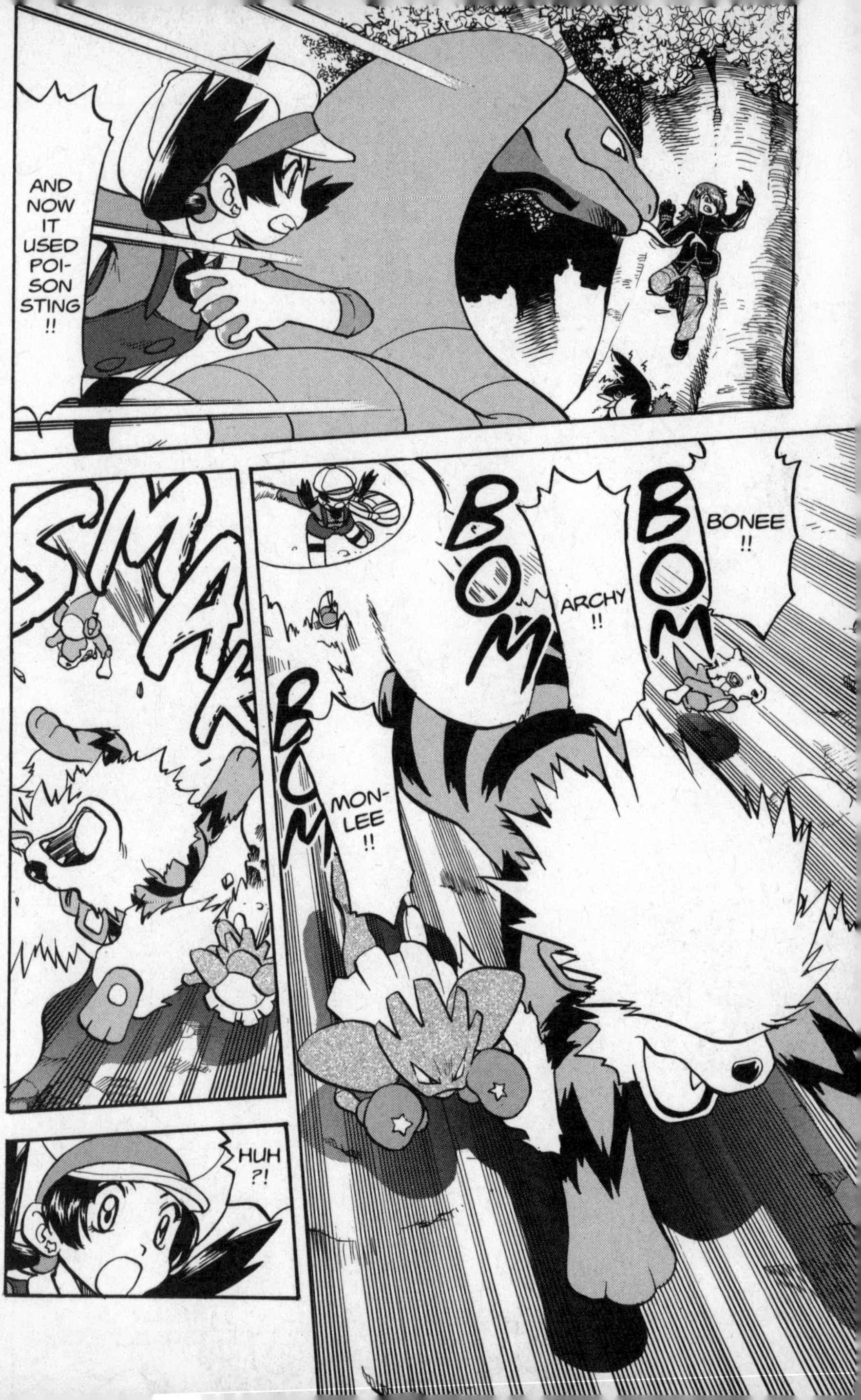
AND NOW IT USED POI-SON STING!!
BONEE!!
BOM
ARCHY!!
BOM
BOM
MON-LEE!!
HUH?!

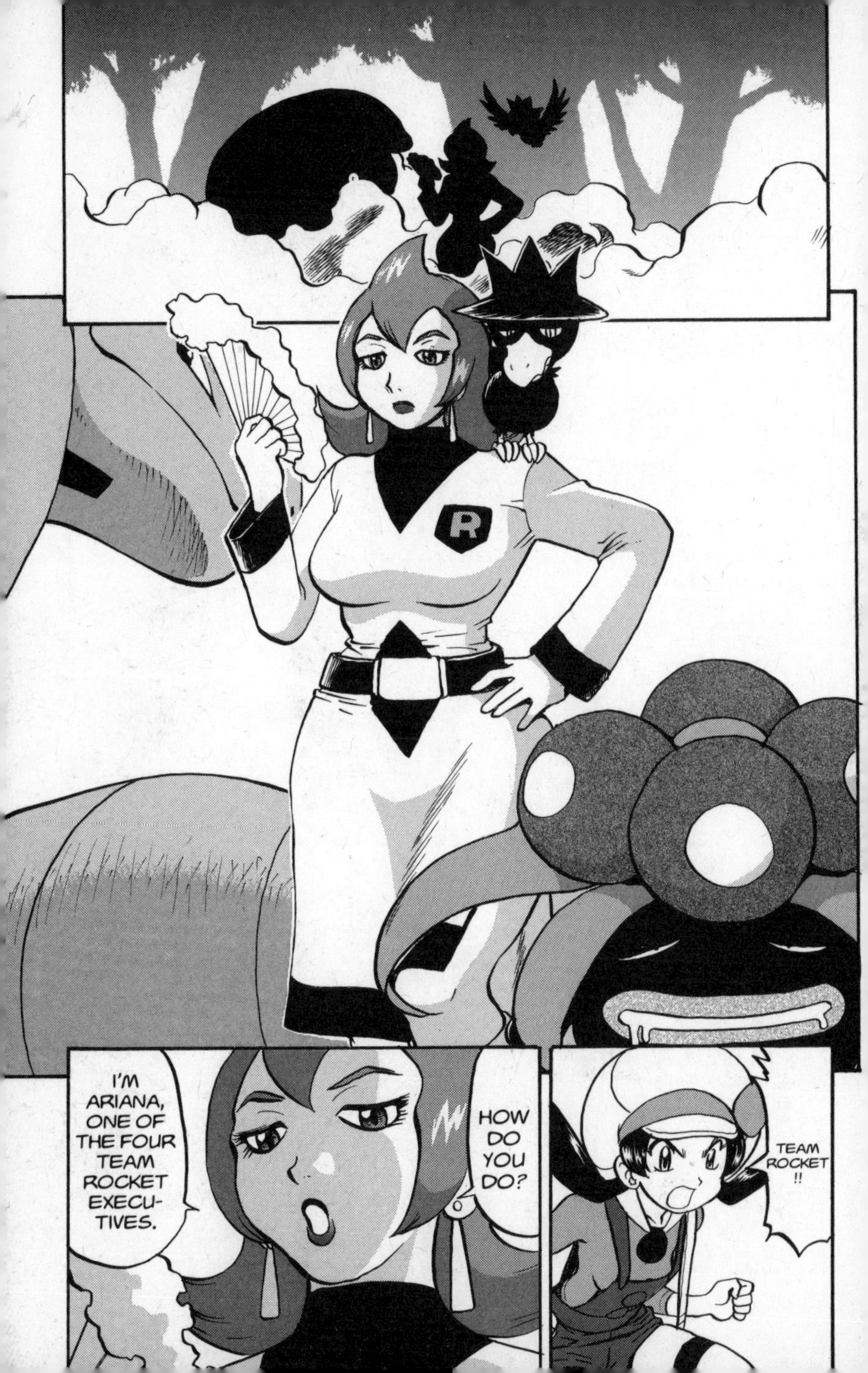
TEAM ROCKET !!
HOW DO YOU DO?
I'M ARIANA, ONE OF THE FOUR TEAM ROCKET EXECUTIVES.

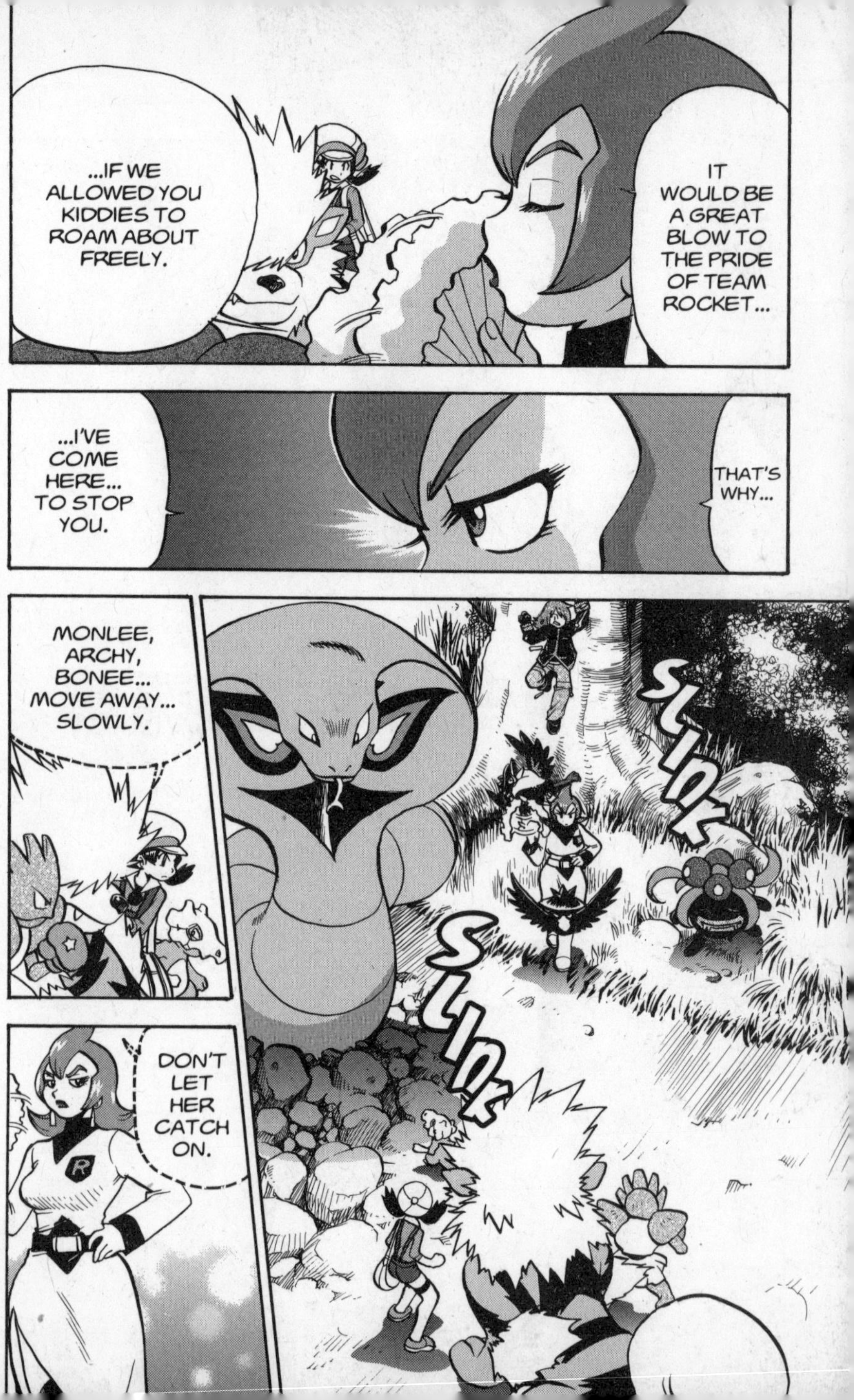
IT WOULD BE A GREAT BLOW TO THE PRIDE OF TEAM ROCKET...
...IF WE ALLOWED YOU KIDDIES TO ROAM ABOUT FREELY.
THAT'S WHY...
...I'VE COME HERE... TO STOP YOU.
SLINK
SLINK
MONLEE, ARCHY, BONEE... MOVE AWAY... SLOWLY.
DON'T LET HER CATCH ON.

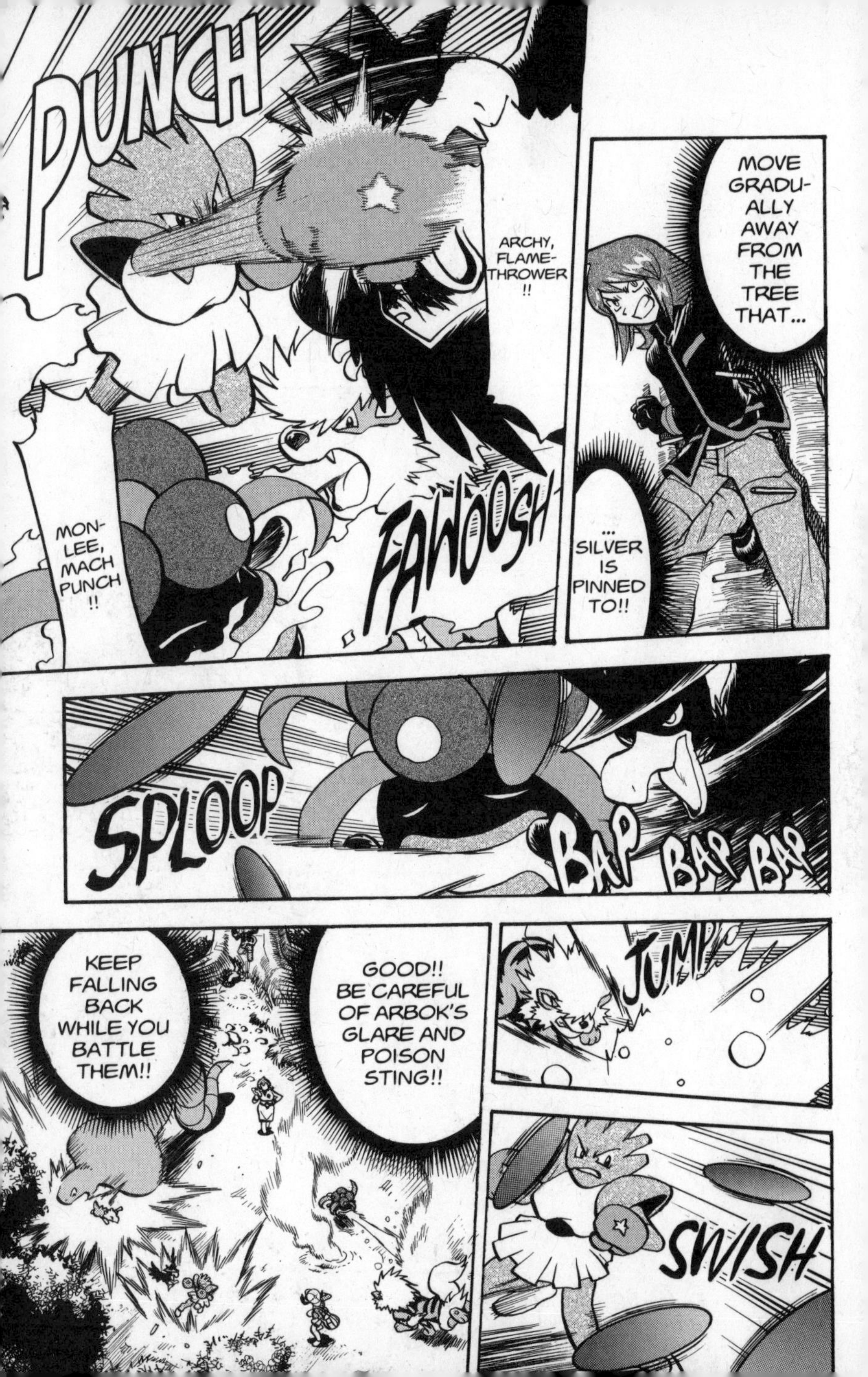
MOVE GRADU-ALLY AWAY FROM THE TREE THAT...
... SILVER IS PINNED TO!!
ARCHY, FLAME-THROWER !!
PUNCH
FAWOOSH
MON-LEE, MACH PUNCH !!
BAP BAP BAP
SPLOOP
JUMP
SWISH
GOOD!! BE CAREFUL OF ARBOK'S GLARE AND POISON STING!!
KEEP FALLING BACK WHILE YOU BATTLE THEM!!

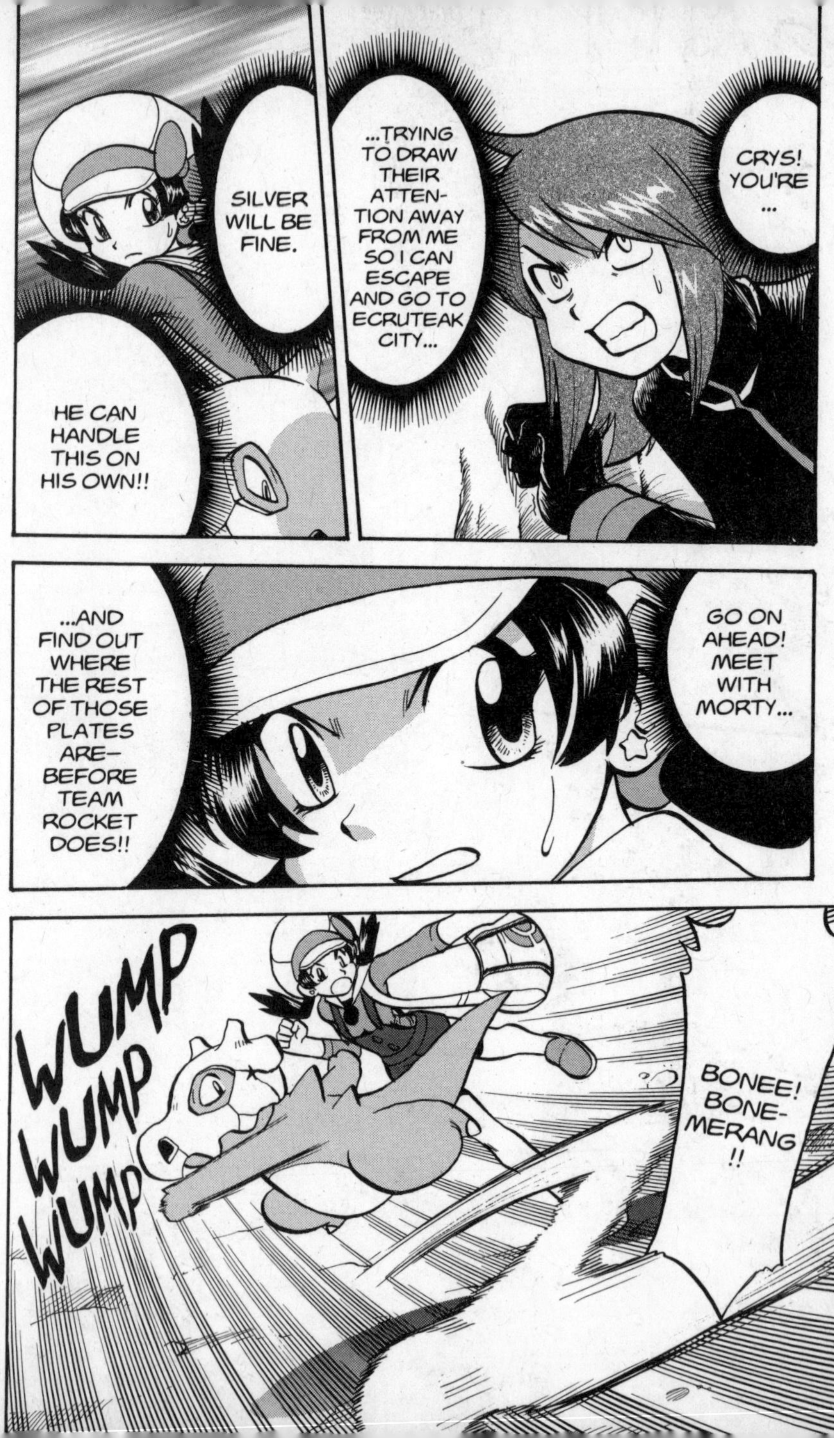
CRYS! YOU'RE ...
...TRYING TO DRAW THEIR ATTEN-TION AWAY FROM ME SO I CAN ESCAPE AND GO TO ECRUTEAK CITY...
SILVER WILL BE FINE.
HE CAN HANDLE THIS ON HIS OWN!!
GO ON AHEAD! MEET WITH MORTY...
...AND FIND OUT WHERE THE REST OF THOSE PLATES ARE— BEFORE TEAM ROCKET DOES!!
BONEE! BONE-MERANG !!
WUMP WUMP WUMP

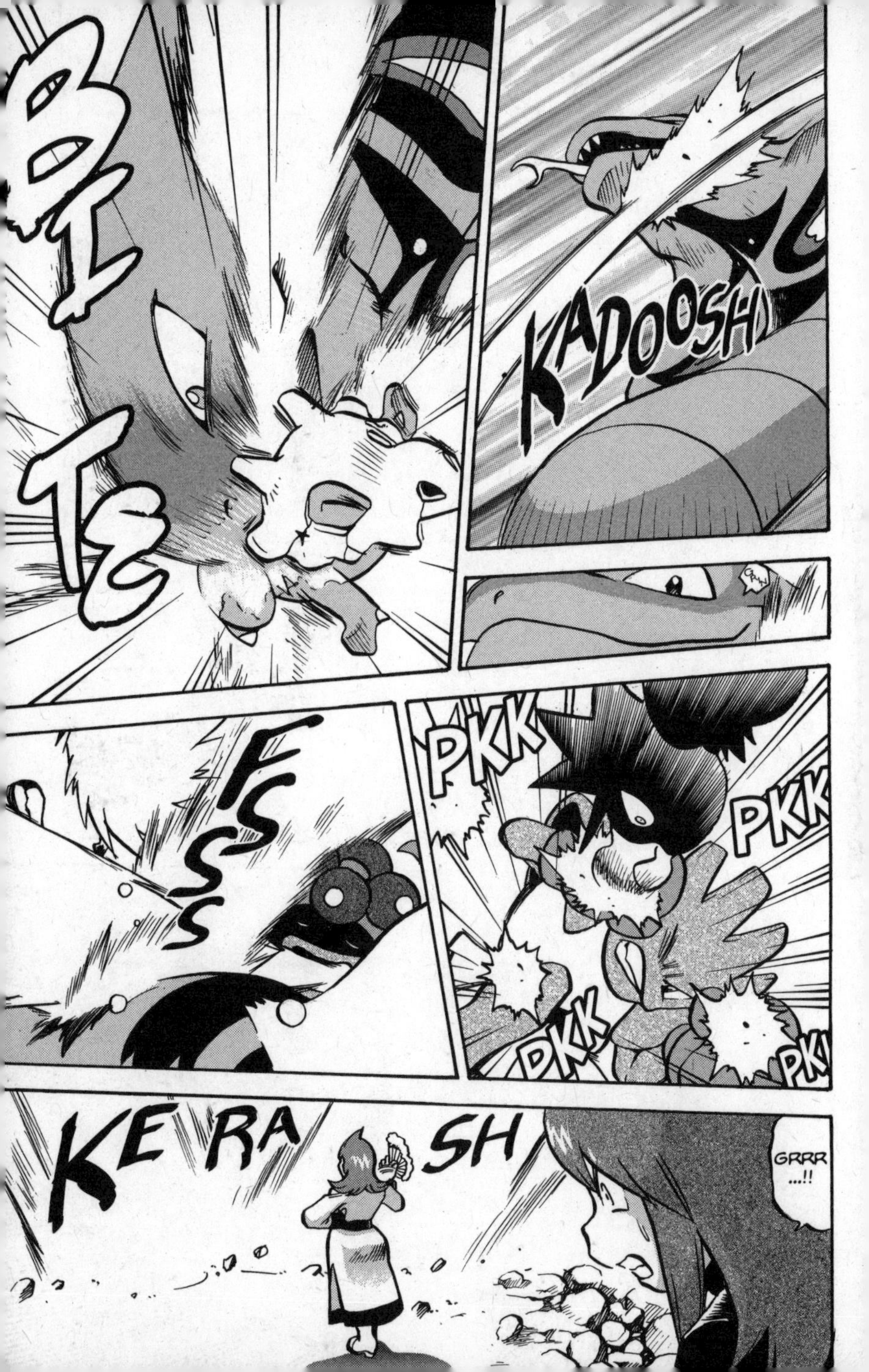
KADOOSH
BOI
TE
PKK
PKK
PKK
PKK
FSSS
KE RA SH
GRRR ...!!

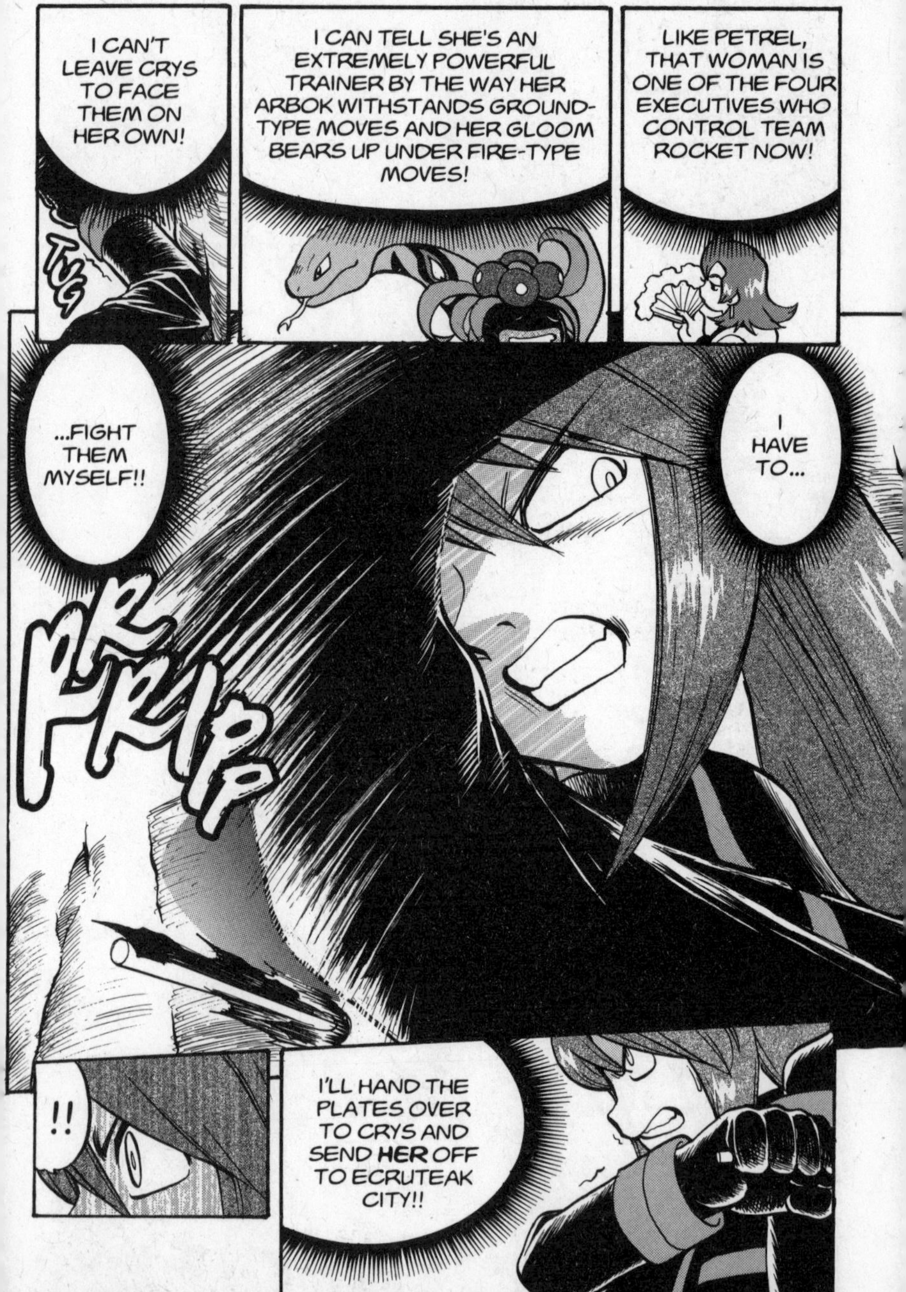
LIKE PETREL, THAT WOMAN IS ONE OF THE FOUR EXECUTIVES WHO CONTROL TEAM ROCKET NOW!
I CAN TELL SHE'S AN EXTREMELY POWERFUL TRAINER BY THE WAY HER ARBOK WITHSTANDS GROUND-TYPE MOVES AND HER GLOOM BEARS UP UNDER FIRE-TYPE MOVES!
I CAN'T LEAVE CRYS TO FACE THEM ON HER OWN!
TUG
I HAVE TO...
...FIGHT THEM MYSELF!!
I'LL HAND THE PLATES OVER TO CRYS AND SEND **HER** OFF TO ECRUTEAK CITY!!
!!

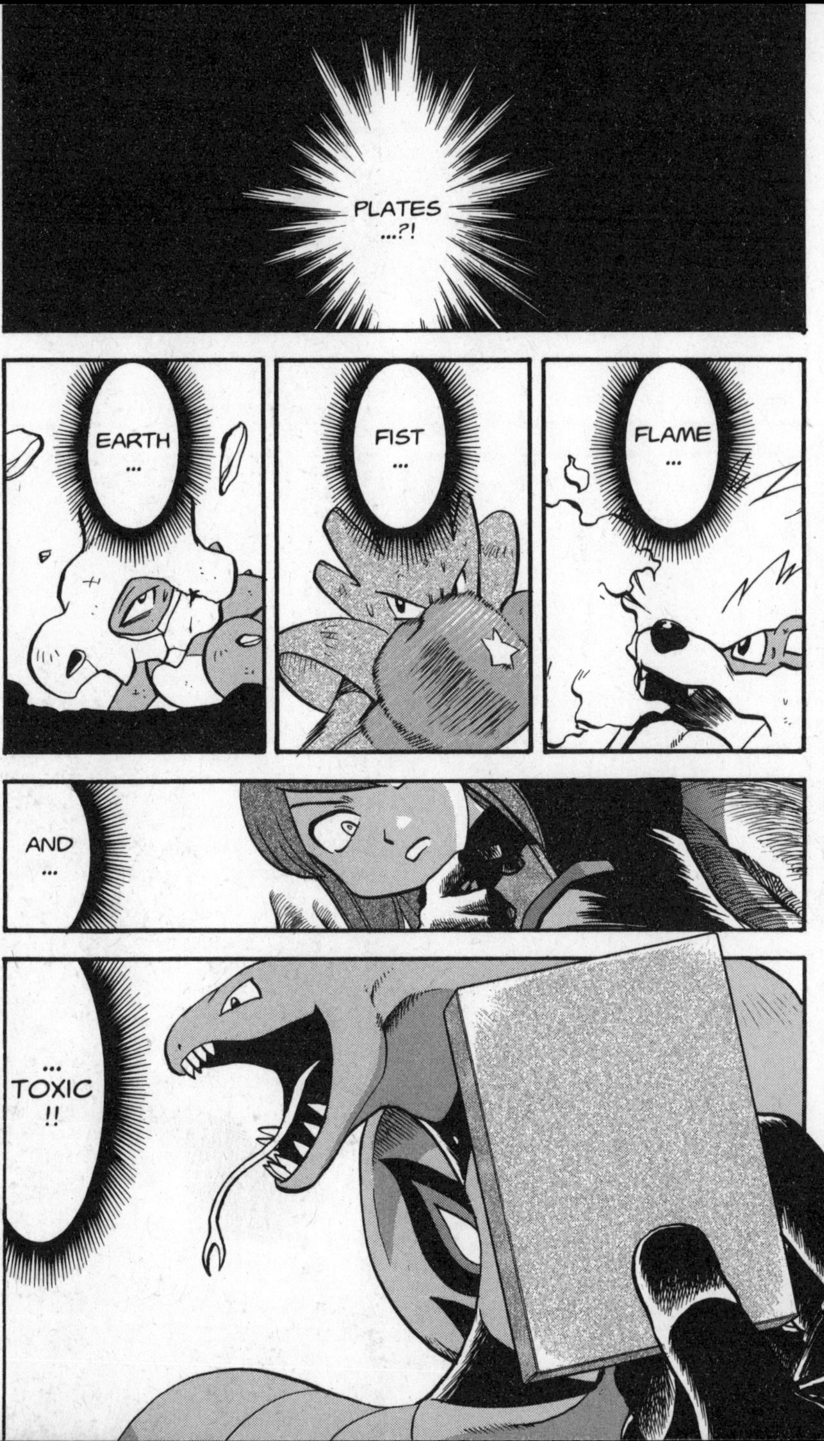
PLATES
...?!
FLAME
...
FIST
...
EARTH
...
AND
...
...
TOXIC
!!

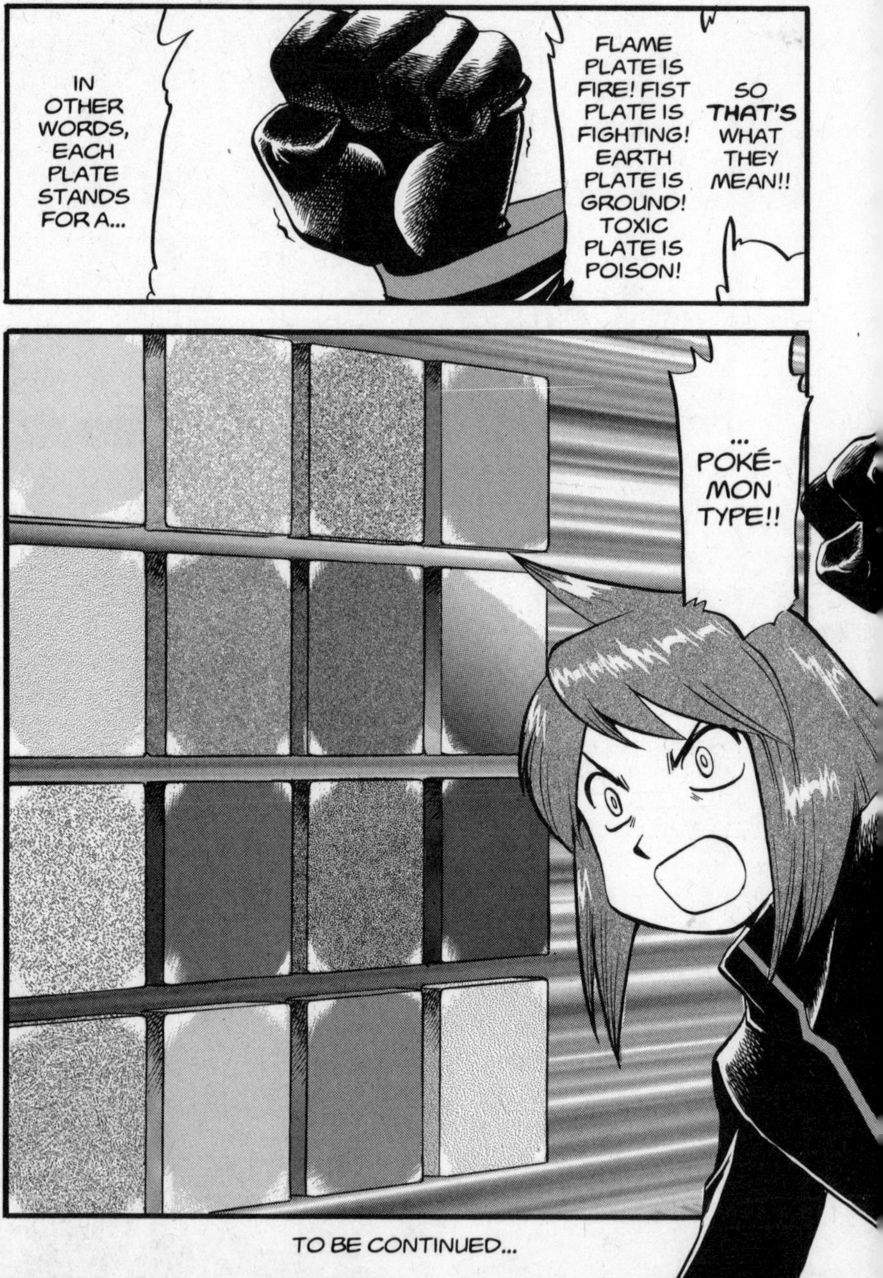
SO THAT'S WHAT THEY MEAN!!
FLAME PLATE IS FIRE! FIST PLATE IS FIGHTING! EARTH PLATE IS GROUND! TOXIC PLATE IS POISON!
IN OTHER WORDS, EACH PLATE STANDS FOR A...
...POKÉ-MON TYPE!!

TO BE CONTINUED...

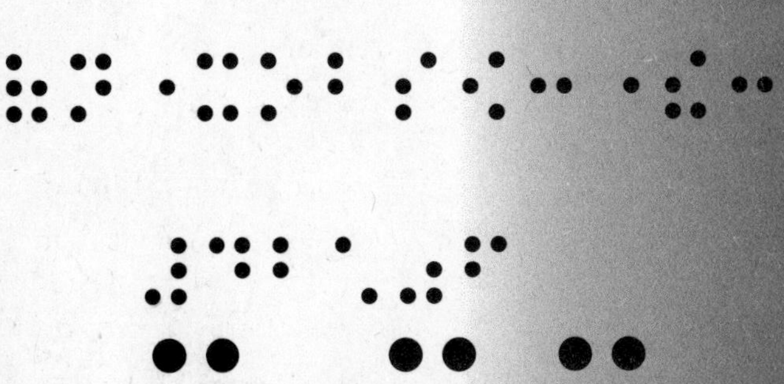

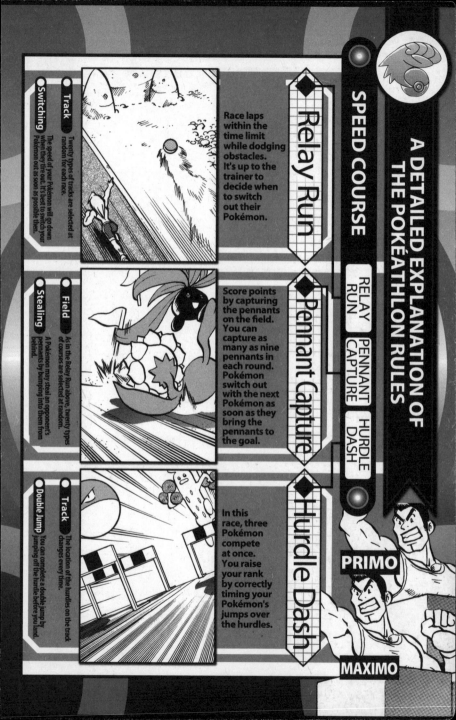

A DETAILED EXPLANATION OF THE POKÉATHLON RULES

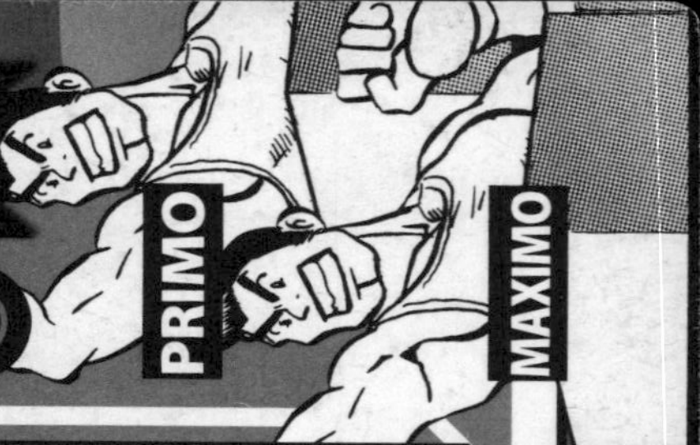
PRIMO
MAXIMO

SPEED COURSE

RELAY RUN | PENNANT CAPTURE | HURDLE DASH

Relay Run

Race laps within the time limit while dodging obstacles. It's up to the trainer to decide when to switch out their Pokémon.

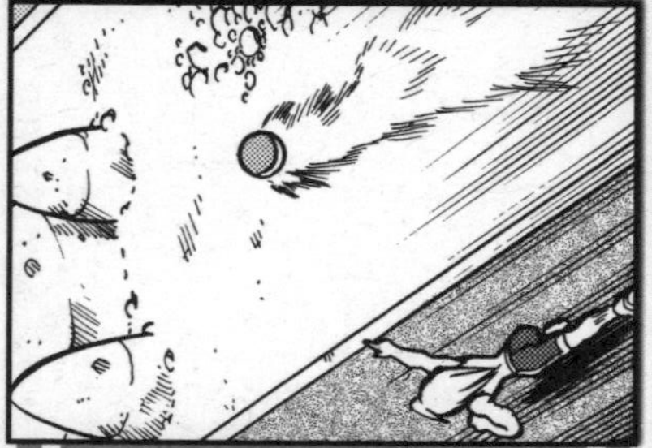

Track Twenty types of tracks are selected at random for each race.

Switching The speed of your Pokémon will go down when they tire out. It's best to switch your Pokémon out as soon as possible then.

Pennant Capture

Score points by capturing the pennants on the field. You can capture as many as nine pennants in each round. Pokémon switch out with the next Pokémon as soon as they bring the pennants to the goal.

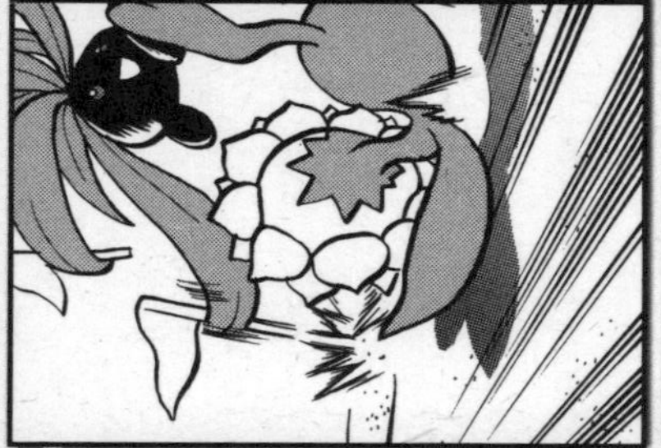

Field As in the Relay Run above, twenty types of courses are selected at random.

Stealing A Pokémon may steal an opponent's pennants by bumping into them from behind.

Hurdle Dash

In this race, three Pokémon compete at once. You raise your rank by correctly timing your Pokémon's jumps over the hurdles.

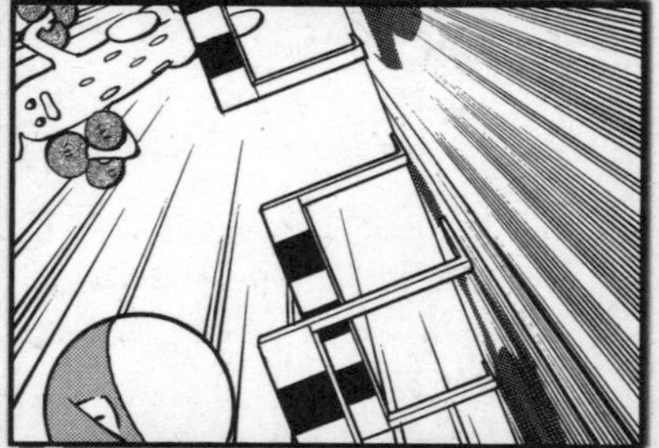

Track The location of the hurdles on the track changes every time.

Double Jump You can complete a double jump by jumping off the hurdle before you land.

STAMINA COURSE

RING DROP | BLOCK SMASH | RELAY RUN

Ring Drop

Score points by tackling your opponents and pushing them out of the ring. The more powerful a Pokémon is, the stronger its tackle will be, and the more likely its opponent will fall out of the ring.

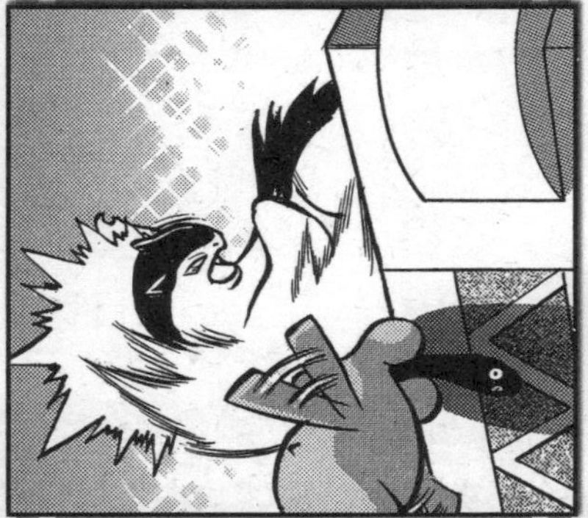

- **Jump Attack** A Pokémon may jump on and attack the Pokémon below it. Pokémon can also dodge their opponent's tackle.
- **Fall** If you fall out of the ring, 10 points are deducted.

POWER COURSE

BLOCK SMASH | CIRCLE PUSH | GOAL ROLL

Block Smash

Smash as many blocks as possible within the time limit. You can raise your Pokémon's Tension by aiming for the crack on the blocks. The trainer's skill will greatly affect the outcome of the game.

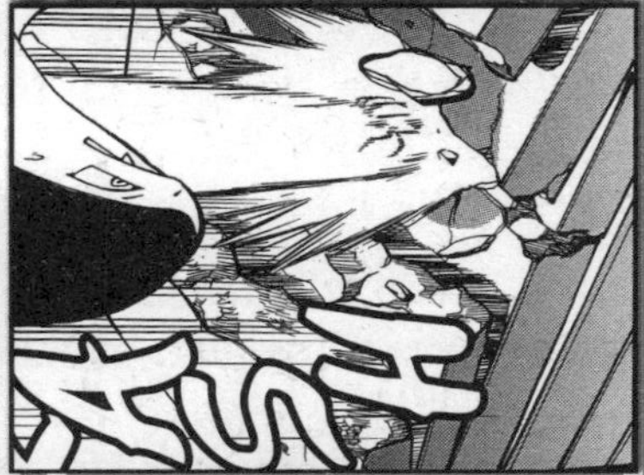
ASH

- **Block** You will receive a new set of blocks after smashing through a set of 10.
- **Switching Pokémon** You can save time by switching Pokémon while you receive a new set of blocks.

Circle Push

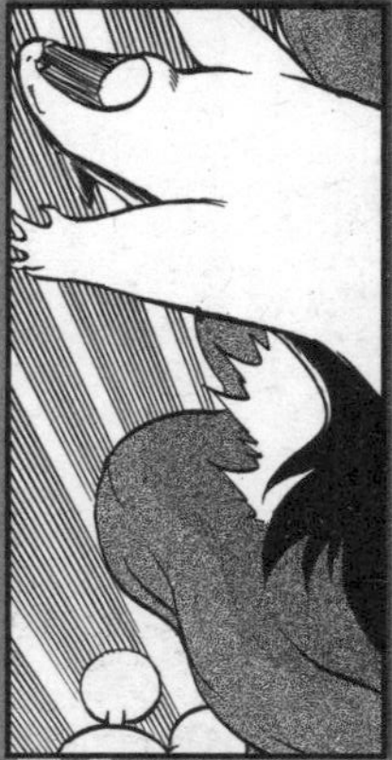

In this game, you push against the opposing Pokémon to remain inside the circle. You score points by remaining inside the circle when the countdown ends. The size and location of the circle differs in each round, so it's important to figure out where to position your Pokémon.

- **Outside the Circle** If you are pushed outside the circle you will be unable to move for a time.
- **Fatigue** Pushing an opponent for too long will fatigue your Pokémon. Make sure to keep an eye on your Pokémon's stamina.

This is the POKÉDEX!!

POKÉDEX DATA

THIS HIGH-TECH MACHINE WAS CREATED BY PROFESSOR OAK. DISCOVER THE FEATURES OF THE NEW MODEL!

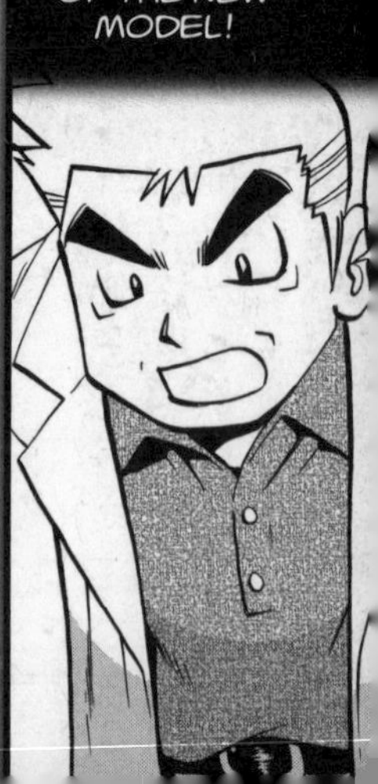

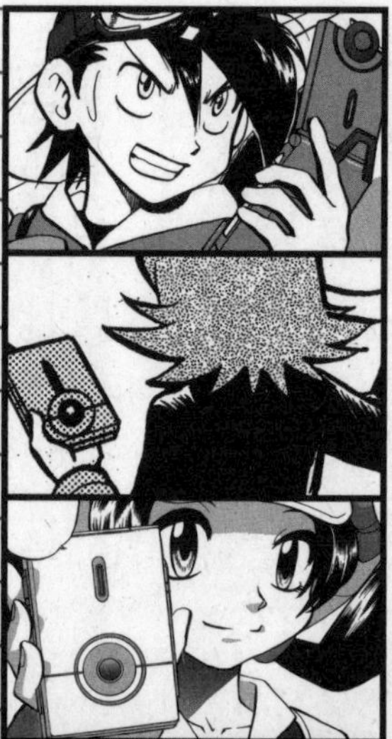

AFTER THE BATTLE AGAINST GUILE, THE POKÉMON TRAINERS TEN POKÉDEXES WERE GATHERED AT PROFESSOR OAK'S LABORATORY. GOLD, SILVER AND CRYS'S THREE POKEDÉXES WERE REMODELED INTO THIS NEW VERSION. GOLD AND SILVER USE AN ORANGE MODEL AND CRYS USES A WHITE MODEL.

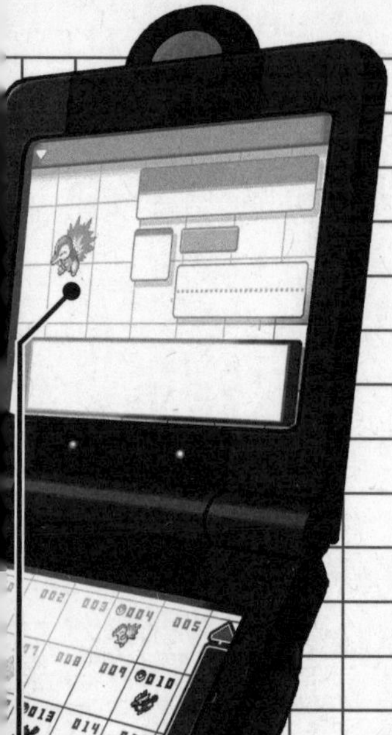

GOLD, SILVER AND CRYS'S POKÉDEXÉS WERE GREATLY IMPROVED BY POKÉMON RESEARCHER PROFESSOR OAK. ▶

01 A NEW SHAPE!

THE OLD POKÉDEX OPENED LIKE A BOOK. THE NEW POKÉDEX OPENS HORIZONTALLY AND HAS TWO SCREENS, MAKING IT EASIER TO SEE MORE INFORMATION AT ONCE.

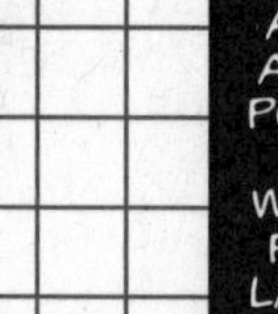
Fire Mouse Pokémon
FIRE
It usually stays hunched over. If it is angry or surprised, it shoots flames out of its back.

▲TOUCH SCREEN MAKES IT EASIER TO SEARCH FOR POKÉMON.

02 COMPARE SIZES.

YOU CAN NOW COMPARE THE SIZE OF A POKÉMON WITH ITS TRAINER TO GET A CLEAR PICTURE OF HOW LARGE OR SMALL THE POKÉMON IS.

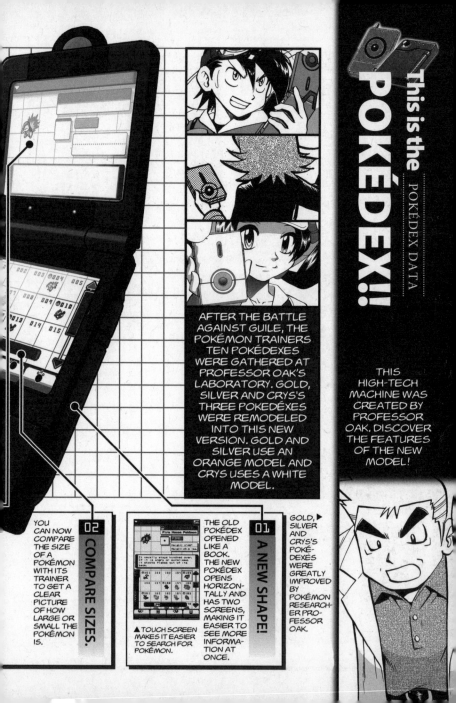

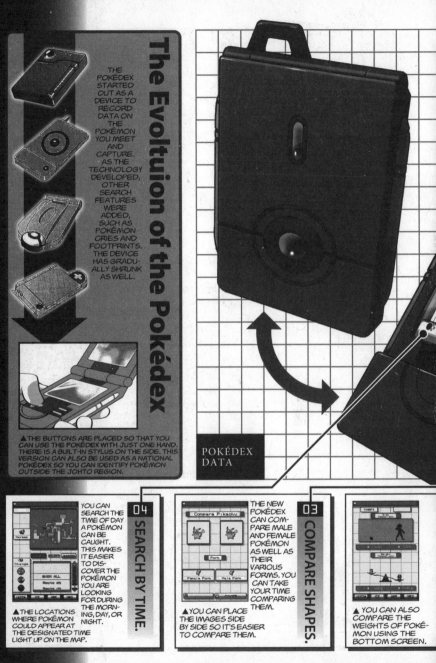

The Evoltuion of the Pokédex

THE POKÉDEX STARTED OUT AS A DEVICE TO RECORD DATA ON THE POKÉMON YOU MEET AND CAPTURE. AS THE TECHNOLOGY DEVELOPED, OTHER SEARCH FEATURES WERE ADDED, SUCH AS POKÉMON CRIES AND FOOTPRINTS. THE DEVICE HAS GRADUALLY SHRUNK AS WELL.

▲THE BUTTONS ARE PLACED SO THAT YOU CAN USE THE POKÉDEX WITH JUST ONE HAND. THERE IS A BUILT-IN STYLUS ON THE SIDE. THIS VERSION CAN ALSO BE USED AS A NATIONAL POKÉDEX SO YOU CAN IDENTIFY POKÉMON OUTSIDE THE JOHTO REGION.

POKÉDEX DATA

▲ YOU CAN ALSO COMPARE THE WEIGHTS OF POKÉMON USING THE BOTTOM SCREEN.

03 COMPARE SHAPES.

THE NEW POKÉDEX CAN COMPARE MALE AND FEMALE POKÉMON AS WELL AS THEIR VARIOUS FORMS. YOU CAN TAKE YOUR TIME COMPARING THEM.

Compare Pikachu
Form
Female Form
Male Form

▲YOU CAN PLACE THE IMAGES SIDE BY SIDE SO IT'S EASIER TO COMPARE THEM.

04 SEARCH BY TIME.

YOU CAN SEARCH THE TIME OF DAY A POKÉMON CAN BE CAUGHT. THIS MAKES IT EASIER TO DISCOVER THE POKÉMON YOU ARE LOOKING FOR DURING THE MORNING, DAY, OR NIGHT.

▲THE LOCATIONS WHERE POKÉMON COULD APPEAR AT THE DESIGNATED TIME LIGHT UP ON THE MAP.

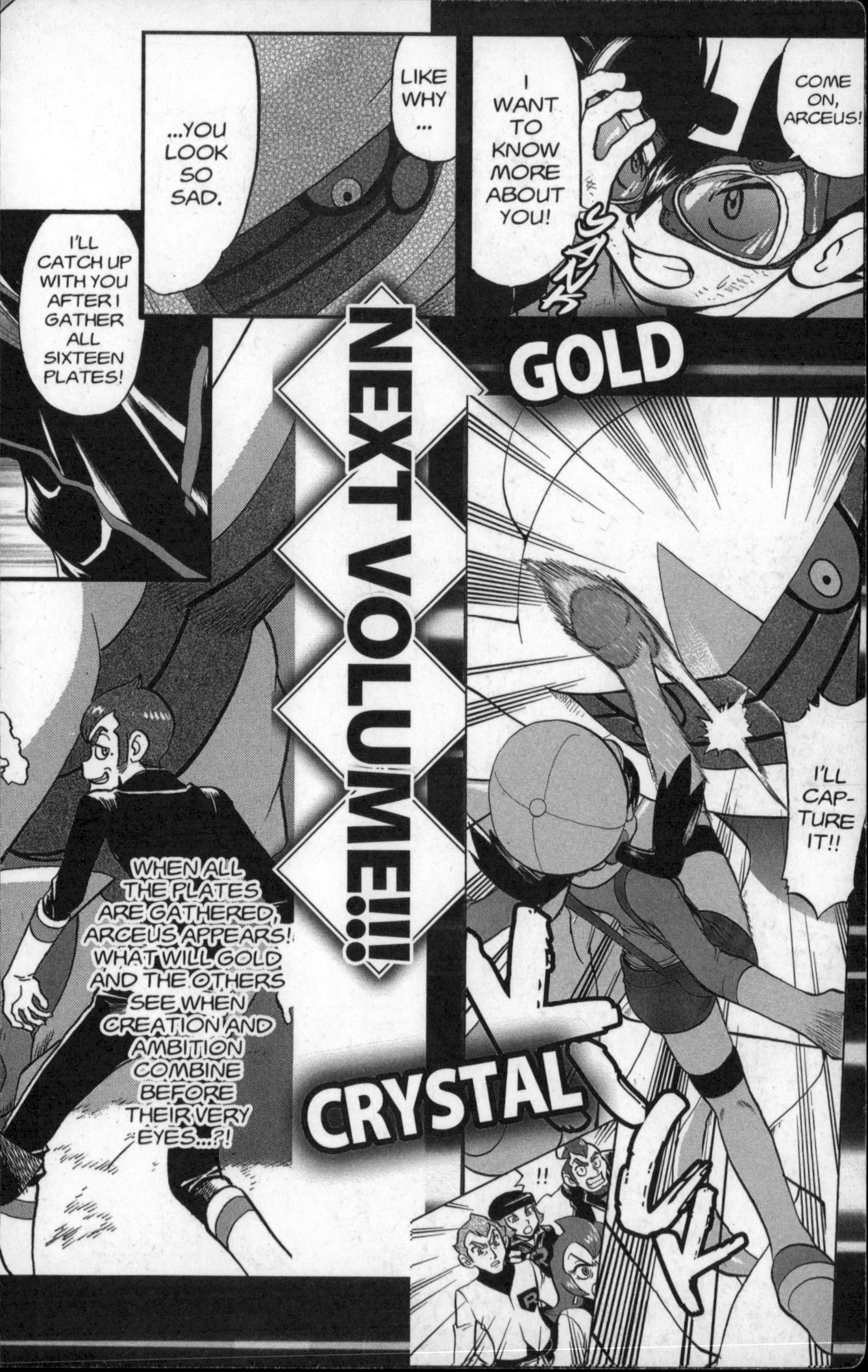
COME ON, ARCEUS!
I WANT TO KNOW MORE ABOUT YOU!
LIKE WHY ...
...YOU LOOK SO SAD.
I'LL CATCH UP WITH YOU AFTER I GATHER ALL SIXTEEN PLATES!
GOLD
I'LL CAP-TURE IT!!
CRYSTAL
!!
NEXT VOLUME!!!
WHEN ALL THE PLATES ARE GATHERED, ARCEUS APPEARS! WHAT WILL GOLD AND THE OTHERS SEE WHEN CREATION AND AMBITION COMBINE BEFORE THEIR VERY EYES...?!

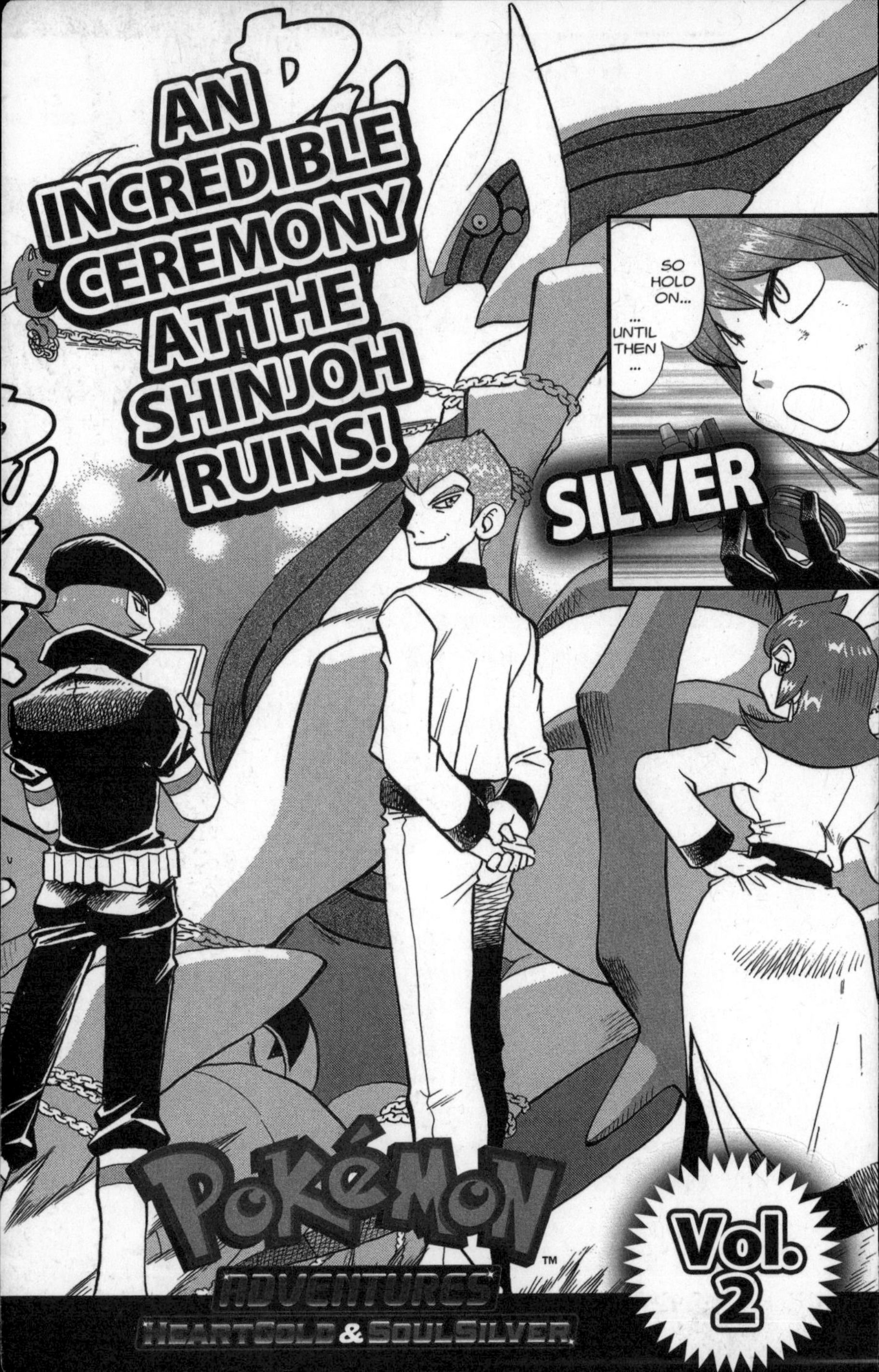
AN INCREDIBLE CEREMONY AT THE SHINJOH RUINS!
SO HOLD ON...
...UNTIL THEN...
SILVER
POKéMON™
ADVENTURES
HEARTGOLD & SOULSILVER
Vol. 2

Message from
Hidenori Kusaka

On rare occasions, I get the opportunity to meet my readers and talk to them. And whenever I meet a young fan, guess what question I'm asked the most... "What is your favorite Pokémon?" of course! They always ask me that. And I always have trouble answering. (LOL) Currently, there are 649 different Pokémon! It isn't easy to choose a number one out of so many! Hmm, I'm still thinking about it... How should I answer that question...today?

Message from
Satoshi Yamamoto

Let the festival begin! Is he a troublemaker who creates chaos wherever he appears? The benchwarmer nobody can rely on? Or actually a tried and true hero?! I'm the one who draws him, but even I'm not sure! I've been waiting for a chance to activate him by drawing him again though. Gold, you outspoken scamp... You're back and ready for more!

HUGE
FINAL VOLUME!

The thrilling conclusion to the story reuniting Pokémon Trainers Gold, Silver and Crystal...and Team Rocket too!

So much fun and adventure it took 272 pages to tell the tale!

Crystal and Gold battle the enemy while Silver collects the 16 mysterious plates that Team Rocket wants to get their hands on to set their latest diabolical plan in motion. Then, a mysterious force field envelops our three heroes—along with Legendary Pokémon Arceus—and transports them all to...*where?!*

Which unwanted companions tag along? And what three new Legendaries will our heroes meet there?

AVAILABLE
NOW!

The adventure continues in the Johto region!

POKÉMON™ ADVENTURES

GOLD & SILVER BOX SET

Includes POKÉMON ADVENTURES Vols. 8-14 and a collectible poster!

POKÉMON™
ADVENTURES
GOLD & SILVER
Bonus Poster Inside!
GOLD & SILVER BOX SET:
POKÉMON ADVENTURES VOLUMES 8-14

Story by
HIDENORI KUSAKA

Art by
MATO,
SATOSHI YAMAMOTO

More exciting Pokémon adventures starring Gold and his rival Silver! First someone steals Gold's backpack full of Poké Balls (and Pokémon!). Then someone steals Prof. Elm's Totodile. Can Gold catch the thief—or thieves?!

Keep an eye on Team Rocket, Gold... Could they be behind this crime wave?

Begin your Pokémon Adventure here in the Kanto region!

POKÉMON
ADVENTURES
RED & BLUE BOX SET

Story by **HIDENORI KUSAKA**   Art by **MATO**

Includes **POKÉMON ADVENTURES** Vols. 1-7 and a collectible poster!

All your favorite Pokémon game characters jump out of the screen into the pages of this action-packed manga!

Red doesn't just want to train Pokémon, he wants to be their friend too. Bulbasaur and Poliwhirl seem game. But independent Pikachu won't be so easy to win over!

And watch out for Team Rocket, Red... They only want to be your enemy!

Start the adventure today!